CHANDLER'S RUN

ABOUT THE AUTHOR

Denise Muir has lived in Whakatane for twenty-five years. She was born and educated in Auckland, married a South Islander, and is the mother of five children, now adult and with children of their own. On two occasions, she has lived in the South Island. More inclined in those days to paint the mountains, it wasn't until some years later, after a serious illness, that she wrote about them. This is her first novel.

CHANDLER'S RUN

DENISE MUIR

HarperCollins*Publishers*

National Library of New Zealand Cataloguing-in-Publication Data

Muir, Denise.
Chandler's run / Denise Muir.
ISBN 978-1-86950-678-0
I. Title.
NZ823.3—dc 22

First published 2008
HarperCollins*Publishers* (*New Zealand*) *Limited*
P.O. Box 1, Auckland

ISBN: 978 1 86950 678 0

Cover design by Louise McGeachie
Cover photos courtesy of Ian Brodie and Getty Images
Internal text design and typesetting by Springfield West

Printed by Griffin Press, Australia

50gsm Bulky News used by HarperCollins*Publishers* is a natural,
recyclable product made from wood grown in sustainable
plantation forests. The manufacturing processes conform to the
environmental regulations in the country of origin, New Zealand.

To my daughter Lynne, without whose
help and patience this story would not
have been written.

Her tireless encouragement and interest
in my efforts to write this first book urged
me on when I might have thought the
task beyond me.

To you, Lynne, my thanks.

Historical note

The story of James McKenzie is true, apart from his involvement with the Chandler family and the Widow Gaunt, which is fiction.

Governor Gore Brown, James Fitzgerald, the superintendent of Canterbury, the Ngai Tahu tribe of Waitaki, and the people involved in McKenzie's apprehension, trial and pardon were all living people.

The *Rajah* did sail from Gravesend on 17 June 1853, and the incidents described during her voyage did actually occur but have been embellished by the writer's imagination.

All other characters and events in this book are fictitious and any resemblance to people living or dead is purely coincidental.

Chapter 1

THE SHIP'S BOW sliced cleanly through the green waters as she ran with the north-east trades. Only those passengers who were fairly recovered ventured up on deck to breathe the clean air and enjoy the sun.

The *Rajah* had set sail from Gravesend on the seventeenth day of June, 1853, with 187 souls aboard; she was bound for New Zealand, on the other side of the world. For almost two weeks many of the passengers had suffered from varying degrees of seasickness and now, tentatively, still unsure of their sea legs, they began to emerge from their cabins.

Lucy Chandler walked slowly along the deck flanked by her two children: Daniel, eleven years of age, and Sarah, who was nine. Adam Chandler, Lucy's husband, had not joined them. He was no longer seasick, but he was listless, very weak, and coughed incessantly.

Released from the stuffy cabins and the lingering smell of illness, Lucy breathed deeply of the sea air and her spirits lifted a little. On the fifth day out, as the ship had headed into a veering westerly on its way to the Atlantic, Adam had succumbed to seasickness, followed soon after by Sarah. Lucy had had strong misgivings then, doubting the wisdom of this venture when Adam, already ill with consumption, could be laid low so soon. She feared for him, wondering as she nodded a greeting to those she passed what other trials might be ahead to tax his failing strength.

~

Adam Chandler, a member of the legal profession, had practised law both in London and in Tenbury, Worcestershire, where the family estate was situated. His health had been of concern for some time and latterly had caused him to consult again with the family physician. The old doctor, after examining him, had been blunt. 'If you would regain your health, you must change your way of life, find a healthier climate to live in and choose a less sedentary occupation.' He had studied Adam silently, then, shaking his head, he had added with regret, 'I can do no more for you.'

Adam Chandler had stared at the old man in disbelief, this man who had cured his ills for as many years as he could remember. 'There must be something you can do.' He had leaned forward in his chair, his two hands clenched on the edge of the doctor's desk.

'Yes, my boy, I know, I could send you off to Switzerland for a while, but what would that avail if in the end you returned to your environment here?' There had been compassion in the older man's eyes.

'Wendon Manor . . . the estate is my heritage — my son's heritage. How can I leave here and where would I go?'

The doctor had risen from his chair and moved to place a hand on Adam's shoulder. 'If you are to survive you must move to a drier climate. I'm sorry. Now,' he continued, 'I think you should consider your uncle's invitation. Ruben, isn't it?'

Adam nodded.

'He has asked you to join him in New Zealand, is this not so?'

'Yes, yes he has.'

'Well, my boy, I think you should go, not only for your sake but for that of your family. Breathe that pure mountain air into these sick lungs of yours, work outdoors with the sheep and who knows . . .'

Adam's uncle, Ruben Chandler, had emigrated to that remote and untamed country seven years earlier after his wife and only son had died of influenza. Within six months of their deaths, he had sold up all his interests and left England to begin a new life in the colonies. Nothing was heard from him for four years, but at last a short missive had arrived from the little-populated South Island of New Zealand. Following the usual platitudes and enquiries after the health and well-being of the family, Adam's in particular, the letter had continued:

I have established a 15,000-acre sheep run in the high country of this island. Chandler's Run. It is the most rugged and the most beautiful country you will ever see. My homestead (sketch enclosed) stands on freehold land; I have purchased the key areas and taken up a pastoral lease on the larger tracts of land. There are few natives here, so they barely warrant a mention except perhaps to say that they are friendly. This is a hard life and a lonely one, but in taking up this challenge I am the stronger for it. I can only regret that Clara and the boy did not live to share it.

On a happier note he went on:

You will be interested to know, Adam, that I am running 5000 head of prime merinos and that the wool-clip each year is most satisfactory. I have a housekeeper and a native girl housemaid, and two native fellows watch over my flocks, so you can see that we are quite civilized here. My dearest wish now is to have some of my family join me in this new and exciting land. There is a mysticism and a presence in this place that causes one to ponder; nowhere else have I experienced this, and a man soon gains a deep respect for the immensity of the mountains, the power of the elements. The air up here is so pure one can believe that only God has breathed it. Perhaps, Adam, you would consider raising your family in this wonderful country: become a sheep man in partnership with me and prosper in health and wealth.

Several more letters had followed over a period of months as Adam's health had continued to deteriorate. Adam and Lucy had read the letters time and again, studying the rough pencil sketch of the homestead, which was similar to a Devonshire farmhouse, and had tried to reach a decision.

For weeks discussion and concerns were passed back

and forth among family members. Lucy's parents, her sisters Amelia and Charlotte, and her brother Christian had all urged caution. 'Should something go seriously amiss with Adam in that godforsaken country, Lucy, there will be little help,' her father had warned. 'Consider the children!'

Mary Chandler, Adam's mother, had wept secretly as she watched her son's declining health. She knew that should he continue as he was she would almost certainly lose him, and should he decide to join his uncle in this country so little was known about she would lose him anyway, and her heart ached. Charles Chandler was resigned. Realizing that only one decision could be taken, he wished his son Godspeed.

There had been tears, excitement, handkerchiefs fluttering, and voices calling back and forth, as the ship made ready to leave. When slowly she began to move and gather way, the figures of family and friends, still waving and calling, seemed to draw closer together as if seeking comfort. They grew smaller and smaller, and when at last they were lost to sight there had come a coldness to the pit of Adam's stomach, a coldness that could have been fear.

As the *Rajah* passed the cliffs of Dover and plied down the English Channel towards the open sea, all that was familiar and dear was left behind and the coldness in Adam's stomach had persisted. A hush had fallen over those passengers who remained at the ship's rail, and as the land receded they had drifted away, in twos and threes, to their cabins. The feelings of hope and excitement and the prospect of adventure that had gripped all aboard became subdued as reality set in; and after the ship had sailed into heavier seas those feelings were lost entirely with the onset of churning stomachs and the exhausting retching that plagued the victims day and night.

Lucy had struggled to ignore the instability of her own stomach as she tended her husband and daughter, but in the close confines of the cabins, and with the pitch and roll of the *Rajah*'s decks as she sailed into the horse latitudes, Lucy too became ill. Daniel remained well and it was left to the lad to minister to his sick family. This he did without complaint.

The sea was calm and the sky was clear as Lucy Chandler walked with her children along the deck. Daniel was chatting, but she was paying little attention to what he was saying, her thoughts on her husband. She could not recall when his robust health had begun to fail. The approach of his illness had been insidious; fatigue, weight loss and finally a debilitating cough that would not go away had indicated that something was seriously wrong.

'Mama.' Sarah's light voice roused Lucy from her retrospection. 'Could we please have tea now? I think I am a little hungry.'

'That is a good sign!' Lucy smiled at her young daughter. 'Come along, Daniel, we will have tea and perhaps fetch something for Papa that will tempt him to eat.'

Food, served to the first-class passengers by a steward in the cuddy or the saloon, was well provided. A sheep and a pig were killed each week, and there was poultry, beef and boiled salmon. Carrots and mashed potato were served at each main meal, followed by green gooseberries, damsons or plum pudding. There was fresh bread daily and goat's milk for their tea.

Adam Chandler had no stomach for food; he had swallowed little but water for many days and this he lost in night sweats. Water was doled out at six o'clock each morning. Daniel would fetch the four quarts, their quota for the day, and Adam, ever-thirsty, would drink his fill but could rarely be persuaded to eat.

When Adam at last felt able to venture on deck he was dismayed by his weakness. He had waited for Lucy and the children to leave the cabin before he would test himself. Now, gaunt and grey of face, he lowered himself onto a hatch-cover with a feeling akin to despair. He made no attempt to speak to his fellows and had not the breath to reply to those who spoke to him; simply sat with closed eyes, letting the sun touch him. Lucy, sitting in a corner of the deck with several other wives and Sarah, put aside her sewing and watched him.

'Your man looks quite poorly, my dear,' kindly little Mrs Truscott, sitting beside her, had whispered. 'I can see you are concerned for him.'

'Yes,' Lucy agreed, 'the seasickness has taken its toll of him.' She did not admit that he had been otherwise ill.

'Well, don't you be worrying. Good food and this delightful weather will soon put him on his feet.' Smiling, the small woman rose to her feet and went to sort out her brood of six, who were playing noisily further along the deck.

Lucy folded up her sewing and rose too. 'Come, dear, we will sit with Papa for a little.' And she took Sarah's hand.

He did not open his eyes at their approach.

'It is almost tea-time, dearest, do you feel you could join us?'

Adam's eyes remained closed. He shook his head.

'Shall I have the steward fetch you something?'

'No. No, thank you.'

'It's a lovely day, Papa.' Sarah pushed up close to her father on the hatch-cover. 'The sun will help you feel better, won't it?'

'Yes, yes. Go with Mama now and have your tea.'

Irritation rose in him as he watched his wife and child move away. Can Lucy not see, he thought testily, that it would be easier for me if she would express her worries rather than attempting to hide them? The possibility of his dying was very real. She must see this; it was his consuming fear. Her continued evasion and carefully chosen words presented a barrier to open discussion or to the comfort he might have derived and indeed expected from her. If he did not recover, or perhaps did not even survive the journey, there were things to be set in place, practical measures to be taken to ensure the safe return of his wife and family to English shores again. These were things they must discuss.

His unhappy thoughts were interrupted by a cry of 'Land ho!' The passengers crowded to the ship's rail as the ship came in sight of Porto Santo, one of the Madeira Islands. Adam half-rose to his feet, then with a sigh he sank down on to the hatch-cover again.

~

Day followed day, and the weather remained fair. Far out in the Atlantic the passengers were entertained by porpoises, flying fish and nautilus with their pink sails erected. All on board were delighted with their antics.

Lucy took advantage of the good weather to sort out the cabins. The larger cabin was well appointed, and Lucy's piano had been placed in it so they could enjoy music on the long journey and perhaps invite others to join them. A small bookcase and some of their books had also been placed in the cabin; among these, three of their favourite authors — Emily Brontë, Thackeray and Dickens. Adam, a little improved, had resumed his habit of reading to the family of an evening and this was much looked forward to.

Lucy stared with distaste at the growing pile of soiled clothing. Fresh water on shipboard was precious; never to be used for washing clothes or bathing in. Salt water was brought on deck each day or two for that purpose and marine soap could be purchased on board. Bathing and attempting to wash one's hair in seawater left one's skin sticky, and the hair stiff and dull. Lucy hesitated to subject their fine garments to such harsh treatment, so the pile kept growing.

The New Zealand Company had issued a list of clothing suited to conditions on board and to the lifestyle in some parts of their new country. The directors of the Company had urged the passengers to avail themselves of these. They had purchased the items on the list, but Lucy, sorting through them again, shook her head and folded them away out of sight. There were twelve calico chemises, four petticoats made of cheap cotton, four flannel waistcoats, eighteen pairs of thick stockings, two pairs of ugly shoes and one pair of boots. She could not visualize herself or her young daughter wearing such apparel. Also there were only three cotton dresses and just two bonnets. She would never manage with so few dresses, accustomed as she was to changing her gown at least twice a day, and calico chemises — oh, never! There was no mention of the unmentionables. Did they perhaps not wear them in this remote country?

Adam, who wore broadcloth and the finest linen, would never be persuaded to wear the rustic garments recommended either: moleskin, fustian, serge and twilled cotton. She folded these articles away, too.

There were many other commodities that the Company urged the passengers to take with them to their new country: an infantry sword, a sheath knife, a billhook, English axes, hammers and nails, etc., and an assortment of cooking and eating utensils. Most of these would already be found at the homestead, and because the passengers were restricted to twenty cubic feet of baggage and that not to exceed half a ton, Adam decided against the tools. He did, however, think it would be wise to purchase the large mackintosh sheets and good Scotch mauds or plaids mentioned on the list, as well as the eating and cooking utensils which would be useful perhaps when they began their journey inland with Ruben Chandler. There were mattresses offered — mean, hard mattresses, measuring seventy-two inches by eighteen — and Adam passed these over, too.

With the exception of the piano, the small bookcase and their trunks, every cherished possession that they could bring with them had been packed into crates and stored below. Their money, all in gold sovereigns, was sealed in a stout wooden box and insured against loss or theft whilst on board. These items had far exceeded the weight and space allowed them, but Adam had come to an understanding with the captain and first mate, who had proved to be very amiable fellows indeed.

Satisfied with the two cabins, Lucy was gathering up her sewing to join the ladies on deck when her eye fell on the tin utensils stacked behind the door. A large box would be required for those: there was a can to hold water, a wash basin, a pot and a teapot, tin mugs and plates, and knives, forks and spoons. Adam would need to speak to the bo'sun or one of the officers about obtaining a box.

As the weeks went by, the poop passengers became better acquainted. For the most part they were well educated, and would be an asset wherever they planned to settle. Mr Johns was a surgeon, and Mr Blackwell was a construction engineer. These two men with their wives and families were to disembark in Lyttelton. Mr Scott was a schoolmaster and taught school on the open deck for two hours daily. Percival Truscott was a tailor, and Mary, his wife, was a dressmaker. They, with their children, would leave the ship at Port Chalmers along with Lucy and Adam.

Many of the folk aboard would sail on to Nelson at the

top of the South Island. Among them, Aubrey Agincourt was a dental surgeon; a pale, unhealthy-looking individual whose many gold teeth most considered vulgar. He gazed into the mouths of those he conversed with rather than their eyes, and Mr Scott thought him 'a deuced odd fellow!'

Most days, Lucy joined the ladies in their shaded corner of the deck. It was very warm and there was still no sign of rain; it had not rained since they had left England and the water casks were emptying rapidly. It was very pleasant, however, to spend an hour or two in convivial company.

The conversation today was in French and everyone took a turn at reading aloud. Lucy enjoyed these times; she did not wish to lose her fluency in that language, and often she would urge Sarah to join the ladies in the hope of advancing her beyond the rudimentary lessons taught by her governess. On other days, as the women worked busily at their sewing, knitting and needlepoint, they indulged themselves in a little light gossip.

The men assembled in their own corner to discuss the things men discuss. Adam was among them that day, as he most often was now. His colour was better and he was enjoying his food again. Of Daniel there was no sign. He was a favourite with the ship's carpenters, who were teaching him carving and woodwork. He was to be found with them most days or with the bo'sun, who showed him how to knot and splice rope.

Mr Cresswell was reading aloud to the men. In his hand he held a copy of the New Zealand Company's list of subjects that they were advised to learn whilst they were aboard ship.

He was an accountant and claimed a touch of royalty in his blood. In a pompous voice, he read out the merits of learning botany, chemistry, agriculture, veterinary surgery, carpentry and the use of the axe — ''pon my word!' He paused for a moment, then read on. 'We are further advised to learn to cure and smoke beef, pork, hams, bacon, etc.—' here he raised his voice '— and the art of self-defence. Ye gods!'

There was general laughter, and Adam, catching Lucy's eye, grinned broadly.

'I think all that laughter will most likely turn to tears when we've stepped ashore,' Mary Truscott said quietly.

Surprised, Lucy turned to face her. 'Why do you say that?'

'Percy and I read everything we could find about this country before we decided to leave home, and we are prepared to do many things that we've been accustomed to paying others to do for us.' Her face was sober. 'Servants in New Zealand are few and can cost one dear. Reliable help is very rare indeed and, because of this, one's cook or housemaid is likely to go off without warning to work for somebody else who will pay her more.'

'Then we must consider ourselves fortunate.' Lucy smiled. 'Uncle Ruben has a housekeeper, a native girl to help with the household tasks and people who work outdoors.'

'Ah, but does he have a cook?' One of the ladies raised an eyebrow.

'Perhaps he awaits her arrival!' Mr Cresswell murmured an aside that Lucy could not hear, and general merriment followed.

Percival Truscott's voice rose above the laughter. 'I would regard the advice written on those pages with all seriousness, my friends. We have left Queen and country to live in a foreign and savage place and will require many of those skills if we would survive!'

There was a hubbub of dissent and more amusement. Matthew Pigott, a general merchant, was heard to say, 'If a man is expected to demean his station in this fashion, I would have to say that this New Zealand is undeserving of such as ourselves and take the first ship home!' There was scorn in his barking laugh.

Percival Truscott was losing his equilibrium. 'Scoff all you like now, gentlemen, but mark my words — calling yourself a professional man will count for absolutely nothing in this country when your belly's empty and you've ridiculed the chance to learn how to fill it. Remember my words — you may have need to!'

The small man scowled at those about him, then shaking his head he turned away and walked to the ship's rail to stare at the unchanging horizon.

Adam was at Lucy's side. 'Take a turn around the deck with me.'

As they passed the galley, the smell of roasting beef caused them to glance at each other and smile. There was a light in Adam's eye and a glow to his skin that had been absent throughout the journey until now, and that night, for the first time in five weeks, Lucy slept in her husband's arms.

～

The heat was intense and the people languishing on the hot decks and in the stuffy cabins of the *Rajah* were out of temper. Still the rain held off and water was rationed to one pint per person per day. Everybody complained, praying for steady rain on the one hand to fill the water casks and berating the captain for his harsh ruling on the other. School lessons had ceased.

The ship was losing way as she moved into the doldrums. The sails flapped emptily and she rolled sickeningly on an oily swell in the stagnant sea. The temperature was in the hundreds and fresh meat was no longer on the menu. Adam was again seasick.

For five days the *Rajah* was becalmed and only the sharks came to watch the passengers' plight. On the sixth day, dark clouds were gathering to the south and sultry air clogged their lungs. All eyes were turned to the approaching dark mass and, when the first whisper of wind was borne to them, the captain sent the deckhands to the ratlines and the women went to their cabins to collect anything that would hold water.

Lucy had noted the position of the sails earlier and knew exactly where she would place her containers. Now, with her eye, she carefully measured the distance from the corner of a tri-sail to the deck below. Bending quickly to place the containers, she cracked heads with Mary Truscott.

'You will have to remove that, Mrs Chandler,' Mrs Truscott said firmly. 'I was here first!'

'I think not,' Lucy replied stiffly. 'I have already placed one of my containers, and you are still holding yours!'

'Only, Mrs Chandler, because you bumped me aside!' Mary Truscott's cheeks were blooming.

'I'm sorry, but you will have to find another place to fill them.' Lucy's voice was unrelenting.

'Mrs Chandler,' the small woman rose to her full five feet, 'I have *six* children, desperately in need of water. I feel that *you* should yield, not I!'

'Mrs Truscott,' Lucy's dark eyes flashed, 'why would you consider the thirst of six children to be greater than the thirst of two?'

Large spots of rain began to fall as the two women angrily faced each other. Then Lucy began to laugh. 'Oh, listen to us — just listen.'

The scowl on Mary Truscott's face dissolved and she began to laugh also, and there they stood, helpless with laughter, the torrential rain soaking them to the skin and filling their containers regardless of where they were placed.

On the last day of August, the *Rajah* rounded the Cape of Good Hope and headed south-east into the roaring forties with a strong following wind. The constellations of the north, the Plough and Cassiopeia, had given way to the Southern Cross; the temperature was dropping. On this side of the world it was winter. Fresh meat was again being served, and school hours from eleven o'clock in the morning until noon and four o'clock until five in the afternoon were resumed.

The coast of Australia was sighted on the fourteenth of September, Daniel's twelfth birthday. Nine days later the ship ran into a terrible storm off Tasmania. The seas were treacherous and the wind howled unceasingly through the rigging. Everything moveable was lashed to the deck and a safety-line was strung across each cabin.

The galley fires were extinguished, leaving only cold fare to comfort the shivering passengers. Leaking skylights in the cuddy dripped constantly on to the food, over the tablecloths, and on to the seats and floors. With this dripping and the tilting of the deck, eating had become a feat of endurance.

Adam was desperately ill. Mr Johns, the surgeon, had struggled along the deck in the teeming rain to attend him when Lucy, stricken with fear, had sent for him. The surgeon had looked at the failing man, made him as comfortable as he could, then floundered back to his own cabin, wondering why the hell a man with a mortal affliction would choose to die on the high seas rather than in the comfort of his own bed. He doubted the fellow would even see the shores of his new home.

But Adam clung to life. Lashed to his bed, he was barely conscious of the mayhem outside his cabin door.

For three days the *Rajah* was beleaguered by high winds and mountainous seas. Spars snapped and the lifeboats were dashed to pieces as the tempest raged. The ship was taking on water and the pumps worked day and night. Then, on the fourth day, the storm abated and the damage to the ship was assessed. The bulwarks and several of the aft cabins had been severely damaged. The lifeboats were kindling, and cargo that had been lashed to the deck was gone. The small amount of sail the ship had carried throughout the storm hung in tatters.

The *Rajah* limped along, battling the heavy swell that the storm had left behind. The pumps continued to labour but each day she settled lower in the water, struggling to lift herself over the bigger waves. The captain's face was bleak as he ordered the galley fires to be lit and warm food to be provided again. Adam, extremely weak, took a little broth.

Anxious eyes watched the rising waterline as day followed day. Then anxiety turned to hope as New Zealand appeared on the eastern horizon, a dark, hazy outline. On the second of October, the land — a bold, hilly coastline ten miles distant — rose up from the sea. A red glow suffused the sky that night from a large fire inland, and a damp peaty smell was carried to the passengers on the offshore breeze.

On the third day of October, the passengers had clearer glimpses of the land. Hills and valleys took on shape and colour and higher ranges towered beyond these. Between the hills was the Otago Harbour; tantalisingly near, but the captain would not venture in without the aid of a pilot to guide his foundering ship.

When, after firing muskets for several hours to draw attention to the ship's presence, there was no response from the shore, the captain reluctantly made the decision to stand out to sea until the following day. Early next morning, it was found that the ship, ponderous with the weight of water in her, had moved in dangerously close to the hilly shoreline. Again no pilot responded to the repeated musket fire, and the captain once more moved the *Rajah* out to sea.

The captain and the first mate pondered their situation. With the ship now perilously low in the water, they knew they must come to a decision within hours. There was much grumbling from the passengers, Mr Cresswell's voice the loudest. 'Are we all to drown in sight of land? Why don't they run this leaking tub on to the beach?'

Adam, resting in the cabin, could hear the overbearing voice and muttered under his breath. Lucy and the children had packed up their trunks several days before and were as restless as everybody else to go ashore. They gazed with longing at the land so near.

At last the captain decided to risk sailing into the harbour without the aid of a pilot, but as they were making their lumbering approach to the entrance a sudden gale sprang up and the ship was driven back, the decks deeply awash and the wind screaming through the rigging. Women and children huddled distraught in their cabins, some crying, while their men, drawn and anxious, could offer no comfort, only wait.

The wind subsided as quickly as it had risen and the sun emerged from behind scudding clouds. The *Rajah* then made her labouring approach to the harbour entrance again, and passengers and crew held their breaths until she had cleared the bar safely and dropped anchor in the outer harbour. All was calm and quiet except for the sound of the pumps. Everybody lined the rails, their eyes fixed on the almost forgotten green of the trees, the distant surf and the gulls. A flagstaff standing on a lone hill was the only sign of habitation; there was no sign of the fire they had seen. Adam stood with Lucy and the children, leaning heavily on the rail, and there were tears in his eyes.

Towards evening a party of natives came to the ship's side in a kind of dugout. They appeared to be friendly. Smiling, they came aboard to sell potatoes, eggs and milk at exorbitant prices.

It was the sixth of October when the *Rajah* limped into Port Chalmers; the wind and the tide being against her, it had taken many frustrating hours to get there.

Chapter 2

THERE WAS A COLD OFFSHORE WIND blowing and the schooner *Henry* pitched uncomfortably in the choppy seas. Lucy was in the small cabin allotted to them, making up the bunks in the event that they would need to remain on board overnight.

If conditions remained favourable they would reach the mouth of the Waitaki River around midnight; there, they expected to be met by Ruben Chandler to begin the long trek inland. The captain had warned that if the weather closed in they would be taking the precaution of anchoring in a sheltered bay until morning.

The cabin was basic and cold. The narrow mattresses were filled with unrelenting chaff, and there was a pervading smell of mildew, brine and wet rope. There was no pretence of comfort.

Lucy finished her task and stood for a moment looking at the grimy walls, feeling strangely naked without her familiar comforts about her. With the exception of the wooden box of sovereigns and their trunks, their possessions remained in Port Chalmers, the captain having refused to load them. 'Ye're like ta lose the lot if the thaw catches yer an' the rivers are up,' he had stated. 'An' Nobby Clark's been known ter leave stuff sittin' on t' beach rather'n put 'is animals at risk. Send down fer 'em beginnin' o' next winter.'

Lucy found her family on deck. Daniel was talking to the man at the tiller with his usual exuberance, and Adam and Sarah were sitting in a patch of pale sunshine, their backs against the cabin hatch, looking far from well.

'The bunks are made up if you need to lie down,' she said, holding fast to the cabin doorway as the small ship pitched and reared through a restless sea.

The captain was approaching as Lucy spoke. He eyed Adam closely and a grin split his swarthy face. 'Aye, yer look ter 'ave swallowed a gob-full o' raw chicken gizzards, ther pair o' ye.'

Adam's throat worked convulsively. Closing his eyes, he slowly stood up. 'Excuse me,' he murmured and turned to the side of the boat.

''Ere now, if yer feelin' a bit squarmy, take me advice, squire, an' stay on deck.' The captain took hold of Adam's arm. ''Ere, come wi' me.' He propelled him towards the bow of the boat. 'Now if yer face the waves, watch 'em comin', yer know what ter expect. Ride wi'em an' ye'll not be bothered by the motion.' The stocky figure turned to Lucy. ''Tis cold up 'ere, missus — they could do wi' a blanket.' He drew Sarah forward. 'Now, if yer man an' lassie 'ere do as Cap'n says, they'll be right fine.' With that he rolled away on short, bandy legs, bawling orders to his crew.

Lucy negotiated the plunging deck again carrying mackintoshes and plaids, acutely aware that the thin rope strung along the deck was all that stood between her and the heaving sea just feet away. Daniel came to help her, moving with the assurance of youth. They settled Adam and Sarah behind the bowsprit and Daniel enquired hopefully, 'May we eat soon, Mama? I'm hungry.'

Meals were not supplied on the *Henry*; one provided one's own food or went without. Percy Truscott had had the foresight to visit the *Rajah*'s galley before disembarking and had pushed a bundle into Lucy's arms as they'd said their goodbyes and exchanged good wishes. Lucy had unwrapped the bundle down in their cabin to find that it contained mutton, bread, tea, pork and crumbling plum pudding. Bless him.

As darkness was falling, the captain made his way up to the bow where Adam and Sarah huddled on a heap of coiled rope. He held a tin cup in his hand and Adam thought wryly that he had the look of a jocular pirate.

'Well, young miss, sir, did Cap'n Jones's recipe work?'

'Indeed yes. We are feeling much better, if a little cold.'

''Ere then, sup a little rum, slow like, sir — let it seep into yer bones.' He patted Sarah's shoulder. 'A sip or two won't hurt ye either, missy, but don't tell yer ma!' He chuckled in the half-darkness.

Midnight had come and gone when Lucy was roused from sleep by the rattle of the anchor chain. She sat up stiffly as Daniel spoke drowsily from the other bunk. 'Have we arrived, Mama?'

Lucy peered through the grimy porthole. 'I think we are at the river-mouth. Adam! Sarah!' she called softly. There was no reply.

The sounds of activity above their heads indicated that indeed their sea journey was over. Without stopping to light the lamp, Lucy hurriedly twisted up her hair, rolled up their bedding and thrust it at Daniel. Then she took the bundle of food from the locker and something small ran over her foot, but there was no time to think about what it had been. They hurried up on deck to find that the longboat was already being lowered over the side with their trunks on board; Adam and Sarah, still wrapped in their plaids, had moved to the schooner's side, watching nervously, shivering in the cold.

'Ahoy the beach!'

The captain's shout was immediately answered from the shore.

'We'll put yer gear ashore then come back fer ye, squire.'

Adam stepped forward as he saw the box of sovereigns in the stern of the longboat. Pointing to the box he said sharply, 'That stays with me!'

In the light from the lanterns his face was cadaverous, but his voice was firm and despite his weakness his upright posture clearly indicated that he would brook no argument. The box was hefted back on deck and the family stood in a tight group as the longboat was shoved away from the schooner's side. There was no moon.

'Was that Uncle Ruben? Is he waiting for us on the beach?' Sarah shivered and crept closer to Adam. 'I don't much like this place.'

'It will seem different in the daylight — no, that wasn't

Uncle Ruben's voice, but he'll be waiting for us, you'll see.'

They heard the sailors' voices on the shore, and shortly the sound of the oars again as they rowed back. Then the longboat was bobbing below them.

'Off yer go! Watch yer step!'

Hands reached up. Lucy stepped down as the boat rose up on the glassy swell and she tumbled in a flurry of petticoats into the bottom of the longboat. Red of face, she was helped to her seat and Sarah was lifted aboard. Adam took his time, then attempting to take the heavy box of sovereigns from a sailor's hands he lost his balance and sat down abruptly. He heard a chuckle and looked up in annoyance to see the captain grinning down at him. In the light of the lanterns, the man resembled a swarthy imp.

Only the pale stars lighted their way as the longboat grounded in the shallows. Then a dark form loomed off the bow and Sarah squealed in fright as she was plucked from her seat and lifted up on to the shore. Adam tried to rise, but again sat down hard. 'Ruben Chandler!' he called. 'Is my uncle there?'

''E's not come,' a rough voice grated. 'Leave 'old.' And the box of sovereigns was wrested from Adam's grasp; then he too was seized and swung up on to dry ground. The sailors were laughing good-naturedly now as Lucy was swept up and deposited beside her husband. Daniel, entering into the fun of it, gripped the big hands and leapt the cold wavelets.

'Good luck, take care, 'ave a safe journey — look arter yerselves!'

The men at the oars were still laughing as they pulled the longboat around and rowed back to the schooner, while the man who had come to meet them could only be identified as a darker mass in the Stygian night.

'I presume you are Mr Clark?'

'Aye.'

'And my uncle, will he meet us along the way?'

The massive hulk did not reply but turned and strode off, a giant of a man to whom the dunes and tangled tussock presented no obstacle. Adam and Daniel, carrying the heavy box between them, tried to keep the teamster in sight but soon his bulk was lost in the darkness.

'Where the devil has he gone?'

'We'd better wait here, Adam, lest we become lost.' Lucy's voice was anxious. 'Rest, you are becoming breathless, dear.'

Then the fellow was back, taking the heavy box from their hands.

'Keep up,' he commanded and was off again.

They stumbled after him, struggling to keep him in view. Then they came on the teamster's camp, a bed of glowing embers in the centre of a clearing. As they approached the warmth the man threw an armload of wood on to it, raising a shower of sparks against the black sky.

'Where is the box?' Adam asked bluntly.

The teamster, setting a tripod over the fire, thumbed over his shoulder. In the flickering light of the reviving fire Adam could just see the big wagon. He walked across to it and slowly raised himself up to the high seat.

'I don't see it.'

''Tis there, under ther seat.'

Adam found it, then cast his eye down the length of the long wagon. It was loaded with sacks, crates and bundles, and he saw their trunks at the end. He walked back to the fire. A blackened kettle hung from the tripod. Lucy and the children stood close to the warmth, but there was no sign of the teamster. 'Where is he?' Adam asked quietly.

'With the horses, I think,' Daniel whispered.

'I am very cold, Mama,' Sarah complained.

The big man loomed out of the darkness then, and set their box of cooking and eating utensils beside the fire along with their plaids and mackintoshes.

'Yer got tea?'

Lucy nodded, holding out the package of food she carried. He ignored it.

''Ave yer tea then bed down. Be movin' out in three hours.'

'Where are we to sleep?'

'On the ground. Got beddin', ain't yer?'

'Only these.' Lucy pointed to the bundle beside the fire. 'They'll not serve us on these stones. Could we not sleep in the wagon?'

The teamster shrugged and turned away. While the family watched silently, he reached out a bedroll from beneath his seat, flicked it open under the wagon, then rolling himself into it he settled to sleep.

Dismayed, Lucy turned to Adam. 'What are we to do? Oh, Adam, where is your uncle?'

'I don't know, dearest.' His voice was weary. 'Let us have our tea, then we'll decide what is to be done. There is no room in the wagon for us.'

There was no milk or sugar, but the hot liquid warmed them a little in the bleak night air. Such was their disquiet, nobody felt like eating.

'Papa,' Daniel whispered, 'could we pull up some of that and lay it under our mackintoshes?' He pointed to the marram grass and tussock that grew in profusion about them.

'It will have spiders and things in it!' Sarah wailed.

'I think it might do very well, Daniel — hush, Sarah! I wish I'd had the wit to buy those mattresses.' And when a bed of sorts had been made and they huddled together for warmth, the children between them, Lucy and Adam lay watching the cold stars and listened to the strange night noises until sleep claimed them.

Adam seemed hardly to have closed his eyes when a boot nudged him. 'Up!'

The taciturn giant loomed over him. It was still dark and very cold; the fire was out. Lucy's tired voice came from the darkness, 'If we can have a fire, I will make the tea.'

'No time fer that — into the wagon.'

Helping Lucy up into the wagon, Adam saw that the driver's seat was cluttered with sundry items, clearly indicating that it was not to be shared. He helped Sarah and Daniel up and they sat where they could among the sacks and crates, still wrapped in their plaids in an effort to keep warm.

Daniel tried to converse with the teamster, but his efforts

were met with silence. Adam, seated on a bag of wheat, his back supported by another, stared at the broad silhouette with dislike.

He must have dozed off. When he awoke it was daylight. His legs were cramping badly and his neck was stiff. Lucy was sitting with the children among the sacks and crates, her hair unpinned, her face rebellious. Adam fumbled for his fob watch; it was half past eight.

'Mr Clark,' he addressed the uncompromising back. 'Can we not stop now? We have eaten little since noon yesterday and we need to alight and refresh ourselves.'

It was as though he had not spoken. Nobby Clark kept driving. Thirty minutes later they came to a wide, shallow wash. The six great Clydesdales drew the heavy wagon diagonally across the shingle to the other side and halted a short distance from the water, snorting steam.

''Alf an hour,' the teamster grated. 'No fire.' He pulled nosebags from the wagon for the horses and, ignoring his charges, took a saddlebag from under his seat and lumbered off along the bank of the wash. Stiffly Adam climbed down and helped Lucy and Sarah to alight. Lucy opened the parcel of food. 'Sparingly, my love,' Adam warned. 'We don't know how long it will take us to reach the homestead.'

'Captain Jones said about three days, saving delays,' Daniel offered.

'Three days,' Adam murmured, rubbing his stiff neck. 'I can't imagine another night sleeping under these conditions!'

To Adam the journey seemed endless. His spare frame felt bruised to the bone as the wagon jolted across the miles. The further inland they travelled, the wilder the terrain became. They had crossed a number of creeks and riverbeds, and the plains around them had the tangled, desolate appearance of unoccupied country. It had been bitterly cold in the night, but as the morning wore on a warm westerly breeze blew in their faces and Nobby Clark pushed his team into a trot.

By noon, the breeze had become an uncomfortable wind that tore at their hair and clothes, and when they made camp, long after the early dusk had come down, the gusts made lighting a fire impossible.

During the night the wind lulled for a time and then a low moaning away in the distance heralded its return. It rose to a roar and the full force of the wind hit them. Rolled tightly in their blankets, the travellers covered their heads to protect their faces from the stinging grit. The wind buffeted them all night. Nobody slept, and when the wind finally ceased an hour before dawn it was followed by heavy rain.

'Get aboard!' Nobby Clark shouted through the downpour as he hitched up his team, and, before his passengers could settle themselves, he was whipping the horses into a trot.

They had travelled parallel to the Waitaki River almost continuously since leaving the beach, but the heavy rain, falling steadily all day, blotted out the river and everything else. Adam, huddled under his mackintosh, experienced an odd sense of disembodiment. The teamster pressed on all day, not stopping for food, and Adam could feel his ire rising. 'How much further before we reach the homestead, Mr Clark?' he called out irritably.

"Bout twenty-eight mile.'

'Can we stop then and take food?' His eyes were on his wife and children crouching miserably in the bottom of the wagon, chilled and wet through. 'My family can suffer no more.'

'Not afore nightfall.'

'Now see here,' Adam shouted at the teamster, 'your treatment of us is not to be borne!' He tried to stand up but fell back as the wagon passed over a rut. 'Why, sir, is my uncle not here to see to us, I ask you again?' His voice shook.

'I'd not be knowing wher' yer uncle is an' if yer not enjoyin' the ride, get yerselves out,' came the surly reply.

Adam was silenced.

In the next two hours they crossed two more washes. The water in the first wash was shallow but swift-running. The second wash was deeper and the current stronger. Another hour passed and the rain had stopped.

As dusk was falling, Nobby Clark brought his horses to a halt on the banks of a broad, rapidly flowing river. The teamster climbed down from his seat and walked to the water's edge. Adam clambered down and joined him. He could see where wagon wheels had made numerous scars in the bank during past crossings, but the river now was running fast and deep, the water a muddy green.

Adam eyed the tumbling waters with misgiving. 'You'll not try to cross here, surely?'

'Why'd yer think that now?'

Nobby Clark strode back to his wagon. Resuming his seat, he flicked his reins along the horses' backs and Adam was obliged to run after the moving vehicle. The wagon moved downstream and shortly came to a place where the teamster halted the horses. 'Make camp,' he grunted.

The Clydesdales were unhitched, watered and tethered to the deep-rooted tussock grass with their nosebags tied on. In the failing light, the weary family clambered down from their cramped positions on the wagon and stood looking across the wide body of rapidly moving water to the rugged, untamed country on the other side. A feeling of deep loneliness was in each of them.

Daniel again collected marram grass and tussock for their bed. There was no dry wood to make a fire, and Lucy knew, as she set out their meagre meal, that there would be no warming pot of tea.

The night came in clear and moonlit, and frost was settling on the ground. Silently, they sat in their damp clothing, chewing their slice of mutton and stale bread and the few remaining crumbs of plum pudding. Nobby Clark had long since retired under his wagon, sharing neither food nor conversation.

When all had finished eating and their rough bed was made, they settled to sleep, again lying close together for warmth. Inexorably, the temperature dropped below zero and, exhausted as they were, the cold seeping into their weary bones would not allow sleep to come. The river rattled and rolled its stones loudly in the sharp air and the monotonous call of a swamp hen seemed very close. Adam's back ached, a deep, unremitting ache, and he fought the urge to cough.

The night was eternal. Finally the cold, pale moon sank from sight and darkness wrapped them in a bitter embrace until the first grey streaks of dawn heralded the day. As the glow of palest pearl showed itself above the plains, Nobby Clark emerged from under his wagon.

A rime of frost lay over the mackintosh, and Adam, throwing it aside, rose stiffly to his feet and bade the children look for sticks to start a fire. The teamster was tying nosebags on the six horses. Hoarfrost lay on the ground and the animals' rough backs were white.

With the resilience of children, Daniel and Sarah scratched about for anything that would make their breakfast fire. Discovering a number of pools covered thickly with starred ice, they traced the patterns on them with fascinated fingers. Shivering, Adam picked up the small pile of sticks they had gathered and began to coax a fire into life. Lucy spread their bedding as close as she could to the warmth and set out the food; they would have tea this morning.

In the growing light, Adam's appearance again shocked her. The skin on his face, drawn tight across his cheekbones, was almost transparent. His eyes were sunk deep in their sockets and the cough he had suppressed during the night would no longer be silenced. It came from deep within his chest, persistent and distressing. The teamster studied him from under his low brow and gave him poor odds for survival in this harsh clime. Seemingly in no hurry this morning, the big man finished his leisurely breakfast of bacon and fried bread with a pipe. Again he had made no offer to share, and the smell of frying bacon was more than Daniel could bear. He watched every great gob-full disappear, scowling darkly, disgust stamped across his young face.

Late morning saw them back in their places on the wagon. They headed downstream; the river quieter now but still moving swift and green over its stony bed. As the wagon rumbled on, the banks on the other side of the river were noticeably closer, and after travelling about five miles the teamster turned his team into a place where the river had narrowed to a roiling, swirling race. 'Hoy, hoy, hoy!' he bellowed, cracking his whip over the horses' heads. The wagon plunged down the bank, tilting precariously, the animals chest-deep in the icy flow. Sarah, taken unawares, was jolted from her seat and began to fall. Daniel and Lucy's hands flew out to grasp the falling child and pull her, white-faced, to safety. Adam, not a swearing man, glared at the wagoner, his lips moving darkly.

The lead horses leaned into their harnesses and pulled strongly, diagonally upstream against the swirling current, taking the brunt of it as the rest of the team hauled the cumbersome wagon. It slewed and bucked across the race, its passengers clinging on for dear life, and then they were across, the Clydesdales slipping and plunging as they pulled their heavy load from the water. While the horses rested, the teamster checked their feet and harness and then they set off towards the scrub-covered hills, leaving the tussock flats behind.

They came to a clearly defined track that ran parallel to a wide body of water. After a time this narrowed into a deep gorge with fluted columns marching up each side of its steep walls, and as the wagon and its passengers moved upwards, the alpine ranges, snow-topped and remote, towered above them.

After two and a half hours of steady climbing, resting from time to time, the horses began to pull more easily as the track became less steep. The sun was high in a clear sky and somewhere a skylark trilled its song. Daniel stood up to move to a more comfortable position and suddenly he was shouting, 'Chimneys — I can see chimneys — look!' He was pointing excitedly.

'Are we on my uncle's property?' Standing up too, Adam raised his voice to be heard over the noise of rushing water in the gorge below.

The teamster jerked his head in assent.

Lucy rose to her feet but in a moment she sat down again, suddenly faint.

'Mama?' Sarah was watching her, worried.

'I'm all right, dear, a little tired perhaps.'

Daniel plucked at his father's sleeve. 'May we get down and run ahead, Papa, and let Uncle Ruben know we have arrived?'

'You may.' Adam grinned. 'Stay on the track.' He felt the tensions of the trying journey fall from him as he watched his two children run ahead, laughing, calling out to each other, glad to be there. Whatever happened now, Ruben would take charge. Lucy guessed his thoughts and, reaching out, she pressed his hand in hers.

They sat close, looking past the back of their taciturn driver to the running children. Then, where the tracks turned towards the homestead, the children were suddenly still, staring at something Lucy and Adam could not as yet see. Daniel turned and looked back at the wagon, his face white.

The teamster did not halt his team but drove past the silent children to the burned-out homestead. Two tall chimneys and the blackened cob walls were all that remained of Ruben's sketch. He lowered his bulk to the ground. 'Stay put,' he ordered. Slowly he walked around the ruin, then disappeared within its walls. Adam sat where he was, stunned, unable to take in the enormity of what he was seeing. Sarah began to cry as she approached the wagon, and Lucy clambered down from her seat to comfort her children, her actions automatic as she saw Nobby Clark scoop up a handful of ash and rub it through his big fingers. 'Burned down afore the rain come,' he stated.

'How has this happened?' Lucy asked quietly. 'And where is Mr Chandler — and his housekeeper and the other people who live here?' Her eyes grew fearful as she turned them again on the blackened walls.

The teamster stared down at her and shook his big head. 'Ther not in ther' anyways.' Turning away from her he faced the hills, cupping his hands about his mouth. 'Hello — *hello!*' His voice echoed around the empty slopes and he listened intently. He shouted again, but his voice, bouncing off the ridges and outcrops, elicited only silence. 'Stay put!' he commanded again and lumbered away towards the rising ground. The waiting family could hear his voice as he shouted up into the vastness above him; it seemed to come from all directions, but no answering call could they hear.

When at length he returned, his words were blunt: 'Barn's gone, musterers' huts, woolshed, the lot — burned out. Nothin' left but the privy!' He threw an axe and a length of chain down on the ground. 'Ther's bits and pieces lyin' in the tussock next t'wher' the barn were — some'un's tried ter save 'em.'

'Are you suggesting somebody did this deliberately?' Adam's voice was unsteady.

'Nah . . . why'd yer think that now?' came the sarcastic reply.

'Where are all the sheep?' Daniel cut in. 'There should be thousands of them, shouldn't there?'

'Aye,' the teamster admitted. 'Didn't see no stock, but ther's a horse runnin' loose up ther', saddle still on him — couldn't get near.'

'What do you think has happened here?'

The teamster's small eyes held Adam's for a moment, then he shrugged his vast shoulders.

'What are we going to do, Adam?' Lucy tried to keep the fear out of her voice.

'We will have to bring the law up here—'

Nobby Clark's laugh was a derisive bark. 'Ye'll get no police leavin' ther' warm orfices this time o' year. Ye'd best be gettin' yerselves back ter the port to buy yer tickets 'ome.'

'We'll not leave until we've discovered what has happened to my uncle — what has happened here!' Two bright spots coloured Adam's cheeks.

'Please yerself.' The big man turned back to his wagon. 'Wher' do yer want yer supplies then? I've ter be gettin' orf.'

'Supplies, what supplies?' Adam stared at the man.

'Yer uncle's dry goods. Ther' paid fer an' I ain't cartin' 'em further.'

'Are you leaving without attempting to help us?' Lucy said in disbelief.

'The thaw's set in, missus. Ther's folks as will be wantin' ther supplies.' He pointed a thumb at the wagon. 'An' I've ter get meself back down afore the rivers get up.'

'You can't just go off!' Lucy glared angrily at the stubborn face of the teamster.

Ignoring her, he faced Adam. 'Yer want me advice — yer go lookin' fer yer uncle up yonder, but keep clear o' them gullies.'

Adam climbed down from the wagon and walked slowly towards the ruined farmhouse. He stood in the doorway for a time, looking up at the sky past the charred rafters, then he turned to the teamster, who was dragging sacks about on the wagon. 'Will you at least stay long enough to help me erect some kind of shelter for my family and a cover for our dry goods? I have no tools.'

Somewhere in the teamster's unrelenting breast, a flicker of sympathy stirred: Poor skinny rooster, I'll lay a bet 'e'll be worm fodder afore summer's done. "Alf an hour — 'alf an hour yer'll get — no more. Up on the wagon then.'

44

The team was turned around and the wagon was driven back the way they had come. After a short distance the horses were reined off the track and brought to a halt beside a derelict hovel, close to the river. 'That ther' shepherd's hut'll cover yer if yer tidy 'er up a bit.'

Adam stared at the hut. He could see through the open doorway that the floor was of mud and he could smell the evil green water that lay in the myriad hoof-prints that pitted it. The single window had never known glass, and the roof, thatched with tussock, was in a sad state of disrepair.

'You can't expect me to house my family in that!' Adam Chandler's voice cracked with outrage. 'It's clear that animals have sheltered in there. It's foul!' He began to cough, a deep, tearing cough that he struggled to control.

'Best decide then if yer stayin'. I'll not be this way again fer a twelve-month — it's that or nothin',' the teamster growled. 'Now, if yer stayin' jump to it.' He turned to Daniel. 'You boy, come wi' me — you too.' He glowered at Lucy and Sarah as he thrust a wicked-looking blade at Daniel. 'Cut the tussock ther' an' lay a floor over the muck — thick as yer like.' Picking up the axe, he motioned to Lucy and Sarah to follow him. Adam, climbing down from the wagon, began to cough again and Lucy hesitated.

'Yer comin'?' Nobby Clark snapped. 'Get movin' — 'alf an hour is all yer gettin'.' He turned his attention to the flax bushes growing in profusion along the riverbank and swung the axe in great arcs. The flax fell in sheaves.

'Gather it up, girlie, and yer ma can beat it 'til it looks like rope. Yer gonna need a heap o' it, so keep at it.'

'What can I do?' Adam asked hoarsely.

'Keep out o' the way.'

Adam watched the tireless energy of the teamster, his wife and children toiling at the man's bidding, and he loathed the frailty of his body. Soon a pile of flax lay before the hut and the teamster showed Lucy and Sarah how to thrash it against the rough surface of a boulder until it was separated into fibres. 'Lay flax over the tussock, boy, soon's yer've covered the muck,' the big man grunted, then taking up his axe he disappeared into a patch of scrub that grew a short distance from the hut. The family could hear his axe and his big body crashing about over the noise of the river. When he returned, he carried an armload of poles and thin branches, trimmed clean of twigs and leaves, and dropped them on the ground. He lumbered away to the patch of scrub again and shortly returned with a second armload of branches.

Four thick poles he set in holes that he dug in the stony ground, two of them close to the shepherd's hut and two more placed three paces back from these.

Working quickly and with obvious bad grace, he set about constructing a framework of the thinner poles and branches. When this was completed, he tied one side of the frame to the poles nearest the hut.

'Get 'ere now,' he said to nobody in particular, 'an' learn 'ow ta thatch.' The family gathered near.

'Keep that tussock comin', boy,' he growled as Daniel put down his blade.

The teamster worked the tussock over and through the latticework for the frame with surprising dexterity. 'Do yer see? — right. When yer've done, lift 'er up and tie this bottom side 'ere to them other two poles.'

'What is this?' Adam asked.

'Cookin' shelter. Build a fire under it an' 'ang yer kettle or cookin' pot from that chain ther'.'

Adam recognized the length of chain that the teamster had brought down from the burned-out barn. It now hung from the middle of the frame. 'I can do that,' Adam said quietly, examining the teamster's handiwork. 'It doesn't appear to be too difficult.'

'Get to it, then.' The man watched Adam for a moment then strode to the wagon. Without ceremony he hefted the four heavy trunks and the box of sovereigns into the hut as easily as though they were empty.

'Wher's yer keys?' Nobby Clark thrust his hand under Adam's nose.

'Why would you want the keys?' Adam asked suspiciously. 'The contents of the box or the trunks are none of your affair.'

The teamster's face darkened. 'Yer wastin' time — empty 'em.'

'I don't understand.' Adam frowned.

'Rats — yer dry goods are goin' in 'em.'

'Rats!' Lucy had come to stand in the doorway of the hut while Adam unlocked the trunks. She watched as the hasps were flung up and the great paws hauled the contents of the trunks on to the floor, her intimate garments among them. With burning cheeks Lucy retreated.

Adam followed her and said quietly, 'Dear girl, I have

47

no right to put you and the children through this. We will go back to Port Chalmers with the wagon, and if Ruben is not to be found we will go home. The *Rajah* will be in port for at least two months, ample time to find out what has happened here.'

'We cannot go home, Adam, you know we can't.' Lucy Chandler raised bleak eyes to her husband's haggard face. 'We will have to make the best of this until we can find help.' She averted her face while Nobby Clark stomped past her, back and forth between wagon and shepherd's hut, unloading and stacking their dry goods. Then when he clambered up the bank and set off up the track on some other mission, Lucy looked quickly at Adam then followed her children into the hut.

'There's not much room in here for us, Papa.' Daniel stood inside the doorway. 'What do you suppose is in those sacks?'

Adam looked at them piled one on top of the other. 'There will be a label on them somewhere. I expect they are full of animal food.'

'Where do you suppose all the animals have gone?'

'I've no idea, Daniel,' Adam replied tiredly.

'Mama,' Sarah said plaintively. 'We can't live in here — it smells!'

The teamster came noisily down the bank. He carried a dripping barrel in his big arms. 'This 'ere's yer meat supply.' He dumped the barrel at Lucy's feet. She raised her eyebrows. 'Ther's two more o' these in the river, marked wi' a stake — can ya cook?'

Lucy shook her head.

'Yer'd best learn quick, then. Yer'll starve up here else.' He wrenched the lid off the barrel and Lucy, seeing its bloody contents, felt her stomach lurch.

'When yer've took out what yer need, put it back in the river afore it goes orf.'

Lucy, who had sat down to her roast beef dinners without a thought to their origin, felt her gorge rise. Was this what the roast dinner on her plate had smelt and looked like before Cook had attended to it? Without warning, she was wretchedly, humiliatingly ill.

'My dear, oh, my poor girl — come, lie down.' Adam drew her towards the hut, but she moved quickly out of the circle of his arm.

'Adam, no, I would rather remain in the fresh air.'

'This has all been too much for you, I fear,' Adam said.

'Yer got a flint an' tinderbox?' Nobby Clark's bulk was between them, his rude stare on Lucy.

'No,' Adam answered shortly. 'But I've matches.'

'Save yer matches. 'Ere—' He thrust two objects at Adam.

'Don't lose 'em.' He considered Adam for a moment, then said gruffly, 'I'm up ter Long Reach now. Effen they know anythin', she'll mebbe come acrost. Yer uncle's likely ther'.'

'Long Reach?' Adam queried.

'The Widder Gaunt's run — the witch — Black Ruby, she's yer neighbour.'

The teamster looked almost amused as he climbed up to his seat. Then he was gone. When they could no longer hear the wagon's departing creaks, the silence and the cold descended on the family. Their isolation was complete and they were ill-prepared for the deprivations they must face. Adam looked down at his wasted frame and his pale, slender hands, and hopelessness filled him. Without much effort, the big teamster had set up their rough abode in less than an hour. Somehow he must carry on with little in the way of tools and no knowledge of how to survive in this wild place. He prayed silently that his uncle would be found not too far away. He shivered involuntarily and his eyes sought the heights above. Would Ruben and his shepherds descend from their cold vastness in due course, driving the missing sheep before them? He turned back to his thatching. 'Let us finish this quickly, son, and light a fire. It is growing colder.'

'Will you not eat something first, Adam?' Lucy was by his side. 'There is a little pork and bread left.'

'No, my love—' A sudden bout of coughing halted his words, then he continued quietly, his eyes on the shelter's roof. 'Save it for dinner lest this is not finished in time.'

Lucy returned to thrashing the flax while Sarah sat miserably watching her. She was shivering and hungry and couldn't understand why they would choose to stay in this place when Uncle Ruben was no longer there.

Lucy's arms ached abominably and she longed to stop flaying the stiff flax, but Adam and Daniel were using it more quickly than she could shred it. She gritted her teeth against the pain and willed her arms to keep moving.

Finally, Adam stood back. 'This will do, I think, Daniel.

Now, help me to hoist it up, then you secure it to the poles as I hold it in place.'

'I shall need to stand on something, Papa, I'm not quite tall enough to reach.'

'Then let us bring one of the bags out of the hut; that should serve.'

The shelter was much heavier than Adam had anticipated. When he strained to lift it, he began to cough. He struggled to breathe as the cold air lacerated his lungs and he lowered the frame, remaining bent double until he gained control. Lucy stood beside him, her hand on his back, waiting. When he slowly straightened, she said quietly, 'Let me help.' Together they raised the thatched frame and held it in position while Daniel fastened it to the poles.

'Firewood, children — gather as much dry wood as you can whilst I fetch the water. Where are the can and the pot, Mother?' With forced cheerfulness Adam went down to the river and Lucy reluctantly entered the hut. The overpowering smell of animal urine and fouled mud was lessened to a degree by the thick covering of tussock and flax, but it was still strong. Listlessly, Lucy gathered up their scattered clothing and belongings and laid them in some kind of order over the sacks of animal feed. Then she laid the mackintoshes on the tussock and flax and placed the plaids on top of these, making one big bed, the head of which would be to the trunks as they slept, and their bodies would be away from the stinking mud walls. This done, she gathered up the now meagre amount of food, the teapot, their precious tea caddy, the tin plates and mugs, and set them out on the bag Daniel had used to stand on. Then she sat down on the other end of the bag and pondered the reason why she felt unwell and when she had begun to feel so.

She cast her mind back and remembered the night she had lain in Adam's arms, then counted the weeks since on her fingers — and the cause of her sickness became abundantly clear. The movement of the ship had certainly been the cause of her illness on board ship, but her present indisposition left her in no doubt: she was with child.

After Sarah, it had seemed that there were to be no more children, and she had long since given up hoping for the larger family she and Adam had planned, but having their wish granted at this time and in this place was a cruel irony and Lucy felt an involuntary anger against the child growing in her womb. Ashamed of the feeling, she rose to meet her husband and children, who at that moment were emerging from the scrub, laden with wood and water.

Lucy lay awake far into the night, her mind on a treadmill of anxious thoughts, the foul smell of the hut an offence to her nostrils. Adam lay beside her, deep in exhausted sleep, his body burning with fever. The children, lying on her other side, were restless, turning constantly and mumbling indistinct words. There were odd rustlings and scratchings in the tussock, and Lucy's tired imagination painted a ghoulish picture of rats gnawing at them as they slept. Wide-eyed, she lay watching the stars through the mean thatching of the roof and listened to the gurgling of the river. The night was still and very cold.

From time to time, Lucy thought she could hear movement

beyond the open doorway. The fire had long since gone out and the moon had set; the darkness was complete as she lay motionless, straining her eyes and her ears. Something moved in the tussock beneath her foot and she brought her heel down in sudden fear — we cannot stay here, she thought, her heart pounding, sleeping with vermin and prey to whatever lurked beyond that door. Panic was taking control as she remembered the teamster's words: *I'll not be back fer a twelve-month.* They were trapped there. She had told herself that she would have to make the best of it for Adam's sake, but in the black hours before the dawn her resolution was wavering.

Deliberately, she turned her thoughts to the evening. They had sat hugging the fire, waiting for two fat hens to cook in the pot that hung from the heavy chain. Adam had declared the pork unsafe to eat, so with rumbling, empty stomachs, they had sipped their tea, making it last as long as they could.

Daniel had stopped Lucy from throwing away the water that the hens had been cooked in. 'Cook would make soup from that, Mama.' So she had put it aside in its pot, wondering how soup could be produced from such fatty liquid and wondering if the last of the stale bread would suffice for breakfast. Adam would have to delve into the contents of a barrel again, she thought with distaste; there was nothing left of the hens.

As dawn's grey fingers brushed the stars from the sky, Lucy fell asleep. She awoke with a start to hear something being dragged about on the ground outside. It was daylight. Daniel, raised on an elbow, whispered, 'There's somebody out there — could it be Uncle Ruben, do you think?'

Lucy rose from the blankets, glancing at Adam, who slept on. Daniel stood up, and Lucy, stepping carefully over Sarah, crept to the doorway to stand beside him. The sight that met their eyes brought disappointment. The horse that Nobby Clark had seen up in the hills was nudging the bag of chaff left near the fire the night before, in a determined effort to get at its contents. It had not seen them.

From behind Lucy, Adam spoke in a quiet voice, 'We'll cut the bag open, Daniel, and if we can tempt her back we'll try to catch her. We are going to need a horse.'

The animal, aware of their presence now, started away as he spoke and then from a safe distance eyed them with distrust. The morning was bitingly cold and a hoarfrost lay on the ground. Two hectic spots of colour dyed Adam's cheeks as he and Daniel dragged the bag from beneath the shelter. They struggled to open it with numb fingers and a blunt New Zealand Company knife. Straightening from his task, Adam watched the mare for a moment. She still wore a saddle, and a broken rein hung from her bridle.

'Whatever has happened here, that animal has been badly frightened,' Adam said. 'It may be some time before we can gain her trust. Let us have breakfast and leave her to eat in peace.' He set about making a fire. 'The water has frozen in the can, Daniel. Set it on the stones here.' He pointed to two flat stones that lay beside his kindling. 'It will thaw in no time and we can have our tea.'

'Mama, I am so hungry.' Sarah came shivering to the fire.

'We will have breakfast as soon as the broth has warmed, dear. Find a forked stick so we can toast the bread.' Lucy reached for the pot of chicken stock, but snatched back her hand when she saw the marks in the remnants of frozen fat that lay on its surface; she had not thought to place the lid on the pot. 'Rats,' she breathed and backed away from the pot.

'Ugh — filthy brutes!' Daniel touched his mother's arm. 'Don't be upset, Mama, I'll throw it away and clean the pot. We can have toast.'

Sarah began to cry. 'Now, now, child,' Adam soothed. 'We will know better next time. Come along and help Mother make the toast.'

'I hate it here — I want to go home!' Sarah sobbed and Lucy silently echoed the child's cry as she looked about her. In the cold morning light, everything was grey and a rime of frost covered the ground. It was a desolate sight, but in a moment the rising sun reached across the plains and slowly rose up to paint the hills gold and festoon the vegetation with diamonds. It was breathtakingly beautiful. In silence the family gazed at the wonder of it, slowly raising their eyes to the mountains. Daubed in rose and deepest purple, the peaks towered above them, immense and mysterious against a brilliant blue sky. The family stood in awe, dwarfed beneath the towering splendour of their majesty, sensing the presence that Ruben Chandler had endeavoured to describe.

Inexplicably, tears welled in Adam's eyes and quickly he bowed his head. Something had touched his very core. Of a sudden, he was keenly aware of his mortality and in that moment he felt the need to be alone, to listen to the silence of those great mountains and glean an intelligence that was just beyond his reach. He recalled Ruben's words: *The air up here is so pure one can believe that only God has breathed it.* And raising his eyes to the mountains again, he felt strongly comforted.

Their frugal breakfast over, Adam carried the scoured pot down to the river where he took two more hens from the barrel. Returning to the cooking shelter he covered them with water, set them over the fire and left them to simmer slowly. Lucy, he knew, would not touch the poultry in its raw state.

He stood for a time staring into the fire, knowing there were things he should be doing to improve their situation, but he had no idea what. He scrubbed at the pale growth on his jaw with a distracted hand. The hut roof would have to be repaired before it rained, but the means of doing this were not at hand. The meat barrels would soon be empty, but he had no way of filling them. Where in God's name was his uncle, who knew how to do these essential tasks? The thought of tackling these problems filled him with despair. Even with the necessary tools, weak as he was he felt it was all beyond him. He thought of Lucy then, delicate and pampered, and of his children forced to sleep in the filthy hovel, and he knew he must try. He called to his son, 'Come with me, Daniel, I'm going to have a look around up there to see if there is anything of use to us. If we are to repair the roof before the rain comes, we must find an implement to cut tussock and construct some kind of ladder.'

'Be careful, Adam,' Lucy said quietly from the doorway of the hut.

'We will be around the homestead and outbuildings. If you are worried about anything, beat a tin plate with a stick and we'll come to you quickly.' Adam kissed her and then, putting his hand on Daniel's shoulder, he turned to clamber up the bank to the track above. Lucy and Sarah stood watching until they were out of sight, then Lucy took Sarah's hand. 'Come, we will go and see what Mr Clark has put in our trunks.' Together, they entered the hut, first tidying their makeshift bed, which had packed down considerably and would need more tussock if they were not soon to be lying on the floor, then they turned their attention to the trunks.

The first three contained large bags of flour, bags of salt and sugar, white and brown, carbonate of soda, cream of tartar, hops, barley, a large jar of malt, saltpetre, dried peas, tins of tea and coffee, tins of tobacco and a large bag of raisins. The last trunk held tins of fluid labelled *kerosene*, boxes of Letchford vesta matches, six bottles of brandy, six bottles of Irish whiskey, tins of sardines, lobster, salmon and other potted meats and fish, two pairs of lace-up boots, a large pair of scissors, packets of seeds, a large piece of pumice and several bars of yellow soap. There was a bolt of canvas and a small coffee grinder. At the bottom of the trunk were folded two coarse grey blankets and a bundle of newspapers. Lucy saw copies of the *Otago Witness* and then she was looking at the *London Illustrated News*, dated nearly six months earlier. A wave of homesickness swept over her as she picked it up.

'There is nothing nice in any of these trunks, Mama. We could just as well have left our things in them.'

For a moment Lucy did not speak, then thrusting the paper from her she said, 'Don't be silly, Sarah. Without those items we will not be able to survive.'

She had spoken sharply to the disappointed child and immediately she regretted it. 'Come now,' she said softly, 'let us put some wood on the fire. Then shall we go and find Papa and Daniel?'

They hastened past the remains of the homestead, afraid to look within its blackened walls, and hurried to join Adam and Daniel who were struggling to drag the skeleton of a cart from the burned-out barn. Even though the sun shone, the air was keen, and Adam, wrestling with the seized wheels, coughed incessantly.

'Could that ever be of any use?' Lucy enquired doubtfully, eyeing the blackened clothes of her menfolk and remembering with distaste the clothing still to be washed, if only she knew how to accomplish this.

'It is only the wooden parts that need to be replaced,' Adam panted. 'Some grease on the wheels should loosen them up again.' His face was flushed and his eyes held a glitter that wasn't entirely due to fever. 'If we can find somebody to rebuild this cart and we can catch the mare, we will have a mode of transport.' He paused to catch his breath then gestured for Lucy to follow him. 'Come and see what else we have unearthed.'

Daniel was grinning. 'This is rather like a treasure hunt, Mama — look.' He held up a blackened object. 'This is a sickle. The handle is not too badly burned.'

'And this —' Adam held up a saw blade. 'The handle is gone but we may be able to use it, and this shovel — I'm sure I can improvise a handle for this.'

Lucy stared at her husband and felt suddenly irritated. What a ridiculous figure he cut in his city finery, ecstatic over a heap of junk burned beyond recognition. She turned away. 'The hens will be nearly cooked. Will you come now and wash before we eat?'

By mid-afternoon the cold was numbing. The small pile of wood, stacked against the wall of the hut, needed replenishing before the early dark came.

Adam had examined the contents of the trunks in his turn and had added a tin of potted meat to the chicken stock to make a kind of stew for tea, adding a little salt. Again Lucy had left the cooking to him, and he was becoming a little annoyed; cooking was surely not a man's domain. But with only one pot to cook in, an already unpalatable task was made almost impossible for Lucy. She had no idea how to prepare a meal for her family and, in spite of Daniel's daily visits to the kitchen, his limited observations of Cook's culinary skills at home were of little help to her here. Added to this, the feel and smell of the meat in the barrels nauseated her so much that she could not bear to touch it.

As she tried to settle to sleep that night, the next morning's breakfast was a problem that loomed large in her tired mind. There was no bread left and she knew that, left to her, there was never going to be any, even though the ingredients to make it were to hand. Tears of despair and defeat squeezed from under her lids and lay cold on her cheeks. How was she to deal with all that lay ahead: Adam so frail, the child, ill-timed, growing within her, her abysmal ignorance of domestic matters, and nobody to help her in this desolate place? She heard the mare return and drifted to sleep at last, thinking that Adam would be pleased that she had come back.

The sun was up when Lucy awoke. With a start she found she was alone in the hut. Hurriedly she pushed back the bedding and scrambled to her feet. As she reached for her shawl, sudden blackness engulfed her and she knew no more.

'Come, dear, come — drink this.' Adam held a mug of hot tea to her lips as she struggled back from the darkness. She heard Sarah's frightened sobs and Daniel's worried face swam in and out of her vision. She tried to speak to reassure them all, but instead floods of tears came and she wept until she could weep no more while Adam held her close. 'There, dearest, there.' He smoothed the tangled hair from her face. 'You'll feel better soon. Try to drink your tea now, it has sugar in it.'

Lucy sat on the makeshift bed on the floor of the stinking hut, sipping tea that was too sweet and too strong, and tried to hide the crushing desolation that consumed her. She reached out a hand to her young daughter. 'I'm all right, pet, Mother is better now.' She drew the child into her arms.

'Why did you faint, Mama? What happened to you?' Sarah stared up into Lucy's face.

'Mama fainted because she has not been having enough to eat,' Adam said.

'Well, we have been making pancakes for breakfast, Mama, and when you eat them you will feel much better.' Daniel spoke with pride.

'Pancakes?' Lucy looked a question at Adam, who was smiling now.

'Yes, pancakes. This lad of ours has sifted through the deeper recesses of his memory and come up with a pancake that resembles Cook's pancakes not at all but it makes passable fare.' He punched a gentle fist at his son's shoulder then turned back to his wife. 'Do you feel you can walk out to the fire? It is far too cold for you in here.'

Lucy, seated near the fire, eyed with some surprise the rounded flat cakes browning on the scoured saw blade that was set in the embers. 'What a clever idea,' she murmured, looking at the saw blade. 'What is in your pancakes, Daniel?'

'Flour and sugar with chicken fat rubbed into it as I've seen Cook do with butter. Then I put in some water and made dough cakes.' He looked at his father. 'We mixed them in the washing basin, I'm afraid.' Plucking a hot cake from the saw, the boy placed it on a tin plate and passed it to his mother. 'Will you try one, please?'

He watched Lucy anxiously as she slowly bit into it, and then she smiled.

'This is surprisingly good. Have you all tried these?'

'Yes,' Adam replied, 'and I'm sure we'll be making more of them. They are sitting very well.'

Lucy felt a deep gratitude to this boy. He was so young, so gently born, yet he seemed to have an instinct for survival and a mind that was capable of grappling with and resolving a problem. To him it was all an adventure. She recalled the conversation around the fire the evening before. 'It should be easy to make a ladder, Papa,' Daniel had said. 'If we cut two long poles for the sides and chip notches in them about a foot apart and then cut short, thick branches for the rungs, set them into the notches and tie them tightly with flax, we would have a ladder.' Adam had nodded, pleased with the boy's ingenuity.

'Yes, Daniel, that should be simple enough, but we need to place new thatching up to and over the ridge of the hut. How will we manage that?'

Daniel had been silent, thinking, his eyes on his father's face; then he had smiled. 'I think we would make a second ladder, Papa, fasten it to the top of the first and lay it on the roof, moving both ladders along as we work.'

'This is a brilliant son we have, my dear,' Adam had laughed. 'But they would have to be safe as well as sturdy, these ladders.'

'Well, Papa, as I am much lighter than you are,' Daniel had replied, 'I would climb up and do the thatching while you passed the tussock up to me.'

They had talked on, discussing ways of utilizing the cart's frame and wheels and how a door might be constructed for the hut. Lucy had listened with small attention, her thoughts occupied by her own problems.

Breakfast over, Adam rose and placed his plate and mug in the basin. 'Sarah, I charge you to look after your mother while Daniel and I go along the riverbank to gather tussock. Today we will mend the roof.'

'Oh, can't I come too, Papa? There is nothing to do here and I could help you carry it.'

'Might be full of spiders and things,' Daniel teased.

'Let her go with you, Adam,' Lucy laughed. 'I am better and I've things to do — but keep away from the river, Sarah.'

When they had gone, Lucy lifted the heavy can of water on to the fire. Then she entered the hut and, gathering up the plaids and mackintoshes, she took them outside and spread them in the pale sunshine to air.

She returned to the hut and methodically sorted through the clothing laid over the sacks of animal food. Soiled clothing was placed by the door and the New Zealand Company's rough garb she laid over the trunks. For a space she stood gazing at them, then selected two pairs of moleskin trousers, two flannel undershirts and two red woollen shirts for Adam and Daniel. Then she set out two calico chemises, two petticoats, two flannel waistcoats and two heavy woollen dresses for Sarah and herself. Last were the heavy boots that had been purchased for each member of the family. She could understand why this attire had been recommended, for not only did she now have a daunting amount of washing to do but there was mending as well. These past months, their fine clothes had become much the worse for wear. She searched for Adam's shaving mug, razor and hairbrushes and her own toiletries, and placed them on the end of a trunk, then checked over the items she had selected. Lucy nodded, satisfied. Today, they would all wash in fresh water for the first time in many weeks and dress in clean, sensible clothing, and, no matter what the circumstance, they would henceforth observe the rules of cleanliness and civilized living as closely as possible.

In a short time her sickness would have left her and she would then be better able to adjust to the necessities of this new life. If Daniel, softly raised and barely twelve years old, could rise to the challenge then so could she. As well, it was more than possible that Ruben and his people were in Dunedin or some other place, availing themselves of materials to rebuild the homestead and the other buildings that had been lost in the fire, and would eventually return to Chandler's Run.

Comforted, Lucy delved into the fourth trunk and lifted out the bolt of canvas and the big scissors. Going to the pile of firewood outside the hut, she selected a straight branch and searched about for strips of shredded flax. She returned to the hut and roughly measured the height of the doorway with the stick. Then, unrolling the canvas, she measured that also and cut a width a foot longer than the height of the door. Having done this, Lucy rolled one end of the canvas several times around the stick and punched a hole through the fabric in the middle and at both ends, then threaded the flax through and tied the canvas securely to the stick. She lifted the stick to the top of the doorway, straining to reach, and wedged it between the mud wall and the rough wooden frame. She stood back, pleased — she had made a door. She knew it would blow about in the wind, but Adam and Daniel could remedy that.

The water on the fire was ready. Half-filling the basin, Lucy carried it into the hut and set it carefully down on the tussock. She looked with distaste at the yellow bar of soap that she'd taken from the trunk. It smelled strongly of carbolic and quickly she replaced it with a cake of her own perfumed soap.

Swiftly she divested herself of her soiled clothing and looked sadly at her soft leather shoes; no cobbler would be able to mend those. The cold air brought goose pimples to her cringing flesh as she stepped gingerly into the basin of hot water and dribbled the water over her body. Luxuriating in the feel of it on her skin and the smell of lavender, she sang softly as she cleansed herself. She was oblivious to the sounds on the track above and did not hear booted feet approach the covered doorway.

'Hello, the house!'

A gloved hand pulled aside the canvas and the ugliest face Lucy had ever seen was thrust through the opening. Desperately, she tried to cover herself.

'Go away, go away — how dare you!'

'Don't take on girl, you've nothin' ther' I've not seen afore,' a deep gravelly voice drawled.

Outraged, Lucy exploded, 'Get out, you dreadful creature — do you hear me? Get out — oh, you are no gentleman!'

'That's right, missus, me name's Gaunt — Ruby Gaunt. No need ter take on — I'll wait outside.'

With hands that shook, Lucy pulled the rough clothing over her wet nakedness and thrust her feet into the stiff leather boots. She did not know how to lace them properly and slowly emerged from the hut trailing the laces on the ground. Scarlet of face, she confronted her visitor. 'What is it you want?'

Raw-boned, with steely eyes regarding her from a countenance that resembled a crumpled burlap bag, the person stood before her, wearing a man's sweat-stained hat, rough trousers and a thick flannel shirt. The name might be Ruby, but to all intents and purposes this was a man.

'I've brought yer gear back.' The person thumbed over its shoulder to the track above, and Lucy, raising her eyes, saw a heavy cart with two big horses in the shafts.

'I don't understand.'

'Pots an' pans an' such. Picked 'em up after the fire afore they were stole — brought 'em back.'

Lucy studied her odd caller with suspicion. 'How did you know anyone was here?'

The slitted grey eyes were quizzical. 'A teamster wi' a big gob tol' me.'

Sudden enlightenment stained Lucy's cheeks again.

'Then you are our neighbour — Mr Clark . . .'

She was suddenly apprehensive. The Widow Gaunt — Black Ruby! Lucy stared at the unlovely face, and the cold slivers of eyes stared back, unblinking.

'Right,' the person grunted. 'Yer won't mind then if I fetch 'em down an' get on me way?' She turned away and, after climbing the bank up to the track, the gaunt figure hoisted itself up into her cart. She didn't look at Lucy as she turned the horses about and drove back the way she had come.

Lucy watched the cumbersome cart turn off the track and drive almost to where she stood. It rattled and squeaked to such an extent she marvelled that she hadn't heard its earlier approach.

'Where do yer want 'em?'

Lucy pointed vaguely to the hut wall. She did not attempt to help as Ruben's possessions were stacked in a pile beside the door. When it was done her visitor seated herself in the cart again.

'Thank you.' Lucy spoke through stiff lips. 'He will be obliged to you.'

The leathery features creased into an expression that could have been a grin or a grimace of pain as she reined the big horses around. 'Ruben Chandler's allus been civil ter me — least I could do.'

She touched her whip to the horses' rumps and as they stepped forward Lucy called out suddenly, 'Do you know where he is? What happened here?'

Ruby Gaunt reined in and studied the young woman on the ground for a moment. 'No, on both counts. Time we got 'ere, weren't no folk nor animals to be seen an' the place were still smokin'.'

'How did you know to come? Do you live near?'

'Two hours' ride away in this.' The woman indicated the cart. 'Boys were checkin' the ewes — smelt smoke an' afore long could see a God Almighty glow as she went up.'

Lucy stood silent, studying the older woman in her turn. 'Would the natives have done this?' she asked.

Ruby Gaunt leaned forward on her seat, her large hands spread on her knees. Her eyes were mere slits. 'The poor bloody Maori gets blamed fer everythin'. Now, I'll tell yer

67

this — 'twere them, they'd 'ave emptied the house, the barn, the pigsty an' the hen house afore they torched it. Yer been up ther', missus, an' seen 'em?'

The ugly face pushed down at Lucy. Involuntarily, she stepped back. 'No,' she murmured.

'A word of advice, lady,' the widow grated. 'If yer know nowt, say nowt!'

To Lucy's ears the words held a threat. She stared at the woman who resembled no woman she had ever known, this Black Ruby, and her nervousness grew. Good manners dictated that she invite her visitor to take refreshment, regardless of what she was, but she hesitated and in her hesitation the Widow Gaunt forestalled her.

'I'll be on me way, then. Ther's a book in one o' them boxes yer might find useful — Nobby Clark says yer can't cook.' With that she flicked her whip and, looking straight ahead, she drove off.

Lucy Chandler sat down suddenly beside the dying fire. The laces of her boots still trailed on the ground and, looking at them, she felt an absurd urge to laugh.

The children had been in bed for an hour, but Adam and Lucy still sat beside the fire, their backs resting against the wall of the hut.

Lucy spoke at length now of her strange visitor and her apprehension in the woman's presence. 'Mr Clark told her we were here and she knew of the fire of course, but she claims no knowledge of anything otherwise. There was something a little sinister about her, Adam.'

'Perhaps only eccentric, my dear. A woman who attires herself to resemble a man would be judged eccentric, no doubt, but probably is quite harmless.' Adam was very tired and the cold night air was troubling his lungs, but he sat on, discussing the accomplishments of the day. Fresh tussock had been placed on a good portion of the roof and new tussock had raised up their bed. The ladders had turned out well, and among the items that Ruby Gaunt had returned was a large zinc washing tub. This had been placed in the hut, half-filled with warm water, and the children had each bathed until the water was cool. Emptying the tub and refilling it had been a heavy task and an awkward one, but nobody complained. The children slept now in clean clothes, in an aired bed, with comfortably filled stomachs; the book that the Widow Gaunt had referred to was entitled *Soyer's Charitable Cookery*. Lucy had cooked her first leg of lamb with some success, and served it with a thin, lumpy gravy and some of Daniel's pancakes. The lamb had been cooked in a large oval cast-iron pot that Lucy had found in one of the boxes.

Adam had bathed before the fire when the children had settled, his tall frame cramped into the small space, while Lucy went through the contents of Ruby Gaunt's wooden boxes. She lifted out sundry cast-iron pots and pans, a meat grinder, and two sad irons with detachable handles; the wood of the handles was charred, but with care, she thought, they could be used. In another box Lucy found a flat round iron plate, its handle also burned, a large iron kettle and three large, round pans. All these items had been scoured. As well there were two pails, a large china crock, crazed and discoloured by the heat, and an iron boiler that showed no signs of having been in the fire at all. Two more boxes carried articles that she could not identify except for cooking spoons, several worn knives of different sizes and the *Soyer's Charitable Cookery* book.

While Adam and Lucy sat quietly talking, the mare, which had not appeared all day, came slowly out of the darkness and stood just beyond the fringe of light, her wary eyes reflecting the fire.

'Hallo, lass.' Adam spoke softly. 'Come for your dinner, have you?' He rose, carefully took one of the large, round pans and scooped chaff into it, then slowly approached the horse, talking to her all the while. He was still several feet from her when the animal seemed to lean away from him and then, snorting, she plunged off into the darkness. Adam placed the pan where the mare had been standing and returned to his seat against the hut wall.

'The poor beast is truly spooked. That saddle needs to be removed but I fear we may never catch her.'

'If we are feeding her,' Lucy replied, 'she must surely sense that we mean her no harm.'

'We are human and humans have done something here that has caused her to distrust them.' Adam looked down at his hands. Lucy, watching his expression in the flickering light, grew uneasy.

'What are you saying, Adam?'

'I don't know, my dear. I don't know what I am saying,

but I do know that the thriving sheep-run that Uncle Ruben described no longer exists and it could be within the realms of possibility that neither does he.'

'Oh, Adam, don't — don't even think such a thing!'

'Then where are the sheep and the people who watch over them? Where are the housekeeper and the native help?' Adam ran his fingers through his hair, his eyes fixed unseeing on his boots. 'Why are there charred corpses in the pigsty and the hen house? What devilry took place here?'

'You have said nothing to me of this — the dead creatures,' Lucy said faintly, 'but that person did, and that it was not a native attack.'

'Did she? Hmm. Well, there seemed no point in upsetting you, but as the hours have passed and there has still been no sign to indicate that we are not the only living souls in this vast place, I think we need to consider our options — and, more importantly, our safety.'

'Are you suggesting, Adam, that whoever is responsible for what has happened here . . . are you suggesting that they may return?'

Adam Chandler turned to his wife and took her two hands in his. 'It is possible, although having destroyed everything I can't imagine why they would. But we need to be on our guard and find a means of protecting ourselves in that event.'

Lucy sat silent, watching the last of the flames flicker briefly then subside into their bed of glowing embers. Withdrawing her hands from her husband's, she stood up and faced him. 'My thinking is this: if Mr Clark was afraid of being caught by the thaw, then surely others would exercise the same caution, wouldn't they?'

Adam nodded thoughtfully.

'Then, if this is so, we should be safe from intruders until the cold weather returns,' Lucy reasoned. 'If by that time Uncle Ruben has not returned and nothing has been heard of him, we must find a way to return to Dunedin and inform the police.'

'Your thinking is without fault, dear, except that the thaw will also prevent Uncle Ruben from coming home, so where does that leave us?'

'It leaves us too tired to sort this out,' Lucy answered, shaking her head. 'Let us retire to bed and leave our timid visitor to eat in peace.'

The mare had come back, and as they settled to sleep they could hear her munching the chaff in the round pan.

Chapter 3

DAY FOLLOWED DAY and Lucy marked each of them in her diary. Nobody came to visit Chandler's Run, friend or foe. Lucy prayed every night for the thaw to come, but the snow-bearing wind still blew down from the mountains and snow had fallen for the past two days, blanketing everything in silence; even the river was quiet.

The mare had been lured closer and closer to the shelter in her quest for food, and that morning she had allowed Daniel to touch her briefly. She stood now, just six feet from the fire, eating her chaff, her rough coat and saddle white with snow.

Lucy talked to her quietly as she went about her work. She was making bread, carefully following the instructions in the *Soyer's* cookery book. A big iron pot with three short legs was her oven, and she placed the loaves in this and set it on the embers, piling more embers on its lid.

Adam had found that a number of the sacks in the hut contained maize, and this morning they had had porridge for breakfast. He had put the grain several times through the coffee grinder. Lucy had then added water and a little salt and allowed the mixture to simmer over the fire until it thickened. With brown sugar sprinkled over it, it was quite palatable and Lucy, reading through her cookery book, felt more hopeful of banishing the spectre of starvation.

Also through trial and error, she was learning how to wash their clothing. Twice the boiler had tipped over and put out the fire beneath it. Now she had the boiler propped against the bank on a firm base of stones and had scooped out a place under it to set the fire: this worked very well.

She had learned also that woollen clothes were not to be boiled, after lifting diminutive items from the water with her stick. In spite of her failures and the drudgery of carrying countless pails of water from the river, Lucy felt she was in some small way getting the upper hand in her unfamiliar domicile.

Adam and Daniel had gone off with the axe to replenish the woodpile, both limping painfully with chilblains. The snow had almost stopped falling and the crusty smell of soda bread wafted through the cold air as Lucy lifted the round loaves from the iron pot. She had no milk or yeast for her bread as the recipe required, but had made the dough with carbonate of soda and water instead. The small, round loaves fitted into the three-legged pot with ample room to rise, and a leg of lamb or pork could readily be roasted in it as well.

Adam was also having some success in his endeavours. From dawn until dusk he and Daniel toiled, fashioning rough handles for the implements that had been burned, and latterly they had taken turns levelling the floor of the hut with the blunt shovel. The pitted mud had packed down hard and they laboured long to level a small area each day. Three iron bedsteads had been found under the rubble of the homestead. They had withstood the ravages of the fire fairly well and it was Adam's intention to bring them down to the hut so that the family might sleep more comfortably as soon as possible. His cough, which had eased, now returned. Day and night he coughed, a dry, rasping cough, and Lucy begged him to rest.

'Soon, Lucy, soon,' he had replied. 'There is not much more to do, then we can bring the bedsteads down.'

Lucy could hear the ring of the axe not too far away. She bent to feed more wood on to the fire and place the kettle on the stones. As she straightened, the sun went in and a breath of wind stirred the ashes at her feet. Lucy stepped from the shelter and looked up to the mountains. Cloud wreathed the peaks and the brilliant blue of the sky had paled; the larks that had been singing a short time before still flitted and dived but were now silent, and the mare lifted her head and stood facing the hills, her nostrils flared.

'The rain is coming, I think, Sarah.'

'Will the roof leak?' The child spoke absent-mindedly as she lifted a tin plate from the basin and placed it close to the fire to dry.

'It is thickly thatched,' Lucy replied, 'and should keep us snug and dry.'

'Do you want it to rain, Mama?' Sarah questioned.

'Yes, I do.'

'Why ever would you want it to rain?' The girl lifted her wet hands from the basin and stared at her mother.

'I want it to rain, Sarah, because . . . well, because your papa will be obliged to rest and it will bring the spring.'

'Oh, yes, I see.' Sarah considered this, then returned to her task.

'When we have finished here, we will go and help Papa and Daniel fetch the wood in.' Anxious as she was for Adam to rest, Lucy longed to sleep in a bed again, and with the levelling of the floor the hut had lost much of its pungent odour. If they did not dally, Lucy was sure that the beds could be installed before the weather changed and Adam could then take the time to restore himself.

When the last of the wood had been stacked, fresh tussock was cut and rolled into the mackintoshes to serve as mattresses. The unwieldy bedsteads were then carried down the hill and the black scrubbed from them. While they dried off in the sun, Lucy cut thick slices of the fresh-baked bread, spread them with dripping, and served them with hot, sweet tea. She insisted that Adam rest for at least an hour after the meal.

As the afternoon wore on, the sky took on a livid hue. Lowering cloud was gathering, moving slowly along the main ridges. The breeze, still blowing from the north-west, was steady with an occasional stronger gust.

'We'd best continue,' Adam said, when barely an hour had passed. 'There is rain on the way.'

The bedsteads were lifted into the hut and made ready for the night. The sacks of chaff and grain were stacked to the roof, and the trunks lifted on to bags of wheat to raise them from the floor and make more space, for there was barely room to move around the bedsteads. Adam looked for a place to hide the box of sovereigns and, finding none, with Daniel's help pushed it under a bed with the zinc tub covering it.

The darkness was coming down early, and Lucy worried about the strengthening wind as she stood before the fire cooking the evening meal. Several times embers had blown around her feet and had to be quickly stamped out. The meat required a half-hour more cooking and she feared that, for safety's sake, the fire would need to be put out before it was done.

Adam and Daniel had gone to the river to get water, while Sarah stood nervously watching the embers glow brighter at each gust and squealed every time the wind sent a shower of sparks towards the shelter roof. Then a stronger gust scattered the embers in all directions and the acrid smell of singeing wool was strong. Frantically, Lucy slapped at Sarah's skirts and at her own, then Adam was there rubbing her scorched hem between his hands while Daniel stamped the glowing coals into black ash.

'We'll have to put the fire out, my love,' Adam said. 'Take the meat off and I'll make the tea. We can eat the outside of the meat and finish cooking it when the wind has gone.' He lifted the kettle from its hook as he spoke.

'Sarah, help your mother take the food into the hut, and Daniel, you can help me make sure the fire is completely out.'

It was dark inside, and darker still when the canvas door had been secured. The family sat on the beds eating their meal in silence, listening to the rising wind.

'We should have fed the mare.' Lucy spoke from out of the gloom.

'There would have been little point putting out chaff only to have it blow away,' Adam replied.

Daniel stood at the small window, his hair blowing wildly about his head. 'She doesn't seem to be out there anyway, Papa.'

The wind lulled momentarily, then a great gust shook the hut, rattling the cooking pots in their boxes outside the door.

'I think we might be wise to bring everything inside.' Adam raised his voice to be heard. 'Daniel, help me undo the door — I'll pass it all through to you.'

Another gust took the canvas from their hands and flicked Sarah where she sat on the end of a bed, leaving a stinging welt across her cheek. The wind lulled again, and Lucy held the canvas firmly while Adam and Daniel gathered the pots and pans into the boxes and pushed them under the beds.

A low moaning stayed their hands as they were tying the canvas on to the doorframe again. It slowly rose to a roar and then the full force of the wind hit them.

'Quickly, Daniel!' Adam shouted as they struggled with the billowing canvas.

'I am trying, Papa, but it is beginning to tear!'

'Sarah, move away from the door, as far away as you can — Lucy sit with her and cover yourselves with the bedding — I have never experienced such a wind!'

The canvas door tore loose as the words left his mouth and flapped wildly until he wrenched it free from the top of the frame.

~

The wind hammered at them all night long while they crouched on their beds. It hurled everything before it. Tussock, branches, scrub and small trees pelted the mud walls and flew through the open doorway and window. In its fury the wind shook the hut until it seemed that it must collapse.

Daylight finally came and the wind ceased suddenly. Then the rain began, torrential warm rain that turned the day back into night. Lightning flashed and thunder rolled around the hills almost continuously. Rivulets of slushy snow, trickling down from the track above, became a rushing river, carrying stones and debris and dead ashes from the fire into the hut. It came through the doorway and swirled around the floor, a soapy, muddy porridge of flotsam that grew deeper as it gathered in volume and surged towards the river.

The family, huddled in their bedding, prayed for the deluge to stop, but it was mid-afternoon before the rain eased and finally ceased. Adam helped Lucy and Sarah over the tangle of mud and debris to the doorway. The sun came through the ragged, fast-moving cloud and a lone lark gave voice. Debris was piled high against the front wall of the hut and the poles of the cooking shelter, which leaned crazily in every direction. The swollen river had pushed its banks back and was a rushing torrent of furious water, crashing into the gorge below. The woodpile was gone, as were the ladders, which had been left leaning against the hut wall.

'So we start all over again,' Lucy said bleakly, surveying the wreckage with weary eyes. 'It becomes plain why this dwelling was left to the animals.'

Adam scrubbed a bristled chin and raised his eyes to the mountains. The towering snow-covered peaks thrust through the mists that obscured the bush-covered slopes and gullies. They had taken on a luminosity, a cold purity; their enormous silence, in contrast to the cacophony below, made a statement of latent primeval threat. Adam spoke his thoughts aloud: 'It would be a daring and foolhardy fellow indeed who would test the forces of nature in this place.' He placed an arm about Lucy's shoulders and said quietly, 'I think we may go about our affairs now without fear of unwelcome intrusion.'

Precious paper and matches were used to coax wet wood to burn. Adam, Lucy and Daniel between them dragged the saturated sacks from the floor of the hut and rolled them laboriously on to piled stones beside the fire to dry. Then Adam and Daniel cleared out the debris and cut load after load of tussock to lay in deep layers over the muddy floor, while Lucy and Sarah searched far and wide for dry wood to keep the fire burning.

They toiled until the last dry sack and trunk in the hut had been raised on to stones and the fading light forced them to stop. There was a dull ache in Lucy's back as she passed the tin plates and cups around. She longed to lie down, to sleep, and in sleep be transported to a place where there was no cold, no wind and no mud. But here they huddled, amongst the wreckage of the storm, gleaning what warmth they could from the sulking fire, silent, barely interested in their food, wishing only to close their eyes and not think of the morrow and its problems and of the mare that had not returned. At last, bone weary, they went to their beds to sink into dreamless sleep. The dull roar of unstable snow plunging from steep faces did not disturb their slumbers, nor did the loosened boulders, sliding and crashing from outcrop to outcrop. They were not aware that a misty rain was falling or that rats of enormous size were gorging themselves on the wet maize beside their fire. They did not hear the mare come to stand beneath the cooking shelter as a grey dawn was breaking, with drooping head and tail flat to her rump, waiting to be fed.

Daniel was the first to rise. He approached the dejected mare, speaking softly. Again she allowed him to touch her. Slowly and with infinite care, the boy removed the saddle and then the bridle and saw the flesh rubbed raw by the wet saddle. When he offered the round tray heaped with chaff, she nickered and came forward.

The rats had gone, but evidence of their presence was found in a myriad holes gnawed in the sacks and maize strewn everywhere. A cold drizzle still fell, and Daniel coaxed the fire into life from the few remaining embers. He hung the kettle from the roof of the unstable shelter, then sat down on a stone to watch the horse eat, wondering what this day would bring and wondering how he would deal with the maddening itch of his chilblains when his feet grew warm inside his boots.

'Ah, she is back.' Adam spoke at Daniel's shoulder. In the grey morning light his face was haggard. 'Not a moment too soon, I'd have to say, poor girl, judging from those galls — how did you persuade her to let you remove her saddle?'

'I think she was quite glad to be rid of it, Papa, and I think now she is glad of our company, too.'

Daniel leaned forward and poked the sulking fire with a stick. 'We had other visitors during the night, too.' He pointed his stick at the ruptured bags of maize.

Adam surveyed the mess, gently pinching his bottom lip. 'Through the long hours of the storm I did some thinking, Daniel, and I have arrived at a conclusion. As we are obliged to remain here, whether we wish to or not, I think we must set about protecting ourselves from the elements and from the vermin that appear to thrive in prolific numbers here. Now — I think that we can build on to this hut with the materials at hand and make a reasonable dwelling. Would you be willing to help me?'

'Of course, Papa, but we don't know how to make walls like the homestead has.'

'Cob walls, Daniel, and no, we don't know how they are constructed, but I am looking at all the stone here, washed down during the storm. I would use that for my walls. There is clay here and mixed with tussock it should make a strong mortar. The roof would be a thatched frame on poles like the cooking shelter.'

'Would the wind not twist your roof as it has the cooking shelter's roof, Papa?'

'No, my boy, because the poles would be inside the stone walls and the frame would be joined to the roof of the hut this side and attached to supporting uprights on its outer three sides. Do you follow me?'

Daniel's toes were beginning to itch as he considered his

father's plan. He harboured serious doubts that his papa, who had never built anything in his life, would be able to construct a building of any kind that would stand beyond the first puff of wind. He was willing to help, though, if only to take his mind off his itching feet. The kettle began to sing and Lucy came from the hut to make the tea with Sarah in her wake. She eyed the scattered maize and shuddered. 'Perhaps you could make some kind of cupboard that would keep those creatures away from our food?'

'Hmm.' Adam rubbed his chin. 'I expect it could be done, though at this moment I have no idea how, but—' and he smiled at Lucy '— we *will* build you a decent hearth, raised a foot high, with a chimney, what do you say about that?'

Lucy smiled tolerantly and turned to lift down the kettle. This morning she felt exhausted and slightly nauseous. She had little expectation that Adam's ideas would amount to much.

'Daniel, will you make your pancake mixture for breakfast, please?' she said.

After breakfast, Adam went for water and tried to find the meat cask. The river ran fast and muddy green, its banks still submerged. Of the barrel there was no sign, and the tussock and flax bushes, twisted and flattened by the surging waters, concealed the marker.

The drizzle cleared as Adam made his careful way downstream. The footing was slippery and unstable, and after a short distance he turned to retrace his steps. He spied one of the ladders then, half-buried in a tangle of mud and broken branches. Slipping and sliding, he struggled to where it lay, and wrenching it free he retrieved the water can and returned to the hut.

'I have not found the casks, so, Daniel, I'll want you to come with me now and help me locate the stakes that mark where the other barrels are.'

'Cutting dry wood should be the first consideration, I would have thought,' snapped Lucy, poking at the smoking fire.

'That will be our next mission, my dear,' Adam replied quietly. 'At this time I am more concerned with what has happened to our meat supply.' Puzzled by Lucy's unusual waspishness, Adam motioned Daniel to follow him.

Recollection of the contents of those barrels turned Lucy's stomach this morning, and determining not to think about it she entered the hut. As she straightened the beds she longed to not be pregnant, to be in charge of her stomach and her emotions and to be rid of the gnawing fear of having to deliver a child in this alien place. She had found no words to tell Adam of her plight, but soon the gentle swelling beneath her bodice would be self-evident.

The barrels were found wedged firmly in the rocks. Submerged waist-deep in the racing icy waters, Adam risked life and limb to retrieve a leg of lamb and a fat hen from one of the barrels, which were only just discernible beneath the littered surface. Chilled to the bone, he prayed he would suffer no ill effects; he was anxious to begin building the structure he had planned, fearing that more storms could descend on them. Stones of all sizes lay ready to hand, and when the wood had been brought in he began setting them in a pile close to where he would build his hearth. That night, while his family slept, he went over the planned construction in his mind again and again. He had gone back up to the homestead and studied the fireplace in the ruined kitchen, measured its width and its depth and noted the broad stone that was the chimney-breast. He was certain that if the mortar he made would bind his work, Lucy would have a safe fireplace and walls to protect them from the elements. Stifling the urge to cough and forcing himself to be still, he at last fell asleep to dream of the Devon homestead as it must have been before the fire.

At daybreak, Adam was up and on his way, axe over his shoulder, to cut the poles and branches for his roof. His plan was to build it in two sections, each measuring ten feet by seven. Heavily thatched, these sections were going to weigh more than the cooking shelter, he knew, but if the roof was to extend the length of the hut he could make them no smaller. When both sections were erected, the area beneath would then measure fourteen feet by ten feet, a good working space for a kitchen.

To his busy mind the night before, building the extension to the hut had seemed simple, but the practical application Adam found rather more difficult. The axe did not bite hungrily into the wood but bounced off, jarring his hands and arms painfully. With growing frustration he recalled the short space of time it had taken the teamster to cut his four poles and the numerous branches he had carried back to the hut.

He picked up the axe yet again, trying to remember the stance of the groundsman on the family estate in Tenbury when he cut down the Yuletide tree. He shuffled back another foot from his target, spread his feet wide and measured with his eye where he wanted to make his cut. Taking aim, he swung the axe in a wide arc, missed the trunk altogether and lurched into the scrub after the flying axe.

'Mama says you must come to breakfast, Papa.' Daniel stood off at a safe distance.

With chagrin, Adam scrambled to his feet. 'I'm not much of a woodsman, I fear, Daniel,' he sighed as he retrieved the axe.

Daniel now stood beside the scarred trunk. 'I think you need to cut a "v" in the bark first, Papa. The wood is softer underneath.'

'How could you possibly know that?' Adam stared at his son.

'The carpenters on the ship told me how they had to cut new masts after a storm and I remembered what they said.' The boy sensed his father's feeling of inadequacy and wished he had not spoken.

Adam, seeing Daniel's discomfort, understood and said quietly, 'Do you think you could show me?'

Reluctantly, he took the axe from his father's hand. Clumsily he struck it at an angle to the trunk, and when it bounced off leaving no mark he squinted an eye at Adam. 'The axe is blunt.' They both began to laugh.

Daylight was fading as the last of the poles for the first section of the roof was set in the ground. Adam was exhausted and coughed incessantly. When he lowered himself to sit by the fire, he was overcome by sudden vertigo and sprawled sideways. 'Don't fuss — don't fuss — just a little dizzy. It is passing,' he said, attempting to make little of it.

'This work is too much for you, Adam. You must not do any more,' Lucy warned. 'We will manage with what we have.'

'The poles — cutting them and setting them in the stony ground is the hardest part, my dear. The rest will be comparatively easy, and when the work is finished you will have your kitchen and we will all be warm and dry.' He smiled at Daniel and the boy saw the glint in his eye. 'Also, I will have a certain satisfaction when Mr Clark and his ilk see what I am capable of — what *we* are capable of doing.'

'If anybody ever comes here again.' Lucy sank down on a stone beside him and knew she had measured her own capabilities this day. She and Sarah had toiled for hours, going further and further afield gathering uniform-sized stones for the hearth and dragging them back to the hut in the maize sack that the rats had gnawed holes in. She looked with sympathy at her young daughter, who sat wilting on her stone, her fair head drooping. The child had surprised Lucy with her stoicism and her cheerfulness as the pile of rocks grew, but she knew Sarah was so spent now that it would take little to make her cry. Lucy's own back ached dully and her hands were bruised.

It was growing colder as night came in, and the mare came closer to the cooking shelter while a flurry of snow eddied around the hut.

❧

Morning dawned fine. The air was sharp and a light dusting of new snow lay over the ground. Adam and Daniel went off to cut flax and tussock while Lucy and Sarah made breakfast. The mare had followed on Daniel's heels. 'She will save us much heavy carrying when those galls heal,' Adam remarked, 'and more so if we can repair the cart.'

By lunchtime, the frame of the roof was taking shape. To lessen the weight of it, Adam trimmed the tussock with the big scissors as each layer was attached. Now it looked much like the thatched roofing at home and he was pleased with his efforts. Sarah and Lucy scraped and flayed the flax until there was enough rope made to complete the first section.

'We will attach this to the roof now, Daniel,' Adam said, 'and raise the outer edge on to the bags of chaff before it gets any heavier.' He turned to Lucy. 'When we have done this, my love, let us then eat. We have all earned our dinner.'

'Once the second piece of roof is in place, Papa, what will become of the cooking shelter?'

'It could be set over the kitchen door, I think, Daniel, or be shelter for the mare. In any event, it won't be wasted.'

The work went on apace when the meal was over, and by late afternoon, as it was growing dark, Adam declared the thickly thatched roof ready to be raised to the outside poles.

'We will all have to lift while Daniel ties the frame securely into the notches.'

On Adam's command everybody lifted the section of roof. It was made heavier by the still-wet tussock, and when Sarah, shorter than the others, could no longer reach, Lucy's strength was severely taxed. She and Adam took the full weight of the frame, straining to set it into the notches at the top of the poles and hold it there while Daniel tied it securely in place. At last, firmly attached to the roof of the hut and its supporting poles, the structure stood strong and immovable. Adam was elated.

'It would take a strong wind indeed to bring this down,' he panted and hugged Lucy to his side. 'While dinner cooks, shall we begin to lay the hearth?' He was performing on the euphoria of success, his exhaustion not registering, and in the light from the fire Lucy noted the spots of colour in his cheeks and wished he would rest. As well there was an odd sensation in the pit of her stomach and her back ached. For the child's sake she knew she should do no more, but a tiny devil of perversity would not allow her to listen to her body's warning. She set about placing the heavy rocks where Adam could sort and lay them, stooping, lifting and carrying until, breathless, she was obliged to sit, unable to go on. That night, as the family slept, she lay awake, prey to a feeling of uneasiness. The ache in her back was much stronger.

When morning came, the ache in Lucy's back had extended to her stomach. She went about her tasks, endeavouring to blot out her discomfort and growing apprehension, but by mid-morning she could no longer deny that something was very much amiss. Instinctively, Lucy knew that her children must not witness what was about to happen to her, and on the pretext of fetching water, she picked up the pails and walked slowly towards the river. Absorbed in the construction of the hearth, nobody paid attention to her going.

She walked slowly downriver, dull hot pain spreading and growing stronger until suddenly a primitive urge made her halt and squat. Very afraid, Lucy remained crouched and, with eyes closed and teeth clenched, she gripped the tussock before her. Her body began to purge itself in spasms and with each pain she bore down, until she felt warmth flow and she knew that the child had passed from her.

Shakily, she rose to her feet to stand dazed, hardly believing what had happened. She stared at the tiny perfect body lying on the scarlet cushion of the placenta and as she stood there she began to realize that she was free; free of the need to tell Adam of the coming child and free of the terror of delivering it. Then her relief was gone and anguish brought her to her knees. Instantly she was crying, tearing sobs of grief and remorse, and her tears fell on the mite she should have cherished.

Lucy knelt for a long time, heedless of the stones that cut into her knees. Then, when her tears had ceased, she began to scrape a hole in the rough ground with her hands.

'I'll tend ter that, child.'

Lucy jerked around and looked up into the face of Ruby Gaunt.

'Shall I fetch yer man?'

Mutely, Lucy shook her head. The shrewd eyes regarded her steadily.

'Then go cleanse yerself at the river — go carefully, 'tis swift-running.'

Lucy came slowly back from the water's edge. The Widow Gaunt waited for her beside a small mound of dirt and stones, a shovel in her big hands. 'Climb into the cart, girl.'

Wishing the woman would leave, Lucy gathered up her wet skirts and turned away. 'Thank you — I can make my own way.'

'So yer can, but I've news yer man will need ter hear.' The big woman picked up the pails and put them with the shovel into the rear of the cart. She held out a gloved hand — 'Come' — and helped Lucy up to the high leather seat. She crammed her felt hat more firmly on to her head, then hefted herself to the seat beside Lucy and the cart jolted forward. They rode the short distance to the hut in silence.

At the sound of the approaching cart, Adam and the children emerged from under the thatched roof. Surprised to see Lucy sitting in the cart and plainly upset, Adam hurried forward. 'Lucy, my dear, what has happened?' He reached concerned hands to lift his wife down and turned to the driver of the cart. 'Who are you?' He bent a look on the raw-boned woman who was tying the reins to the side of the cart. 'What has happened?'

'Name's Gaunt, from Long Reach over yonder.' She thumbed over her shoulder to the south.

'I see. Well, madam,' Adam frowned, 'perhaps I can ask you again — what has happened?' He was experiencing a feeling of hostility as he addressed the run-holder, which surprised him.

Ruby Gaunt lowered herself to the ground before replying. 'I've news — news that bodes none too well fer yer uncle.' The steely eyes regarded Adam and she held up a hand as he began to speak.

'A swaggie came a-callin' yesterd'y an' when 'e'd been fed 'e unloaded a saddle on me doorstep an' tried ter sell it ter me.'

She went then to the back of her cart and lifted down a saddle with an ornate oak-leaf design tooled into the leather. She placed it on the ground before Adam. 'Coupla times afore, I've seen this saddle. It were yer uncle's.'

Adam's face hardened. 'If what you say is true, where did the fellow come by it?'

Unwavering eyes looked back at him. 'Son, yer can believe me or not as yer please.' The leathery features were expressionless. 'The swaggie were persuaded to own that the saddle weren't 'is. Story goes, 'e took it from the carcass of a black horse he found in the lower reaches of this 'ere river . . . Yer uncle rode a black horse.'

Turning back to the cart she reached out the pails and placed them on the ground beside the saddle. 'Yer've been told, so I'll say good-day.'

'Are you telling me that my uncle is dead?'

'I'm tellin' yer what I've been told — nothin' more.'

With that, the Widow Gaunt climbed up to her high seat and, looking down on Adam, said, 'Yer missus 'as 'ad a shock. She'd do well to rest up a bit.' The gravelly voice was blunt. Picking up the reins she turned the cart about and, without another word, drove off.

Adam watched the woman's departing back, a frown creasing his brow, then he turned to his children who had stood silent throughout. 'Daniel, build up the fire, and Sarah, make the tea. We are all in need of a warm drink.' He placed an arm about Lucy, who stood staring at nothing. 'Come, dear, come and rest and don't upset yourself. I would give little credence to anything that strange creature said.'

Lucy allowed Adam to divest her of her wet skirts. He did not ask her how she came to be wet as he tucked her into bed, saying only, 'Try to sleep, dear.' Lucy turned to the wall and closed her eyes, making no reply. The possibility of Ruben's death had not touched her. Her consciousness was focused on the pale scrap of humanity she had left in the stony ground — she knew the image of it would stay with her to the end of her days.

The hearth and the chimney slowly took shape. It had taken much searching to find a suitable stone for the chimney-breast, and when they found it, the stone proved too heavy to move. Frustrated, Adam cast about for something that would replace it and enable him to continue building his chimney. He and Daniel probed through the ashes of the barn but found nothing. The following day they unearthed the wide grate of the parlour fireplace, and that same day found a smooth stone slab where perhaps the scullery had stood. Blackened and slightly pitted though it was, Adam was elated with the find; it would serve his purpose well. The construction of the chimney continued without any more delays, and four days later Lucy's hearth was completed.

It was raised a foot high as Adam had promised, and the parlour grate was set on a stone hob a foot higher and to one side of the open clayed hearth. Lucy's pots would sit on the grate and her three-legged oven would be set in the embers of the open hearth. The chain from the cooking shelter was mortared into the stones of the chimney and the kettle hung from this. Adam and Daniel were justly proud of their accomplishment and, when the first fire was lit on the ample hearth, Adam opened one of the bottles of brandy and they each took a nip in their evening cup of tea.

During the days they had been building the fireplace, the wind had blown steadily from the south, bringing with it flurries of snow and bitter nights, followed by cold, clear days. That night, as they sat sipping their tea, the wind veered to west-north-west and fast-moving clouds scudded across the mountain tops, silver in the moonlight. 'The weather is about to change, I fear,' Adam observed, 'so tomorrow we will make an early start and erect the second section of the roof, before the rains come — God willing!'

'Do you think the water might come inside again, Papa?' Daniel questioned.

'I've no way of knowing, son, but we'll pray that the storms will stay away until we have built our walls.' He glanced at Lucy as he spoke, wondering if she would be equal to the following day's task. Since the widow's visit, she had been oddly withdrawn and had made no reference to Ruben at all. She performed her daily work with a listless air, and at night she no longer slept in his arms. At a loss to know how to deal with this behaviour, Adam had tried to reassure her. 'Dear girl, if Ruben should not return by next winter, I promise you we will leave this place and go back to Dunedin; we will find a way.'

Lucy had looked at him, her eyes darkly inscrutable, but she had made no response. Adam had other concerns as well. Of late, he had been conscious of a feeling within himself that was unsettling. It was a feeling he could not have described; different to anything he had experienced before in relation to his illness. He knew that something had changed and the knowledge was making him fearful. As a result, a sense of urgency made him hurry to complete the extension to the hut. If Ruben Chandler was unlikely to return, he must see to it that his family were housed and provided for until they could leave this place. The meat in the barrels would not feed them past another week or so; they must be replenished. And the box of sovereigns — a secure hiding place must be found for it because Lucy and the children would need every penny in that box should his fears be realized.

Daylight came in cold and grey, heavy cloud descending from the peaks and settling on the lower hills. Breakfast was eaten hastily, the tin plates and cups left unwashed as everyone hurried up-river to cut more poles and branches and gather armloads of flax and tussock. Mid-morning arrived and Lucy stopped flaying the flax to make a pot of tea. Lunchtime came and went and the work continued, everybody acutely aware of time passing.

The rain still held off but the wind was coming from the west now, blowing an icy, moisture-laden breath down on the family as they worked. With numb fingers and empty stomachs they toiled on. The second section of roof was taking shape much more quickly than the earlier one had, and when the last bundle of tussock was tied in place the roof was pronounced ready to be lifted.

The rain came as the last corner of the roof was being secured. A flash of lightning, a great clap of thunder, and in the moment it took for Daniel to clamber down the ladder he was soaked to the skin. Adam watched the rain for a time, then turned wearily to the fire. 'We can do no more tonight, but tomorrow I will dig a trench in which to set the foundation stones for our walls.' The rain fell steadily all evening, but by bedtime it had dwindled to a chilling drizzle. As Adam sank into exhausted sleep, he thought of a hiding place for the box of sovereigns.

Work on the walls of the kitchen took precedence over everything else, and Lucy was happy to have it so. The mindless monotony of mixing mortar and sorting stones allowed her to settle into an unthinking apathy where yesterday and tomorrow were not a consideration.

She and Adam spoke little as, stone by stone, the walls rose. Adam's preoccupation with his building was almost obsessive as he pushed for completion. The children noted their parents' uncharacteristic countenances and murmured unhappily to each other.

The door to the kitchen faced north, and when the cooking shelter was erected over it, Adam decided to wall that in also. In the event of another violent storm, the structure would deflect runoff from the track above and offer shelter for the mare which, during the construction of the kitchen, had spent most nights within its walls. Daniel groaned inwardly as he visualized the number of painful trips that would be needed to bring down enough stone to build the walls. His toes were so badly swollen with chilblains that it was agony now to push his feet into his boots, but, seeing his father's drawn face, he knew he would remain silent and do whatever was required of him. He promised himself, though, that when the last stone was in place he would sit, his feet unfettered by his boots, for a long, long time and devise canvas covers for the two small windows. But it was not to be. When the building was finished, Adam needed his help to carry the heavy box of sovereigns up to the homestead.

'There is a hollow place up inside the kitchen chimney where it will never be found.' Adam coughed a short, harsh cough as he turned to Lucy. 'Come with us, my dear, you will need to know where it is.'

The box was heavier than Adam had remembered as he and Daniel, carrying it between them, struggled up the hill, Lucy and Sarah following. Several times they were obliged to stop while Adam caught his breath, and Daniel's concern for him was growing as they entered the burned-out ruin. He glanced at his mother, but she seemed unaware of his father's distress.

'There now, see up inside there, Lucy?' Adam stood on the broad hearth and Lucy stood beside him. She peered into the black depths of the chimney but could see nothing.

'There is a niche that will just hold the box. Do *you* see it, Daniel?'

'Yes, Papa, but it is quite high — how can we lift it up there?'

'We'll manage between us. Come now, pick up your end and we'll heave it up.'

Twice they lifted the heavy box, but there simply wasn't enough room for both of them to stand inside the chimney, raise it to shoulder height and push it into the hole.

'This is awkward,' Adam gasped. 'I'll have to do the last bit on my own — now, lift with me as high as you can, then let go and try to steady me.'

They lifted the box up, then, alone, Adam gripped it and wedged it with his body-weight against the rough stone while he gathered his strength, then he heaved it higher and with a tremendous effort thrust the box into the cavity.

Slowly, he stepped down from the hearth and lowered himself to its edge, his face ghastly. Daniel reached a hand out to him as he began to cough, a deep, wrenching cough that doubled him over. Lucy turned then and saw the crimson spots splash onto the blackened timbers of the floor. 'Mama!' Fear was in Daniel's voice as Adam, silent now, leaned against him. 'What is happening to him?'

Lucy was looking at death. Adam, so still and so white, seemed not to be breathing; she did not know what to do. Panic gripped her. Her apathy was gone and Daniel's eyes pleaded for reassurance, his young arms supporting his father's dead weight. Then she saw Adam's eyelids flicker, and quickly she knelt before him, chafing his cold hands.

'Sarah, run and fetch a blanket — hurry, child!' She raised her eyes to her son. 'Can you hold Papa a little longer?' Daniel nodded. Lucy's mind was racing. Somehow she must bring Adam back to the hut and warmth. She thought of the mare, then dismissed the idea: even if they could lift him onto her back, it would be difficult to hold him there. She cast about in her mind for a way to carry him down the hill. The ladder — if they laid him on the ladder, would she and Daniel be able to carry him?

'Lucy.' Adam's voice was a croak. His eyes were open, sunken back into his head, his lips chalk-white.

'Don't try to talk, dearest.' Lucy brushed the fair hair back from his brow and was startled by the coldness of his skin.

'I need to get to my bed.' Adam's weak voice held urgency.

'Daniel and I will try to carry you in a little while.'

Lucy touched her son's shoulder. 'I will take him now — go and bring the ladder back.'

Sarah was back with the blanket, held out half-fearfully.

'No,' Adam said faintly as Lucy began to object. 'Support me. I will walk — now!'

It was a painfully slow journey, with many stops on the way, but placing one dogged foot after the other Adam gained the hut and the warmth of his bed. There his frail strength left him and he lost consciousness.

Throughout the long night, Lucy watched over him, his body burning under her anxious hands while he cried out and thrashed about in delirium. Some time after midnight a westerly wind rose to gust occasionally through the uncovered windows, and the gusts became a strengthening wind, shaking the dwelling and rattling the pots and pans beside the hearth. Daniel crept from his bed to move them from the path of the wind and put more wood on the fire. He did not return to his bed, but hobbled to sit with his mother. In the flickering light he could just discern his father's ravaged face. The eyes he turned on Lucy were fearful. 'Is Papa going to die?' he whispered.

Lucy looked directly at her son, knowing it was pointless to soften the truth. 'I think it is possible, dear,' she replied. 'Your papa is very ill.'

'What will become of us, Mama?'

Lucy did not answer, could not answer; her gaze was on her husband who lay quietly now, his shallow breathing barely stirring the covers. Her throat was choked with grief and the certainty that Adam would soon lie with her lost child. What was to become of them then, she dared not contemplate.

Outside, the wind rose to a roar and battered the small structure with relentless force. Speech was impossible. Sarah crept to her mother's side, alarmed by the violence of the storm, and together Lucy and her children kept vigil, huddled close until the wind suddenly ceased just before daybreak and the heavens opened.

The rain fell steadily in a solid vertical sheet. Lucy sent the children to their beds as it grew colder, and soon she too began to doze. Some time later she started awake to realize that the rain had eased. In the gloom she looked quickly at Adam. He lay unmoving, his eyes open in a bloodless face. Her breath stopped in her throat. Had he died while she slept? Then weakly he turned his head and whispered, 'Has the water come inside?'

Lucy released her breath. 'No.' Her tears were close. 'No, dear heart, it hasn't.'

For three days Adam drifted in and out of consciousness. He took a little sweet tea and an occasional spoonful of broth made from the last of the hens, but he could eat nothing of any substance. Blood was on his lips when he coughed.

On the morning of the fourth day, the rattle of an approaching cart was heard coming up the track. Lucy pushed the children out of sight and crept to a window.

'Hello, the house!' Lucy recognized the deep, gravelly voice before the cart came into view, and with mixed feelings she bade the children stay indoors and went to meet the widow.

'Good mornin' ter yer, missus.'

The big woman did not leave her seat on the cart but sat regarding Lucy with sharp eyes. 'I'll be needin' ter speak with yer man. Is 'e about?'

'My husband is ill and cannot leave his bed.'

'Knocked 'imself out building this, did 'e?' The narrowed eyes flicked over the stone and thatch addition, then rested again on Lucy's face as the widow silently considered. Then in low tones she began to speak.

'Now, I'm supposin' that yer man is in somethin' of a bad way — consumptive is me guess?' The steely eyes probed. 'Aye,' she went on, 'then yer'll need ter use yer judgement whether you should pass on what I'm about ter tell yer, but it has ter be told.'

She was quiet for a space, her eyes never leaving Lucy's face, then said abruptly, 'Do yer mind if I step down?'

Lucy shook her head and stepped back a pace. Her legs felt weak with the certainty that she was about to hear something that she'd rather not.

The widow faced her. 'Ruben Chandler has been found— No!' as the younger woman's face lightened. 'No, girl, he is not alive. The Maoris found 'is body in a creek aways down river from 'ere; been in the water a while.'

Lucy swayed and a gloved hand reached out to steady her. 'Stay with me, ther's more ter come — all right?' Lucy forced herself to focus on the craggy face.

'The body's in a shepherd's hut on my lower boundary. I've no doubt it's Ruben Chandler but my word ain't worth rhubarb in these parts, so he has to be officially identified by a relative or someone who knew him. With yer man ill, missus, ye're goin' ter have ter do it.'

Horrified, Lucy stared at the older woman. 'No — no — oh, not at all — I couldn't!'

'Ther's no *couldn't* about it, girl — it's got ter be done, an' soon: the poor bugger needs burying.' Ruby Gaunt took Lucy's arm and walked her to the kitchen doorway. 'I'll take a look at yer husband. Is he spittin' blood?'

Lucy freed her arm. 'Yes, he is, and you must excuse me but your looking at him will hardly help — he needs a doctor.' Her chin was firm.

'A rarity in these parts,' the woman grated. 'Take me in.'

Reluctantly, Lucy entered the kitchen and Ruby Gaunt followed her to Adam's bedside. He lay quietly, seemingly unconscious of the widow's presence. 'Send the children out,' the woman commanded as she bent over the sick man.

'Damned dark in here. Is he taking nourishment?'

'A little tea and chicken broth.'

Lucy saw the big hands move over her husband with deft competence, and Daniel, standing beyond the doorway, politely asked, 'Are *you* a doctor?'

'No.' The reply was blunt. The widow turned to Lucy. 'Your husband must have fluid, as much as he will take, water, beef tea, chicken broth—'

'We have little meat left.'

The big woman grunted, considering the man on the bed, then she turned to Lucy Chandler. 'Termorrer mornin', early, I'll be on yer doorstep. Be ready ter come with me.'

'I can't leave my husband—'

'Yer can. I'll bring somebody with me who will look after him and she'll do it well.'

Lucy's mind was in turmoil. Everything was happening faster than she could deal with it. She shrank inwardly at the prospect of viewing a dead body; she knew she could not face that, and she also knew she could not leave Adam with a person she did not know. If the widow's claim proved to be true, Adam and the children would have to be told. They would have to leave, but with Adam so ill it would be out of the question.

Ruby Gaunt saw the anguish on the younger woman's face and the sternness on her own softened fractionally. ''Ere, now, don't ye be goin' into a decline, girl. I'll be back o' yer all the way — we'll get it over and done an' put behind yer.'

Chapter 4

As GOOD AS HER WORD, the Widow Gaunt had arrived on
Lucy's doorstep a little before seven o'clock. With her
were two dark-skinned natives: a man, short, nuggety and
proud of bearing, and a young woman of unusual beauty.

'This 'ere is Moana.' Ruby Gaunt had drawn the girl
forward. 'And this young fella is Rewi. Moana don't speak,
but she is very able an' will watch over yer man while we're
gone.'

Lucy had stood uncertainly as sundry items, including a
deal table and bench seats, were carried past her into the
kitchen. The widow had bellowed from the cart, 'Where's
yer meat barrels?'

'I'll show you where they are,' Daniel had offered.

Lucy, realizing that the bundles still on the cart contained
meat, was discomforted. 'This is kind of you, but we can't
accept all this.'

'Yer can, girl,' the widow had rasped. 'Yer payin' fer every
ounce of it. Go with Rewi, lad — what's the matter with yer
feet?' And Daniel had replied that he had chilblains.

～

Lucy sat on the high leather seat of the cart and her stomach was a palpitating lump beneath her bodice. She turned in her seat to look back. They had left the precipitous fluted walls of the gorge far behind and continued to travel ever downwards, yet the mountains seemed no further away. She shivered with nerves, apprehensive and uneasy for her family left with those primitive people. She faced forward and stole a glance at the weathered profile beside her. How could this unlovely creature be sure that they would not harm her children and her helpless husband? The further they went, the stronger her agitation became, made more so by the woman's silence. No word had passed between them since they'd set out, and in Lucy's overwrought state this appeared to be more than a little sinister. She started when the widow spoke suddenly, pointing with her whip. 'Down ther' — we come down to the flat off this 'ere hill an' the hut's beside a bit of a creek.'

Shortly after, the track levelled out and the horses broke into a lumbering trot towards a primitive hut. Two horses stood dozing before it and, as they drew nearer, two dark figures rose to their feet and stood waiting. Lucy had not seen them squatting against the hut, hidden by the tall tussock, nor had she noticed the tall, caped figure standing a little way from them. Here on the sheltered flat, the temperature was noticeably warmer and Lucy felt sweat break out on her nape; the moment she had been dreading was at hand. She gripped the front of the leather seat with shaking hands, feeling she might suffocate. The widow pulled the horses to a halt before the hut, and stepping to the ground she turned to help Lucy down.

'I can't — do this.' Lucy stared down at the older woman with terrified eyes.

The seamed face was uncompromising. 'Yer can. Get down!' Hard fingers gripped her arm and Lucy was stumbling towards the open doorway of the hut. The smell of carrion was in her nostrils and blowflies flew in her face. She stopped walking to turn a beseeching look on the widow, and the grip on her arm tightened. 'Come, 'tis nearly done. Hold yer breath and take a quick look.'

A rough-hewn box stood open on the packed dirt floor. Ruby Gaunt thrust Lucy towards it. 'Now — is this yer man's uncle?'

Lucy's eyes shrank from the thing in the box. It was grossly swollen and resembled little that was human. The only concession to her sensitivity were the pennies pushed into the eye sockets.

'The little finger—' the unrelenting voice grated in her ear. 'Look! Was Ruben's finger broken like that? And the ring?' Lucy looked with fading sight and nodded as her senses left her.

She came to herself lying beside the cart. Ruby Gaunt was patting her hands. 'There, 'tis over. Come now, on yer feet, yer all right.'

Lucy rose shakily and the widow pushed her up on to the leather seat.

'With yer permission, we'll take yer uncle home an' bury 'im on 'is own land. Termorrer, Kahu here will take a note ter the magistrate in Dunedin town, signed by yerself. All right?'

Lucy nodded dully. The carrion smell seemed to linger in her hair and in her clothes. She turned slowly to see the pine box, its lid now closed, directly behind her. The tall native in the feathered cloak was seated beside it.

'He must be buried properly,' she said faintly. 'A minister must be sent for — my husband would wish it.'

Ruby Gaunt barked a harsh laugh. 'As with doctors, ministers also are a rarity in these parts.' She stabbed a thumb over her shoulder. 'The tohunga ther' 'as agreed to do the honours.'

Lucy turned to look at the seated man. His skin was walnut brown and he was very old, with a head of fine white hair. He nodded slowly, his face solemn.

'It is most kind of Mr—'

'He is a tohunga, girl, a Maori priest, an' he will pass yer uncle into the hereafter as well as any minister could. Ye'll get no reverend riskin' 'is neck comin' ter a funeral this time o' year.'

Lucy looked at the young Maori riding ahead of them. 'If *he* can travel to Dunedin to take the note to the magistrate, why can't he fetch a minister?'

'Yer nose'll give yer the answer ter that question,' the widow grunted.

Lucy Chandler stared at the mountains and the rough track that led back to Adam and the children. She knew that Adam would not approve, but the situation had a nightmarish quality and Lucy badly needed to think. She wondered what Ruben himself would do under these circumstances, and, remembering his warmth and his down-to-earth common sense, she thought he would not be dismayed. 'Very well,' she said quietly.

~

Later, Lucy recalled little of Ruben Chandler's interment. The old tohunga had rambled on and on, performing rituals that held no significance for her, and the monstrosity in the box held even less. She was in no doubt that it was Ruben they were burying — the small gold band on the broken little finger had been Clara's wedding ring — but the strange assembly of people gathered around a roughly dug hole in unconsecrated ground, the ancient who presided over it with many clearings of the throat and alien words, were to Lucy the embodiment of a farce and she felt an inappropriate urge to laugh. Fearful though she was of what she might find on her return to the hut, Lucy felt the urge to surround herself with things familiar.

It was early afternoon when the cart drew to a halt beside the porch. Lucy climbed quickly down and hurried indoors, unmindful of the widow or the old man. She was immediately aware of changes within the rough walls. There was warmth, orderliness and the smell of lamb roasting. Adam lay in one of the single bedsteads beside the window on the far side of the hearth. He had been bathed and shaved, and wore a fresh nightshirt. He appeared to be sleeping comfortably. Daniel was quickly beside her, a question in his eyes. 'Was it Uncle Ruben?' he whispered.

Having given only the vaguest explanation as to why she must accompany the widow, Lucy was surprised by the boy's

astuteness, so she replied without any attempt at evasion, 'Yes.'
She reached out a hand to this son of hers who demonstrated
an understanding well beyond his years. Her gaze rested
again on Adam and tentative hope was in her voice. 'Papa
seems a little better, Daniel. Has he spoken to you?'

'No, Mama, but he doesn't seem to mind Moana. She has
fed him some broth and sips of water each time he wakes,
and he's hardly coughed this last hour or so.'

Ruby Gaunt was at Lucy's elbow, her hand on Adam's brow
and her strong fingers pressing under his jaw. She nodded
then and drew Lucy away from the bed. 'He is cooler and his
pulse is steadier, but make no mistake, your man is gravely
ill and more'n likely is past savin', but if you'll put 'im in my
hands, missus, I'll do me best fer 'im.'

Lucy stared at this strange woman, need and distrust at
war within her. 'There must be a hospital somewhere, where
he can be given the care he needs. Why can't we try—'

The widow shook her head, 'Even supposin' we could find
a safe way ter get 'im ther', 'e'd not stand the trip. No, girl,
yer lookin' at the only person near enough ter 'elp 'im an' I'll
make yer no promises.'

Lucy turned away in despair. It had now been put into
words: Adam was likely to die, and this rough creature,
despite what she claimed, had little more hope of preventing
his death than did Lucy herself.

The Maori girl was holding a tin cup out to her and
indicating a bench placed beside the deal table. The old
man sat on the other side, his wrinkled hands enveloping
his own cup, his gaze on Daniel, whose eyes were on his

father. As Lucy seated herself she wondered vaguely where the other three natives were. The gravelly voice broke in on her thoughts. 'Whatever you decide, you must not share your husband's bed again, and his eating and drinking utensils must be kept separate from yours and your children's. Any cloths used to wash him and his bed linen must be boiled and not used by anybody else.'

Lucy was bewildered. She understood nothing of what this woman was saying, and her bewilderment turned to anger at this intrusion into her privacy. 'I don't know what you mean or why you are saying these things to me,' she said coldly, 'but I thank you for your help today and if you will allow me a few minutes, I will pay you what I owe.'

'Child, child!' The creases in the leathery face grew deeper. 'I'm not meaning to interfere in personal matters or to frighten you, but you have to understand that this illness can be passed on to you and your family, unless every care is taken. His sneezing, coughing — the cloths that come into contact with his mouth and nose and are touched by you — can pass the disease. Are you understanding me now?' The steel-grey eyes held Lucy's and Lucy was suddenly still.

'Could we already have it?'

'Only time can answer that.'

'I don't know what to do.' Lucy pressed her fingers to her temples and Daniel came to place his arm about her shoulders. His face lowered to hers, he said softly. 'Let her try, Mama — let her try, won't you?'

After a moment Lucy raised her gaze to the big woman. 'I think I must,' she said.

~

In the days that followed, Lucy came to appreciate the gentle, unobtrusive presence of the girl, Moana. Ruby Gaunt had not called again but had sent Rewi back with a jar of red pulp labelled *Titoki Berries*, to lessen blood spitting, and a small wooden box that held a quantity of dried leaves. The instruction on that label read: *Manuka Leaves. Infuse in hot water to allay coughing and lower fever.* There was also a small jar of dock-root ointment for Daniel to apply to his chilblains.

Moana administered these strange medications to Adam and attended to his other needs, bathing and shaving him, feeding him, and boiling his dishes and linen with a silent efficiency that Lucy knew she could never match. The mud floor of the dwelling was swept clean daily, good food was on their table, and the young woman's sleeping mat was placed close to Adam's bed so that Lucy's sleep was rarely disturbed. There was time now for her to spend with her children, time to sit with her husband, and time to reflect on the widow's abandonment of the rough vernacular as she had spoken of Adam's illness and the precautions that must be taken for their safety. Lucy also had time to reflect on the fine writing on the document that was taken to the magistrate in Dunedin and the writing on the labels.

Rewi had cleverly devised covers for the windows, canvas-covered frames that swivelled on a central pivot and could be turned to allow the passage of air while keeping the rain out. On the widow's instruction, Adam must be near a window, which would remain open day and night. Only clean air was to enter his diseased lungs, and when the sun shone he was to be carried to a sheltered place outdoors to benefit from its healing rays. 'Should he recover to the point where he is willing to eat meat,' the widow had further instructed, 'Moana will keep his portion aside until it is strong of odour and glows with phosphorus when the lamp is extinguished. Only then will she cook it for his consumption.'

As Adam slowly grew stronger, Lucy did not question these unusual instructions but went about her tasks with a lighter heart. Each day now the children had a period set aside for lessons, and Lucy learned how to cook under Moana's silent direction. She learned also that nothing was to be wasted, whether it be food or material items. Empty sacks were to be opened and joined together to make a mattress or floor mats. Flour bags, bleached white on the frosty ground, would be made into bed-sheets or table linen. An empty tin filled with mutton fat, a stick pushed into it when it was set, served as a lamp. She and the children learned how to weave flax, and with Rewi's help they made a screen that enabled them to take their Saturday-night bath in privacy. Rewi went off each evening but returned again in the morning to chop the wood and dig a garden in the rough ground. He made a stout door for the kitchen out of thick branches and canvas, and brought the privy from behind the homestead and set it up a discreet distance from the porch.

On the day that Adam was able to leave his bed and sit for a time beside the fire, Lucy gently told him of Ruben.

She told him nothing of her ordeal and very little about the burial. He seemed to accept that Ruben was dead and sought no details of the event. He also accepted Moana's and Rewi's presence without question, and made no objection to Moana's ministrations to his more intimate needs.

Even though Adam was gaining strength daily, Lucy felt that his interest was removed from them. He was oddly remote, speaking little; and when he sat outside in the warming sun his attention was fixed on the mountains, his gaze roving endlessly over their majesty as though he searched for something.

'Perhaps Papa will cheer up for Christmas,' Daniel remarked on the morning Ruby Gaunt next came calling. Lucy had not written in her journal since the day before she had lost the child, so she had no way of knowing when the festive season would be.

The widow stooped through the low door and moved to where Adam sat dozing by the fire. 'How does he?'

Lucy and the young Maori woman looked at each other before Lucy replied. 'Each day he appears a little stronger, but he seems to suffer a deep melancholy and is quite withdrawn. This worries me.'

'He aha hoki te painga o te maharahara?' The big woman dismissed the use of worrying, and turned to Adam. 'Mr Chandler, I am pleased to see you much improved. Your cough is troubling you less?'

The deep voice roused Adam but he did not reply. He stared dully at the widow, and she spoke again, leaning down to him.

'You seem better, Mr Chandler. Do you still feel a need to cough?'

Adam shook his head slowly, as though it were too heavy for movement.

Ruby Gaunt watched him for a moment, then turned away and asked in a low voice. 'Does your husband move about of his own volition or does he sit like this all day?'

'He is as you see him, all the hours he is awake. Why is this, when he seems so much better? He coughs very little and there is no blood.'

Ruby Gaunt did not answer, her attention held by Moana, who was making signs with her hands. The widow nodded. 'E hore ano e whakaroatia e ia ona ra he atarangi nei te rite.' She turned back to Lucy then. 'Let us go outside.'

Lucy followed the tall figure out into the brilliant sunshine and together they walked slowly along the riverbank.

'I have three items of news for you,' Ruby Gaunt began. 'As a result of your signed statement being delivered to the magistrate in Dunedin, the plodding machinery of bureaucracy has duly informed Ruben Chandler's lawyer of his demise. He in turn has informed Ruben's housekeeper who, it seems, has been staying with her sister these many weeks. It appears that the sister broke her leg badly and Agatha Brand had gone to tend her until the leg healed; she knew nothing of happenings here.' The widow reached into the pocket of her jacket and withdrew a plain white envelope. 'Kahu has carried a letter from her for your husband but, under the circumstances, you'd best read it.'

Lucy took the envelope and looked from it to the face of

the woman walking beside her. 'You have not answered my question. Why is my husband so strange?'

The widow was silent while they moved around a fall of rock, and then she replied quietly, 'Moana speaks to me with signs. You saw her doing this?'

'Yes.'

'The Maori people are a very spiritual race and often they perceive things that we cannot.'

Ruby Gaunt stopped walking and her keen grey eyes were on Lucy's face. 'Moana was saying to me, "I tend a body only; the eyes are empty." My reply to her, child—' the woman's voice was low '— was "Neither shall he prolong his days which are as a shadow."' She took Lucy's arm and turned her back the way they had come. 'Your husband has lost the will to live, is what I am saying. In his poor state of health, he is finding it easier to simply give up.'

Lucy stopped walking and stared down at the river. She stood silent for a space then turned to Ruby Gaunt, her eyes hard. 'No,' she said, through clenched teeth. 'No — I will not let this happen. We have worked too hard to save him — all of us. We have gone through too much hardship in this place and before to allow Adam to just give up. No!' Lucy faced the widow. 'Christmas is coming. We will celebrate it; have a tree, singing, laughter. It must rouse him, bring him back to us.'

'Christmas has come and gone, girl. Tomorrow is the second day of the New Year,' the widow said drily.

Lucy bowed her head and walked on. 'What other news were you to tell me?' she asked at length.

The widow pushed the battered hat back from her brow

and wiped the moisture away with a sleeve. It was hot in the sun.

'Word is, come April or May, the constabulary will be callin' — too late by far, but they'll plod around on their flat feet an' ask fool questions. 'Twill only be a token gesture so don't be bothered by it. Don't feed 'em too well an' they'll be on their way the sooner.'

In spite of herself, Lucy smiled. This ugly woman might be rough and strange, but Lucy was beginning to feel a sneaking regard for her.

'The other bit o' news,' the widow went on, 'is that sheep, masses o' sheep, 'ave been sighted on the northern end o' the Barrier Range, by a sundowner passin' through. They've not been shorn, poor brutes, so I'm guessin' they're yer uncle's stock. Now, they've to be dipped against the scab — yer'll not be wantin' ter be fined fer neglectin' that.'

They had reached the hut and Lucy stopped at the entrance to the porch and looked into the leathery features. 'Should Adam die,' she said in a low voice, 'I will be taking my children home. I will have no further interest in this place, its stock or the creatures who have destroyed Ruben's dreams. You will understand this, I'm sure.'

'Aye, lass, but now, think on. Sheep are money on the hoof and money will be useful whatever happens. As well, sheep are stinkin', movin' life an' ther showin' up in ther thousands might spark a bit o' interest in yer man.' Ruby Gaunt rammed the hat down on her head. 'I'll be takin' a cup o' water, missus, an' be on me way. An' if I can find yer a coupla musterers, are yer up to payin' 'em?'

'Yes, but I need time to consider.'

'Not too much time, girl — the poor buggers are like to die of the heat wi' all that wool on 'em!'

It was nine days since Ruby Gaunt's visit and eight days since Moana and Rewi had returned to Long Reach. Today was the eleventh day of January and, as Lucy sat to write in her journal, she felt indescribably lonely. She was keenly aware of her isolation in this vast expanse of empty country where her nearest neighbour was more than an hour's ride away. Months had passed since their arrival on Chandler's Run and not another living soul had she seen here apart from the widow and the natives. Even though Adam moved about a little now, he remained withdrawn. He still slept in the kitchen and seemed content to do so. He made no reference to Moana's departure, except to lift her flax sleeping mat with his toe and murmur, 'Shouldn't she have taken this with her?'

Lucy bit the end of her pen, her thoughts on her husband. At this time of day, when the sun touched the highest peaks with rosy fingers, he was to be found in his usual place beyond the entrance to the porch, sitting with his back against the warm cob wall of the hut. Always his gaze was fixed on the mountains and sometimes his lips moved as though he spoke. Rarely, though, did he speak to his family, and Lucy wondered if he also was lonely, isolated in his need to be done with life. Her sadness for him was beyond tears, but sometimes she felt anger — anger against a merciful God who did not release him — release them all.

She dipped her pen and scanned the few lines of writing on the page. It was not easy making a daily entry when one day was much like another. Her journal was no longer a calendar of social events and family gatherings but now recorded only the mundane: *Today the weather was fine and the washing dried quickly. Sarah is doing well with her samplers, but I fear that my roughened fingers do the silks no kindness. Daniel chased the mare off the garden this morning. She found nothing to her taste but trampled several plants.* For the most part Lucy's entries avoided observances that pertained to Adam.

With Moana's departure, Lucy set about maintaining a routine. Monday was washday. Tuesday, ironing, mending and sweeping the floor filled the day. Wednesday, she and the children worked in the garden that Rewi had dug and planted, carefully weeding and watering the precious vegetables. There were rows of potatoes and kumara (the Maori sweet potato), pumpkin, rock melon, watermelon and Spanish onion plants — and woe betide anyone who pulled these as a weed. Thursday, Lucy and Sarah made soap as Moana had taught them. Leaching lye from the wood ashes, they added melted fat and took turns in stirring the mixture until it was of creamy consistency; then a small handful of salt was added to harden it, unless they were making soft soap, when the salt was omitted. Friday was baking and bread-making day.

The children did their allotted tasks and spent two hours at their lessons each day except Sunday. It was Daniel's task also to chop wood for the fire.

Lucy followed this routine as closely as possible and in this way she attempted to preserve normality in their lives. It also kept her thoughts from things she would rather not contemplate.

Agatha Brand's letter had been brief in her condolences. She had warned Adam to keep the carbine handy and beware the Widow Gaunt, whose husband had died in unusual circumstances some years ago and whose medicinal dabblings were regarded by many as witchcraft. The letter ended with the advice that she would remain with her sister permanently and with the wish that any future enterprise on Chandler's Run would be successful.

Lucy finished her entry. Turning to put the journal away, she was stilled by Daniel's excited voice. 'Mama, Papa — look!' Hurrying outside, she looked where Daniel pointed, already hearing the bleating of many sheep and the barking of dogs. She saw them then, coming up the track, led by a black-and-white dog.

As the mob grew in volume, Adam slowly rose to his feet and came to stand beside Lucy.

'Are those our sheep, Papa?' Sarah's voice was high.

Adam did not reply, and when Sarah looked at her mother, Lucy answered quietly, 'I believe they are Uncle Ruben's sheep, yes, dear.'

'You don't know that!' Adam's voice was sharp.

'Yes, Adam, I do. The Widow Gaunt told me they had been seen when she was last here.' She moved to touch his arm, but Adam stepped away from her and turned to go indoors.

'I don't want that woman coming here again,' he said sourly and unexpectedly. After a moment, Lucy followed him. He lay on his bed, his eyes closed, and quietly she went to stand beside him.

'Adam, dear, won't you talk to me — about the sheep and what must be done with them?'

'I don't want to talk at all, about sheep or anything else.' Adam's voice was querulous. 'Can't you see—' He waved a dismissive hand and turned his face from her.

Slowly, Lucy walked outside again. The widow's notion that the sight of Ruben's sheep might lift Adam's melancholy had been proven vain. Lucy felt a flicker of panic. She would be entirely on her own if she were to obey her husband. The children were nowhere to be seen, so she turned to the place where Adam had been sitting and sat down to watch the sheep pass, hundreds of them, moving towards the homestead and the upper pastures. She heard a horse whinny and the children's voices, then the *clip clop* of shod hooves, and Rewi rode around the porch followed by Daniel and Sarah. 'Kia ora,' he greeted.

Lucy stood up. 'Hello, Rewi. How many sheep are there?'

Serious brown eyes looked down at her as the Maori passed a folded piece of paper to her. 'More come tomorrow. Many — many.'

Lucy unfolded the paper and read the widow's script:

I've had no success finding workers for you. Ruben's boys are not to be found. Since this is so, I would suggest that you allow my lads to set up a temporary arrangement to shear these animals as

quickly as possible. They must be washed and dipped as well.
Rewi will bring your reply.

Only for a moment did Lucy hesitate. 'Wait, Rewi.' She hurried into the kitchen to write her reply. Adam lay on his side but she sensed he was not sleeping. With a hand that shook, she penned her acceptance, and in doing so she removed Adam's authority. She almost ran from the kitchen to thrust her note at Rewi, then resumed her seat against the wall of the hut and closed her eyes. At home she would have been ostracized for her disobedience, but while they remained on Chandler's Run and Adam was so strange, she had little choice. If they were to survive she would be totally reliant on the widow's help, whatever she was. Lucy was only vaguely aware that the children had gone away.

It was hot sitting against the cob wall, and in a while Lucy got to her feet and moved into the shade of the porch. Sheep were still filing past on the track above her, and as she watched a lone horseman appeared. He was tall and lean and rode a rangy chestnut. He was not a native, even though his skin was mahogany; his hair and rough beard were much the colour of his horse. Lucy stepped quickly out of sight, reluctant at this moment to be obliged to speak, her mind occupied totally with Adam and what she had done. While she stood there, another horse passed on the track and she could hear Daniel and Sarah chattering happily as they came running around the corner of the porch.

The following morning Chandler's Run was alive with men, horses and dogs. Rough pens and staging were erected, plus a race where the sheep were hand-washed and then left to dry for eight days before shearing. Each animal was examined for scab, but all were found to be clean. Daniel was a keen observer and reluctantly tended to his tasks and lessons before being set free to join the men. Sarah sulkily remained with Lucy and her father, wishing that she had been born male.

As the wool was shorn from the sheep, it was carted away. Lucy needed to ask somebody about this, but shrank from the idea of approaching any of the workers. Daniel had asked the question of two natives who had simply stared at him and pointed vaguely south. Lucy held no expectations of seeing the wool again.

The day came when the workers had left and all was quiet again. A man left to guard the sheep was seen only occasionally, and only at sunset when the flock moved up into the hills for the night; then they saw his fire's glow. Adam was more morose than ever and would stare at Lucy unblinking for a minute at a time. Disconcerted, she had tried to explain her action to him on several occasions and beg his forgiveness, but each time his face had remained closed and he'd turned away, unable to accept her disobedience. Lucy had gone against his wishes and he saw her now as someone he could no longer trust. But does it matter? he thought tiredly. I will soon be gone and my going will not be easy for her.

Lucy understood, but knew she'd had no choice. With sadness, she set about putting her household in order and no longer tried to appease Adam. She accepted that in his eyes she had disgraced herself, and now she applied her attention to the business of surviving. The tasks she was obliged to perform were oft-times too heavy for her, and maddeningly repetitive. Daily, she battled with anger and resentment. Adam's health seemed to be improving, yet he made no attempt to help her even in the smallest way, clearly uninterested and disapproving.

Then, on a clear warm day, she allowed Daniel to persuade her to leave her tasks and see the sheep at close quarters, and in doing so she discovered that the homestead garden was thriving. She had not been tempted to venture close to the homestead or the outbuildings again, even though Adam and Daniel had been in the area many times. She had felt unnerved by the burned-out buildings and the eeriness that seemed to surround them.

Now Lucy found that what she had thought was a patch of scrub proved to be a tangle of berry canes. Raspberries and red- and blackcurrants grew in profusion, and close by Sarah found a strawberry patch. Dried and wilted weeds that Daniel pulled aside carried mature potatoes on their roots, and searching carefully now, they found pumpkins and Spanish onions and self-seeded tomatoes. Peas, ready for picking, struggled through the overgrown garden to reach the sun. Beyond the garden, hidden by a thick stand of scrub and cabbage trees, Sarah discovered four fruit trees: two apple trees, a nectarine tree and a peach tree, all of which bore fruit. Two more trees beyond these Lucy thought might be lemons.

Lucy watched her children begin to pull the weeds away from the vegetables and the irony of the situation was not lost on her. Here, in the midst of violence, fire, trampling feet and storms, this peaceful garden had survived to furnish them with the food that would keep them alive. With the discovery of the potatoes, Lucy could now bake proper bread as Moana had shown her. She would shred flax and boil it together with potato and a little sugar, then strain off the liquid and leave it to ferment. The resulting yeast would make light, crusty bread that would keep fresh longer than the soda bread Lucy had customarily baked.

'Fetch the shovel, Daniel, and a bucket for the potatoes. Sarah, you can help me pick some peas and a few strawberries.'

'We should buy a cow, Mama,' Daniel said happily. 'If we had a cow we could have cream on our strawberries.'

'Yes, Mama, and hens,' Sarah added. 'I would gather the eggs each morning for breakfast and Papa would get well again much sooner.'

Lucy nodded. It would be nice to have milk in her tea again and butter on the table and a bowl of brown eggs each day. Perhaps the widow could advise her? Suddenly Lucy laughed. 'Could you ever see your mama squeezing milk out of a cow? — Oh!' And her clear laughter rang out. The children were laughing with her, and through his laughter Daniel was spluttering words and holding his sides: 'I *can* see you, Mama. I can see you pumping her tail—' he was overcome with laughter, clutching his sides harder. 'And when no milk comes out—'

Gasping for breath, Lucy pushed her son away. 'Stop, Daniel — oh, *will* you stop — my ribs are splitting!' She wiped her eyes on her apron. 'Come, let us tend to the task at hand and decide what is to be for dinner.' She smiled after her children as they went off to do her bidding. Oh, it was good to laugh; laughter had been a rarity since they had come to Chandler's Run.

She raised her eyes to the mountains. Bronze-gold cirrus clouds gilded the high peaks and a cooling breeze stirred the flax and cabbage trees along the riverbank. The sheep were moving slowly towards the higher ground as the evening drew nearer, and beyond them, almost invisible against the scree slopes, stood the lone figure of a man with his horse. Lucy could not discern whether he was a white man or a native, but his silent presence was somehow reassuring.

Chapter 5

HEARING A LONE HORSE approaching, Lucy put aside her mending and rose to her feet. She urged the children to continue their lessons as she walked slowly to the kitchen doorway. Ruby Gaunt was dismounting when she stepped into the porch.

'I've some figures 'ere fer yer to peruse.' The widow tapped the satchel she was untying from her saddle.

'Figures?' Lucy queried.

'Estimated figures for the sale of yer wool and a list o' me charges.'

With some trepidation Lucy bade her enter the kitchen where Adam sat at the table. His brooding gaze rested on the widow, but he remained silent as she sat down opposite him and, emptying her satchel on to the rough table, pushed a sheet of paper towards him.

'Yer wool clip — eighty-eight bales, will fetch a fair price—' she began, but Adam, swinging slowly around on the form, turned his back to her, rose from the table and went to lie on his bed. Lucy coloured.

'I am so sorry,' she whispered.

'Pay it no mind,' the widow growled. 'Now, 'ere is what

yer owe me, which I've deducted from yer total, given that the market's not changed.'

Lucy took the sheet of paper from Ruby Gaunt's hand and looked at the substantial list of charges. On it was the deal table, the forms, the old straw broom that Moana had left behind, the meat and medication, the small bag of potatoes left over from the garden Rewi had planted, even the flour-bag sheets on Adam's bed; and Moana's and Rewi's wages. She had no way of knowing if the charges were fair, and as her eyes moved down the list she was astounded to find a charge for Ruben's funeral, including the rough coffin. Lucy looked sharply at the raw-boned woman and noted the glint in the steely eyes and the grimace that might have been a grin. Lowering her eyes, she drew another sheet towards her and examined the figures written on it. Itemized were the number of bales to be sold, their combined weight of forty-five thousand pounds and the market price. Against this was the widow's charge for droving, washing and shearing the sheep, pressing the bales, and the hire of the three wagons that would be required to transport the wool. Even though the balance was satisfying, Lucy suspected that Chandler's Run had paid in full for services rendered. This last paper was yet to be date-stamped and receipted.

'Things are only middlin' in regard ter yer shepherds.' Ruby Gaunt's gravelly voice broke in on Lucy's thoughts. 'Been down to the Ngai Tahu kainga but the boys are spooked about this place an' refuse ter work 'ere again.'

'You saw them then?'

'Aye — briefly.'

'Did you ask them what had happened here?'

'I asked 'em — in a roundabout way so's I'd not scare 'em. Before the words were out o' me mouth, they'd vanished.'

Ruby Gaunt was looking at the figure on the bed. Lucy spoke quickly.

'The man who is with the sheep now, could I not keep him for a while until we find somebody?'

'E's not one of my fellas. Ther's no 'arm askin', girl, if yer can afford ter pay 'im. 'E's a master drover, I'm told — name o' McKenzie.'

'Goodness, when he came with your people I assumed you were paying him and feeding him — oh, dear!'

''E'll not be starvin' up ther'. Don't you fret.' The widow barked a short laugh. 'A fat lamb or wild pig'll feed a man royally, an' if he's no tea fer 'is pot, the leaves of the manuka tree will serve very well.'

'Do you mean to tell me that this man is killing our sheep?'

'Effen yer've not been feedin' 'im . . .' The widow raised an eyebrow.

'I see.' Lucy digested this then asked, 'Why would he stay if he is not being paid? Is this not rather odd?'

'More'n likely 'e's between jobs an' yer lucky ter 'ave 'ad 'im this long, eatin' yer sheep as may be. 'E'll move on soon, I expect.'

'Then what am I to do when he does?'

'Like I said, girlie, ask 'im.'

'How am I to do this when he stays up there in the hills?'

'Yer got legs, ain't yer? Better still, put that fat mare ter work afore she founders.'

Lucy was silent for a time, then looked into the ugly face and smiled her best smile. 'Would you approach him for me? I would be so grateful if you would.'

The widow's creases deepened and her eyes were pinpoints of steel. 'That I'll not, lady. Move fer yersel' or do wi'out.' Ruby Gaunt rose slowly to her feet, and pulling on her gloves she growled, 'I'll do yer one more favour — that fella up yonder wants ter go off, yer can 'ave Kahu tend yer flocks fer a while. 'E'll be 'appy on a pound a week an' found.' So saying, the widow strode to the door and was gone.

Adam Chandler reclined on his bed, watching his wife knead the dough that would make their bread supply for the week. She had always been considered pretty as became an English lady of breeding, pale and delicate, but as he watched the rhythmic movement of her body, he realized that she was comely indeed. The sun had burnished her skin, her dark hair shone with health, and she was supple and more shapely than hitherto. He was surprised by a sudden surge of desire, which it caused him to grimace inwardly, sure as he was that Lucy would not encourage intimacy. The boiling of his eating utensils and his linen, and the gentle distancing of his family, had not gone unmarked, and he'd guessed rightly who the author of these precautions would be. Nevertheless, the old harridan's witchery seemed to be having some effect, he grudgingly conceded; he seldom coughed now and he felt altogether stronger. Perhaps soon he could be his own man again and take charge of his affairs once more. The thought heartened him.

He swung his legs over the side of the bed and stood up. Feeling his eyes on her, Lucy looked up. 'Are you going for your walk?'

'Yes, and when I return, I think we must discuss our situation here and make some decisions. Do you agree?'

'Indeed I do.'

Lucy had watched the gradual improvement in Adam's health with growing hope. She still cooked his meat as the widow had instructed her to, not understanding how it could be helping him but sure that it was. Latterly he had worked a little in the garden and carried in small loads of wood for the fire. Daily now he walked along the riverbank or down the track, going a little further each time as his confidence grew; as it grew, his demeanour was changing, his remoteness and melancholy affecting him only rarely. God bless Ruby Gaunt, was Lucy's heartfelt thought.

She shaped the dough into round loaves and set them down on the hearth to rise, then stood absently staring into the fire, wondering what it was that Adam wished to discuss and what decisions would be arrived at. A wave of homesickness swept over her and she found herself wishing that Adam would decide to return home. Guiltily, she dismissed the wish and upbraided herself for even entertaining it. She heard him enter the porch and quickly busied herself about the hearth. When he entered the kitchen, he bade Lucy sit and, seating himself opposite her, he began to speak. 'I think I must find a way to see Uncle Ruben's lawyer. The legal ramifications of his death — the stock, the land, where we stand — all these things must be looked into as soon as possible.'

'You are hardly fit to travel such a distance, Adam,' Lucy warned. 'And besides, many of the rivers will be impassable.'

'Nevertheless, Lucy, I would wish to make the trip very soon and have considered asking the Widow Gaunt for a man to accompany me as guide.' He thought for a moment, then said slowly, 'There is also the matter of our possessions. We need to know that they are still safely stored.'

'Then we must all go, Adam. I could not in conscience allow you to go alone.'

'And how do you propose to manage that, my dear? We have but one horse and one saddle.'

'We could surely hire a cart, as well as a man from our neighbour—'

Adam held up a silencing hand. 'I would as soon walk, dear girl, every inch of the way, than subject these fleshless bones to that kind of torture again. No. I will travel alone and go the faster for it.'

Two days after this, young Kahu rode over from Long Reach carrying two battered oil lamps, a tin of colza oil, and a crumpled note which read: *Throw out those foul-smelling slush lamps; not good for the lungs. No charge.* It was not signed. Adam was quick to take advantage of the Maori's visit and sent him back with his own note.

~

It was suffocatingly hot; the slight breeze coming off the scree slopes was a searing breath. The heat from the boiler's fire penetrated Lucy's skirts, and sweat ran into her eyes and between her breasts. Impatiently she pushed the damp hair off her brow and unfastened the top buttons of her bodice.

Washday was her *bête noire*, a task which that day was more unpleasant than usual — her washing-stick had snapped in half as she had lifted the clothes from the water, and she was, as a result, drenched to the skin. Uncomfortable, dishevelled and out of temper, she flung the two pieces of stick from her and cast about for another. Suddenly she became aware of movement on the track above, and looking up she saw a horseman reining his mount to a halt. He sat relaxed in his saddle, his intense blue eyes sweeping her from head to foot, and Lucy, with cheeks blooming, clutched the neck of her bodice together and dragged the clinging skirts away from her legs. She realized that this was the drover, McKenzie. All thoughts of negotiating for his services fled. Deeply embarrassed, she dropped her eyes, wishing he would ride on, but his voice came down to her, deep and slow. She could understand not a single word of what he said, and, completely flustered now, she shook her head and turned quickly away, bumping into Daniel who had come to stand beside her. Rubbing his arm, the boy looked up at the horseman. 'Hello,' he said. 'You're the chap who has been minding the sheep, aren't you?'

'Aye.' He turned clear eyes on Daniel and, dismissing Lucy, waved a hand towards the hills and spoke again. He then touched two fingers to the brim of his hat, pressed heels to his horse's flanks and rode off down the track. A black-and-white dog ran beside him.

'Dear me,' Lucy said breathlessly. The one word she had understood was *beasties* and it was clear that he was moving on.

'He is Scottish, I think, Mama, and maybe speaking the Gaelic.' The boy chuckled. 'Do you remember the gardener at home, Mama? He used to make noises like that when we ran over his flowerbeds and *he* came from Scotland.' Mother and son looked at each other for a moment, then both began to laugh.

'Oh!' Lucy wiped her eyes. 'I didn't think to pay him. Oh, Daniel!' Then she fell silent and listened to the diminishing sound of the horse's hooves until she could hear them no more. There was a sense of emptiness as the silence folded around her.

The meal that night was eaten without appetite. Adam had left for Dunedin the day before with Rewi as his guide. Lucy had lain sleepless throughout most of the night, listening to noises she could not recall hearing before, whilst taking comfort from the presence of the man on watch above them. She had watched Adam ride off with misgiving; Rewi's stocky frame had accentuated her husband's frailty as they had ridden side by side down the track, and she had prayed silently as he went from her sight that all would be well.

In the lamplight Lucy watched the downcast faces of her children. Sensing her own disquiet, they were anxious and tense. She tried to make light of their isolation. 'How can you think we are alone when there are thousands of woolly souls all around us?' But as she made the joke she was keenly aware of the many miles separating them from their own kind. With the drover gone, the solitude weighed heavily.

'Come, let us clear away these dishes and we'll read a story before we go to bed.'

The night was warm and sleep eluded Lucy again. Sarah's soft breathing beside her told her that the child was asleep, and Daniel had not stirred for an hour. She slipped out of bed and went into the kitchen. The water in the kettle was simmering and, careful not to make a noise, she made herself a cup of tea and sat sipping it slowly, gazing into the fire. She wondered where Adam was sleeping at this moment and looked across at his empty bed. There was a strong foreboding in her that she could not dismiss despite the fact that the weather was warm and his path would be overland for the most part, following tracks over pass and mountain that only the Maori knew. He would sleep in friendly villages — the widow had assured her that as Rewi's companion he would be made welcome — but Lucy's uneasiness persisted.

Suddenly, she was listening. Faintly on the still night air came the sound of a horse cantering. Was it one horse? She held her breath and listened intently. Were there more running on the grass that she could not hear? Lucy felt her heartbeat accelerate. Who could be coming to Chandler's Run at this hour? Slowly she stood up and looked about for something to arm herself with. The straw broom leaned beside the hearth. She took it up and stood waiting. The rhythmic beat of hooves was drawing closer and Lucy prayed it would be the drover returning to the untended sheep. Clutching the broom, she crept to a window. The moon went in as she peered around the cover and she strained her eyes to see in the darkness. The animal slowed to a walk on the track above, and when it drew level with the window it halted. Lucy stood rigid, fearful, then heard Kahu's smiling voice call goodnight softly: 'Po marie.'

She was shaking as she replaced the broom and sat down again. Into her mind's eye came, unbidden, an image of the thing that had been Ruben Chandler, and she shivered. Some time later, she went to her bed and composed herself for sleep, knowing that Kahu stood guard up in the hills.

Lucy and the children were working in the garden when Rewi returned. He rode up the track then around the porch to the garden, leading the mare. Lucy went cold. 'Where is my husband?'

'Him in hospital, missus.'

'What has happened? Tell me!'

'We coming home — two day. He fall down, say take him back.'

Rewi's brown eyes were doleful. Lucy's forebodings had become a reality.

'What are we going to do, Mama?'

'I don't know, Daniel, at this moment I just don't know.'

Lucy was thinking, planning. She needed to be with

Adam and she would have to take the children with her. Would the widow oblige them with transport to Dunedin? Rewi passed the mare's reins to Daniel and rummaged in his saddlebag.

'Words for you,' he said, holding out a battered roll of paper. 'Inu —' he made a sign of drinking, 'then we go.'

'Sarah, bring water for Rewi please, and water for the horses, Daniel, if you would.'

Lucy hurried into the kitchen and quickly thrust onions, potatoes and pumpkin into two flax kits. These she took out to Rewi, then bade him wait.

In the shade of the porch she read Adam's letter. It was scrappy and a little disjointed, but she caught the sense of it. He had searched out Ruben's lawyer, John Hamilton, on arriving in Dunedin. There he had learned that Ruben had named him sole beneficiary in his will and that there was some doubt as to whether he had inherited the leasehold on the larger tract of land. He went on to say that Mrs Brand had visited him in hospital and that he had commissioned Nobby Clark to carry their belongings up to Chandler's Run as soon as the rivers were passable. The doctor at the hospital had advised against attempting the journey home at this time, but had given no opinion otherwise of Adam's condition, except to warn him that he must rest. He ended the letter saying:

Should I not be able to do so myself, Mr Hamilton or Mrs Brand will keep you informed. Under no circumstances must you try to come to Dunedin. A hellish journey, my dear. Even with

Rewi's knowledge of the terrain, we still had to make our way on occasion through thickets of speargrass and matagouri which punished both horse and rider, and we risked our lives time and again negotiating steep and narrow passes and fast-running waters.

Lucy folded the letter and pushed it into her pocket, then returned to Rewi, who stood waiting beside his horse. 'Thank you for your help.' She held out her hand and took the Maori's hand in hers. 'There will be no letter for Mrs Gaunt. We will stay here.'

Sarah was watching her mother with wide, worried eyes. 'Is Papa not coming home, Mama?'

Lucy saw the child's fear and quickly placed an arm about the small shoulders. 'Not for the present, dear. The journey to Dunedin has made Papa very tired so the doctor has said he must rest for a while.'

'But he will come home?'

'Of course.' Lucy made her mouth smile. 'Don't you worry now. Papa is in the best possible place, Sarah. And do you know what we are going to do?' She gave the child a gentle squeeze. 'We are going to buy a cow and some hens to surprise Papa when he does come home.'

Some days later when the Widow Gaunt came calling, riding her big bay mare, Lucy negotiated the purchase of a cow and six hens, over a pot of tea. 'Don't leave 'em runnin' loose, missus,' the widow warned. 'Wild pigs an' dogs'll 'ave 'em effen yer do, an' the rats'll eat yer eggs. Yer'll need ter make a fowl-house an' run.'

'We'll make a cow byre out of stone and mud,' Daniel said quickly, 'and the hen house can be built on to it. Do you think we could do it, Mama, the same way we built the kitchen?'

Lucy looked doubtful. 'I don't know, Daniel. I had not envisaged having to build anything.' She looked at the big woman and slowly shook her head. 'Maybe it would be wise to wait until Papa comes home.'

'I can do it, Mama,' Daniel replied stoutly, 'and I'll weave reeds or something along the front of the hen house to keep the rats out.'

'Rats'll chew through yer reeds, boy — make a lattice of thick branches ter keep off the dogs an' the pigs an' set yer layin' boxes atop poles taller than yersel'. Think yer could do that?'

'I'm sure I could. Do rats climb?'

Ruby Gaunt chuckled deep in her chest. 'Aye, an' that's why yer put a tin collar around yer poles, two-thirds o' the way up an' two feet deep.' She turned to Lucy. 'I've some nails an' some tin yer can buy from me, missus.'

Lucy accepted the offer, knowing she would more than likely be paying twice their value. 'You have had no success in your search for a shepherd?' she asked.

'None,' came the gruff reply. 'Rewi took my note to the *Otago Witness* but I don't expect a swift reply.' She squinted at Lucy. 'Shame in a way, 'cause I could do with Kahu on my place right now.'

Lucy didn't rise to the bait; she was learning. She had no intention of paying anything other than the Maori boy's wages. There was a short silence, then the widow stated tersely, 'Yer cow an' hens'll be across in a while an' I'd get yer man out o' that place as quick as yer can. It's a hotchpotch o' diseases all lumped tergether — odds are 'e'll 'ave a couple more when 'e gets out o' ther'.'

After delivering that grim piece of advice, Ruby Gaunt drained her mug, pushed her hat down more firmly on to her head and strode to the door. 'Yer can pay me when I bring the livestock an' tin.' With that she was gone, and Lucy sighed inwardly.

The task of gathering suitable stone and digging a shallow trench for the foundations of the cow byre and the hen house was begun, and every hour that could be spared was dedicated to their construction. Without Adam's help, progress was slow and Lucy feared that the cold months would be upon them before the structures were completed. Kahu, with his perpetual smile, would stand and watch their labours when he came down from the hills to collect his dinner-pail, but he offered no help and, though Lucy had been tempted to employ his strength to cut the poles, she decided against it. Her money would remain where it was.

From dawn until past dark, Lucy and the children toiled, attending to their usual tasks as well as the erection of the stone walls. With mind-numbing fatigue they fell into their beds each night, too exhausted to think of anything but sleep. There was no further word from Adam, and Lucy had no time to reflect on what might be happening to him in Dunedin. Sarah's tenth birthday passed unmarked.

Progress on the stone walls was so slow that Daniel decided to make his laying boxes first. He laboured for hours to chop the poles with the blunt axe, and eventually, with painfully blistered palms, he dragged them out of the scrub and dropped them within the unfinished walls of the hen house. He then set about making a roost. Never having seen one, he could only guess how it would look, and when after a number of false starts it was finally finished, he doubted the hens would ever use it. Ruby Gaunt, arriving with the cow and hens the day after its completion, viewed the roost with arms akimbo and eyes narrowed.

'Puts me in mind o' a funeral pyre,' she commented drily. 'When the buggers go off the lay they can commit *suttee*.'

Daniel was crestfallen and Lucy glared at the ugly face.

'Pay me no mind, lad,' the widow rumbled. 'Ye've done a damn fine job. Put some grain in them boxes an' those birds'll feel right at home. Now, 'ere's yer tin an' nails. I'll show yer what yer do wi' 'em — are yer makin' a brew, missus?' Unabashed, she grinned at Lucy.

Lucy ignored her, giving her attention to the cow tied to the back of the cart.

'Milk 'er mornin' an' night. Get me a pail and summat ter sit on an' I'll show yer, then you can try yerself.'

The widow demonstrated. Lucy was very nervous. She seated herself on the box and with trepidation squeezed the teats gingerly.

'God in Heaven, girl, she'll be dried off in no time if

yer do it like that. Look now — the milk's up ther' an' yer squeeze it down like squeezin' paint out o' a tube — see?' The big hands went to work and twin jets pinged into the tin pail.

'Can I try?' Daniel was fascinated. He sat down carefully on the wooden box and rested his head gently into the cow's flank as the widow had done, then slowly imitated the movement of her hands. The milk began to flow and he felt a sense of peace and unity with the animal as his hands fell into the simple rhythm. He smiled at the raw-boned woman.

'You'll do,' she grunted. 'Leave off now an' help me unload the hay while yer ma makes me that cup o' tea — with milk.'

'Does she have a name?' Daniel asked, as he followed the widow to lift the hay down from the cart.

'Cow' came the laconic reply, and Sarah giggled.

When the tea was made and they all sat at the table, Lucy was given instructions on how to separate the cream from the milk.

'Them big round pans yer've got ther', those're settlin' pans. Leave the milk stand in 'em overnight then skim the cream off in the mornin'. Yer've got a skimmer — big flat spoon wi' holes in it?' Lucy nodded. 'Yer'll need butter pats,' the widow continued, 'an' a butter churn — order 'em from Nobby Clark when 'e's next up this way. Meantime whip the cream by hand an' don't fergit the salt.'

Lucy's head was beginning to spin. After showing Daniel how to store the hay and how much to put in the bail at each milking, the widow finally took her leave and Lucy looked at her son with dismay. Milking, skimming, churning, fashioning butter pats; hens to be housed and fed; a cow bail to be built — dear God!

'I can't do all this, Daniel,' she wailed. 'I had no idea that a cow and hens would mean so much more work.'

'Mama, there are three of us — Sarah is able to share in the daily tasks very well now. Between us we will manage until Papa comes home.'

Lucy looked at her boy. Not yet thirteen, he was a pillar of strength and so sensible. She felt a little ashamed in the face of his sturdy optimism. 'Of course, you are right, Daniel. It's simply a matter of arranging each day a little differently and getting used to these new tasks.'

Daniel nodded. 'May I milk the cow? I have thought of a name for her. Do you think Ruby would suit her?'

Remembering the colour of the animal, the red-brown so dark it was almost black, Lucy agreed. She would have agreed to any name, in fact, so long as she was not required to touch the bearer of it.

The days passed and the walls of the byre and hen house began to take shape. The hens were using Daniel's roost and were laying in the tussock-filled egg boxes. All pride in his handiwork was gone, however. Now when he looked at it he saw only its resemblance to a Hindu funeral pyre.

'It doesn't matter what it looks like, Daniel, so long as the hens lay in the boxes,' Lucy told him. 'I think the roost will need to be covered because there is a change coming.'

A cool southerly wind was pushing cloud along the ridges

as she spoke and the sheep were moving with purpose to the lower slopes. The mare had come to stand in the porch entrance.

'Milk the cow as soon as you can, dear, and we will need more wood in.'

～

The rain came during the night, heavy rain that fell steadily. Some time before morning, Lucy was awakened by the sound of horses on the track above. Raising herself on an elbow, she listened intently. Daniel, awake too, slipped from his bed and went quickly to a kitchen window.

'Can you see anything?' Lucy was beside him.

'No, but it sounded like two horses, at least, up there,' the boy whispered.

'Let me see if I can see anything.' Lucy peered out into the streaming darkness but could see nothing.

'Go back to bed, Daniel. Come, Sarah, there is nothing to see.'

The young girl stood close to her mother in the darkness, clutching her arm. 'Who is out there, Mama?'

'I don't know who it was, pet, but they have gone. Come along, into bed with you.'

The rain continued to fall and Lucy dozed fitfully. She rose before daybreak and stirred the fire into a blaze. The rain had subsided to a grey drizzle that obscured everything beyond fifty yards, and as daylight came Lucy donned her cape and went outdoors. The mare and the cow were grazing peacefully and there was nothing untoward to be seen. Low cloud cloaked the hills and she could hear the sheep bleating. If mischief had been afoot last night, there was nothing to show for it in the morning. Whoever the unknown riders were, they would probably have been unaware of the family's presence or not seen the stone dwelling in the pitch darkness and teeming rain — but what of Kahu? Lucy went back indoors, anxious for the safety of the smiling Maori.

Plainly tired, both Sarah and Daniel were up and setting about their tasks. 'Could you see anything amiss, Mama?' Daniel asked.

'No, with this misty drizzle one can see very little, but all seems as usual so far as I can tell.'

'If people are going to ride around, why can't they do it in daylight?' Sarah asked plaintively.

When Kahu had not appeared with his dinner-pail by late afternoon, Lucy was afraid that all was *not* as usual. The misty rain had cleared away, leaving low banks of cloud that obscured forest and scrub-land; the mountain peaks rose disembodied out of their moist embrace. Lucy pondered the wisdom of leaving the safety of the hut and the children, but Kahu's non-appearance played on her mind until finally she said, 'I will walk a little way up the lower hills.' She pulled on her boots and cape again as she spoke, and shook her head at Daniel, who was reaching for his jacket. 'No, Daniel, stay with Sarah and don't worry — I will be careful.'

Sheep ran from her path as she walked quickly towards the foothills, keeping her eyes on the pockets of scrub and rocky outcrops. As her path became steeper, she moved with instinctive stealth, sensible of the danger she could be in.

She did not call out. Of Kahu, his horse and his dogs, there was no sign. Thick silence surrounded her.

Winded, Lucy was forced to rest. She sat down under a limestone outcrop and was surprised to see the distance she had come. Far below, through scarves of mist, she could see the burned-out homestead and outbuildings. Her gaze followed the track past the hut to where it disappeared around the bend, and she tracked the river between its fluted columns until it was lost to sight where it crashed into the gorge below. It emerged again away in the distance in the intricate patterns of the Waitaki River where it flowed, milky green, across the parched brown plains. As she sat there surveying the landscape, Lucy came to understand something of Ruben's feeling for this wild and beautiful land. Anger rose in her against the interlopers who had brought him to his end in this place that had held so much hope for him, and her anger included those who might still be skulking in the hills. Her gaze swept the broad landscape but nothing moved except the cropping sheep.

Slowly she rose to her feet and, stepping out from beneath the outcrop, looked up at the towering mountains. Only pockets of snow lay on their rugged peaks and the lowering sun picked them out and painted them a blinding copper. Before the beauty and majesty of those peaks, man's violence and ugly death were a cruel dissonance, and Lucy prayed that those responsible for Ruben's death would be found and made to pay.

∼

A week had passed and Kahu had not put in an appearance, but at night the glow of a small fire could be seen again up in the hills. Lucy assumed that the Scotsman had returned to eat her sheep, and worried no more.

For the past few days, work on the cow byre and hen house had ceased to allow bruised and blistered hands to heal. Daniel had attempted to cut the poles for the roof, but his hands were raw and Lucy had stopped him, saying that she would prevail upon Kahu to cut them when next she saw him. The stone walls had risen to only half the height required and she feared the work would never be finished unless she could employ somebody to help them. There was still no word from Dunedin but Lucy would not dwell on this silence; she was not ready to face the prospect that Adam might not return, reserving her energies for the preparation and maintenance of their home for when he did.

The children had resumed the pastime of watching the sheep these past few days, and Lucy took advantage of their absence to quietly assess their stock of food. She sat at the table now and, quill in hand, made her list. The fresh meat was finished, but there was still some potted meat, potted fish and lobster, and the hens were laying. Onions were strung from the kitchen roof as the widow had taught her to do, and the pumpkins and potatoes were stored against foraging rats in two of the trunks.

Lucy was making butter with some success and kept it in the stone crock in the shade of the hut to keep it from turning rancid. They had dined well on apple and berry tarts and stewed fruit served with lashings of cream, but having no containers to store the fruit in or to make jam or jellies, a good quantity had been wasted. Ruby Gaunt had shown them how to dry peaches and apples by splitting them in half, removing the stones and pips, and threading them on to white cotton, then hanging them on rows of nails to dry in the sun. Lucy's concern, however, was keeping food on the table during the winter months. The meat barrels needed replenishing, and her supply of flour was low, as was the tea and sugar. She had not seen the Widow Gaunt since the delivery of the cow and hens, and she found herself listening for the sound of the cart. She needed to know how to replace her stock of dry goods and she needed the meat barrels filled before the cold months set in. More than this, in her isolation Lucy needed the companionship of another woman and Ruby Gaunt was the only candidate, unsuitable as she might be.

Her thoughts turned to Adam. Lucy was making a tentative plan to journey to Dunedin when the rivers were again safe to cross. The gold sovereigns were still untouched in their hiding place, and the money from the wool, when it came, would be placed in Adam's tin box and hidden in the same place.

She would somehow buy a cart and two strong horses to pull it, and she'd hire Kahu from the widow to drive them. Determined to see Adam for herself, she would make the long trip, talk to the doctors at the hospital and perhaps find him well enough to bring home.

Home — how odd that she could now think of this place as home, and odder still that she would contemplate making such a journey with a young Maori who, to her mind, was a savage with strange customs and little English. Lucy smiled ruefully. Five months they had been on Chandler's Run and in that time she knew she had changed in many ways herself, especially in appearance. If she were to pass her mother in the street today, that dear lady would not recognize her with her rough clothes, toil-worn hands and undressed tresses. She was aware also that the genteel niceties of home would find no place here, and even were they to stop to chat with each other they would find no common ground. Saddened, Lucy put down her quill and rose from the table. The shadows were lengthening; the children had been away a long time, longer even than the day before. She walked to the kitchen doorway and out into the porch to hear Daniel's laughter and Sarah's giggle as they came crashing down the bank. It was a happy, carefree sound. Mama would not recognize her grandchildren either.

'You have been gone for a long time,' Lucy said. 'You must have been enjoying yourselves.'

'Yes, Mama. Sheep are entertaining creatures but they are rather silly. If one runs down the hill, they all run down the hill. If one jumps over a rock, they all jump over the rock. It seems as though one does the thinking for all of them.'

'I see. Well, I'm doing the thinking for all of us and I think we must have more wood for the fire.' Laughing, Lucy tousled the boy's hair and turned indoors. 'Come, Sarah, we will start making dinner.'

On the track above, the man sat still in his saddle listening to the laughter and the voices, then he reined his horse about, called softly to his dog and turned towards the hills.

Chapter 6

LUCY AND THE CHILDREN resumed building the byre and the hen house at the end of a week's rest. They worked at a more leisurely pace, having experienced the consequences of pushing too hard for completion.

'If the byre is not finished, Ruby can share the porch with the mare,' Lucy said. 'It is more important to make a shelter for the hens and I have been thinking, Daniel, that thinner poles should suffice for the lower, smaller roof.'

'I agree, Mama.' Daniel took up the axe. 'I shall go and cut them now before the rain comes.'

Lucy and Sarah continued placing stones on the hen-house walls. A chill wind was blowing from the south, and ragged cloud obscured the peaks as they worked. As the first spits of rain began to fall, Daniel threw down the last bundle of branches from the track above and looked up at the sky. Because of his momentary inattention, his ankle turned under him as he stepped down, and with a shout of pain he was falling, landing heavily on the stony ground below. He lay still for a moment and Lucy and Sarah ran to him.

'Are you hurt, Daniel?' Lucy touched him anxiously.

The boy groaned and slowly sat up. 'I'm all right — it

knocked the wind out of me and my ankle hurts.'

'Come, let us get you inside out of the rain. Can you stand?'

With an effort Daniel rose to his feet, then yelped when he placed his weight on the painful ankle.

'I think I may have broken it, Mama,' he gasped.

Dismayed, Lucy stared at her son's crumpled face. She knew nothing about broken bones. What was she to do? Panicky thoughts skittered through her brain as she cast about for a way to get help. Daniel was watching her, waiting, anxious, and Lucy pulled herself together. There was nobody to help him but herself.

'Can you hop, dear?' She made her lips smile. 'You are too big to carry. Lean on Sarah and me — carefully now.'

Once inside, Daniel lowered himself on to a bench beside the table and stretched his injured leg along it. Gingerly, Lucy removed his boot and sock and saw with misgiving the discoloured and swiftly swelling ankle.

'Is it broken, Mama?'

'I have no way of knowing, Daniel. We'll have to wait and see.'

In pain and not entirely satisfied with his mother's reply, Daniel frowned. 'When George Potter broke his leg at school the doctor put a board on it to keep it straight.' His gaze moved from his ankle to Lucy's face. 'Shouldn't we do that?'

Lucy stood up slowly and moved to the fireplace. With her back to her son she said quietly, 'Daniel, I am not a doctor. If I touch your ankle not knowing what I am doing, I could make matters worse.'

The boy was silent. Sarah took his hand and patted it. 'Don't worry, Danny. It may be better in the morning.'

~

Morning dawned cold and wet. Daniel had slept little. His ankle had throbbed painfully throughout the night, and by morning the swelling and discoloration were worse. Lucy stood at the fire stirring the maize porridge, her anxiety for Daniel growing. She thought of the man up in the hills and was tempted to enlist his aid, then thought better of it. Sarah brought in the eggs and put them carefully into the basin to wash them. 'Listen to Ruby, Mama,' she said. 'She is mooing again.'

Lucy had heard the cow in the early hours of the morning and had wondered briefly what was disturbing her. Now, suddenly she knew. 'The cow was not milked last night!'

'Mama, I'm sorry — I should have remembered,' Daniel spoke from his bed. 'If you'll help me out to the porch and bring her in, I'll milk her.'

Torn between her fear of the cow and her conviction that he should not try, Lucy helped Daniel to swing his legs out of bed but the pain was so intense when he lowered his foot, he quickly raised it again. 'I can't, Mama, I'm sorry.'

Lucy squared her shoulders. 'Never mind. Bring me the box to sit on, Sarah, and the pail.' She donned her cape and boots and went out to drive the bellowing cow into the porch, muttering to herself as she went, 'Like squeezing paint from a tube.'

The udder was distended, the teats taut. When Lucy's

hands began to squeeze, a hind leg lashed out and the pail went flying.

Shaking from head to foot, Lucy leapt up from her seat on the box and stood helplessly, looking at the distressed cow.

'Hello, the house!'

The rough call had never been more welcome. Ruby Gaunt strode into the porch and took in the situation at a glance. Her gloved hand patted the damp quarters and stroked the heaving sides and she spoke in soothing tones, ''Tis all right old girl, 'tis all right.' She stripped off her gloves and talked to the cow in a low crooning voice, her hands calming, then picked up the pail and straddled the box. Her hat fell off when she tucked her head into the cow's flank. The thin grey hair was drawn into a tight knot on the top of her head and without the hat she seemed somehow vulnerable. Her big hands moved gently over the bulging udder and the gravelly voice crooned, and soon the bellowing ceased and milk began to flow. 'There, my beauty, there, 'tis easier now, my beauty.'

Lucy was no longer shaking, but stood entranced, watching the ugly face grow almost comely in its concentration. The cow's eyes had closed and slowly she began to chew her cud. Sarah moved closer and her hand crept into her mother's.

The pail was full of warm frothy milk. Moving it aside, the widow reached for her hat. Ramming it on to her head she stood up and faced Lucy. 'Where's yer boy? Thought he were the milker.'

'Daniel fell down the bank yesterday. His ankle is swollen and painful.' She gestured for Ruby Gaunt to enter the hut.

'Would you be able to tell us if it is broken?' The widow strode to where Daniel lay.

'Aye, yer've done a job on that — let's 'ave a look.'

Daniel clenched his teeth as big fingers probed. 'Well, yer lucky, lad, 'tis only sprained.' The widow glanced at Lucy. 'I've a lotion in the cart. We use it for sprains, wounds, sores and joint pain. I'll want you to apply hot, then cold packs to the ankle, ten minutes or so for each, twice a day, then stroke on the lotion. When that is done, bind it firmly for support and keep it bound until the swelling has gone — yer understand?' Lucy nodded.

'Right, then come with me.'

Oblivious of the rain, the widow rummaged about in a box under the cart's high seat and at last produced a small bottle containing an oily green substance. 'Keep what you don't use.'

Lucy accepted the bottle. 'What is this?' She extracted the cork and sniffed carefully at the contents.

'An extract from the titoki tree.' Ruby Gaunt swung up into the cart and squinted down at Lucy. 'Yer boy'll be off that ankle fer two or three weeks so yer'd best learn ter milk.'

She untied the reins from the side of the cart and sat down on the leather seat. 'I come over ter remind yer that the muster's ter be done end o' the month.'

'Muster?'

'Aye, an yer goin' ter need two bush hands ter put up yer huts, repair yer yards an' build a barn an' woolshed. Then yer'll need a couple o' musterers an' a camp cook, less'n yer doin' the cookin' yersel' — an' yer'll need a packie ter fetch an' carry an' tend the dogs an' horses.' Ruby Gaunt looked down on Lucy's consternation, the seams in the brown face deepening; she was enjoying herself.

'Must we have a muster?'

'No avoidin' it, girl — stock count every April and check fer scab.'

'The sheep have already been checked, and weren't they counted when they were shorn?'

The widow eased herself around on her seat and placed a booted foot on the side of the cart, her steely eyes on Lucy's face. 'My thinkin' is this,' she said, ignoring the younger woman's question. 'Seein' yer've no workers still, we'll do the muster fer Long Reach then yer can hire my lads ter do yours an' the dippin' if it's needed — providin' yer can pay.'

Lucy did not reply immediately and the sharp eyes above her narrowed.

'What will all this cost me?' she asked finally, remembering that if she was to journey to Dunedin she was depending on the good graces of this woman. 'And I've no food to feed all these people.'

The wrinkles on the widow's face deepened still further, the eyes all but disappearing. 'Well now, Nobby Clark will be bringin' me dry goods early May so yer'll be all right. I'll see ter yer meat.'

'And the cost?'

'Will be fair — as always. Well?'

Lucy looked up into the unrelenting face. It bore no resemblance to the face that a short while before had been comforting the cow.

'Very well,' she replied briefly.

~

When the Widow Gaunt had driven off, Lucy did not go indoors but made her way up to the track and walked slowly towards the ruined homestead. The rain had stopped. A fleeting thought had disturbed Lucy as Ruby Gaunt had made her dubious offer, and she needed time on her own to examine it. There were the occasions when she had noticed an inconsistency in the woman's mode of speech when dealing with things medical. She spoke then as an educated woman and she was obviously literate. Yet at other times she appeared ill-bred, rough and coarsely spoken, and this was but part of the enigma. The sequence of events following the fire seemed too ordered somehow, too coincidental, and the widow's involvement in all of them seemed a little sinister to Lucy's mind. Had the Widow Gaunt advertised for a shepherd or *was* that her man up there in the hills?

Lucy stopped walking and her eyes swept the rugged terrain where the flocks grazed. She could not see the drover, but, feeling he could be watching her, she turned and walked quickly back the way she had come. The smell of burned porridge assailed her nostrils as she climbed down the bank, and on entering the kitchen she found Sarah scraping out the pot, her face glum. The questions in Lucy's mind remained unanswered.

The tasks of the day, accomplished in their order, moved Lucy inexorably closer to milking time. Her apprehension was interfering with her concentration, causing her to make mistake after mistake as she worked. By milking time she was in such an agitated state that the cow, sensing this, rolled her eyes warily and was reluctant to enter the porch. Sarah patted her and coaxed her with hay, but Ruby was plainly unhappy.

Lucy lowered herself onto the box and quickly thrust the pail beneath the cow's udder. She could not bring herself to rest her head into the animal's flank. Shaking visibly, her icy fingers gripped the teats and squeezed hard. An outraged tail whipped out and Lucy leapt to her feet, pressing fingers to the rising welt on her cheek. Blindly, she stepped backwards, fell over the box and sat down hard on the ground. The cow, turning a startled eye on her tormentor, seized her opportunity and backed out of the porch, then trotted with purpose towards the higher ground.

Refusing Sarah's help, Lucy struggled to her feet and walked gingerly into the kitchen to set about preparing the evening meal.

'Fetch some wood in, Sarah,' she said dully. 'I'll see to the cow later.'

In a moment the child returned. 'There is no more wood cut, Mama.'

'No more wood! Is there to be no end to the tribulations of this day?' Lucy did not look at Daniel as she left the kitchen.

'Come with me, Sarah.'

She picked up the axe and turned towards the riverbank. At a glance she could see that Adam and Daniel had cut out any useful wood near the hut, so retracing her steps she climbed the bank, dragging the heavy axe behind her. She headed towards the burned-out barn and Sarah pointed out an area of scrub where Daniel had been cutting his firewood and the branches for the hen house.

Lucy was daunted by the thickness of the stunted trees as she approached them, but it was obvious that Daniel had been here. If he had managed, so, surely, could she.

'Stand back, Sarah.' Lucy raised the axe and swung it towards a thin trunk. The blade bounced off leaving no mark and she gasped as cold water showered down on her. Again she tried, hurling the axe mightily. Her hands and arms were jarred painfully and she dropped the axe.

In frustration she cast about for anything that might be easier to chop and her eye fell on a fallen branch. Where it lay under the ferns it looked brittle and dry and she dragged it clear in triumph. The wood shattered under the blunt blade until the branch was broken up into useable lengths. Then she spied another fallen limb and, dragging it clear of the undergrowth, she attacked it with enthusiasm. This one, however, resisted her blade, and no matter how she chopped and hacked at it she made little impression. Lucy rested briefly to catch her breath, then gritted her teeth, raised the axe and brought it down with all the force she could muster. The axe slewed off the branch and turned in her hands, and the head struck her shin an excruciating blow. She dropped the axe and, gripping her leg, she watched as a great lump rose up under her stocking. 'Oh!' she cried. 'Oh damn — damn, damn, *damn!*' She snatched up the axe and turned, then hobbled past Sarah and furiously made her way down to the hut. Ignoring Daniel, she went to the trunk where the brandy and whiskey were stored. Lifting out the brandy bottle that Adam had opened, she carried it to the kitchen table, poured a good measure into a tin cup and gulped it down.

'Mama,' came Daniel's shocked voice from his bed, 'what are you doing?'

Lucy waved her hands ineffectually as she choked on the raw liquid. Through tear-blurred eyes she saw Sarah come into the kitchen carrying the wood that had been cut; watched her place it beside the hearth then, with a quick sideways glance, leave the kitchen again. Lucy poured more brandy and drank again, beyond caring, then slowly she placed the cup on the table and stared down at her work-worn hands and rough clothing. Her shin throbbed in exquisite pain. So I have come to this, she thought angrily. Through no fault of my own, I have come to this. Lowering her head into her hands, she began softly to cry.

Lucy registered little of that evening, her fury and her pain melting into an alcoholic haze. She woke some time during the night to hear a dog barking and heard Sarah whisper to Daniel, 'It's Friday.'

Vaguely, Lucy thought: It can't be Friday — did I not do the ironing and the mending yesterday — it's Wednesday. She remembered groggily that the cow had not been milked, then drifted back to sleep.

≈

Dawn came in cold and fine. As Lucy prepared breakfast,

her head and her shin pounded in unison. The last of the wood was on the fire, and she knew that today, somehow, she would have to cut more; and that today, even if she had to tie its tail and its legs together, she would milk that cow! She was deeply angry at the unfairness of what was happening to herself and her children. *My anger,* she decided as she served the porridge, *will now be my strength.* She would no longer hope for Adam's support, but would face up to dealing with the realities of their situation herself. She would be on her guard against the Widow Gaunt and — when she could find a way of obtaining experienced shepherds and shearers to operate Chandler's Run, people she could trust — she would no longer allow the widow to manipulate her. She and Adam would become run-holders in their own right and, God willing, he would be spared to live a decent life here with his family.

For the present, Lucy knew she had no option but to agree to Ruby Gaunt's terms, but in time she was determined to gain the knowledge and the skills to survive and manage the holding successfully. When this was accomplished, the widow's visits would be discouraged. In that moment Lucy made the decision to make her own way to Dunedin. When Nobby Clark arrived, she and the children would be ready to return with him.

Lucy straightened her back and lifted her chin. 'Sarah, wrap up warmly now and come with me.' She threw her shawl about her shoulders and tied it in a tight knot, then opened the kitchen door. She stood stock-still. Stacked against the far wall of the porch was a pile of manuka, the wood that had yesterday resisted her efforts. Beside the wood was the pail, two-thirds full of cream-topped milk. She did not hear Sarah's soft intake of breath or see the swift smile she turned on her brother, but limped forward to touch the pail. The milk was cold. Lucy walked slowly outdoors and looked about. The cow was browsing beyond the garden and the mare grazed on the edge of the track. Lucy turned to the bank and carefully picked her way to the top, Sarah following close behind.

She scanned the track to the south then turned towards the hills. She could see nothing, only sheep. She returned to the hut, deep in thought. Could it be that Ruby Gaunt had relented and sent somebody to milk the cow and cut her wood? Lucy frowned. The widow could not have known of her abortive attempt with the axe, so it seemed unlikely that she had sent anybody to help. That then left only the man up in the hills, or Daniel.

'No, Mama, *I* am not your good Samaritan.' Daniel presented his clean bandage as proof — and the mystery deepened when Lucy discovered that the axe was missing.

The following morning, more wood had been added to the pile in the porch but there was no milk. The pail stood empty beside the hearth where Lucy had left it after a fruitless attempt to entice Ruby into the porch.

That night, before retiring to bed, Lucy placed the empty pail outside the kitchen door and sat in the firelight silently waiting, her ears tuned to every sound. The hours crawled by and finally, when nothing had happened and she could no longer stay awake, Lucy made her way to bed.

~

'Mama!' Sarah was calling her from sleep. 'Ruby has been milked.'

Lucy pushed herself up on one elbow. 'Did either of you hear anything?'

Both children shook their heads. A cold south-westerly wind soughed about the porch as Lucy stood looking at the pail of milk. The woodpile, she saw, was as it had been the night before; no wood had been added.

Later in the day as she worked at her soap-making, Lucy was suddenly still, listening. Faintly, borne to her on the wind, she heard the ring of an axe.

It was barely dusk when Lucy retired to bed that night. She had asked Sarah to lead the cow into the porch and tie her securely. No pail had been left out.

'Why must we go to bed so early, Mama?' Sarah had questioned.

'Because I wish to rise early, pet.'

The moon was on the wane when Lucy slipped out of bed and dressed quickly before the embers on the hearth. She crept to the kitchen door and opened it a crack. She could see the dark outline of the cow. Satisfied, she pushed the door to and tiptoed to sit at the table, the unlit lamp and a taper close to her hand.

She did not have long to wait before she heard stealthy movement beyond the door, wood being placed carefully and the slight scrape of a boot. Lucy lit her taper in the embers and touched it to the wick with a hand that trembled, then picked up the lamp, swiftly crossed the kitchen and pulled open the door. The dog's eyes glowed red in the light, and the man, slowly straightening, turned to face her.

'Would you be so kind as to tell me what you are doing here?' Lucy asked stiffly.

The drover, still holding an armload of wood, waved at the woodpile. 'Ca' ye nae see, lassie? Ah'm stackin' wood.'

The red beard twitched minutely and Lucy set her jaw.

'I'd be obliged if you didn't come skulking around at night, and I can stack my own wood!'

In the lamplight, cool blue eyes were levelled at her. 'Aye. But ca' ye cut it?'

He turned from her and unhurriedly placed the remaining logs on the pile. Piqued, Lucy stood silent. Somehow the situation had been reversed and it was she who felt like the interloper. This would not do at all.

'And it's you who has been milking my cow,' she accused baldly.

'Aye, an' will ye nae leave the pail where a body ca' find it?' he drawled. ''Tis a bluidy waste puttin' guid milk into the groond.' He pushed his hat to the back of his head and held out his hand. 'Would ye be fetchin' it noo or will ye be milkin' the beastie yesel'?'

Lucy glared at the Scot, then turned on her heel and went back into the kitchen. Placing the lamp on the table she picked up the pail, marched back to the doorway, thrust it at the man with one hand and with the other, shut the door.

She was shaking as she sat at the table and listened to the milk spurting into the pail, and she didn't move until she heard the pail being placed beside the door and the low voice call to the dog. She had been unpardonably rude, but if the fellow was indeed the widow's man then she would be justified in resenting his unsolicited presence on Chandler's Run.

Lucy rose stiffly from the table and lifted the big iron kettle on to the fire. Pushing pieces of wood beneath it she stood watching them catch and burn while she pondered her situation. In a little less than three weeks Nobby Clark would be delivering their dry goods. If she offered him enough money, Lucy was certain that he would take them back to Dunedin on his return journey. She would see Adam, she would enlist Mr Hamilton's help and, most importantly, she would find lodgings where they could safely stay until the many issues troubling them on Chandler's Run had been resolved. The sovereigns in the homestead chimney posed a problem, however. She would not consider leaving them there in her absence, but she could think of no safe way to remove them while there was the possibility that the redheaded man might see them do it. From his many vantage points high in the hills it was now apparent that he saw and heard a great deal more than was desirable, and she had learned tonight that the Scot could understand English and speak it passably well.

The days went by, and in time Daniel could walk without pain. He ventured outdoors on a day when the sun shone and a cold southerly wind blew.

'We must finish the hen house, Mama,' Daniel said while he gathered up the branches he had cut on the day of his mishap. 'Why didn't you chop these up for the fire?'

Lucy chose not to see the Scotsman again. She had developed the habit of remaining awake until she heard him deliver the milk and the wood, and the last time she heard him was the morning following Daniel's sojourn outdoors. He seemed to stay longer in the porch than usual, and when Lucy went to fetch the milk she found a good three days' supply of wood stacked high inside the porch wall with the axe leaning against it. That afternoon, Kahu rode past the hut. 'Kia ora,' he smiled, and Lucy knew that the Scot had gone.

It was the end of May and Lucy was ready to leave. Everything they would need she had packed into one trunk and two boxes. Remembering their uncomfortable sleeping arrangements on their last journey, she had sewn empty sacks together and stuffed them with tussock, making three narrow mattresses. Then she had rolled their plaids and blankets into the mackintoshes and tied their pillows to the roll. Lastly she had baked enough bread and pumpkin pies to feed them over the days they would be travelling. These she packed into one of the boxes with potted meats and fish and their eating utensils. Satisfied that all was in readiness, she settled down to wait for the teamster to appear. While they waited, she and Daniel went up to the homestead to bring the box of sovereigns out of the chimney but found, as she had feared, that it was too heavy to lift down safely.

'We will have to trust Mr Clark, Daniel,' she said. 'He will lift it down easily enough.'

'Who will milk Ruby while we are gone?' Daniel asked.

'Kahu,' Lucy replied. 'I will pay him extra if he agrees and he may have the eggs as well.'

Neither child had asked how they were to return to Chandler's Run, a question Lucy hoped would not be asked. If there was unthinkable news awaiting them on their arrival in Dunedin she was sure she would not wish to return here. She was not ready to face this possibility, however; nor was she ready to prepare her children to face it. Turning her thoughts to other things, Lucy wondered if they would meet anybody who had been on shipboard with them. She would like very much to know what had become of Mary and Percy Truscott. By this time, both husband and wife would be established in their separate callings, she imagined, and her thoughts turned to new dresses for Sarah, who was rapidly outgrowing her present ones. With this thought, Lucy realized that her thirty-first birthday was but a week away and it was possible she might be with Adam on that day.

Lucy was roused from her reverie by the sound of the big wagon rumbling up the track. The children ran to meet it, then stepped aside as the great horses drew the wagon past the hut and turned its ponderous weight around to face the way it had come. Slowly, Lucy approached it. 'Good-day, Mr Clark.'

The teamster's small eyes swept over her then past her to the hut. He made no answer while he tied the reins to the brake handle and swung his bulk to the ground. As unmannerly as ever, Lucy thought, as she watched him.

'We wish to travel back to Dunedin with you,' Lucy began

without preamble. 'I will pay you well. My husband—'

'No need.' The big man thumbed over his shoulder. 'Brought yer man home.'

Lucy stared, uncomprehending, then her gaze flew over the objects in the wagon to where Adam huddled. She picked up her skirts and ran to him, urgent questions on her lips, questions that remained unuttered as she looked at him.

'Papa!' The children had seen him too, and clambering up to touch him became suddenly still, seeing something in their father's face that made them uneasy. The teamster pushed past them. 'Let's be gettin' yer indoors.'

Adam did not attempt to stand but let the giant lift him bodily from the wagon bed. His arms and legs as thin as sticks, he looked like a wooden puppet in the big man's arms as he was carried into the hut. Shocked and breathless, Lucy led the way. Adam closed his eyes as he was laid on his bed. It had been a gruelling journey and he was beyond exhaustion as Lucy tucked the thick plaid about him.

'Would you pay Mr Clark, my dear,' he whispered. 'He has my satchel — there is mail in it from home — legal papers—'

Her eyes on the wasted face, Lucy's mind was flying in all directions; send Sarah to fetch in the eggs — milk — Daniel must milk the cow. She must have meat to make broth — whatever Ruby Gaunt was planning, it did not matter now: Lucy needed her as quickly as she could get here. She must send a note with the teamster. Adam's eyes opened and they rested on her face. 'They told me they could do no more for me, Lucy, and I thought I could accept that.' His voice was barely audible. 'But then I knew . . . that I couldn't . . . not ready yet to let go.'

Lucy took his cold hands in hers and struggled with the fear in her heart.

'The Widow Gaunt — will she help me?' Tears welled in the hollow eyes, and Lucy gathered her husband's brittle frame into her arms.

'She will, my love.' She tried to keep the despair from her voice. 'She will, and you will grow strong again. Rest now. You are home and safe.'

Daniel and Sarah stood at the foot of the bed; they did not look at Adam but at their mother's face, and Lucy could not meet their eyes.

Adam slept as the stores were unpacked and the piano was manhandled into the kitchen, badly out of tune and rocking on the uneven floor. Their other possessions were stacked against the far wall to be sorted later. Daniel and Sarah barely glanced at the familiar items that they had been denied for so long, such was their apprehension.

Nobby Clark left, carrying Lucy's note to the widow and a further order for goods to be delivered in August. He had not charged for Adam's passage, and an expression close to compassion was on his craggy face as he took his leave, certain in the knowledge that he had brought only grief to this remote place.

Two days later Lucy heard a cart approaching and relief washed over her as she went to meet it. It was not Ruby Gaunt, however, but a heavily laden cart pulled by two heavy bays. It came steadily up the track, flanked by two riders on horseback and several dogs. Another horse was tied to the rear of the cart. When the driver of the cart saw Lucy, he reined in his horses and, removing his battered hat, called down to her. 'Good-day to ye, mistress — understand yer lookin' fer shepherds an' such?'

Nervously, Daniel and Sarah came to stand beside their mother.

'Yes,' Lucy said firmly. 'Have you come in response to my notice in the Dunedin paper?'

'Nay, missus, the Scot sent us,' the man replied.

'The Scot — the drover?'

'Aye, McKenzie. Now — I'm Willie Good, camp cook, an' these two fellas, Tom Masters an' Jack Tanner, are shepherds. At yer service, missus. The packie's down yonder catchin' a few salmon fer dinner. We'll work fer one pound ten shillin' a week, board an' billet, an' the young fella' — he pointed down the track — 'ye'll pay a pound a week an' found. Would this be suitin' ye?'

Lucy studied the weathered brown face grinning down at her with its crinkling blue eyes and decided that here was a man she could like. She cast a quick look at the two nondescript riders, who also had removed their hats and sat silent in their saddles, waiting. 'If you are prepared to work on a trial basis,' she said slowly, 'for three months, shall we say, perhaps we can come to an agreement.'

The grin on the cook's face broadened. 'Right yer are, missus. We'll set up camp. Anywhere in particular?'

Lucy shook her head. 'No, Mr Good, you may set your camp where it will best suit you.' She began to turn away, then on a thought she faced the cook again. 'My son will bring eggs, milk and bread up to your camp directly. I regret I have no meat to offer you.'

'The milk an' eggs'll be a treat indeed mistress, thank 'e. Fer the rest we are well supplied, needin' only a side o' hogget from time ter time wi' yer permission.'

During the next two days, Chandler's Run came alive. The packie, a quiet young man affectionately nicknamed Pitchin, set to work replacing the smashed and burned rails of the yards and holding pens. A rough hut of canvas and pit-sawn planks was hurriedly erected some way beyond the charred remains of the barn, to house the four men. The jovial cook was quick to assure Lucy that it was only a temporary arrangement, as was his cooking shelter. 'Soon as we've settled in, missus, the boys'll build quarters that'll gladden yer eyes.'

The sounds of barking dogs, the sharp whistles of the shepherds and busy hammers at work echoed back from the hills as Ruby Gaunt drove up to the hut five days after Adam's arrival home.

'Couldn't get 'ere sooner, girl. An outbreak of scrofula in one o' the villages kept me tied.'

She followed Lucy into the kitchen. Adam turned hollow eyes towards her.

'So yer back, Mr Chandler,' she rasped and surveyed him silently for a moment, then turned to Lucy. 'Bare 'is chest.'

She laid two fingers on the shrunken chest and tapped them gently with the fingers of her other hand, listening intently as she moved them from place to place.

'Sit 'im up,' she commanded and repeated the procedure on Adam's back.

'Take a deep breath.' Her ear was against his back. 'Another — and one more. Yer can lay him back down.'

The widow stood back, her keen eyes on the sick man's face.

'I'll not gloss over the truth. I have to agree with what I daresay you were told at the hospital — there is little to be done for you now.'

Adam closed his eyes and for a space did not reply, then whispered, 'Will you not even try? Your treatments helped me before.'

'And I will help you again. That is why I am here, but understand me, Mr Chandler, both lungs are compromised and, at best, all I can do is give you a little more time.'

Adam turned weary eyes to Lucy, who stood behind the widow quietly weeping. Sarah and Daniel listened to the fateful words but only Daniel realized the gravity of them. He went to his mother and placed an arm about her, his eyes meeting his father's. What he saw there shook him to his core: fear, grief and a terrible courage burned deep within their faded blue depths, and an unspoken question. For a heartbeat father and son looked at each other, then Daniel, slowly and softly, made answer far beyond his years. 'Papa, what you are now unable to do, I will do in your stead. This is my promise to you.'

Ruby Gaunt began to speak, cleared her throat and began again. 'I've some prime beef in the cart an' two boiling hens. Start 'im on broth from the hens an' beef an' give 'im egg custards. Feed 'im thin porridge each morning with a little cream — buttermilk will help to sustain 'im also. He is not to drink tea, only water, as often as he can swallow it.' She watched Lucy wipe her eyes surreptitiously on her apron before she went on. 'Have that window open at all times, as before, and he should sit in the sun for a time each day, weather permitting.' The widow touched Adam's shoulder briefly. 'Rest up, lad, and leave the work to us. I'll be back in a day or so ter see 'ow yer doin'.'

Lucy walked out to the cart in silence, and as she accepted the beef and hens she asked quietly, 'How long does Adam have?'

The creases in the brown skin deepened and she realized that the widow was smiling. 'If yer can get 'is spirits up an' keep 'em ther' — longer than 'e's any right to, I'd expect.' The big woman stepped up into the cart and, taking up her whip, she pointed in the direction of the homestead. 'See yer've found some help.'

Lucy stared up at the ugly face. 'You did not know?'

'Should I?' Ruby Gaunt shot her a quizzical glance and Lucy held her eye, plainly disbelieving.

'The Scotsman sent those men up here. Do you say you knew nothing of it?'

'I do. I'm not privy to McKenzie's confidence.'

'Weren't you paying him to work here?'

'Not I, girl, not a penny.'

'Then who is he? And why would he want to work here unpaid?'

'Who knows? James McKenzie is summat of a mystery. 'E comes an' goes ter suit 'isself; showed up last year.' The widow chuckled deep in her throat as she recalled the event. 'Thought 'e were a sundowner.'

'A sundowner?' Lucy queried.

'A swaggie — bush tramp — fella who arrives on yer doorstep wantin' yer ter sew a shirt ter 'is button and give 'im a feed.' She chuckled again. 'A swaggie 'e were not. Best bloody drover yer'd find in a mighty long mile — 'im an' that dog of 'is — ran circles round my fellas an' 'e never took a penny, just 'is tucker an' a place ter rest 'is 'ead.' She met Lucy's doubting gaze for a long moment, then rasped, 'I'll be on me way then — pay Kahu off an' send 'im home.' She rammed the battered hat down on her head, gathered up the long reins and, nodding briefly, set the big horses in motion.

Lucy watched the retreating back for a time then walked slowly inside. Either the widow was telling the truth or she had a reason for lying, and Lucy suspected the latter.

Adam slept for three days, waking only to take the broth Lucy fed him. The children were torn between anxiety for their father and the excitement of the muster as thousands of sheep were driven down from the hills. There were lambs among them, and more were born as the ewes settled in the lower pastures. Curiously, Daniel pointed them out.

'Aren't lambs always born in spring?'

'Aye, lad,' Willie Good explained. 'But up here, an' other places, too, autumn lambing is sometimes encouraged so that lambing don't clash wi' shearing in t' spring.' He shook his head and added, 'Never could see the sense in it meself, though, 'cause losses, due to the freezin' cold, are allus high.'

The plump cook was ever-patient with Daniel's many questions, and he held the children enthralled with his endless stories of adventure in the high country and of the people who lived and worked there. They would sit beside his cooking fire as he stirred his thick soups and stews, their eyes never leaving his round, flushed face; completely absorbed and temporarily removed from the uncertainty of their own lives, they hung on his every word.

When Ruby Gaunt returned after a few days, the girl Moana was with her. 'Thought yer could do wi' some help,' she rasped. 'Yer'll be needin' relief now an' then, an' Moana's good wi' 'im.'

The lovely brown face was serene. Moana smiled at Lucy and, taking the bowl of broth from her hands, she seated herself beside Adam's bed. As his eyes drifted over her face, a fleeting smile touched his pale lips.

'There now,' the widow murmured, "e's all right with her. Come wi' me now, ther's stuff in the cart fer yer.'

There was more beef and a number of hens, which would help to replenish the meat barrels.

'Tell yer cook ter kill a couple o' lambs fer yer table an' an old wether ter make yer man's broth.'

As she spoke she pulled a soft sheepskin from the cart

and held it out to Lucy. 'Put this under 'im fer comfort —
help ter stop 'im gettin' bedsores. I'll not charge yer fer this,'
she added gruffly.

Daniel and Sarah clambered down the bank and came
shyly towards them. Ruby Gaunt turned to the boy. 'Been
keepin' an eye on them fellas 'ave yer son — makin' sure they
earn ther keep?' And she laughed her raucous laugh.

Daniel smiled. 'Mr Good has been telling us stories,' he
replied politely. 'Stories about the folk who live in the high
country.'

The widow looked at Daniel, her eyes steely slits in a
suddenly stony face. Abruptly she turned away. 'I'll look at
yer man now,' she grated, and heaving the bundle of meat up
on to her shoulder she strode towards the porch.

Adam seemed to rally a little and, as before, Moana tended
to his needs. Her sleeping mat was beside his bed, and if he
coughed in the night it was she who made his bed comfortable
so he might rest more easily and who administered the
manuka tea to soothe his cough. Sometimes Adam would
talk to the girl, and, even though she couldn't reply and
her comprehension of English was limited, they came to
understand each other reasonably well. Although extremely
weak, on days when the sun shone Adam forced his trembling
legs to carry him outside to his seat against the hut wall. He
swallowed pints of broth daily and bowls of custard (which he
was not partial to), and followed Ruby Gaunt's instructions to
the letter, even though the effort of doing so exhausted him.

Lucy was heartened by his determination to become stronger, and heartened still further when he began to show an interest in the muster and the men who were performing it.

It was at Adam's request that Willie Good submitted the final stock count to him in person when the muster was completed, and it was Adam, sick though he was, who established himself in his workers' eyes as run-holder, fully in charge. His legal experience and Ruben's letters stood him in good stead, and the men came to view with growing respect this fleshless caricature of a man who asked pertinent questions and expected explicit answers.

'Come shearing time,' Willie Good stated one day, 'the wool off them merinos'll fetch a tidy sum but ye'll be needin' ter 'ave yer woolshed up before then, gov'ner, an' shearers' quarters built. Ther'll be no idle hands this winter.'

Adam waited impatiently for the time when he hoped to be strong enough to walk up to the homestead. In the back of his mind a plan was forming. The sketch of the homestead as it had been was still among Ruben's letters, and he drew endless floor-plans trying to establish where the original rooms had been situated and where the staircase up to the attic bedrooms had stood, but with little success.

'I will be requiring a competent builder,' he said one day to the cook. 'Do you know of one such?'

It had become Willie Good's habit to sit with Adam for a space when he took his daily sunning, to give him a progress report on the activities of the run.

'Aye, I do.' The cook scratched his head and a frown creased his brow. 'Sam Curry would be yer man, but I'm blessed if I'd know where ter look fer 'im these days. Moves about a bit, 'e does — busy fella.'

'I want to rebuild the homestead as soon as possible — put a decent roof over my family's heads. One of the men must travel to Dunedin and make enquiries and put a note in the *Otago Witness*. Will you see to this, Mr Good?'

'Leave it ter me, squire.'

The cook stood up to take his leave. 'I'll send young Pitchin. 'E'll be glad of the chance ter do summat else besides slappin' muck atween boards. Yer ever seen cob walls bein' made, sor?'

Adam shook his head.

'Well 'ere's 'ow it's done — bit messy, but works a treat.'

Willie Good seated himself again, warming to his subject. 'Yer 'eave clay an' gravel into one o' the pens wi' a heap o' manure — horse, sheep, it don't matter what kind. Then yer add straw, tussock — whatever's ter hand — and water. Then yer shut two or three horses in the pen fer the night and in t' mornin' ther've mixed up a fine porridge wi' ther feet. Then yer make a mould wi' yer boards an' slap the muck atween 'em. When it's dried, them boards are raised higher fer the next lot an' afore long ye've got four good walls that nothin'll shift.'

'This is what the homestead's walls are made of?' Adam asked faintly.

'Aye, an' that's why they're still standin'.'

'Would it not be wiser to send one of the older men to Dunedin, Mr Good?' Adam was suddenly weary. 'The boy seems very young for such an undertaking.'

The cook saw Adam's waning strength and, pushing himself to his feet, he held out a broad hand. 'Will ye not let me help yer indoors, sor? I can see I've near talked yer ter sleep. 'Ere, that's the way now — lean on me.'

Adam allowed himself to be half-carried into the kitchen and lifted on to his bed. Moana was quickly in attendance and Lucy thanked the plump cook, who lingered for a moment, his jovial face sober.

'Now don't ye be worryin', gov'ner. Pitchin's young but 'e's a head on 'is shoulders an' if Sam Curry's ter be found, the lad'll find 'im — I'll send 'im off termorrer.'

Lucy wondered briefly who Sam Curry was and why it was important to find him, but her attention was on Adam, who was having difficulty breathing. A sheen of sweat had broken out on his face and his fingers plucked agitatedly at the plaid covering him. Fear flickered in his eyes and was mirrored in Lucy's, but Moana remained calm. She raised Adam gently and piled pillows made of sacking and chaff at his back to support him. Then she filled his tin mug with hot water from the simmering kettle and indicated that he should breathe the steam. In a while his breathing was easier and he drifted into sleep, still raised on the rough pillows. Many incidents of this kind would follow in the days ahead, which left Adam exhausted, but his resolute determination saw him through each time.

Daniel had given himself the self-appointed task of riding the mare out each day to oversee the ewes in the lower pastures, and he would return each afternoon with a tally of the lambs born that day. Soon it became the highlight of

Adam's day to sit with his son and listen to the happenings on the run, recounted in humorous and colourful detail, and enjoy Willie Good's imaginative tales retold word for word.

As day followed day, life settled into a comfortable pattern. Adam's condition grew no worse and he was in fair spirits. With Moana and Sarah to help her, Lucy at last unpacked their precious possessions. It was an emotional task for Lucy as her hands touched the familiar objects that had been packed in their boxes for nearly a year. Adam's large leather chair was drawn up to one side of the hearth while her smaller chair was set on the other, and the joy of reading was again theirs as the bookcase was filled with their favourite books. Lamps, linen, woollen blankets, eiderdowns and Lucy's good crystal and china were discovered again; sadly there were breakages and the chiffonier was bruised on its edges where the ropes had held it secure during the storm.

Moana's exploring fingers moved gently over objects that were strange to her, and when Lucy and Sarah laughed at her wonderment she laughed with them, a soft husky sound that delighted them. They set the small carriage clock to Adam's fob watch, which kept excellent time, and placed it on the chiffonier. Its busy tick seemed loud in the quiet room.

Autumn's cooler days had arrived, and three weeks after Lucy's birthday the Scotsman returned. She heard a horse pass some time after midnight; the night was still and cold and the sound of shod hooves striking stone was loud on the clear air. She supposed it was young Pitchin returning from

Dunedin, but when she went out in the morning to feed the hens, she saw the chestnut and its rider moving across the lower hills towards the grazing sheep, the black-and-white bitch at the horse's heels.

An hour or so later, the young packie did arrive, accompanied by an older man whom he brought directly to the porch doorway. 'This here is Mr Sam Curry, missus,' the boy stated, quietly proud of his achievement.

The older man removed his hat and bowed slightly. 'I fear I've kept your lad away longer than I would have wished, but I had a task to complete, you see.'

Lucy bade him enter while Pitchin went off to attend to the horses. She took him into the kitchen where Adam dozed by the fire, and as she made tea to warm the traveller she listened to the conversation that ensued between the two men. She understood then why Sam Curry was here.

'From what I could see as we rode up, Mr Chandler, there is little but the walls and chimneys left standing.'

Adam produced Ruben's sketch, then leaned back in his chair, his earnest gaze fixed on the other man's face.

'Can you build it to look like that again, and have the rooms and staircase as they were before the fire?'

Sam Curry studied the drawing in silence for a moment, then directed a question at the sick man. 'Are the interior walls still standing?'

'Yes.'

'Shouldn't be too difficult, then. Makes me homesick does this — I was born in Devon and learned me trade building such as this.'

Adam closed his eyes and didn't speak for a while. Moana moved to stand behind his chair. With her dark eyes on the builder, she shook her head and moved her hand in a small gesture towards the door. Sam Curry nodded imperceptibly as Adam spoke again.

'How long will the work take?'

'Let me have a look first, sir, then I can better give you an assessment of time and cost.' He turned to Lucy. 'Thank you for the tea, mistress. If you would excuse me now, it's been a long journey and I'd like to be settling myself in.'

'Yes, yes,' Adam whispered. 'Daniel will take you up and present you to Mr Good.'

Alone again, Adam went to his bed and Lucy sat by the fire wishing she could ask the questions that jostled in her brain.

Why had he not discussed this with her? Did he believe she would wish to stay here, isolated in this lonely place, her children isolated with her, when he finally succumbed to his illness? The cost of rebuilding the homestead would surely take every penny they had. Why would he want to do this? Lucy was bewildered and a little angry. Did he not understand that she would want to return home to the bosom of her family, that this money would ensure that they could?

Adam had not rested well during the night and morning found him in poor humour, so Lucy did not tax him with her questions. Sam Curry came with his estimates in the late afternoon, and Adam was plainly upset that the work would take so long to complete.

'End o' spring, sir, savin' unforeseen hold-ups, is the best

I can give ye. I've only the lad up yonder to help and there's timber to be brought from the mills, and glass and suchlike to be sent away for.'

'By my count, there are four able men on this property,' Adam replied testily. 'Can they not be put to work now that the muster is done?'

Sam Curry shook his head as he picked up his hat to leave. 'I'd not even consider it. Sheep men can knock up passable quarters for themselves, but I would not enlist their help if you want a quality job done. No, sir, and as I understand it, Mr McKenzie will be movin' on in the morning.'

Adam sank back on his pillows and closed his eyes. The thought that death might claim him before the homestead was finished sent a dart of fear through him.

'We'll do our best, sir,' Sam Curry said with sudden insight. 'You may depend on that.'

Lucy saw the builder to the door, wishing she could find a way to stop him from doing Adam's bidding, but when he said quietly in an aside, 'We'll begin removing the rubble tomorrow mornin', mistress, and when that's done I'll be back to Dunedin to fetch the timber and so on as quickly as is humanly possible', she knew it was useless to try.

Work on the cow byre and hen house continued apace, and when Daniel declared that the roof for the hen house was ready to be lifted into place, Lucy suggested storing some of the maize within its walls to make more room in their crowded bedroom. The Scotsman did not move on. Inexplicably he remained, dividing his time between boundary riding and helping to demolish the homestead's burned-out interior. Fleetingly, Lucy wondered why this was so, but with more pressing things on her mind she decided to puzzle over the enigma that was McKenzie some other time. Her immediate need was to know Adam's reasons for rebuilding the homestead. At each gentle attempt to question him, Adam had appeared reluctant to discuss the subject with her and she was obliged to remain in ignorance.

As the work in the homestead progressed, Adam worried that the box of sovereigns was no longer safe and sent Daniel to fetch the builder.

'Ah.' Sam Curry nodded. 'Just ten minutes gone, young Pitchin found a tin box tucked inside the chimney in the kitchen, and there's a box you say, as well?'

Clearly agitated, Adam began to cough. Between spasms he gasped, 'Both are to be — brought — down to me—'

'Count on me, sir, they'll be in your hands within the hour — intact.'

Lucy saw the builder to the door, where he drew her attention to the lowering cloud, which heralded rain soon to fall. 'Daniel, we will secure the hen house roof now and move in some of the maize. Sarah, stay with Papa while Moana and I help your brother. Perhaps you could read to him — let him choose.'

Sarah sat down obediently, resigning herself to reading to her father, but Adam lay silently staring past her at the flames on the hearth, his mood sombre and distracted. Wistfully she glanced out of the window, wishing she could be outdoors too. She was uneasy in her father's presence, and left alone with him she was more than a little afraid. The child could not rid her memory of the blood and Adam's deathly face when he had collapsed on the homestead's hearth. It haunted her dreams and her waking hours, and latterly she found herself wishing that Papa had not come home, that he had stayed in the hospital where there were people who did not mind seeing him spit unspeakable stuff into a bowl, or seeing his pillow yellowed by his breath, or smelling the metallic sweat of his body; these people would not be terrified at the sight of bright, frothy blood. Nobody had told her that Papa was dying, but she knew that it was so and she was fearful of what he might look like when he did. Her emotions swung between love, pity, revulsion and apprehension, and she shed guilty tears each night as she said her prayers.

It was growing darker, and still nobody came and still Papa lay, staring at nothing. Tensely Sarah waited, her shoulders climbing up to her ears. The small clock on the chiffonier ticked loudly in the silent room, and it seemed to tick louder and faster until she could remain still no longer. She stood up hurriedly, not looking at Adam, and crept to the door. Stepping through, she gulped hungrily at the icy air, trying to fill her empty lungs, growing giddy suddenly and very frightened. When Moana came to the porch entrance, she saw and understood. Strong brown arms gathered the child to her and a gentle hand stroked the fair hair until the tears came and, with them, relief.

Chapter 7

WHILE LUCY AND SARAH were preparing breakfast, Daniel went to milk Ruby, and Moana set off to fetch water, her cloak drawn close about her. The morning was crisp and golden and the tarns had long since frozen solid. The small waterfall where the water cans were usually filled was now a cluster of stalactites and it had become necessary to climb down to the reduced flow of the river. This was a dangerous undertaking, the riverbank being slick with hoar frost, but Moana chose her path carefully, filling the two cans then hefting them up the bank, slipping and sliding until she reached the top. Here she lowered the cans to the ground and stood for a moment to catch her breath, her eyes on the mountains. A persistent southerly wind, driving a cold rain before it, had made conditions miserable for everybody this past week, but in the night snow had fallen on the mountains and a soft blanket of white had crept down below the bush-line, broken only by black outcrops of rock and patches of scrub. The wind was gone and the sun on Moana's back was pleasantly warm as she walked back to the hut.

Adam had again passed a restless night and the Maori girl was tired; it seemed that she had barely closed her eyes when it was morning and time to rise. The man in her care spent many such nights, and there were times now when she longed just to be able to lie warm and secure in Rewi's arms and sleep the whole night through. Sometimes when sleep evaded him Adam would talk to her, rambling on until his voice failed. She could understand only a little of what he said, but she knew that here was a being in torment, a being possessed of such anguish that his tired heart was driven to keep beating even though his diseased body had ceased to fight. She marvelled at the strength of his spirit as she devoted herself to yet another day of perpetuating a cause that was already lost.

She placed the cans in the porch and entered the kitchen. Lucy smiled at her and set a plate of porridge on the table.

'Have your breakfast, Moana. Mr Chandler wishes to rest. He does not want porridge this morning but says he will take a little broth later.'

Daniel came into the kitchen, grinning broadly. 'Ruby has been milked,' he said, placing the pail on the table.

'You managed that very quickly.'

'It was not I who milked her, Mama, and there is something else: the cow byre is finished!'

A small frown creased Lucy's brow. She served Daniel's porridge before she spoke. There was an image in her mind's eye of a man and his dog in her porch in the dark of night.

'Finished — *properly* finished — are you sure, Daniel?'

'Down to the last stick and stone, Mama. I found the pail propped in the hay in a newly built bail. The milk is still warm.'

Why would the Scot concern himself when there was now no need? Lucy felt vaguely irritated.

'It *must* be Mr McKenzie,' Sarah piped. 'He has helped us before, so it must have been him.'

'It could have been Mr Good, who is a most kindly soul, or even Pitchin,' Lucy murmured.

'I shouldn't think so, Mama, and Mr Tanner and Mr Masters were up in the hills last night and Mr Curry is in Dunedin so I think Sarah is right.'

'Do you really — I can't think why he would trouble himself.'

'I think we must arrange to pay this man, Lucy.' Adam's voice came weakly from his bed. 'For as long as he is working here, he must be paid.'

'Yes, of course,' Lucy replied absently. 'I will walk up later today to see what can be arranged.'

What an odd person this Scotsman is, she was thinking; pointedly unsociable, unmannerly, yet unexpectedly capable of kindness. Glancing at her calloused palms, she knew she should be grateful to the man, and politeness bade her tell him so. 'Come with me this afternoon, Daniel, and I will talk to Mr McKenzie.'

Later in the day when they went in search of the Scot, he was nowhere to be found. 'I've not seen 'im the day, mistress,' Willie Good said. 'Likely 'e's up ther' startin' the wethers for lower ground.' He squinted up at the sky. 'We've precipitation on the way again, I'm thinkin' — next couple o' days or so.'

'Perhaps then, when you do see him, you could tell him

that Mr Chandler wishes to speak with him.'

McKenzie did not come down to the hut that day or the next, but two nights later shots were carried on a strengthening wind to the ears of those below. With daylight came the rain, mixed with hail that sent the mare crashing down the bank to the shelter of the porch. The rain soon changed to driving sleet and the temperature in the hut plummeted. Adam began to cough, and Moana stooped quickly to fuel the fire with the wood stacked beside the hearth.

'No!' Lucy spoke sharply. 'No, Moana, you must bring the wood in from the porch.' She spoke more softly then: 'You must not use that wood — not touch — do you understand?'

The Maori girl was plainly affronted and instantly Lucy regretted raising her voice. For lack of a hiding place in the hut, she had stacked firewood over the box of sovereigns, reasoning that anyone looking to steal it would least expect to find the box under a pile of wood beside her hearth.

By mid-afternoon the weather had begun to clear, and Willie Good, stamping cold feet in the porch, called a greeting. When Lucy opened the door and bade him enter, he carried a heavy sack into the kitchen and set it down on the floor. 'Haunch o' wild pig, missus. McKenzie shot it last night along wi' two dogs worryin' the flock this past day or two.'

Adam pushed himself a little higher on his pillows. 'We heard the shots. Would you thank Mr McKenzie for his diligence and—' He coughed harshly, struggling for a long moment to regain his breath, while the people in the room waited. 'And remind him that I wish to see him,' Adam continued hoarsely.

'Aye, squire, I will that.'

The plump face was sober as the cook turned to leave. At the door he faced Lucy and murmured, 'Anything I can do ter help, anything at all, yer'll let me know won't you, m'dear?'

Lucy nodded, smiling faintly as the door closed on the man's kindly back. There is nothing anyone can do, Mr Good, she was thinking as she turned back into the kitchen, nothing at all.

Willie Good pulled himself up the bank and plodded along the track, puffing steam into the freezing air. The ewes had moved down to lower ground along with the wethers, and were grazing close to the shepherds' huts and the partially built woolshed, but Willie didn't see them. He had been dismayed by the appearance of the sick man; he had not seen Adam since the colder weather had driven him from his seat in the sun, and the change which had taken place in that short time was appalling. That the comely young woman down there was soon to become a widow was plain to see, and Willie's charitable heart grieved for her and her children.

Moana's lovely face was without expression as she attended to Adam's needs, but there was pain in her heart, her dignity bruised. The wahine Pakeha had damaged her mana in the manner of her address to her. Wood was wood, wasn't it, wherever it was taken from? There was a longing in her now to be in her own home; to be with her hoa tane, but she knew she must stay until the wairua had left this ravaged body. The dark eyes filled with tears for her own mokemoketanga and then for the same loneliness that was to come for the pale woman.

As Moana moved away from Adam, Lucy went quickly to her. Working at the kitchen table she had seen the hurt she had caused, and now she took the slender brown hands into her own. 'I am sorry — so very sorry, Moana,' she said simply.

The two women stood facing each other in silence, then in a spontaneous gesture their cheeks were pressed together and tears were in the eyes of both. In the moment of that embrace, there was born a wealth of sympathy and understanding, and a bridge was built that spanned their very different worlds.

'Mama, we have rats again!' Daniel burst through the kitchen doorway.

'Did you see them?'

'No, not actually, but there is maize scattered about the hen house floor. There are holes in three of the bags that I could see — the hens have been having a feast!'

'Then I think you must go and talk to Mr Good. He must have had to deal with rats from time to time, so he may be able to advise us. Go now, dear. Wrap up warmly and come back quickly because it will soon be dark.'

As she finished speaking, Lucy saw Adam gesture to Moana. 'Raise me up—' His voice was urgent.

'What is it, dearest?'

Adam held up a hand. 'Listen, can you hear it?'

Everybody was still, and in the silence a faint rumbling could be heard.

'That is a large vehicle or vehicles approaching.' Adam's voice cracked with excitement. 'Daniel — go and see — see if it's Sam Curry returning.'

The boy was through the door as the words left Adam's lips. Donning their cloaks, Lucy and Sarah followed more slowly. They scrambled up to the track and stood facing the sound of the distant rumble. Whatever was coming was moving slowly and would be some time yet coming into sight. Lucy and Sarah waited, shivering, until they could stand the cold no longer. Daniel was gone from sight, around the corner.

'Come, Sarah, we will go in.'

Adam was propped up in his bed and two bright spots of colour burned in his sunken cheeks as he strained his ears to hear. 'It can only be the timber for the homestead,' he croaked. 'It cannot possibly be anything else.'

'Yes, Adam, I expect it is; it sounds heavy and slow-moving as a loaded dray would. We will know soon.'

Lucy regarded her husband's face with misgiving. She had seen that hectic colour before and it did not bode well. 'Would you take a little broth while we are waiting, dear?' she asked quietly. 'It will pass the time.'

'No, no. I don't want anything — just let me listen.'

Eventually, in the silence, they could distinguish the sound of iron-shod wheels and the plodding of many hooves. As the sounds drew nearer, Lucy pushed a window wide and thrust her head past the canvas cover. In the failing light she could see a large dray pulled by many bullocks, coming around the corner of the track. This was followed closely by a second dray. Both were piled high with lumber and bulky items covered with canvas. Daniel sat between Sam Curry and the driver of the first dray. Lucy shut the window again. 'There are two drays coming, Adam, drawn by bullocks. They are loaded with timber. Mr Curry is on the first dray.'

'Did I not say so?' Adam's voice was a whisper. 'Now the building can begin.' He lay back on his pillows and closed his eyes.

The drays came to a halt opposite the hut, the bullocks blowing clouds of steam into the cold air. Sam Curry climbed stiffly down from his seat and followed Daniel into the kitchen. Adam opened his eyes.

'You have been gone for an age,' he said querulously.

'Aye, there were a lot to do an' it were a slow trip back, sir.' He declined the mug of tea Sarah offered. 'We've everything we need, so ther'll be no delay gettin' ter work as soon as the drays are unloaded in the morning.' He turned to Lucy. 'The drivers will stay overnight and rest their teams, then they'll set off back to Dunedin tomorrow. If you've any letters, give them to me an' I'll see that they take them an' post them off for you.' He fumbled in the copious pocket of his ulster as he spoke, and produced a packet. 'I took the liberty of fetching up your letters too.'

'Will the weather hold you up?'

Adam's anxious question was answered with a tired smile.

'Nay, sir, 'twill serve to make us have the roof up quicker. Now, I'd best get the lads off those drays and settled in.'

As the builder left, Lucy held the packet of letters to her breast; letters from home. Should she read them to Adam or would news from home and family upset him? She wasn't sure he had realized what Sam Curry had given her, absorbed as he was with the rebuilding. Daniel and Sarah were looking at her expectantly, but with a brief shake of her head she placed the letters on the table.

'Should I go and see Mr Good now, Mama?' Daniel asked then.

'No. Leave it until morning.'

Daniel went to a window and watched the drays move away. Sixteen bullocks pulled the first dray and eighteen drew the second. He would see what each carried, apart from the timber, when he went to see the cook in the morning. Lucy glanced at her husband. In these few moments he had drifted into sleep so, picking up the letters, she nodded to the children and taking a candle from the table she moved into the bedroom. By the written word, they entered again the familiar world they had left behind, a lifetime ago it seemed to Lucy. In reality it would be one year, the month after next, since they had passed down the Thames.

There were a number of letters from Lucy's mother and Adam's father, and several from other family members, including letters from her sisters and her brother, Christian. All asked the same question: had Adam's health improved? Lucy's heart sank at the tidings she must impart.

In the dim light her eyes devoured her mother's words, and

as she visited in her mind's eye the places so familiar and the family and friends she knew and loved so well, homesickness overwhelmed her and she bowed her head.

'Mama,' Sarah whispered, 'are you crying?'

'A little, Sarah, only a little.' Lucy gave a small laugh and folded the letters away. 'The light is too dim. Shall we finish reading these tomorrow?'

'Could we not read them at the table?' Sarah pleaded. 'Moana has lit the lamp.'

'No, love; if Papa asks me to read the letters to him, then I shall, but until he asks we will read them only between ourselves.' Lucy touched the child's cheek. 'Do you understand?'

In the faint light, Sarah studied her mother's face. 'I think so, Mama.'

When Adam had taken a little broth and was settled for the night, and Moana lay curled in her cloak on the floor beside him, Lucy took up her pen. All evening, the words that she would write to Adam's father had chased one another around in her head, but now her pen was unmoving, her mind void. She stared at the barren page before her as the night wore on, searching for the words that eluded her, then finally wrote a simple postscript to the letter she had written weeks earlier.

Wide-eyed, Lucy lay long into the night, pondering a future without Adam and longing to be home in the haven of her mother's arms; but the following morning, at Adam's bidding, Lucy sat beside her husband and learned what her future was to hold.

'While I was in Dunedin town lying in my hospital bed not knowing what lay ahead of me, I had Mr Hamilton draw up a new will. I know you have wondered at my plan to rebuild the homestead, my dear, so I will now answer your questions.' Adam drew a shallow breath and lay quietly for a space, then continued.

'Ruben had amazing foresight and many dreams when he chose to settle in the high country.' He paused for breath again then went on. 'My wish is that our son may benefit from that foresight and make his own dreams in this place.' Adam paused again for a longer time, then turned his sunken eyes to his wife's face.

'The new will has been written to that end. When Daniel reaches his majority he will take up the reins as the owner of Chandler's Run; until that time, I have encumbered you with his stewardship.'

Lucy sat speechless, trying to take in what her husband had said. Were they to remain here then after his death, unable to return home? She could not envisage the long years that would need to pass before she was freed of her burden — long, empty years, embittering years that would take her youth and her vitality. Surely he did not intend this? Sarah's chances of making a suitable marriage would be negligible; she would be doomed to spinsterhood.

Adam saw her dismay. 'My dear, don't look so,' he whispered. 'Daniel would never have this chance at home. This country is new and holds immense promise — do not deny him his part in it.' Adam closed his eyes. His breathing was becoming troubled.

The minutes ticked by and Lucy sat waiting for him to speak again, to explain why he had taken all options from her and placed her in this impossible position. She sat watching his still face, her hands clenched in her lap. Slowly Adam's eyes opened and he spoke with effort, 'I do not denigrate you in this, Lucy — you are young and comely, and in time . . . you will perhaps remarry.' He began to cough. When the paroxysm had passed, there was blood on his lips and Moana was quickly by his side.

'Do not try to talk any more, Adam. Rest now,' Lucy murmured.

'I must explain — let me finish — if you remarry and the run is willed to you — it could be lost to Daniel — if there is other issue.' Adam gasped the words. 'Do you understand?'

'Yes, yes, dearest, now you must rest.'

Lucy stroked the pale forehead until Adam fell into exhausted sleep; then, taking her cloak, she left the hut. She needed to walk and try to come to terms with Adam's wishes, to grasp and try to accept the enormity of what he was asking of her.

Her feet took her down the track, out of sight of the hut. A biting wind flayed her skin and stung her eyes as she walked, and soon she was very cold; but she went on, needing to dispel her distress and bitter thoughts in action. Desperately, she cast about for ways to reverse Adam's decision. If she was not to inherit the run as Adam's widow, then she would not be able to sell it. Daniel would not be able to sell it either until he reached the age of twenty-one years. The sovereigns in the box would be gone in the intervening years if Chandler's Run failed, and her dream of returning home with her children would vanish. Unless the will could be disputed, they would have no choice but to remain in this alien country.

Lucy's feet faltered as a feeling of utter hopelessness came on her. She raised her eyes to the flying clouds and stood thus for a long time, watching them jostling each other into ever-changing shapes as they sped eastwards. Then she looked about her. She had come a long way, and after a moment she realised where she was; she recognized the low hill. Ruben was buried up there, and on impulse Lucy climbed up to the grave and stood staring down at the shallow mound overgrown with stunted tussock and weeds. It still awaited its headstone and she knew with chilling certainty that soon Adam would be in this desolate place, in an unmarked grave also. Her tears came then and she wept unrestrainedly, releasing her grief and pent-up misery with only the bleak mountains as witness.

Emotionally spent, Lucy wiped her eyes and, turning away from the grave, she clambered down to the track and began the long walk back. She felt empty and did not want to think any more. Her immediate need now was to be warm as she plodded up the rough track on frozen feet, unseeing eyes on the ground. Then the rumble of a cart behind her penetrated her consciousness, and she turned to see Ruby Gaunt sitting high on her leather seat, whipping her horses into a shambling trot to come alongside. 'Gracious, girl, what in the name of sanity are yer doin' walkin' about in the freezin' cold?' The widow's nose was cherry-red and her eyes were slitted against the wind as she peered down at Lucy.

'Get yersel' up 'ere an' we'll get yer home afore yer blood sets — hup, that's it.' Lucy was pulled up by her hand to sit beside the driver and share the rough canvas that draped the woman's shoulders.

'I've some chickens an' a side o' beef in the back ther' an' some more titoki pulp fer yer man. How is 'e doin?'

Lucy did not raise her head. 'He grows weaker daily.'

Ruby Gaunt had noted the red and swollen eyes, but she made no comment. She flicked the whip over the horses' backs. 'C'mon, yer lazy hulks, pick 'em up!'

They rode in silence for a time, then the widow said slowly, her gravelly voice almost soft, 'Yer know, in the times ter come, I'll not leave yer ter face yer trials alone. Yer know that, don't yer?'

Lucy kept her gaze on the horses' backs. 'Thank you.'

She was tempted to confide in this woman but remained silent, realizing that she would be completely vulnerable when she was finally alone if she softened her stance at all. She couldn't afford to do so if the widow's bona fides proved to be false. Ruben's grave was a mute reminder that the marauders of Chandler's Run had not been brought to book, and nor had her suspicion of Ruby Gaunt been allayed. Distressed though she was, Lucy realized it would be folly to forget this.

When they pulled in beside the hut, the widow jumped down from her seat and moved around the cart to help Lucy alight. She was in so many respects a man, Lucy thought, and it was impossible to guess her age.

'Get yer cook ter cut this beef up today and store it in yer barrels,' the widow grunted. 'Now, let's be lookin' at this man o' yours.' She hefted the side of beef on to a shoulder and strode towards the porch.

'Leave the chickens, girl, yer lad can tend ter those, but bring the jar.'

Adam stirred as they entered the kitchen and the side of beef was dropped on to the table. He attempted to raise himself as the widow approached his bed.

'Don't disturb yerself — lie back an' let me have a look at yer.' She picked up the thin wrist and held it for a space while she regarded Adam's face. 'You eatin'?'

'When I can.'

'Do you feel there has been any change in yourself in this past week?' Ruby Gaunt released Adam's wrist and lowered herself on to the side of the bed.

'No, one day is much like another.'

'Good. Now see you keep taking your berry pulp — the less blood yer part with, the less strength yer'll lose.' Her wrinkles deepened in a smile. 'Well, I'll not dally.' The big woman stood up. 'I've more sick 'uns ter see to — kids down in the village been eatin' dried tu tu berries — stupid little buggers never seem ter learn.'

'What are tu tu berries?' Daniel asked.

'Deadly poison is what they are! These kids 'ave 'ad more kerosene down 'em than yer'd use in a twelve-month ter light yer way.'

Lucy and Daniel walked with her to the cart and watched her drive away. 'If she's not a doctor, why does she visit the

198

sick?' was Daniel's next question.

'Perhaps she is a kind of bush doctor — a person who has learned from experience rather than training.'

'Or a witch, as people claim. I think it's jolly odd, Mama.'

The afternoon was cold and still. Lucy and Moana sat beside the fire darning socks and mending frayed hems. Moana had learned quickly; her deft fingers could turn a seam as neatly as Lucy's could, and her darning was even and flat. Adam was sleeping at last. He spent his days listening to the fall of the hammers and asked constantly what part of the homestead Sam Curry was working on.

Daniel and Sarah had gone to gather chips and off-cuts for the fire, and in a while Lucy heard their voices on the still air as they returned to the hut. Then she heard a deeper voice and the children's laughter, and her hands became still as she listened.

'. . . an' the wee sleekit beastie ge's a whiff o' tha' cheese an' — *bang!* — doon drops tha' end.'

Sarah squealed and Daniel was heard to ask as they entered the porch, 'Will it break the rat's neck every time or could it sometimes be a bit messy?'

'Nay, laddie, 'less 'tis a creature tha' walks backward tae its denner.'

Daniel was laughing as he pushed open the kitchen door and bade the Scot enter. 'Mama, Mr McKenzie has come to see Papa and he's made some traps to catch the rats in the hen house — look!'

'Come in, sir, come in.' Adam struggled to pull himself up on to his pillows. 'Lucy, pull a seat over.'

The Scotsman stayed Lucy with a gesture. 'Ye'll nae mind if ah stand.' He moved to stand a few feet from the end of Adam's bed, then waited for him to speak.

'I understand you have been performing a very useful service for us these past weeks. You must allow me to pay you . . .' Adam's voice faded for a moment, then with an effort he continued. 'I would like to come to an arrangement with you, Mr McKenzie. Would you consider filling the position of manager on Chandler's Run?' Adam coughed harshly, struggled to speak, then whispered, 'I will pay you well.'

The tall Scot studied the man in the bed, then slowly shook his head. 'I'm nae ya man. Ah'm a drover, ye'll mind, an' dinna care tae be o'er long i' one place.'

Adam closed his eyes and lay silent for a moment, then looked at the auburn-haired man and drew a trembling breath. 'I'm more disappointed than I can say. I did not expect you to refuse, your having found people to work here — I felt you had some interest in Chandler's Run. I am in no state to do this myself, as you can see.'

'Aye, ah ken, but ah'll nae be stayin' an' ah'll nae be takin' ya money.' Startled by the blunt words, Lucy glanced sharply at the Scot. The unkempt beard hid the man's expression, but the blue eyes were steady as they rested on her sick husband. She could see no remorse in them, and a flicker of uneasiness made her heart beat a little faster. Who *was* this man? If he had no interest in Chandler's Run, why did he keep returning and why had he troubled to send men to work here? Did Ruby Gaunt really know as little about him as she claimed?

Lucy dropped her gaze quickly as McKenzie's clear eyes rested on her briefly before he turned his attention back to Adam. 'Ah'll gang awa' in a bit an' if in ma travels ah see a guid man, ah'll send him awa' up.'

Adam nodded, closed his eyes and turned his head away; the interview was over.

Lucy rose from her chair and in silence opened the door. The Scot nodded tersely, scooped his hat from the floor and left. There was a sense of anticlimax in the room as Lucy resumed her seat. She glanced at Moana, who had continued with her darning throughout the short visit. The Scot had not acknowledged the young woman's presence, which in view of his having worked on Long Reach seemed a little odd, even a little sinister, and she wondered if Masters and Tanner were in fact only shepherds. Then as the image of Willie Good's jolly face came before her mind's eye, she smiled ruefully and picked up her sewing.

'I suppose I could bait these traps with maize, Mama.'

Lucy had forgotten the traps. She turned now and looked at them.

'Did you say Mr McKenzie made them?'

'Yes. Shall I show you how they work?'

'No, no, Daniel, I'm happy to accept that they do.'

'Lucy,' Adam croaked from his bed, 'tomorrow will you go up to the homestead — tell me what progress has been made?'

Lucy sighed softly. 'Yes, dear, if you wish me to.'

Sam Curry made his report every day or so, but Adam failed to be satisfied with this, needing almost hourly to know what work was in progress.

⁓

Lucy and Daniel hurried up the hill, pushed along by a strong south-westerly wind. They could see the skeleton of the new roof and hear the hammers at work somewhere within the homestead. As they approached, Sam Curry emerged from the doorway with an armload of off-cuts.

'Ah, Mrs Chandler, you have chosen a cold day indeed to come visiting — come in out of the wind, dear lady.' Placing the wood on the ground, he ushered Lucy and Daniel inside the cob walls.

'There is not much to show you yet, but we start thatching the roof very soon. You will see that the joists for the attic bedroom floors are in place.' Lucy, following the builder's finger, raised her eyes aloft and met the shy gaze of young Pitchin. Beyond him, straddling a crossbeam, was the Scot. He paid them no heed, his attention fixed on the work in hand.

'How many bedrooms will there be?' Lucy raised her voice to be heard.

'There will be three bedrooms, Mrs Chandler, as there were in the original structure, and the staircase will be here, back from the front door.'

'Is the floor here going to be the same as the floor in the hut — dirt?' Daniel questioned, scuffing his boot on the packed earth under his feet.

'No sir,' Sam Curry laughed. 'Your mama's floors will be made o' pine, here and upstairs.'

Lucy moved to a doorway that she imagined would open into the dining room, and crossing the empty space she looked through a doorway opposite into the kitchen. The stone fireplace had been scrubbed clean of all traces of the fire and the metal bars set into the chimney gleamed dully.

'You will see that with the rubble gone 'tis much easier to imagine what the rooms were like.' The builder stood at Lucy's shoulder.

'It must have been a fine home.'

'And it will be again, have no doubt.' Sam Curry beamed at her.

Lucy turned away. The man could not know what this house was to her, that it would be her prison unless she could have Adam's will overturned. 'I will take up no more of your time, Mr Curry, thank you,' and, nodding to Daniel, she turned to leave, needing suddenly to be outside these walls.

Adam was awake and waiting when they entered the kitchen. 'Well, tell me what is happening up there — in detail, Lucy, if you will.'

'The roof is nearly ready for thatching.'

'And the beams are up for the ceiling, and the bedroom floors, Papa — the floors are to be made of pine,' Daniel went on. 'The fireplace in the kitchen—'

Lucy walked into the bedroom to remove her cape. She had no wish to talk about the homestead or hear Daniel's account of the progress being made. Anger flickered in her bosom and, try as she would, she could not extinguish it. She sat down on her bed and tried not to hear Daniel's enthusiastic words. Sarah came to sit with her. 'Shall I be allowed to come with you next time, Mama — to see our house?'

'I expect so, as long as you wrap up warmly.' Lucy touched the fair hair. Poor child, she could have no conception of what the future held for her if they were forced to stay here.

'Can we go tomorrow, Mama?'

'Perhaps, dear, if it is fine.'

'Take her tomorrow, Lucy — let her see for herself,' Adam urged from his bed.

So Lucy found she was obliged to trudge up to the homestead daily. To save her patience and Adam's frustration, she drew small sketches of the various stages of rebuilding. Adam pored over these endlessly, and endlessly required her to elaborate on what she had drawn.

'If the Good Lord would only grant me the strength to go and see for my own satisfaction, my dear, I would no longer need to trouble you,' he had said querulously on one occasion when Lucy had failed to hide her exasperation. Her guilt then drove her to greater effort.

Sam Curry watched Lucy's daily pilgrimage with misgiving. 'That young woman will make herself ill coming out in all weathers as she does, trying to appease her man — 'tis a great disservice he does her.'

'The puir devil is dyin' an' 'is brain is dyin' ahead o' him,' James McKenzie grunted.

Sam Curry shook his head. 'It will not bode well for the children should both parents perish,' he muttered as he turned back to his labours.

The short winter days passed slowly, and when the thatching was completed the Scot went his mysterious way. Lucy found that she was missing his silent presence and was surprised that this should be so, for he rarely spoke to her, choosing most times to ignore her presence as she sat with her drawing. With Daniel, though, he would converse at length, and surreptitiously Lucy would listen, intrigued by his dialect.

Chapter 8

WILLIE GOOD HAD TAKEN to his bed. He had caught a chill several days earlier and his condition had steadily worsened.

'He's right poorly,' Sam Curry had informed Lucy, 'and young Pitchin is like to poison us — that lad is no cook.'

He had looked at Lucy with expectation and she, with reluctance, had offered to relieve the lad of the task.

'The Widow Gaunt will be calling in a day or so to see Mr Chandler. Perhaps Mr Good would allow her to tend him also.'

She stood now in the lean-to that served as the cookhouse, stirring a large pot of stew over a primitive hearth, wishing she had been slower to saddle herself with this undertaking, heavy as it was proving to be. Even though the day was bitter, the heat in the confined space was uncomfortable; her hair clung in damp tendrils to her neck and her bodice was stained with perspiration.

Earlier, Ruby Gaunt had looked in on the ailing cook and the lines in her seamed face had deepened with amusement as she'd then watched Lucy from the doorway before she took her leave.

"E'll be on 'is feet again in a few days,' she'd rumbled. 'Ye seem ter be managin' well enough — best not ter rush 'im, I'd say.'

A deep chuckle had come back to Lucy on the wind as the widow stalked back to her cart.

Strong gusts tugged at the sacking that covered the doorway, and whistled and moaned about the walls. Lucy was suddenly conscious of her isolation. The shepherds were up in the hills driving the sheep down from gullies and bluffs where they were sheltering, and Sam Curry and Pitchin were still at work in the homestead. The sound of the wind was unnerving and she longed to be standing safely at her own hearth. She placed the ladle beside the rough hob and, going to the doorway, pulled an edge of the sacking aside and peered out at the darkening day. The wind, sleet-laden, was driving fog up the valley in grey swirls. Shivering suddenly, Lucy pushed the sacking back into place, wishing Sam Curry would come.

From time to time the gusts rose to an eerie shriek and there were brushing sounds and odd thumps against the walls outside that could not be readily identified. Lucy was becoming uneasy, straining to hear over the wind. Was that a footfall? Was there somebody out there skulking about, moving along the wall? Or—?

'Oh, stop it, you silly creature,' she admonished herself. 'Stop scaring yourself senseless!'

She turned to lift the iron pot from the embers and in that moment the sacking in the doorway was tugged aside and the wind gusted in. Lucy leapt, the pot tipped, and scalding liquid ran over her fingers. She shrieked in pain and fear as a figure loomed out of the gloom. 'Gi' it tae me.' The heavy pot was taken from her and the pail of water that stood beside the door was lifted quickly on to the rough table and Lucy's hands thrust down into its icy depths.

'Bide there noo.'

McKenzie secured the sacking. 'Is the cook nae aboot?'

'He is ill.' Beneath the water, Lucy could see the angry darkness of her fingers.

'Well, ye canna cook wi' those.' McKenzie peered into the pail.

Lucy began to lift her hands.

'Nae, let them be.' The Scot pushed them back into the water. 'Twa more minutes then gang away doon, ye'll nae be seein' ye way home in a wee bit.'

'The bread—'

'Ah'll see tae it.' McKenzie lifted the oven from the embers and deftly emptied the loaves on to the table, then put the iron pot back on to the hearth and passed Willie Good's apron to Lucy to dry her hands. When she had done, he lifted down her cloak. 'Se' off noo an' mind ye way.'

Lucy fastened her cloak with difficulty while the Scot untied the sacking. He held it aside and she passed out into the biting teeth of the wind, the grey fog soon swallowing her from his sight.

～

The roof of the homestead was finished, thatched with strong red tussock, and the floors of the attic bedrooms were in place. Daniel went daily to bring back off-cut timbers for the fire and deliver in detail the progress reports Adam craved. Moana had returned home for several days: Adam was no better, and yet no worse, so Lucy felt she could spare her for a time. This meant that Lucy went less often up the hill and she missed the opportunity now to be away from the hut for an hour and talk to somebody other than Adam and the children. On occasion McKenzie was at the homestead and Lucy would linger a little longer. The man held an odd fascination for her which she would have denied even to herself, but nonetheless she found she was drawn to him, to the mystery that seemed to surround this dour, solitary man. He carried an air of authority that the shepherds seemed not to question, sensing perhaps that he would not be one to cross. Nor would one attempt to intrude on his remoteness; yet she knew that, in Adam's stead, she should be asking the Scot to explain his continued presence on the run.

She was within her rights to do so and chided herself for the reticence that made her reluctant to do this. As a result the Scot was in her thoughts more often than was seemly. To dismiss a faint sense of guilt, Lucy paid more attention to Adam's needs and those of the children, diverting her mind from the Scot and succeeding to some extent, until the night when the quiet of the high country was shattered by the pounding of many hooves, the sound of shouting and a barrage of gunshots. Dogs barked, horses squealed in fright and the sheep stampeded.

'Daniel, Daniel — no!' Lucy hissed. 'You must not show yourself.'

'The mare, Mama, and Ruby. They will be running frightened and get shot!'

'Better them than you! Come, sit quietly by the fire — Sarah, come, sit with your brother, quietly, until we can find out what this is about.'

Lucy went to Adam. Before she could speak more shots rang out, echoing around the hills, and voices shouted back and forth, distant now. Two more shots and then silence, broken only by the sporadic barking of the dogs.

'I wish I knew what was taking place out there.' Adam's voice shook. 'Perhaps you should leave, take the children, Lucy — find a place to hide —' He smothered a cough.

'We will stay together.' Lucy spoke softly. 'If it's the marauders returned, remember they do not know we are here and won't, so long as we are quiet.'

She went to the windows then, secured them, and sat in Adam's big chair beside the fire, Sarah tucked in beside her.

They waited, listening, hearing only silence as time slowly passed. No more shots had been heard, and Lucy peered at the clock on the chiffonier: half an hour had passed since anything had been heard and the quiet was rubbing at their nerves. Daniel moved closer to the fire. 'They will know someone is here, Mama — the smoke from the chimney will tell them that.'

The boy's voice was barely above a whisper but Adam heard him.

'Go and hide — all of you. Take your bedding and hide down among the flax—' Adam's hoarse whisper ceased and they listened intently.

'Hello, inside. Is everybody safe here?'

'It's Mr Curry!' Daniel ran to let the builder in while Lucy hurried to light the lamp on the table. As the wick burned brighter, they could see that the builder's cheerful face was sober, his hair in disarray, and he had obviously dressed in haste.

'By — it's as well those blighters went right past here. They were bent on running us off, dragging young Pitchin and myself out of the hut and shooting at us ter set us running. I don't care to think how they'd have treated yourself, sir, or your family.'

'Who were they?' Adam struggled to sit upright. 'Where are they now? Did they torch the homestead again?'

'Nay, sir, the homestead is safe.' Sam Curry turned a careful eye on Lucy and the children. 'We don't know who these people were, but we know where they are — three of 'em.' He cleared his throat. His eyes still on Lucy, he went on. 'Tanner and Willie were asleep in the other hut. Masters and McKenzie were out boundary riding. We were taken completely by surprise.'

'Did they attack Mr Good and Mr Tanner?' Daniel asked.

'Didn't get the chance.' The builder smiled sourly. 'McKenzie came out of nowhere — him an' that dog of his — and set about evening the odds. He downed three of 'em and, with Masters and Tanner, chased the rest of 'em up into the hills.'

'Have they returned safely?'

'Masters an' Tanner have, sir. They lost their quarry in

the dark, so McKenzie sent them back to round up the flock while he's gone on to Long Reach to warn them to be on their guard.'

Lucy spoke for the first time. 'Surely that was not wise — out there on his own — he could be set upon by those creatures. Would he not be worried about this?'

'I think, missus, that they'd be the ones to worry if McKenzie was to come upon them, keeping in mind that our man is something of a pathfinder, which would give him the advantage.'

'Where are the three men that were caught?' Adam coughed, then added hoarsely, 'Are they secure?'

'Aye.' Sam Curry glanced at Lucy again. 'Two of McKenzie's bullets found their mark. The third man has a shoulder wound.' The words were quietly spoken and Lucy, about to place a mug of tea before the builder, stayed her hand and stared at him.

'Mr Curry, are two of those men—?'

'Aye, Mrs Chandler, they are, and McKenzie I'm afraid suffered injury — not serious, as he was able to carry on, but injury all the same.'

Lucy placed the mug of tea carefully on the table and as carefully lowered herself on to the wooden form beside it. Her face had blanched.

'See, now, you take a sip o' this yourself, m'dear,' Sam Curry said, gently placing the mug in her hands. 'It's all come as something of a shock, has this, but you've not to worry — 'twill all get sorted come morning.'

'Would you think it is possible that these are the same

hellions who destroyed Chandler's Run?' Adam murmured, as though to himself. He addressed the builder then. 'The police must be sent for. If these *are* the perpetrators and someone can recognize them, they must be brought to book and Ruben will surely then rest in peace.'

Morning came and went, and Lucy did her daily tasks automatically. She had listened most of the night for the sound of McKenzie's horse on the track above and had watched throughout the morning for his return.

She had kept the children in her sight, fearful that the horsemen might appear again. Willie Good had trundled down the hill mid-morning; his plump cheeks were pale and carried a stubble of beard. 'Come ter let yer know, squire, we're all shipshape up ther' so ye're not ter be worryin'.'

'Where is the wounded man?'

'We've tied 'im in one o' the bunks — one of us allus wi' 'im.'

'And the others?'

'In the big shed.'

The cook had not stayed long. Adam was exhausted and had said little, and Lucy's questions about McKenzie's whereabouts had elicited nothing more than a shake of the head. 'No way of knowin', missus, 'til 'e shows up — 'e weren't hurt bad as Masters tells it.'

It was an hour after the midday meal had been eaten when Lucy heard the sound of an approaching cart. She knew it was the Widow Gaunt, able now to identify the grindings and squeaks of the old vehicle, and in a short time she heard the gruff voice beyond the porch. 'Hello, the house!'

Lucy glanced at Adam, who did not rouse from his sleep, and hurried to open the door. The widow entered after kicking the snow from her boots, and Daniel turned back from the window. 'Was that Mr McKenzie riding on up the track?'

'It was, son.'

'He wasn't wearing his beard.'

The widow chuckled. 'That subject's best left — he's not well pleased to have been shorn.' She chuckled again. 'Bullet clipped 'is jaw an' it needed a stitch, so off it came.'

'He was not badly hurt then?' Lucy murmured, not looking at the older woman as she lifted the kettle from the hob.

'Only 'is vanity.'

Adam had woken and turned his head to address the visitor. 'Does Mr McKenzie know who those riders might have been?'

''Tis possibly three brothers, name o' Rafferty, an' their followers.'

'How does McKenzie know of them?'

''E don't personally, but 'e's come across homesteaders run off ther land an' ther stock taken — most times they're burned out like yer uncle was — 'e's seen a picture of 'em at the courthouse so 'e'll like as not recognize one o' them fellas up there.'

Lucy was thoughtful as she made the tea. If the Scot suspected that the intruders were those known to the authorities and still he had ridden in pursuit of them, she could only applaud his courage. The thought that he had actively protected them gave her a warm feeling of gratitude and a sense of security. Was it possible that the Scot felt more regard for Chandler's Run and its people than he'd allowed? And, if this was so, might he now be persuaded to accept Adam's proposal?

'Oh, I do beg your pardon.'

Ruby Gaunt's narrowed eyes regarded her. 'Ye'll not mind if I go up and see to that fella's wound, is what I was saying?'

'No, oh no, by all means.' A thought occurred to Lucy then.

'What are we to do with him — with them? They can't stay here. The children—'

'All taken care of. Rewi has carried McKenzie's note to the village down below and from there it will be carried to the next village and so on until it reaches the constabulary in Dunedin — quickest way to get 'em up here and get shut o' yer unwelcome guests.' The widow turned to Adam. 'How are you after last night's goin's-on?'

Adam raised frail hands and smiled faintly. 'I was not required to do anything so I had no active part in the proceedings.' He looked through the window to the mountains. 'I wonder where the bounders went?'

'They'll be headin' west to the coast — if they can find the pass. No loss if they can't.' Swallowing the last of her tea, the widow rose from the table. 'I'll go an' tend to the gent up ther' so's 'e's fit ter travel when the law gets 'ere.'

'Perhaps I should go with you and thank Mr McKenzie,' Lucy murmured.

'Mr Masters and Mr Tanner, too,' Daniel reminded her.

'Yes, of course. I'll get my cape.'

'May I come, too?'

Lucy looked quickly at Adam.

'I can see no harm in his going,' he said quietly.

'Then Sarah will stay and read to you. We shan't be long.'

Resentment rose in the girl as again she sat beside her father's bed and picked up the book she had read to him twice before. 'Shall I read this again?'

Her voice was sullen, but Adam, not noticing, answered absently, 'Yes, pet, it will do very well.' He had noted Lucy's heightened interest and her concern when he had spoken of the Scotsman, and, wondering why this should be, he felt vaguely uneasy. Sarah's voice droned on, the words not registering, as Adam puzzled over his wife's inattention to her morning tasks; her distraction had been obvious, as had her vagueness when spoken to. Had she shown as much concern for the other men as she had for McKenzie? He couldn't remember and felt too weary to pursue the thought. Frowning slightly, he drifted into sleep.

Sarah continued to read, glancing from time to time at her father. He appeared to be asleep but she couldn't be certain. Eventually she lowered the book and whispered, 'Papa, are you awake?'

When he did not reply she continued to sit, studying the pallid face on the pillow. When will he die? she wondered. Would he slip into sleep as he had just done and not awaken, or would he gasp and rattle? She had heard somewhere that people sometimes did this before they died. Was he dying now? Uneasiness was growing in her and it was becoming more difficult to breathe. Quickly she rose from the chair, dropped the book on to its seat and went to open the kitchen door. She stood there, fearful of what was happening to her, panic growing, knotting her stomach, filling her head. Then slowly the panic receded, leaving her shaken and clammy. Where was Mama? Where was Daniel? When would Moana come back? Not daring to go back inside, Sarah stood in the porch waiting for someone to come.

Lucy was disappointed when she found that the Scot was not at the homestead. She went in search of Willie Good and was informed that McKenzie had taken a supply of food and his swag an hour earlier and ridden off into the hills.

'Is he still searching for those men?'

''Appen 'e is, 'appen 'e's lookin' fer strays — 'e don't never say.'

Lucy made her way back to the homestead, where Daniel had remained. She wandered from room to room on the lower floor, noting the white of the pine floors and the stack of totara that stood ready to line the walls. A fire blazed on the kitchen hearth and even though there was an absence of doors and windows yet, it was warm within the thick cob walls. There was no staircase in place at this time and Lucy stood below the opening in the ceiling wondering how Adam, in his weakness, would manage if he were to occupy one of the attic bedrooms.

Objects covered with hessian and canvas were everywhere,

leaning against the walls and piled in corners, and as she walked into the unfinished parlour Lucy wondered idly what they were. She stood where the rear window would be and searched the hills for McKenzie. The flock had settled on the lower pastures and in that vast setting the sheep were the only things that moved. Then she saw the widow step out of the shepherds' hut and climb up on to her cart. Quickly Lucy moved from sight and presently the cart rattled to a halt outside the front doorway. 'Hello, the house! Could a body step down and view the grand abode?'

Lucy went to greet her and stepped back while the older woman kicked off her boots whilst looking pointedly at Lucy's. 'Ye'll learn ter leave yer footwear at the door, lady, less'n yer want ter spend your days scrubbin' the muck off them white boards.'

Taken aback, Lucy looked at her wet boots and the marks she and Daniel had left on the floor. She glanced at Sam Curry's feet as he came across the hallway; he was bootless, wearing soft leather slippers.

'Oh, I am sorry,' she said. 'I didn't realize — I'm truly sorry!'

'No need to take on, girl,' the widow grunted. 'It's your floor.'

Sam Curry hid a smile and, bowing to the two women, he excused himself and went about his labours.

'That chap you tended,' Daniel asked, 'was he badly wounded?'

''E'll survive,' Ruby Gaunt muttered. 'That's the pity of it; the likes of 'im an' 'is ilk, we'd all be better off without.'

Lucy, regarding the seamed face, realized that now she probably had no cause to be suspicious of this woman; that her knowledge of the terrible events on Chandler's Run was indeed coincidental; her involvement purely out of concern for the beleaguered family. Yet there was Nobby Clark and his cryptic remark, and Agatha Brand's less guarded statements. Perhaps she would be wise to keep these in mind.

'Ye're impatient I expect ter move yer family under this roof.'

Ruby Gaunt's words broke in on her thoughts.

'No,' Lucy said quietly, 'I'm in no hurry — the stairs will be difficult for Adam—'

She turned abruptly and walked to the doorway of the parlour. 'Come and see the view we will have from this window — one will be able to see the mood of the mountains while sitting warm beside the fire.'

'Aye, an' keep an eye on yer flock an yer shepherds. Yer man would be best in 'ere, where 'e can see all the goin's-on—'

Lucy looked sharply at the widow, but the woman's face was bland. 'Come along then, what's in these other rooms?' And she strode back to the parlour doorway.

The days passed and McKenzie did not return. Adam, lying in his bed, noted again his wife's distraction and the repeated question each time Daniel returned from the homestead, and his uneasiness grew. Naïve as she was, Lucy was not skilled in deception and, despite his illness, Adam was becoming more and more aware of her interest in the Scot. He was filled with dismay. As a result, his tenuous health went into a decline and Lucy forgot everything as his condition worsened. Exhausted and fearful, she at last sent Tom Masters to fetch Ruby Gaunt, and when Ruby came and had made her examination, she walked Lucy outside and spoke bluntly. 'Yer man is losing ground and his chances of rallying this time are slim. Can you think of anything that could set 'im back like this?'

Lucy avoided the widow's eyes. 'No — no, nothing.'

Ruby Gaunt pushed the battered hat back off her forehead and regarded Lucy in silence, then said, 'I'm askin' yer this because I've not expected 'im ter turn the corner just yet.'

Lucy did not speak.

'Well, it could be reaction to those blackguards raisin' Cain 'ere, I suppose.'

With that the big woman stalked back indoors. 'Now, you rest easy, lad.' Her hands were busy mixing her potions. 'Yer've ter worry about nothin'. I'll be sendin' Moana back ter help yer good lady here and see that yer takin' yer medicine.' She touched the thin shoulder gently, then raised Adam up a little. 'Drink this now an' sleep.'

When he was settled, the widow gathered her concoctions into their box and turned to the door where Lucy waited. 'Poliss not come yet?'

'No. When will Moana come?'

'Rewi'll bring 'er in the mornin'.' Ruby Gaunt stepped from the porch and, pushing her hat firmly on to her head, she squinted at Lucy. 'You all right with this?'

'No — I don't know — how can I stand it?'

'You will. When the time comes, you will and I'll be back.' The Widow Gaunt turned to leave. 'Where are the children?'

'At the homestead.'

'Good. Keep them out of it as much as you can.'

When Lucy returned to the kitchen, Adam lay quietly, his eyelids heavy. He turned a little on his pillow. 'Lucy,' he murmured, 'I feel so odd — as though I might drift away now — not unpleasant.'

He was silent for a while then whispered, 'I wish I could have seen you settled . . .'

'Oh, Adam, don't say such things — you are drifting because Ruby Gaunt has given you a sleeping draught.'

'No more pretence, love — stay . . .' The soft whisper was lost in sleep.

Lucy awoke with a start. Dawn had not yet broken, and she was cold and stiff. The fire was a bed of dull embers and the lamp on the table burned low. She moved slowly to sit upright in the big chair and became aware of the stillness, aware that Adam had not coughed through the night to awaken her and there was no sound of breathing other than her own. Turning fearful eyes on the figure in the bed, she could see that the eyes in the pale blur of the face were open and her heart began to pound. Her hand to her throat, Lucy rose slowly from the chair and made herself move nearer to the bed, made herself lean closer, then started violently as Adam's faint whisper came up to her. 'I hoped not to waken you.'

She could barely speak. 'The fire has died — is nearly out — are you cold?'

'A little.'

Lucy went to the hearth to revive the fire and put the kettle on the hob; the activity steadied her. 'Could you drink a little tea?'

She moved to the bedside and touched Adam's brow. 'I think your fever may have lessened. Do you feel a little better?'

'Yes, I think I do. Can I have some broth rather than tea?'

Lucy fed him carefully, a little at a time, but the mere effort of swallowing tired him quickly and he turned away to sleep. She sat for a time, the bowl of broth cooling in her hands while she gazed at the frail man in the bed and wondered at the strength of the spirit that brought him back to her time and again.

Later that morning, Moana was back in the hut and resuming her tasks so smoothly it was as though she had never been away. In spite of herself, Lucy found her thoughts turning to the Scot again. No matter how she busied herself she could not dismiss him from her mind, and three days after Moana's return she accompanied the children up to the homestead. McKenzie was there, helping Pitchin to hang the kitchen door. With diffidence, Lucy approached him, her gaze fixed on his beardless face, the roughly trimmed moustache and the healing wound on his jaw. Clear blue eyes were turned on her as she moved nearer and the words she had imagined herself saying fled from her mind. There she stood, bereft, unable to utter a sound, and Daniel spoke from beside her. 'We think you were very brave chasing those bad men, Mr McKenzie.' He glanced at his mother. 'Mama was worried when you were up in the hills on your own—'

'Hush, Daniel.' Lucy's cheeks were burning but she'd found her tongue. 'For all our sakes, I wish to thank you for coming to our assistance.'

'Nae need.'

McKenzie turned his attention back to the door, clearly dismissing her, and Lucy stood uncertainly, looking at his back.

'Ah, Mrs Chandler.' Sam Curry stood in the doorway opposite. 'Come through, dear lady, and tell me where you would like your linen-press to be placed. I thought perhaps under the stairs . . .'

Lucy turned to the builder, colour staining her cheeks: the man had virtually snubbed her. Disbelief and anger warred within her as she went with Sam Curry into the hallway.

'See now,' he was saying, 'the bedrooms are not over-large and there will be no room on the landing, so I thought perhaps that here would be the best place to store your linen. Would you agree?'

Lucy tried to concentrate and visualize the staircase that was yet to be built.

'Yes, I'm sure that you are right,' she murmured, raising her eyes to the floor above. 'When will you be building the stairs, Mr Curry?'

'When we're finished lining the walls in here. Have you been through into the kitchen yet?'

'No, Mr Curry, I haven't.'

'Then you'll want to come and see. The walls are finished and the windows and doors are in place. Come, it will only take a moment.'

Reluctantly, Lucy passed the Scot, careful not to look at him, and entered the kitchen. The walls glowed from the fire in the hearth and it was now a room, which even unfurnished welcomed you into its warmth.

'Is it not handsome? And we are making better time than I had expected, due largely to the extra pair of hands, I have ter say.'

Lucy made no comment and shortly after left the homestead, leaving Daniel and Sarah to gather wood-chips and off-cuts. While she struggled to lace her frozen boots she could hear her son talking animatedly with the Scot, hear the man's deeper voice in reply and his rare laugh. Smarting, she stepped out into the snow and walked as briskly as was possible back to the hut, promising herself with each step that she would not attempt to speak to that man again. Churlish, ignorant and — yes — ugly! She would not leave herself open to further rebuff.

Within days, however, she found herself remembering the clean-shaven face, the skin paler where the beard had been removed, and the firm, unsmiling mouth that was no longer hidden. What was wrong with her to permit herself to dwell on the man again? She would *not* think of him. When she found, however, that she could not dismiss him so readily, she was dismayed. Angrily, she worked harder and devoted more time to Adam. She increased the children's studies and fell on the pile of mending, planning her spring garden while she plied her needle.

The police duly arrived. With the exception of Adam, they questioned everyone on the run several times and were finally satisfied that the dead men had met their end as a result of their attack on Chandler's Run. Three days later, they removed the two frozen corpses and the wounded man to their wagon, and left with a warning for everyone to be on their guard. The Rafferty brothers were still at large.

Adam was weaker than ever and could no longer stand. Lucy and Moana lifted him from his bed daily to change the sodden sheets, and the few moments he sat propped in his big chair brought him close to collapse. Ruby Gaunt spoke a gentle warning to Lucy. 'Prepare yerself girl, 'e's living on guts alone now — 'is body is all but fallen in on itself — blessed if I know how 'e's still 'ere.'

And the day came when Adam whispered, 'Lucy, there is something I would do now, and soon.'

'What is it, dear?'

'Will you find a way to have me taken up to the homestead?'

Lucy and Moana exchanged startled looks.

'To go out in this cold, Adam, would be to kill you — you must not ask this of me.'

'I am dying. What does it matter?' Adam's eyes closed. Without opening them he whispered, 'Don't deny me this, Lucy. Go now — up the hill — see what can be done.'

~

A cold wind whipped about Lucy as she stumbled towards the homestead. Swirling flurries of snow blinded her, stinging her eyes, and the tears froze on her lashes. Twice she fell. Daniel, watching anxiously as she left the hut, saw her fall the first time as she climbed the bank; she had refused to allow him to accompany her, and soon she was lost to sight in the flying, billowing whiteness.

Lucy followed the edge of the track and, when that disappeared, sought rocks and familiar rises and falls in the ground only to find that under its heavy mantle of snow the landscape looked very different. Somehow she found the homestead, its new front door closed against the wind. Inside her stiff, wet gloves, Lucy's hands had lost all feeling and failed to turn the big brass knob, hard as she tried.

Desperately she called and hammered at the panels, and when the door suddenly opened she fell into the arms of the Scot. Hardly able to stand she lay against him, panting, her heart bursting, and she heard the strong beat of his own beneath her cheek. For a moment she stood in the circle of his arms, then slowly she raised her head and looked up into blazing blue eyes, eyes that held an expression of such intense dislike that Lucy reeled back from him. Sam Curry hurried forward. 'My dear Mrs Chandler, come to the fire, your skirts are saturated — come, before you catch your death!' He pulled a wooden box forward for her to sit on and quickly drew the gloves from her hands. Sober-faced, young Pitchin stood watching. Without turning, Lucy felt the Scot's hostile stare on her back.

'What has happened, my dear?' the builder asked gently. 'Is something amiss with Mr Chandler?'

Lucy nodded, making no sound, her teeth clenched against the violent shivers that now shook her. 'Bring Mrs Chandler a mug of tea, lad,' Sam Curry said to the boy. 'Plenty of sugar.' He knelt before Lucy. 'This is not the weather to be abroad in,' he tut-tutted as he unlaced her boots. Aware that McKenzie had not moved, she sat silently and watched the steam rise from her skirts while the builder propped her boots and gloves where they would dry. Pitchin returned and shyly offered her a brimming mug. Sam Curry hovered over Lucy as she sipped the scalding liquid; then, as her shivering abated, he asked gently, 'Feeling a little better, my dear?'

'Thank you, yes.'

'Can you tell us what has happened to bring you out on such a terrible day?'

'Yes.' Lucy nodded again. 'Adam, my husband — he is failing, is very low — but he insists that he must see the homestead. He has charged me, with your help, to find a way to bring him up here.'

'Dear me, dear me.' Sam Curry rubbed his jaw. 'This requires some thought . . . Insists, you say?'

'Yes — I could not dissuade him. I tried.'

The builder frowned. 'Not an easy undertaking under the circumstances; the weather—' He turned from Lucy. 'What say you, James, could we build a litter or somesuch?'

'There will not be time — I fear . . .' Lucy bowed her head.

'Dear girl,' the builder commiserated. 'I *am* so sorry, but now don't you worry, we will find a way.'

'He'll weigh nae mair tha' a wisp.' James McKenzie spoke then. 'Ah'll carry the wee mon ma'sel'.'

~

The wind had ceased and a pale sun shone when the Scot and Sam Curry came the next day to take Adam up to the homestead. Wrapped in his plaid and a coarse woollen blanket, a thick scarf covering his nose and mouth, Adam was almost euphoric as the tall McKenzie lifted his shrunken form from his bed and carried him carefully up the snow-covered track. Lucy, Moana and the children walked silently with Sam Curry in his wake. Young Pitchin waited to open the door, and when everyone had entered he quickly closed it to retain the warmth from both kitchen and parlour hearths.

Adam turned his head weakly, taking in as much of his surroundings as he could, his eyes unnaturally bright and two hectic spots of colour burning in his cheeks. The Scot carried him slowly, the builder quietly explaining where the cupboards, lamp brackets and bookshelves were to be set and describing the three attic bedrooms in detail. Adam did not speak but nodded fractionally from time to time. They were leaving the parlour when his body went limp, his frail endeavour at an end.

'Tis time, aye, ta gang away hame wi' ye',' the Scot said softly, and motioned with his head for Pitchin to open the door. Lucy moved to his side and touched Adam's face with trembling fingers. She did not speak but stayed close all the way back to the hut, her anxious eyes on her husband, who seemed no bigger than a child in the tall man's arms.

Adam drifted back into consciousness as McKenzie lowered him carefully on to his bed. 'I thank you,' he whispered. '— has meant a great deal — seeing for myself.'

The Scot nodded, then, touching two fingers to the brim of his hat in salute to Adam, he turned from the bed and walked to the kitchen door. Involuntarily, Lucy hurried after him. 'Mr McKenzie.' The tall figure turned. 'May I express my gratitude — my husband, due to your kindness, will rest content now.' She extended a diffident hand. McKenzie's pale eyes dwelt on Lucy's face briefly, then ignoring her hand he nodded curtly and stooped through the door.

Rattled again by his open dislike, Lucy walked swiftly into the bedroom, there to hide her hot cheeks and her humiliation. This was insufferable — not to be borne! With an effort she composed herself, took off her cloak and returned to the kitchen. Sarah sat at the table, looking absently at the lessons she had been set that morning but not attempting to do them. Daniel was building up the fire and Moana was tending to Adam. Nobody, it seemed, had seen what had transpired. Lucy went to stand beside Moana to watch her husband's troubled breathing. His eyes were closed and he was very pale now. He coughed harshly and Sarah raised worried eyes to her mother's face. Lucy did not notice her child, nor did she really see Adam; her thoughts still focused on the Scot. Why should it matter to her if he shunned her? It was obvious that she was only incidental to the place while it suited him to remain. And when he left again and this time did not return, no doubt it would be for the best.

It was then that Lucy Chandler faced several truths. She did not wish McKenzie to leave, and she admitted now that she was no longer harmlessly intrigued by him — she desired him. It had been a long time since Adam's arms had held her; a long time since she had been needed as a woman. Her gaze rested on her husband as she stood there, seeing the frail travesty of the man she had known and loved with gentleness and respect since childhood. Soon now he was to leave her, and with grief and shame she owned to the truth she had tried to deny. A wild throbbing filled her breast as once again she felt McKenzie's hard arms about her. She wanted him. It was a fierce need, and the intensity of it frightened her. She had never experienced this powerful emotion with Adam; would not have believed herself capable of it. Moana's dark eyes were on her, compassion on the lovely face. Knowing she didn't deserve it, Lucy turned abruptly away.

Chapter 9

THE MORNING AFTER Adam's visit to the homestead, James McKenzie rode off. Riding the mare, Daniel went with him part-way down the track, the dog Friday loping between their two horses.

There had been no warning of the Scot's departure, but seeing the full saddlebags and the bedding roll, Lucy knew with cold certainty that he was leaving. Would he come back?

When Daniel returned, he unsaddled the mare and entered the kitchen, a gloomy expression on his face. Sarah followed her brother into the bedroom. 'What did Mr McKenzie say, Daniel?'

'He said he had a flock to drive over some pass somewhere before the thaw, and then he said he would go up to Long Reach for the lambing and probably the shearing.'

'But is he coming back here?' Sarah squeaked. 'We have lambing and shearing too.'

Daniel shrugged. 'I don't know, Sarah — when I asked, he answered in the Gaelic I think. I didn't understand what he said.' He shrugged again. 'I thought he might be here for my birthday.'

Lucy, sitting sewing, had become still, her attention on her son's words. When he said no more, she lowered her head and her thoughts turned inward. If the Scot did not return she would have no chance to win his regard and perhaps, in time, his love. The thought chilled her as she visualized the void of loneliness opening before her and the long empty years stretching ahead in that place up on the hill. Adam lay watching her; feeling his eyes on her, Lucy raised her head. As their eyes met, she saw with a shock that he knew what was in her heart and hastily she averted her gaze. From that moment, Adam spoke no more.

Lucy's remorse was a physical pain. She hovered over Adam, her contrition tinged with anger, feeling that had his will been written in her favour she would not have been drawn to the Scot or any other. When the time came she would have buried her husband, rid herself of the run any way she could, and taken her children and her grief home to England where they belonged. By his action, Adam had brought all of this about and there were no words of comfort she could say to him now. He would not have welcomed them anyway, turning from her whenever she came near. Moana watched with sadness, not understanding why the man would part himself from his woman before death brought this about.

～

On the day that Daniel turned thirteen, James McKenzie returned to Chandler's Run. He gave no explanation for his return, but Lucy's heart sang.

The boy had gone to milk the cow, and when Lucy heard his exuberant whoop and the sound of a horse cantering past the hut, her heart missed a beat. She made herself walk slowly from the kitchen and, from the doorway of the porch, she saw the Scot rein in his horse and wait while the boy clambered up the bank. She could not hear the words they spoke, but she saw a package change hands. McKenzie then rode on and Lucy walked slowly to meet her son as he scrambled back down the bank. 'He's come back, Mama — I knew he would — I just knew!'

Hurriedly, Daniel stripped the heavy brown paper away and held up a gleaming knife. 'It's a hunting knife, just like his, Mama.'

Lucy duly admired the horn handle and the long sharp blade and did not ask the question she was burning to ask. Instead she turned back to the porch. 'Finish your milking, Daniel. Dinner will be on the table in half an hour.'

Adam lay with his eyes closed when Lucy re-entered the kitchen but he was not asleep. He had watched her leave, had heard his son's excited shout, and somewhere deep within him, his soul wept.

The following day, Sam Curry sent word with Daniel requesting Lucy to come and advise him where her work-benches were to be situated in the lean-to that had been built on to the kitchen's west wall. This extra room was where Lucy would separate the cream from the milk, where she would make her butter, and later, when she had learned how, where she would make their cheese. It would also be used to store her preserves, jams and dry goods.

Lucy's first impulse was to go immediately. Adam, she knew, had heard Daniel's words. Glancing quickly at him she saw that his eyes were fixed on the mountains beyond the window, as they always were now when he wasn't sleeping, and a deep pity stirred in her. 'Tell Mr Curry, Daniel,' she said quietly, 'to build the benches on the south and west walls. It will be cooler on the south wall for setting the cream, and the bench on the west wall is where I will work.'

'You will not be going up then, Mama?'

'There is no need.'

Lucy restrained herself from going up to the homestead for three days, caring for Adam, making extra tasks for herself in an attempt to turn her thoughts away from the Scot. Lambing had started and she told herself that even if she went up to the homestead she would not find McKenzie there. For three nights she lay wide-eyed, physically spent after working herself to the point of exhaustion, and listened to Adam's harsh breathing and Moana's soft movements as, countless times, she rose from her mat to tend him.

On the afternoon of the fourth day, with nerves stretched to breaking point, Lucy left the hut, taking Moana with her as a concession to Adam. 'Come, the walk will do you good. You have been cooped up in there without a breath of air for days.'

Moana looked doubtfully at the sick man.

'We shan't be long,' Lucy added firmly, 'and Sarah will sit with her papa.'

A north-westerly wind blew in their faces as they trudged up the hill. Moana noted the swirling, restless cloud about the peaks, but Lucy saw nothing, intent on reaching the homestead.

McKenzie was not there and she dared not ask his whereabouts. Covering her disappointment with bright chatter, Lucy took the Maori girl slowly through the rooms. Playing for time in the hope that the Scot would put in an appearance, she explained everything in minute detail. Sam Curry, enjoying the company, offered them tea and Lucy accepted.

As time went by and the day grew darker, Moana was becoming anxious: they had been away for a long time and this was not good. Pointedly she went to stand by the front door and Lucy was obliged to return to the hut.

Sarah sat beside Adam in the deepening gloom. The wind gusted around the hut, rattling the open window in its frame. She seemed to have been reading for a long time, but she continued on because the sound of her voice covered the sounds she was afraid to hear. She doubted that her father was hearing her words, and she wished that her mother and Moana would return so she could at last be freed from this task which she hated. The sick odour of the man in the bed and the face on the pillow that bore little resemblance to that of her papa's unnerved her, as did his feverish sunken eyes forever fixed on the mountains.

The child read on, her ears tuned to exterior sounds.

Daniel would be finished milking soon, she comforted herself. Adam coughed, a harsh, tearing bark which made Sarah jump. She started to read again but stopped when an odd gurgle came from the bed. She raised apprehensive eyes to her father's face; his eyes were on her, huge, starting from his head. He tried to speak, reaching out to grip her hand. The gurgle was in his throat and suddenly he coughed again. Bright blood bubbled from his mouth and nose, and Sarah screamed. She tried to free her hand but Adam, with the strength of a drowning man, held her fast, coughing his life's blood into her face and on to her hand. Sarah screamed and screamed again, until no sound came; her lungs were empty and the sound was only in her head. Terrified, all reason gone, the child lashed out with her free hand, blindly, frantically, until the nerveless fingers released her. Then, with unseeing eyes, she fled from the room, colliding with her mother and Moana as they came through the door.

Lucy barely saw her as she walked towards the bed; saw only the blood and Adam's eyes. They seemed to watch her as she approached, accusing eyes, even as they glazed in death. Involuntarily, Lucy turned away and Moana, moving past her, gently closed the lids as Daniel came hesitantly into the room. Moana set up a soft wailing as she washed the blood from the waxen face and hands, and Lucy, huddled in her chair beside the fire, wished she would stop.

It was Daniel who helped Moana attend to his father, and it was Daniel, when it was done, who said, 'Mama, we must find Sarah — she's not come back.'

Roused from her apathy, Lucy stared at her son. Sarah —

was it an hour or longer since the child had rushed past them? It had grown dark. Uneasily, she rose to her feet. 'Daniel, light the lantern. We must go and find her.' Averting her face from where Adam lay, Lucy went to the bedroom to gather up her cloak and Daniel's long coat.

The wind beat about them as they moved through the darkness, the flame in the lamp flickering erratically. They looked in the cow byre and the hen house and called up and down the track, the wind whipping their voices away. If Sarah replied, they did not hear her. She was not in the homestead and now Lucy's concern was turning to alarm. They hastened their steps then, turning towards the hut where the men would be eating their evening meal. Lucy hammered on the door with a clenched fist and quickly entered when it was opened to her, Daniel close behind. 'Has anyone seen Sarah?' was her urgent question.

Willie Good stepped forward. 'We've not seen her this day, missus,' he said, turning to the other men in the room, 'have we?' Heads shook.

'My husband passed away a little over an hour ago while Sarah was alone with him. Now she is nowhere to be found.'

There was no emotion in Lucy's voice; her face was the colour of parchment. Sam Curry was at her elbow.

'This is sad news indeed. Sit, my dear, sit down here — young Daniel. A hot mug of tea, Willie, if you please. Now, she'll not be far — don't you worry.'

'We must go now — *quickly*,' Lucy urged, as a strong gust shook the hut. 'Sarah is out there somewhere. We must find her. Somebody must go and fetch Mrs Gaunt, and whoever she can bring, to help us look!'

'All will be done that needs to be done.' Sam Curry spoke gently. 'Was young Sarah dressed warmly?'

Lucy shook her head. 'No.'

'Then we'll not waste time. Willie, would you ride to Long Reach?'

The plump cook nodded. 'Aye, I'll find me way — a deep sorrow is this, missus.'

'Pitchin, mount up and alert McKenzie and Jack Tanner,' Sam Curry ordered. He placed a hand under Lucy's elbow and guided her to the table. 'We will find the child, Mrs Chandler, never doubt it. Sit down now and drink your tea — this is men's work.'

Tom Masters shrugged into his oilskins and reached for his hat.

'I'll head sou'west, Sam. Jack and McKenzie are somewhere west or nor'west.'

'And I'll ride north-east, Mrs Chandler.' Sam Curry raised his voice as another gust shook the hut. 'When the folk arrive from Long Reach, tell them where we are, my dear, so they can cover as much ground as possible, spread out between us.'

'I will saddle the mare.' Daniel spoke quickly. 'Where should I look, Mr Curry?'

'No, my boy.' The builder shook his head. 'Your mama will need a man to stay with her, too.'

❧

The anxious hours passed and the wind grew stronger, hurling itself down into the gullies and ravines and battering the walls of the small hut, shaking it until Lucy feared it would collapse. Then over the wind a horse was heard to neigh and shortly a voice shouted at the door. Daniel leapt to open it and Rewi filled the doorway. 'Boss lady come soon. Us fellas go find tamaiti — which way?'

Lucy was confused; she could not recall Sam Curry's words and looked at Daniel for help. The boy stepped out into the blustery darkness and raised an arm. 'Go up there, Rewi, and all the way along there.' His arm made an arc. 'There is nobody looking down there, either.'

'Matau,' Rewi nodded his understanding. 'We look for tamaiti there.' The Maori quickly remounted and rode off, the darker shapes of horses and riders close behind him.

Daniel shut the door. 'I hope they find her soon, Mama, it's very cold.'

Lucy did not reply. Dread was in her heart; she knew that when the wind dropped finally and the rain followed, Sarah would have little hope of surviving. She sat with head bowed and hands clenched in her lap and silently began to pray.

Another hour passed and suddenly Daniel was listening. 'Someone is coming.' The wind lulled, and Lucy heard the familiar creaks and rattles of the widow's cart. She rose stiffly, pulled open the door and stood waiting while the wind, with renewed force, tore at her hair and skirts.

The big horses drew the cart alongside the hut and Ruby Gaunt jumped down. Two lanterns either side of the footboard lit up her craggy face as she dragged something from under the seat. 'Here, lad!' she shouted. 'Give a hand.' Thick canvas covers were thrown over the horses' backs, flapping wildly, and Daniel hurried to help with the straps. The widow then stepped into the hut, her keen gaze resting on Lucy's pale face. 'Are ye just goin' ter stand ther' or will yer make me a mug o' tea?'

'I'll make it.'

'Yer *ma* will make it,' Ruby Gaunt growled. 'Move about, girl, and get yer blood movin' — yer as white as a parson's neck-gear.'

She sat down and motioned to Daniel. 'Sit, boy, an' talk ter me.'

Pushing the battered hat back off her brow, the widow tucked a strand of grey hair behind an ear. 'How long has yer sister been gone?'

'She ran off at the end of milking.'

Lucy placed the tin mug before the older woman, then resumed her seat. 'It's too long to be out there, isn't it?' Over the wind her voice was toneless.

'Aye, a body would have to say so, but that's not to say she don't have a chance — tucked away somewhere out o' the wind. Why did she run off?' The steel grey eyes were fastened on Lucy.

'I don't know — my husband — Adam — Sarah was reading to him while we — Moana and I — went up to the homestead.' Lucy's halting words stopped. She saw again Adam's dead eyes and a shudder ran through her.

'Her papa died while she was there alone with him. Is

this what you are saying, Lucy?' The gruff voice softened. Lucy nodded.

'Aye, well, I can see what has happened, and yer blaming yerself — this so?'

'It is *my* fault if she dies out there tonight.' Lucy's voice was suddenly shrill. 'My fault, nobody else's, and I won't be able to live with that either!'

Ruby Gaunt stood up slowly, and grasping Lucy's shoulders she shook her, none too gently. 'Get a hold o' yerself, girlie, ye're frightening the lad. Whatever yer think yer've done, it's done — can't be undone — and hysterics'll serve no useful purpose.' The widow waited for a space, then continued. 'Ther's things ter be discussed an' the next day or so ter get through — are yer with me now?'

Lucy nodded.

'Good, then I'll only say this. Even though we all knew it was inevitable, it's the harsh reality that the knowin' can't make easier. I'm sorry it had ter be.' Lucy lifted her head. The widow's steely eyes looked steadily into her own, and something in their depths conveyed a comfort that no words could have.

'Thank you.'

The words were a whisper and the three people in the hut realized that the wind had ceased.

'We should go back,' Lucy said with reluctance. 'Moana is down there alone.'

'She has things to do and is well able ter manage. She has seen Rewi briefly and will go home to him when all this is over.' Ruby Gaunt rose to her feet. 'I've things ter do also.

Stay here and wait — sleep if yer can.'

When she had gone, Lucy and Daniel sat in silence. After a time, the boy began to nod off. Lucy tucked him into one of the bunks and there he fell into exhausted sleep. Soon the wind returned, a low moaning in the distant hills that came steadily closer until it was a roaring, battering onslaught against the walls of the hut. It ceased as suddenly as it had begun, and the rain was on them, falling in torrents; sleet-laden rain that turned the air in the hut bitterly cold within minutes. Lucy's faint hope for Sarah was gone; no eleven-year-old girl, exposed to the elements for these many hours, could survive in this. She bowed her head then and gave way to her grief. Daniel, woken by the downpour, went to his mother and there, in the rough shepherds' hut, they clung to each other, crying openly.

Just before dawn the rain ceased, and a short time later Ruby Gaunt walked through the door. She did not speak, but grim-faced she took the battered teapot from the table and went outside again. A little later, weary riders began to come in from every direction. Silently, they dismounted and held their frozen hands to the fire in the cooking hut while the widow poured scalding tea into tin mugs and cut thick slices of Willie's bread. Soon she came into the hut with a freshened pot. She placed it before Lucy, then lowered herself wearily on to a wooden stool. Lucy poured a mug for each of them.

'Did yer sleep any?'

Lucy shook her head. 'Daniel slept a little—' Sudden movement outside the hut silenced her, and she started as a shout went up. Ruby Gaunt stepped outside and in a moment her voice boomed out over the men's excited calls: 'Get yerself out 'ere, girl — 'ere's a sight fer ye!'

Lucy and Daniel hurried to stand beside the widow and look where the gloved finger was pointing. They saw the sheep running willy-nilly down the hill, the mob scattering east and west, then they saw the bitch Friday, swift and unerring, turn the steaming, bleating mass and sweep them towards the lower ground. Following them came a lone horseman, and behind his saddle a small figure clung for dear life as they negotiated the treacherous slope.

'Sarah — he has Sarah,' Lucy breathed.

'Aye, an' thank God for McKenzie.' The widow's voice was rough.

Wordlessly, Daniel hugged his mother then turned again to watch the Scot's approach.

When the rider reached the barn, Lucy began to run.

'Wait!' Ruby Gaunt was clambering up into her cart. 'Ride with me — come along son, in yer get.'

Sam Curry, Tom Masters, Jack Tanner and Willie Good mounted their horses and followed, and the sheep milled about them as they met the Scot. Lucy scrambled down from the cart and ran to reach up to her child who sat, swaddled in a thick blanket, pale and still.

'Thank you,' she whispered. 'We thought we had lost her.'

'Where did you find her?' Sam Curry lifted Sarah from the horse's back and set her down before her mother, and Lucy held her as though she might lose her again if she let her go.

'This is indeed wonderful, James.' Sam Curry was exuberant. 'We thought we had covered virtually every foot of the place!'

McKenzie did not reply immediately. His pale eyes, cold and condemning, rested on Lucy's face. When at last he spoke, his voice matched his eyes.

'Behint yon howe,' he said slowly and with deliberation, 'abeen yon hame, ah heard a beag mane. Friday sniffed her oot, the wee lassie scarce girded, hurklin' laich, cauld a' deith, wi twa een startin' frae her kin.'

'Will you say again, my dear chap — in English?' Sam Curry, looking up into the grim face, saw the man's exhaustion and something else he didn't understand.

McKenzie turned his pale glance on the builder then and, slowly shaking his head, turned his horse about and cantered back towards the hills.

Ruby Gaunt muttered to herself then touched Lucy's arm. 'Come, let us get this child home.'

Sarah went rigid in Lucy's arms. 'No!' The single shrill cry startled everybody. The child's eyes were huge and she looked fearfully at Lucy, pushing away from her.

'Ah,' Ruby Gaunt breathed. 'No surprises here — don't be upset.'

She took Sarah's arm firmly in her gloved hand.

'Perhaps your mama will let yer come home wi' me fer a spell — would that suit yer?'

The blue eyes that looked back at her were vacant, looking inwards.

''Tis all right, lass, yer don't have ter go in ther' — are ye listenin'?' The widow shook her arm.

Sarah stared blankly at the craggy face close to hers, not speaking, then gave an almost imperceptible nod.

'Then let us go down and pack yer bundle. You can stay in the cart, child — don't get fussed — come.'

The widow hefted Sarah up to the high seat and helped Lucy up beside her.

'In the back, lad —'

Rewi and six riders from Long Reach rode silently behind them as they trundled down the hill, breaking into a canter only when they had passed the hut.

'Stay wi' yer sister, boy — we'll not be long.'

Lucy entered the porch reluctantly. The widow's hand cupped her elbow and pushed her to the closed kitchen door. 'Yer've nothing ter bother yer in there, girl,' she rumbled. 'Rewi an' Moana 'ave seen ter things.'

She pushed open the door and Lucy's shrinking gaze fell first on Moana, sitting with her mending beside the fire, then her eyes jerked to the pinewood coffin that sat on two rough trestles with tall candlesticks placed at its head and foot. The coffin lid rested against the trestles: Adam's bed and bedding were gone.

'Come, Lucy, lay your ghosts and fears to rest. Adam is at peace.' The widow guided her to stand beside the coffin, and Lucy looked down on the face of her husband. In death it was smooth and tranquil; his earthly trials were at an end. And mine are just beginning, was Lucy's unbidden thought. This man whom she had loved and had betrayed was no more — but the memory of McKenzie's cold eyes was destroying her. She was more alone now than she had ever been in her life, and her future was taking on a new and frightening dimension.

She turned away from the coffin, empty, drained, her thoughts turning to Sarah so nearly lost: how could she relinquish her to this rough woman? Her instincts cried out against abandoning her daughter to the care of this person of questionable repute while her own arms ached to soothe her and keep her safe. She stood irresolute in the bedroom doorway. 'I don't know what to do—' She turned to stare at the widow as Agatha Brand's words slipped into her mind: 'Her husband died in unusual circumstances — medicinal dabblings . . .'

'What you need to do, girl, is trust me. The child should be away from all this and there's nowhere else she can go *except* Long Reach.' A heavy silence filled the room until Lucy said bleakly, 'I will pack Sarah's clothes.'

She picked up the lamp from the table and walked into the bedroom. The widow stood in the doorway. 'Funeral, day after tomorrow?'

Lucy nodded.

'Moana will come with us now. You want the coffin closed?'

'Yes.'

Ruby Gaunt moved back into the kitchen and Lucy heard the lid being put in place.

~

Daniel had long since retired, wearied by his grief. Lucy

sat beside the fire, her mind a kaleidoscope of fragmented images: Sarah's small frame seated beside the widow as they drove away; Adam's eyes accusing; the Scot's eyes bleak and damning. Adam blood-spattered; Daniel's tears; her tears; the battered teapot in the hut. The images whirled around in her head endlessly. She tried not to look at the coffin, but it was always in the periphery of her vision no matter where she stood or where she sat; a mute indictment against her, the condemnation in its silent presence palpable in the quiet kitchen.

Lucy bowed her head. Forgive me, Adam. My need of this man is a sickness in me. I want to go home, take our children home — forget him. Anger and grief were tangled together in her heart. If I am to obey you, I cannot go home; you have made my life impossible. In your wisdom, did you know you were making my life impossible?

Lucy rose from her chair and moved to stand beside the coffin. Placing her hand on the rough wood she whispered, 'I cannot obey you, Adam — forgive me.'

∾

They stood at the graveside in the grey and cheerless afternoon. The cold wind tore at their hair and clothes. Lucy clasped Daniel's hand as he wept silently beside her. Tom Masters stood next to Daniel and the Widow Gaunt was at Lucy's other side.

Sam Curry officiated, and his voice drifted in and out of Lucy's consciousness as she kept her gaze just short of the coffin.

The Lord is my shepherd, I shall not want . . .

She had not cried. Dry-eyed she stood there, and the irrelevant thought came to her that it must have been difficult to dig the grave in the frozen ground. She wondered, glancing briefly at the five men present, who had dug it.

McKenzie was not in evidence.

Though I walk through the shadows of the valley of death . . .

A horse snorted on the track below and harness jingled.

Lucy's mind turned inward again, reliving the slow procession down the hill, the coffin behind the high leather seat that she shared with the widow and with her son, and she remembered the other coffin that had sat on the floor of the cart behind that seat, just months before. She could see Ruben's grave, almost concealed by tussock and weeds, and she thought that it would not be long before Adam's grave was lost in the tussock too.

She was suddenly aware of silence. Sam Curry had stopped speaking and was looking at her. 'Will you say your good-byes now, my dear?'

Lucy drew Daniel close to the coffin and together they stood in silence. Briefly she placed her hand on the pine box, and when she stepped back Daniel moved with her, stumbling, his vision dimmed with his tears.

'Come.' The widow took their arms. 'It is over.' And she drew them down the hill to the cart. They rode in silence for a time, then Ruby Gaunt began to speak. 'I have talked with your people here and told them that you will be coming back with me to Long Reach for a while.' She held up a gloved hand. 'Now, before you say anything, I must tell you that young Sarah is in trouble.'

'What do you mean?' Lucy turned on the seat to stare at the rugged profile beside her.

'I mean that something ails the child beyond the death of her papa — seeing him die. She will not speak of it but remains closed away from everybody, almost cataleptic. I think you should be with her, you and the lad here.'

'Should she not come home rather than be in a strange place where everything is unfamiliar?'

'My opinion is that different surroundings may help her to disassociate herself from what has caused this, assuming that your husband's passing or something else on Chandler's Run has brought this about.'

'Then we must be with her.' Lucy looked at Daniel. 'There are things to attend to, the cow, the hens — will you—'

''Tis all in hand. Willie Good and young Pitchin will tend to the cow — she's almost dried off, isn't she? — and the hens and your bit of garden, so all yer'll need ter do is pack yer things an' we'll be on our way.'

The house stood on a plateau high above the plains, its high gables giving it an imposing appearance. It was built of timber and cob, and a wide veranda ran around three sides. Smoke rose from several chimneys, and as the cart halted beside a wide side door people seemed to come from everywhere. The cart was unloaded and driven away, and, as they followed the widow indoors, their bundles were taken from their hands by a young Maori woman whose black hair fell in braids to her hips.

'Go with Parani,' Ruby Gaunt said. 'She will show you where you'll be sleeping.' An older Maori woman hovered in the dimness of the hall.

The room was austere but clean. Lucy was vaguely surprised to see lace at the windows and a snowy counterpane on the bed. She unfastened her cloak and, draping it over the high footboard, she went to the ewer and basin standing in a corner of the room and splashed water over her face. In the mirror above the cabinet she looked pinched and white. Smoothing her hair quickly, she turned to the door. Daniel and the young Maori woman were waiting, and together they went downstairs.

In the small parlour, Sarah sat on a chintz sofa, a book in her lap. She was not looking at the book but at something beyond the window, and she did not move or speak as Lucy and Daniel entered the room. Moana was sitting beside the fire, her fingers busy with her sewing, stilled for the moment as she smiled a welcome. Lucy sat beside her child and reached to take her hand. 'Hello, pet, are you having a nice holiday with Mrs Gaunt?' The words sounded trite in her ears.

The girl nodded.

'We have missed you, so we have come to stay for a few days.'

Daniel picked up the book from Sarah's lap. 'This looks like a jolly book — are you using this for your lessons?'

Sarah did not reply and her eyes slid past Daniel to gaze

beyond him through the window again.

'Won't you talk to us, Sarah — are you not happy to see us?'

There was absolutely no response to Lucy's questions, and Sarah, withdrawing her hand, moved surreptitiously away from Lucy's closeness. At that moment Ruby Gaunt entered the room. 'Cook has made a seed cake and there are bowls to be scraped.' Her voice was raised slightly, as though she spoke to someone with impaired hearing.

'Run along, lass, and take your brother with you.'

Sarah stood up and moved towards the door without enthusiasm.

The widow lowered herself into a chair.

'Did the child speak to you?'

'No. It is almost as though she would rather we hadn't come.'

'Hmm. Well perhaps Daniel will be able to penetrate the barrier she has erected; children have more insight than we give them credit for. Let us wait and see. Now, shall we have our tea?'

Parani padded into the room on silent feet and placed a tea tray beside the older woman, and Lucy focused now on Ruby Gaunt with some surprise. The widow had changed her rough attire for a long black skirt and black leather slippers. Her thin hair was no longer covered by the battered hat, but was drawn back into a tidy bun. A soft cream shawl was caught in a fine cameo brooch below a high black collar, and her words, though deep and gravelly still, were those of an educated woman. It seemed she could abandon the local vernacular and rough exterior to pour tea in her own parlour.

'With lambing season beginning, I will not be able to be with you as often as I'd wish, but enjoy your days at Long Reach nevertheless and try not to worry too much about the child.' The widow turned to the young Maori woman. 'Moana will be close by should you need anything.'

Sitting in this room, taking tea with this unusual woman, Lucy imagined she could be back in her own country. The furnishings, the paintings on the walls, even the bellows reflecting the fire on the hearth were English, but as her gaze rested on Moana she knew that the illusion of civilization was only that, an illusion that could not disguise the treacherous beauty of this wild country. Nor could a few trappings from home disguise the fact that there were forces in this place that were a constant threat to survival. Suddenly, Lucy was deeply homesick. I need to go home, she said to herself. I need to take Sarah away from this trouble that plagues her; take her back to the people and places she has known all her life where she can be well again. Dear God, let us go home.

Ruby Gaunt watched the face of her guest and perceived something of the misery she was feeling. She did not speak but waited quietly until Lucy, sensing the widow's eyes on her, turned and said quietly, 'I don't know how to help my child. She has gone beyond my reach.'

'For the present she is closed to all of us, Lucy, locked in shock, the nature of which we can't even guess. There *is* a key to her illness, and with patience and understanding we will find it, but be prepared — it could take a while.'

'How can you know this?'

'Past experience, Lucy. Take heart, girl, and keep her days as normal as you can. Don't let her sense your own turmoil.'

Lucy stared at the older woman. Abruptly she stood up, placed her cup and saucer on the tea tray and went to stand at the window. She was facing the terrain they had covered earlier in the day. Somewhere to the north, two hours' cart-ride away, were Chandler's Run, Adam's grave and James McKenzie — and pain, grief, bitterness and shame. Turmoil? Yes, it was all there, two hours away, to be faced again in a few short days.

'Would you care to go up and rest, Lucy?' The widow broke in on her thoughts. 'Dinner is at eight o'clock.'

'Yes, thank you.'

'With your permission, I will speak to Daniel about Sarah.'

'Yes, of course. I do not know how to speak of his sister to him.'

~

Birdsong outside the window awakened Lucy. A rime of frost edged the windowpanes and the muted bleating of sheep was the only sound to disturb the deep quiet. The fire that had burned in the grate the evening before had gone out and the room was cold.

She lay against the pillows, her mind going back to the previous evening. Sarah had sat with Daniel, herself and the widow at the long dining table, eating without appetite, answering dully when spoken to. When Lucy bent to kiss her goodnight the child had stood stiff and unresponsive, then followed Moana from the room in silence. Ruby Gaunt had watched but not commented. Again Lucy wondered who this woman was. In retrospect she could not reconcile the woman who had sat at table with them the evening before with the creature who dressed like a man, worked like a man and swore like a man. Here was an anomaly that left her perplexed and uneasy. Pushing back the covers, Lucy rose from the bed. She dressed quickly, washed and tidied her hair, then went in search of Daniel.

Five bedroom doors stood open, the rooms unoccupied, so she turned to the stairs. In the lower hall, three closed doors were on her right and Lucy couldn't recall which one opened into the parlour. She paused at the first door, then moving on she knocked softly on the second. When nobody answered she turned the knob, and slowly pushing the door open she found herself standing on the threshold of a large room furnished with dark leather chairs and sofas, and thick Persian rugs. Polished floors reflected the colours of a striking stained-glass window that rose up to a high cathedral ceiling. The room was bitterly cold; no warming fire burned in the wide grate.

'So ye've risen.'

Lucy started as the rough familiar voice spoke at her elbow.

'I'm sorry, I did not mean to pry. I hoped to find the children or Moana.'

'Yer'll not find Moana in this room,' the widow said grimly. 'Silas Gaunt met 'is end in 'ere.'

Again she wore her rough garb, her speech in accordance. The steely eyes riveted Lucy's wavering glance and the widow barked her harsh laugh. 'Yer can ask if I did fer 'im an' I can mebbe tell yer the truth or I could mebbe lie — which shall it be, eh?'

Reaching a gloved hand past Lucy, she pulled the door shut.

'Yer'll be wantin' yer breakfast.' The widow took Lucy's elbow and steered her down the hall. There she opened another door and pushed Lucy through.

'Help yerself from the sideboard ther' — I'll join yer when I've cleaned up.' And she was gone.

Lucy approached the array of dishes with diffidence and lifted the lids of two chafing dishes. One contained broiled kidneys and bacon; the other, porridge. There seemed to be no one else about; no sound came from behind the adjoining door. Feeling rather unreal, Lucy spooned a little porridge into a dish, added milk and sugar, and carried it to the table. Ruby Gaunt's words were in her ears as she sat down, and the craggy, unrelenting face glared up at her from her plate. Suddenly her appetite was gone. Where were the children? Lucy stood up. They should leave — and quickly.

The door opened and the widow strode in. 'Sit, girl — tuck in. Breakfast is a meal I look forward to, starting my workin' day afore dawn. That ther' on your plate wouldn't feed a fly.'

'Where are the children?'

'Fed already, I expect, an' gone off with Moana.'

'I think we should return home.'

At the sideboard, Ruby Gaunt continued to pile food on to her plate.

'Today—'

The widow turned sharp eyes on Lucy. 'Sit down, girl — eat yer breakfast. We'll find yer children when we've eaten.'

Lucy remained standing, staring at the woman's set face; and Ruby Gaunt stood, plate in hand, waiting, unbending, for Lucy to do her bidding. There was an odd dignity in the widow's stance — and anger.

Slowly Lucy took her seat, irresolute and apprehensive.

When the meal was over, the Widow Gaunt rose to her feet and, standing very erect, spoke in a low, harsh voice. 'We will search out your children now and then I shall endeavour to lay to rest one of many ill-founded myths — a courtesy I have extended to nobody else. If, then, you still wish to leave, I will not detain you.'

Ruby Gaunt seated herself opposite Lucy beside the newly lit fire. The silence in the room was palpable, the cold bone-chilling, and an atmosphere of something equally chilling hung in the air. The face of the older woman seemed to have collapsed as she stared into the sputtering flames, collecting her thoughts. Then, still staring into the fire, she began slowly to speak.

'You are aware that Moana does not talk even though she has a fair understanding of the English language.'

'Yes.'

'At age fifteen I brought her into this house to train her as my housemaid. Mrs Samuels, my housekeeper, kept an eye on her and she learned our ways quite quickly, except for one thing.' Here the widow's lips twitched slightly. 'She had her own small room off the kitchen, but she never learned to sleep in the bed.' Still staring at the fire the Widow Gaunt went on, her voice very low. 'On a cold winter's day, Moana was sent to the woodshed to bring in wood for the kitchen fire. She did not return. Rewi, who did odd jobs about the place in those days, found her in the woodshed drowning in her own blood. He and Moana had what we would call an understanding, and when he carried her in to me he was in a terrible state: she had been raped, you see, and her tongue had been cut out so that she could not tell.'

'Dear God,' Lucy breathed.

'We fought for the girl's life for nearly five weeks. She had lost a dangerous amount of blood and her state of shock was deep.' The widow stopped speaking for a moment as she remembered, then continued, 'At my bidding, Rewi took word back to his village that Moana had contracted a white man's disease that was both serious and contagious; a tale designed to keep people away, because after six weeks it was obvious that the girl was pregnant and it was Rewi's fear that she would be banished from the tribe. At the end of nine weeks, when she was stronger, Moana and Rewi agreed that I should terminate the pregnancy, which for reasons of my own I was anxious to do.'

Lucy studied the older woman's profile in silence for a time, then said slowly, 'You *are* a doctor then?'

'No. But that is another story.' The widow leaned forward in her chair to place more wood on the fire. 'Moana went home to her village for a while when she was well again and her people accepted that she had lost her tongue as a result of her illness. When, after several weeks, Rewi brought Moana back to continue her employment, she would not venture outdoors or remain alone indoors, which strengthened the suspicion I was already harbouring.'

Ruby Gaunt pressed an index finger to her temple, then, leaning back in her chair, went on. 'When some time had elapsed, I asked my little housemaid if she would like me to teach her her letters — you may guess my reason for doing this — and so our lessons began, an hour each day when her morning duties were done. Mrs Samuels had gone for her afternoon nap and Cook was ensconced in her kitchen, the house otherwise empty — this was our time.'

The widow stood up suddenly and walked to the centre of the room to stand looking down at the rug at her feet. 'The girl learned quickly and very soon could write her name and a few simple words. We were thus occupied one afternoon at the table there when Silas Gaunt burst into the room, his musket aimed at Moana, his face scarlet with fury and his eyes on me. "I know what ye are about, ye ugly bitch," he shouted, "but ye'll not!" And he stormed towards us with his finger on the trigger. One more step he took—' Ruby Gaunt stopped speaking. Still looking down at the rug, she pushed her booted toe under its edge.

'One more step and he caught his toe and was falling, the musket butt slamming down against the floor, his finger still tight on the trigger. The ball went in under his chin and took the back out of his head.'

Slowly the widow walked back to her chair and sat down, facing Lucy now. 'They took me away, though for lack of evidence and motive they had to release me — but the dirt stuck.'

'Why did Moana not use her learning to spell out what had happened?'

'At that time she had not learned to string words together and her unintelligible cries when they were taking me away would have served only to make her appear addled. However, last year, when the police were here due to your trouble, McKenzie climbed up to the cornice there and dug out a flattened musket ball which, when presented to the sergeant, gave credence to my story. But, as I said, dirt sticks.'

Day followed day and Lucy made no further mention of leaving. She saw little of Ruby Gaunt but much of Sarah, on the widow's advice.

'Continue her schoolwork, go for long rambles, sing songs at the piano' — Lucy had not noticed the piano in the big living room — 'do anything you can think of that will draw her mind outside herself.'

'I wish I had your knowledge in these matters, a knowledge which I feel cannot be put down to experience only.' Lucy's glance was quizzical.

'I will not equivocate, girl. If there is time before you go home I will explain, on the understanding that my confidence is respected.' The widow had grimaced her strange smile. 'I'm somewhat partial to the title of *witch*, you see.'

When the weather permitted, Lucy and the children walked over the lower pastures. There were many lambs among the sheep, and Lucy gave a fleeting thought to the lambs that would be on Chandler's Run. They did not venture where cattle wandered free among the flax and cabbage trees on the flats further away.

Moana took them to a walled garden at the rear of the house on one of their walks, and at the sight of it Sarah showed the first signs of emerging from her withdrawn state. She wandered among the bluebells, violets and pansies — English flowers all — her closed expression momentarily absent. Homesickness flowing over her, Lucy sat down on the damp stone bench and watched Sarah wander about the garden, randomly picking flowers.

'Is Sarah getting better, Mama?' Daniel sat down beside her.

'It's hard to tell, Daniel. Sometimes she seems to be, but at other times I feel she is much the same.'

'When do you think we might go home?'

'I think we must go quite soon, Daniel,' Lucy said thoughtfully.

The homestead was nearing completion and soon the builder would be gone. Before that occurred, Lucy had a letter to write to John Hamilton, and she would entrust that letter to Sam Curry to deliver. As well, Nobby Clark was due any day and she must have her order ready in case they were unable to quit Chandler's Run.

'I will discuss our return with Mrs Gaunt when next the opportunity presents itself, although she may not be able to spare the time just now to take us home.'

∼

Lucy raised the question of returning home two mornings later when the widow put in one of her rare appearances at breakfast.

'Aye, there'll be much to do over there now — yer'll not want to delay longer.'

'Will Sarah be well? Eventually?' Lucy asked the question that tormented her.

'We'll hope so, girl — just wish we could 'ave rooted out the cause. Her recovery would be certain then.'

The night before they were due to leave Long Reach, Ruby Gaunt joined Lucy at the piano. After a while she reached over Lucy's shoulder and picked out a melody with one finger. 'Do you know this?'

Lucy nodded.

'Shift over, then.' The widow's gnarled hands moved with surprising dexterity over the keys as she played the introduction. 'Sing,' she nodded at Lucy. The song came to its end and Ruby Gaunt said, 'Ye've a sweet voice, girl. We'll do this again, but now—' She swivelled around on the piano seat. 'You young 'uns get off ter bed, yer mama an' me want ter talk.'

Sarah had sat beside the fire throughout the evening, brooding into the flames. Now, slowly, she stood up and walked from the room, ignoring her mother's outstretched hand. Lucy turned troubled eyes on the older woman, who shook her head slightly. 'Tis plain she does not want to go home, my dear, but she will have to face it sometime — we can only wait and see.'

Daniel said goodnight, and when they were alone the Widow Gaunt indicated the chairs flanking the fireplace. Leaning forward in her chair, she placed a log on the glowing coals and was silent for a moment, watching the shower of sparks disappear up the chimney. Then she turned to Lucy. 'I will tell you my story now, if you would care to listen. Honesty and trust are necessary ingredients in any friendship and I think that you and I, Lucy, will in time become friends. So now, in confidence, I will speak.'

Lucy sat, her hands resting in her lap, her attention on the ugly, seamed face opposite, and waited.

'I am the product of a genteel background,' the widow began. 'You will have guessed this. My father was a doctor, as was his father before him, and I, though female, was an only child and so hoped to follow my father into the profession. During the fourth year of my training, I met Silas Gaunt. He was something of a rolling stone, a handsome fellow, and five years my junior. My father disliked him on sight but I was besotted with him, and against my father's advice we began courting.' She ceased speaking for a moment, her slitted eyes reflecting the fire. Then she faced Lucy. 'You are wondering why a young man endowed with the countenance of an Adonis would pursue such as me, but pursue me he did. Soon after our marriage, the reason became clear: he had a habit you see — opium — and I was to be instrumental in obtaining the drug for him under threat of his leaving me if I did not comply.'

'You did not, of course, do as he demanded?'

'Ah, but I did. As I said, I was besotted with him, could not see past my need of him. In the end, I was caught. My father set a trap for Silas, assuming it was he who was the thief, but caught his daughter instead. My father disowned me on the spot — my career in medicine was ended.'

'Surely your father understood that you were under duress — extreme duress!'

Ruby Gaunt barked a derisive laugh. 'Not he! And Silas, in fear of the law, set sail for the colonies. Fool that I was, I went with him.'

A log rolled forward in the grate and the widow pushed it back quickly with her foot, then, leaning back in her chair, her hands spread on its arms, she looked across at Lucy. 'We arrived in this country the year after the natives signed a treaty with the Crown, but we lived in fear of our lives. We had disembarked at a place where it was rumoured that cannibalism was the rule rather than the exception, and we left that place in haste, heading south in a bullock-drawn wagon, arriving eventually in a place named Akaroa. We found lodgings of a sort, and a source that supplied Silas with opium. Our money was fast disappearing when I happened to overhear some men talking of the high country and a system of leasing land, endless acres of it, to run sheep. I found out where one went to apply for a grant, but, being a woman and an unappealing one at that, I was not taken seriously. That was the moment when I decided to don male apparel.'

'Your husband, could he not have applied for the grant?'

'My dear, his only interest was in feeding his habit and frequenting the drinking houses. I went with him to these places, and, by listening and asking questions, I learned the rudiments of making a living running sheep, where to obtain them and what my initial outlay would cost me.'

Ruby Gaunt glanced down at her gnarled hands and sighed. 'We were told that the Maoris up here were friendly. That was good enough for me. For the first two years we lived in a raupo hut, the most basic of dwellings; no doors or windows, no fireplace — dirt floor, much like your beginnings. I worked like a man with only native help, and the only white faces I ever saw were the shearers each January. And Silas — until his supply of opium needed replenishing — then he would be gone for weeks at a time.'

With dawning respect and a sense of awe, Lucy looked at the older woman. 'Were you not terribly afraid — living up here, a woman, mostly alone?'

The widow laughed harshly. 'In appearance and deportment I was no longer a woman, and I found life to be much easier once I had adopted the male role. I learned to swear and roar as well as any of my rough counterparts, and it served me well. Even Silas walked with care around me, although I never could get him to do a day's work. He was a leech and an addict and I accepted him as such, giving him just enough money to ensure that he kept out of my way.'

The widow sat silent, reflecting on the past, then she continued. 'After eight years of hard toil, Long Reach was firmly established and flourishing. Having sent home for the materials that were unobtainable in this country, the house, much as you see it today, was finished. Built by old Tom Butland — he's gone now. And from that time on I fed most of my profit back into the land and stock. A large part of Long Reach is now freehold.'

'Does your father know what you have accomplished?' Lucy asked softly.

'No, my dear, and he never will, presuming he is still alive. Nor will he ever know how I practise medicine, without qualification or the instruments of the civilized world.' She barked her harsh laugh again. 'He would be mortified to see me funnelling kerosene into a child who has eaten the tu tu berry, or to see me inoculating children with cowpox to prevent them dying of the smallpox which is prevalent here—'

Ruby Gaunt rose to her feet and stood, looking down at Lucy.

'I have told you my story, knowing I can trust you to keep my origins in confidence, and in the hope that we might be friends.'

Lucy stood up too and extended her hand. 'I will be proud to be your friend, Ruby Gaunt. I am indeed privileged to know you.'

Chapter 10

THE CART RATTLED and creaked its ponderous way up the hill, and as they passed Adam's burial place the impact of what returning here could mean hit Lucy like a clenched fist to the stomach. She cast a furtive glance at the woman beside her. Was she destined to become like Ruby Gaunt, hard-bitten, coarsened by hard work and the harsh climate, ever-lonely? Lucy looked back at Sarah huddled in the bed of the cart. The child's face wore a mask of misery, and as they drew nearer to the hut her expression became hunted. Daniel touched her arm. 'It's all right, Sarah,' he said quietly.

The widow drew the horses to a halt and, turning on her seat, reached a gloved hand to the child. 'Up here, girl, 'tween yer mama and me — quick now.'

Sarah hesitated, then slowly made her way forward to sit hunched on the high seat as they drove on, not looking at the hut as they approached it, not realizing they had driven past it, until she heard the widow's voice. 'Willie Good an' 'is merry men 'ave moved into yer old dwelling — more convenient 'e says, an' it leaves the huts fer the shearers.' She cleared her throat. 'Took the liberty o' movin' yer bits an' pieces up to the homestead — piano needs tunin', by the way.'

Lucy stared at the craggy profile, then suddenly she was laughing. 'Ruby Gaunt — will you ever cease to amaze me?'

Daniel seated on the side of the cart stood up suddenly, pointing ahead. 'Look at the lambs, Mama, there must be hundreds of them — look! But I can't see the mare — or Ruby — can anyone see them?'

'You'll not see yer cow, lad,' the widow grunted. 'She's found 'erself a fancy man down in my bottom pasture.' She glanced at Lucy and flicked the reins along the horses' backs. 'Pick up yer feet yer great tired things, we've not got all day.'

'When will Ruby come home?' Daniel persisted.

'When she's a calf in 'er belly,' was the blunt reply.

Quietly, Daniel digested this, then turned his gaze towards the homestead.

'That wasn't there when we left!' he exclaimed. 'Look, Mama, Sarah!'

A long, deep veranda had been built along the front of the homestead, and Sam Curry stood on its wide steps awaiting them. Beyond the homestead, two horsemen were riding across the lower pasture. Lucy looked away quickly; she had no desire to see McKenzie if he was one of them.

'Welcome home,' Sam Curry beamed. 'Good-day to you, Mrs Gaunt.'

The widow nodded and pushing back her hat she turned to Lucy. 'I'll not step down, my dear, but in a day or so I'll stop in to see how you're settling in.'

'We will look forward to that. Thank you, Ruby — for everything,' Lucy replied simply.

Sam Curry helped Lucy down from the cart and took their bundles from Ruby Gaunt's gloved hands. Daniel reached a hand up to Sarah, who still sat on the high seat. 'Are you coming down?'

'Ther's a few odds an' ends o' stuff I've no use fer,' the widow said gruffly, 'to tide yer over 'til yer can get yer own. Burn 'em if yer don't want 'em.'

With that, she raised a hand to the group on the ground, then turning the horses she set off on the long journey home. Lucy watched the widow's departing back for a moment and the builder watched with her. 'A fine woman is that,' he murmured.

There was a dignity in the straight back of the solitary figure that tightened Lucy's throat and brought a stiffening to her own spine. 'Yes, indeed,' she answered. 'Let us go in.'

A small fire burned in the parlour grate and the hearth was flanked by Adam's big chair on one side and Lucy's chair on the other. An ancient horsehair sofa faced the fireplace. The piano and their small bookcase were set against the wall opposite. A round wicker table stood beneath the big window that framed the mountains, and on its top was a potted fern. The floor of the room was raw white and, remembering the deep polish on Ruby Gaunt's floors, Lucy had a fleeting thought that this floor should be burnished in the same way.

Holding Sarah's hand, Lucy followed the builder across the hall, through the unfurnished dining room to the kitchen. Here stood a large trestle table and six chairs, scarred with age. Beside the fireplace was a sturdy sideboard and Lucy's chiffonier stood beneath the kitchen window. On the opposite wall a tall storage cupboard had been built, and before the hearth was a faded rag rug. Lucy's kettle sang on the hob.

'Your deal table and forms are in the lean-to, Mrs Chandler, as is a box of sundry dishes and such that Mrs Gaunt thought you might find useful. Now,' Sam Curry said cheerfully, 'would you care to see the bedrooms?'

The builder was enjoying himself. As they ascended the stairs, Lucy was feeling a little emotional: how kind people were. The builder was justly proud as he walked them from room to room; even she could see he had spared no effort in building this dwelling. And the widow must have made a number of treks across to Chandler's Run to bring all these items and move their belongings from the hut. She wondered when the widow had found the time, but in doing so she had endowed this empty place with a feeling of home.

Sam Curry opened the first door on the landing. The big iron bedstead faced the window and at its foot was one of the trunks. The second bedroom was bare except for a wooden trundle bed covered with a faded pink quilt, and the third room, Daniel's, was bare also except for his single bedstead.

Downstairs again, the builder turned to Lucy. 'Well, my dear, I have finished my work here, so unless there is something else you would have me do, I will be on my way in the morning before the rivers become too difficult to negotiate.'

'We will miss your cheerful company, Mr Curry,' Lucy said. 'And my husband would thank you as I do if he could see this homestead as it is now.'

'It has been my pleasure to build this home for you and your children, Mrs Chandler. Should you need my services again, I will be very happy to oblige. Here is my card; the address on there will find me eventually.'

He turned to Daniel and Sarah. 'Take care of your mama and each other, eh? One day, perhaps, I'll see you all again. Oh, yes —' he reached into his pocket a little diffidently and passed a folded sheet of paper to Lucy, 'my itemized bill, my dear. Settle in the morning if you wish.' He gave his kindly smile and turned to leave. 'Goodbye to you and be happy.' Then he was gone.

Lucy sat down at the trestle table and ran her eye down the column of figures. This will be the first substantial bill I have ever paid, she thought with a sense of pride. Then she froze. 'The box —' she whispered '— the box of sovereigns: where is it?'

'It will be here somewhere, Mama. It will have been carried up with everything else, I expect.'

'Then we must look for it. I'm sure if it were here we would have seen it!'

There were not many places a box of that size could hide, and after ten minutes of frantic searching Lucy had to accept that the box of sovereigns and the money-tin were not in the homestead.

'Shall I go down to the hut and ask Mr Good and Mr Curry, Mama?'

'Oh, Daniel,' Lucy cried, 'in the time we have been away the firewood will have been used and the box discovered — what am I going to do?'

'I don't understand — firewood, Mama?'

'I hid the box and the money-tin in the pile of firewood beside the hearth; that is why I insisted on wood being taken from the porch only. Our money should have still been safe . . .'

'If it has been found, Mama, nobody here would steal it. Let me go down and ask.'

'We don't really know any of these people, Daniel,' Lucy said quietly, the face of McKenzie swimming before her mind's eye. 'We don't know what they are capable of doing.'

Silence greeted her words, and into the silence came the tick of the carriage clock that was set on the mantelpiece above the hearth. All eyes turned to the sound at once and saw the folded piece of paper tucked behind it. Lucy reached up slowly and, taking it down, she unfolded it. With relief washing over her she read the brief message: *The trunk in your bedroom holds the things you treasure most*. It was not signed.

Without a word, Lucy ran upstairs and opened the lid of the trunk that stood at the foot of her bed. The clothes that had remained in the hut were wrapped about her crystal, her good china and her lamps; she had missed none of these. Carefully lifting the items out of the trunk, she placed them on the floor. Beneath the woollen blankets and an eiderdown were the box of sovereigns and the tin box, the contents of which remained undisturbed, with Adam's fob watch lying on top where she had placed it. She picked up the watch and looked at it dully for a moment then, placing it to one side and with a silent apology, she began to count out the money owing to the builder.

Later that night when the children had gone to bed, Lucy sat at the trestle table and wrote her letter to John Hamilton. When Sam Curry had delivered it, perhaps in a little while they would be able to leave this place. She wrote then the difficult letters to Adam's father and her parents.

Chandler's Run was the scene of much activity. Young life frolicked on the rolling hills and pastures, and the shearing shed was nearing completion, but Sarah had retreated into herself again and was aware of none of it. The nightmares began on their third night home and recurred with worrying frequency; nightmares that left the child wild-eyed with terror, incoherent and bathed in perspiration. During the daytime, Lucy tried to rouse Sarah from an apathy that was still close to being catatonic; Sarah performed her tasks with a dull acceptance which made Lucy's concern for her grow stronger daily. Ruby Gaunt admitted she had no answers.

One morning, Daniel said, 'Come for a walk, Sarah. It's too nice to stay moping indoors.' Listlessly, the girl followed him outside, but wouldn't budge further when he began to walk down the track towards the hut.

'Come on, Sarah — don't be an egg — there's nothing to bother you. What *is* the matter?'

Without replying, Sarah turned back to the veranda.

'Well, let's go up to the barn then.'

They walked slowly, Sarah dragging behind, not seeing the golden spring day or listening to her brother's chatter. They reached the barn just as McKenzie rode into view. 'Och there, Daniel, wou' ye gie a hand here?'

Two small lambs, bleating continuously, were carried in sacks, tied either side of his saddle. A third lay quiet across the Scot's knees. Gently he lifted it down and Daniel took it from his hands.

'Are these lambs orphans?'

'Aye, an' we've a ewe there wi' dead lambs.' McKenzie pointed.

'Would she look after these?'

'Wi' the scent o' her bairns on 'em, aye.' The Scot dismounted, and unfastening the sacks from his saddle he laid them down beside Daniel.

'Gie tha runt to ye sister, lad.'

He strode across to the ewe, picked up the two dead lambs, and brought them back and laid them beside Sarah, who eyed them uncertainly.

'Noo — wi' these pelts we gird tha mites, ye ken, an' tha ewe nae doot wi' be fuiled tha' the lambs ah her ain.'

He picked up a small carcass and Sarah averted her eyes. 'I don't want to do this,' she whispered.

'Ye wou' nae le' the wee beastie die?'

The Scot's keen knife skinned the dead lamb with a few deft strokes and Sarah's face blanched.

'Haud it still noo.' And he draped the skin over the lamb she held, leaving bloody smears over her hands. Sarah stared at the blood, her colour ghastly, then letting go of the lamb she turned abruptly and vomited on to the ground. Without haste, McKenzie tied the pelt securely to the small body and pushed it towards Daniel. 'Bide wi' it.' Then he placed a hand on Sarah's shoulder where she still crouched on the ground. 'I mind ye are troubled,' he said quietly. 'But we canna ge' inside ya' haid lass. Why winna ye speak — wha' are ye afeart of?' Gently he pressed her shoulder. 'Tell us, we fain wad ken.'

Sarah remained silent; shudders visibly passing through her, her eyes fixed on the blood on her hands.

''Tis tha blood, ah've nae doot,' the Scot persisted. 'Ah mind tha blood on ye face an' hands in yon howe — ya da's blood, ah ken.'

Sarah raised tormented eyes to McKenzie's direct gaze.

'Wa ye tell us noo wa' ails ye, lassie?' He pressed harder. The girl twisted away, clenching her hands, agonizing, not looking at him now, and the silent moments passed. The Scot remained still, waiting, his pale eyes compelling her to speak.

Sarah's whispered words came out of the silence: 'I killed Papa.'

Daniel crouched behind them, not seeing the ewe pushing at the lamb under his hand. He held his breath, shocked.

'Nae doot ye own ta it,' the Scot spoke softly, but said no more. Time passed and still he waited, his eyes never leaving the child's face. Then through white lips, Sarah began to wail.

'I didn't want to be left alone with him. He didn't look

274

like Papa any more. I was frightened — he began to make dreadful noises and he held on to my hand. He was staring at me, gobbling his blood — it splashed everywhere.' Her voice rose. 'It was on my hand — in my face — he wouldn't let go — I hit him and hit him — until he died.' The last words were barely audible.

McKenzie regarded the bowed head for a space then spoke softly, 'Ye canna kill wa' deith ha' a'ready claimed, lassie; he wou' nae be knowin' anythin' o' ye or o' this world.' He tilted the small face upwards and smiled his rare smile. 'Ya da' were clingin' ta tha han' o' the Lord, do ye ken, so he didna stray frae the guid path. I mind ye were afeart but ye cou' nae ha' killed ya da — he wa' a'ready gone.'

The sense of the Scot's words began to penetrate the haunted mists in Sarah's mind, and with the release from her horror the tears came; healing tears that ran their course while McKenzie cradled her in his arms.

'Be afeart nae mair, lassie, an' gang awa' hame noo,' the Scot said gently as he set her on her feet. As he watched her go, his gaze moved ahead to the homestead and his eyes grew cold.

~

Lambing season was over and the men paid, with the exception of McKenzie who was not to be found, thus obliging Lucy to walk down to the hut to leave his dues with Willie Good.

She had had no cause to enter the hut since their return to Chandler's Run and she felt a sense of dread as she approached its door. However, the cook had wrought such changes in its rough interior, and filled it with such appetizing aromas and warm cheerfulness, that Lucy had no difficulty crossing its threshold again.

McKenzie departed the following day, and any regrets Lucy might have felt at his going were diminished by the relief of not having to face him again until she was more in charge of her emotions. Now she felt she could visit Adam's grave at last. His dead eyes reproached her still, but slowly she was coming to terms with the memory and was better able to deal with it.

Knowing the children were in the barn tending orphaned lambs with Tom Masters, Lucy quickly picked snow berries and snow marguerites, put them in a tin mug and set off down the track. She trod quietly on the grass as she passed the hut, somehow reluctant to be seen, then hurried on, mindful of the water in the mug.

She seemed to have been walking for a long time and was wondering if she had missed the small hill when she recognized the stony path just discernible among the tussock and flax. She scrambled up to the top and slowly approached the mound of stone and soil where her husband lay. She stood looking down at the rough grave, the flowers in her hand forgotten, as in memory she passed through the years of their growing up, their courtship and marriage: the good times and not so good times, which had always been buffered for her by those who loved her. She lived again through the hardships of their time on Chandler's Run, through the tragedies and near tragedies which had occurred in the space of a few short months, and she remembered the wording of the letter she had sent to John Hamilton. She could not feel she was betraying Adam in the writing of it. They had come to this place for his health's sake; now he lay dead in a foreign grave, and by the drawing up of his will he had condemned his widow and his young daughter, with small compassion, to a life of struggle and loneliness in this wild and savage country. No, she could not feel she had betrayed him.

Somewhere above her in the clear blue of the sky a lark sang, and her memory swept her back to the green fields of home enclosed in their tidy stone walls; to the great oaks and wide carriageways and the tall elegance of her home; to the Adam fireplace in her drawing room, and she felt it was she who had been betrayed.

Lucy bent and placed the flowers on the grave, then stood erect and spoke aloud, 'I'm sorry, Adam, but when Mr Hamilton acknowledges my letter and the will goes through the due process to invalidate it, I will sell this place and its stock for Daniel. He will have his legacy, then I'll take the children home where we belong.' She turned then, and without looking back picked her way carefully down the path, wondering vaguely why, at this moment, she felt nothing: not grief, not anger, just emptiness. She had loved Adam; they had shared a gentle, considerate union, their children conceived in tenderness rather than passion. He had supported her and protected her always, which made the content of his will the harder to understand.

'Please God,' she muttered as she trudged up the track.

'I know I have sinned in my heart. Forgive me and let us be free of this place as quickly as possible.' When she had passed the hut, again on silent feet, she raised her eyes to the mountains. Cloud was wrapped about the glittering peaks like a scarf and at that instant the sun went in. A cool wind blew in her face as she neared the homestead, and she stopped for a moment to watch the sheep. They seemed undisturbed, moving uphill as they ate; a sign that rain was not yet imminent.

On entering the homestead, Lucy walked through the empty dining room into the kitchen. If things went as she was anticipating, she would not be needing to furnish the dining room or any of the other rooms. A small thrill of excitement went through her at the thought. The shearing would be followed by an early muster, and then she would arrange the sale of the stock and the property with John Hamilton. She sat down at the trestle table and, resting her chin on her hands, allowed herself to dwell on the prospect of going home to England.

'Hello, the house!' The familiar call broke into Lucy's reverie, and she heard the creaking approach of the cart as it came around to the back of the homestead. Lucy rose to open the door and greet the widow. Two cows were tethered to the back of the cart; one of them was Ruby.

'Did yer mean ter name yer cow fer me?' The widow cocked an eyebrow and Lucy laughed.

'If it pleases you to think so, lady, but I rather think the children named her for her colour.'

'Well, in any event, your Ruby cow is in calf an' this old girl here, while getting on a bit, is a good milker — yer welcome ter keep her until your cow has calved.' She untethered the animals as she spoke, and slapping their rumps with a gloved hand she asked, 'Kettle on?'

'It is, and thank you, we have missed having milk on the table.'

'How is young Sarah?'

'Did Mr McKenzie not tell you?'

'McKenzie? No, I have not seen him — what would he be telling me about the child?' Ruby Gaunt pulled a chair out from the table and plumped herself down.

'I assumed he'd left here to go on to Long Reach.'

'We will not see him until early January for the shearing, if indeed we see him then.'

Lucy poured the tea before she spoke, then, seating herself opposite the widow and leaving out no detail, she relayed Daniel's account of the events that had brought about Sarah's recovery.

'You must be vastly relieved, my dear, and grateful to McKenzie for having the nous to recognise what the problem was.'

'I am as grateful as it's possible to be under the circumstances,' Lucy answered in a low voice. 'He does not approve of me and clearly blames me for what happened.'

'I'm sad to hear this, Lucy, but I'd not take it to heart. He's a strange fellow in many ways and those of the fairer sex are not his favourite people, I've been told, but I think that under that hard-nosed exterior there hides a good man.' The widow held out her cup. 'Fill that again, girl, an' then I must be off.'

She sipped the strong tea. 'Ah, that's a good drop — have yer sorted out yer furniture an' such fer the house? Nobby says 'e left 'is catalogue wi' yer.'

'I have sent a letter to Mr Hamilton, Ruben's lawyer, with Mr Curry and await his reply. In it I have asked that Adam's will be overturned so that we may go home.' Lucy raised a hand as the widow started to speak. 'Adam has left Chandler's Run to Daniel in its entirety and he has charged me with overseeing the running of the property until Daniel reaches his majority — I have no rights whatsoever. If Adam's will cannot be overturned, we will have to stay here for years. Sarah will be terribly disadvantaged, as will Daniel. His education is at an end — I can take him no further; he will grow up in ignorance. As for myself . . .' Lucy's voice faltered.

Ruby Gaunt studied the younger woman in silence, then said, 'It is most unlikely that your appeal will fall on sympathetic ears in this man's world. Rather will your request be viewed as disobedience, a violation of the male domain, so prepare yourself for a refusal.'

'But surely,' Lucy rejoined hotly, 'Mr Hamilton, the judge, whoever decides these matters, must see that my situation here and my children's situation are impossible!'

'That may well be — I know little of these matters. For your sake, feeling as you do, my dear, I hope your letter is viewed with favour.'

The widow finished her tea and rose slowly to her feet, her face expressionless. 'I'll be off, then,' she rumbled. 'Want to be home afore dark.' She pushed her hat down on to her head and, without looking at Lucy, strode to the door. Lucy followed and watched as the big woman climbed up on to the cart, lifting her hand briefly as she turned the big horses around. Something about the solitary figure penetrated Lucy's preoccupation and she hurried after the cart.

'Mrs Gaunt — Ruby — wait!'

'Whoa.' The widow reined in and turned on her seat.

'I don't know what you must think of me. I am sorry — I have not considered your feelings at all.'

Ruby Gaunt did not reply.

'We are friends now, are we not?' Lucy went on. 'And if we are able to go home, back to England, come with us — sell Long Reach and make your peace with your father—'

The widow laughed abruptly. 'You don't know my father, girl, an' all else aside 'e's like to 'ave shuffled off by now — seventy-three 'e'd be.'

She picked up her whip and faced forward again. 'Ther's nothin' back ther' fer me, Lucy; this 'as been my home fer more'n thirteen years an' in my way I'm happy here.'

Out of respect for Adam Chandler's family, Christmas was not celebrated by the shepherds, but Willie Good discreetly delivered a dressed lamb and a brandy pudding to the homestead on Christmas morning. Over-warm in her widow's weeds, Lucy stood before the glowing hearth spooning the juices over the tender meat and blessed the man's kindness while her thoughts turned to home. It would be snowing there and the family would be gathered about their wide fireplaces celebrating Christmas, unaware that Adam was dead, unless her letters had found an early ship. There would be few willing to travel in the heat of summer, risking life and limb crossing broad rivers where quicksand could catch the unwary, battling swarms of sandflies, to bring John Hamilton's reply to her letter. She would be obliged to wait until Nobby Clark arrived at the beginning of winter.

Lucy contained her impatience as best she could, busying herself in her garden, sewing, mending, making sheets and tablecloths out of her empty flour bags and piling them in her cupboard ready to be spread out on the ground to bleach in the frost when the winter cold arrived.

The building of the shearing shed was completed and Lucy had walked through it with Ruby Gaunt. To Lucy's mind the shed was a bit like a church: the pens each side of the aisle were the pews and the long shearing platform at the end the altar; the only things to spoil the illusion were the chutes beyond the shearing platform.

'You'll get a goodly profit this year, girl — fifty-five, sixty thousand pounds of wool,' the gravelly voice stated. 'Yer must be pleased.'

Lucy nodded absently, remembering Daniel's enthusiasm and excitement as he'd joined the men to bring the wethers and the straying ewes down to the lower pastures to be shorn. He worked the hours the men worked, and at day's end both he and the mare, who had grown plump, were barely able to stand, but the next day he would be as keen to work as ever. She was dismayed by his adaptability and his enjoyment of life on Chandler's Run, and was forced to consider the prospect of his not *wanting* to return to England. Sarah too, surprisingly, had settled into life in the high country. It was she who had taken up the tedious task of skimming the cream from the milk each morning and kept the lean-to and kitchen scrupulously clean after butter- and cheese-making, washing shelves and tables with salty water to keep the flies away. It was she, too, who picked and cleaned the berries and stone fruit to make jam. Ruby Gaunt had shown Daniel how to make jam jars from empty bottles by heating an iron ring in the fire then placing it carefully over the neck and dipping the bottle into cold water. A sharp tap then separated the neck cleanly from the bottle. And so, after several burned fingers, Daniel had become expert at making jam jars. The widow also showed Sarah how to cover the filled jars by dipping squares of paper into milk and pressing the paper, still wet, across the top and down the sides of the jars so that when dry the paper made a strong air-tight seal.

'The results of yer next muster will surprise yer, I think.' The widow's words broke into Lucy's thoughts. 'Yer lamb numbers are well up on last year.' She chuckled as they turned to leave the shed. 'If yer not careful, girl, yer'll soon be needin' more territory an' more men ter work it.'

Lucy did not reply immediately, her mind turning to the Scot. He had not returned for the shearing, and she wavered between relief and longing.

'We've more than enough acres for a few extra sheep,' she said finally.

'Aye, but Ruben's fifteen thousand acres are shrinking with each lambing season. Keep in mind that yer wether requires one and a half ter two acres an' yer ewe only slightly less, so unless yer planning ter sell stock next lambing, yer'll be lookin' sooner rather than later.'

'Perhaps by next lambing it will be somebody else's decision,' Lucy replied.

They emerged into the late afternoon sun, and Lucy raised her eyes to the mountains set against an amethyst sky. The gullies and crevices were mauve deepening to purple, the western slopes a blinding copper, and as she looked she prayed she would not be here to gaze on the beauty of it next summer. The hot north-wester, which had been particularly trying today, was slowly dying away as the widow climbed up into her cart. 'Think about coming over for a few days before the garden is past its best,' she said. 'It'll help to pass the time 'til yer letter gets here, an' I'd best make the most of yer company while it's still available, eh?'

'I wish you could be persuaded to change your mind, Ruby, to come home and run your sheep in a civilized country—'

''Tis no good, girl, I'd stifle wi' postage-stamp fields and stone walls about me, an' I'm not about ter change me appearance or me ways — I'd not be accepted.'

'Then forget about sheep, finish your studies, become a qualified doctor.'

'Too old, lady — too old by far. No, I'll be stayin'; this wild place suits me — I can stretch out in all directions here an' bump nobody.'

'Then I'll press no more, but know that we shall miss you

sorely.' Lucy smiled her rare smile. 'Send the cart the day after tomorrow. We will come for a visit.'

When the widow had rumbled away, Lucy began to walk slowly back to the homestead. It seemed that, contrary to what she had said previously, Ruby Gaunt was now facing the possibility that the family might go home. This cheered Lucy enormously and she viewed the prospect with more confidence and a growing excitement. Of course they would go home; any other consideration would be ludicrous. She did not hear the larks or see the robins flitting ahead of her, or feel the vibrant life about her as she walked; her thoughts were in another place.

January was ushered in on a hot, blustery westerly, and low cloud moved along the main ridges hiding pockets of sheep on the higher ground. Daniel was excited; the shearing was soon to begin, and that morning, against her better judgement, Lucy had agreed to his joining the men to bring the sheep down, as long as he rode with one of them. She had checked his saddlebags several times to ensure that he was well prepared should the weather change, and Tom Masters and Jack Tanner had assured her that Daniel would be under the eye of one of them at all times.

After an early breakfast hurriedly eaten, Lucy watched the four riders canter towards the hills, Pitchin and Daniel in the wake of the two older men. Sighing, Lucy turned from the parlour window to begin her own day. From time to time she would stop what she was doing to look for Daniel and the mare, her gaze scanning the rough terrain up to and beyond the scrub-line, but there were only sheep to be seen.

'Are you worrying, Mama?'

'No, dear, of course not.'

'You were looking worried.'

'Daniel is with experienced men. He will be all right.'

At sunset, Lucy again stood at the parlour window, all pretence now gone. Deeply uneasy, she watched the westering clouds turn from pink to orange then to smouldering bronze; the tussock was a molten gold as the sun's red orb dipped slowly from sight. Soon it would be dark. Where was Daniel? She turned away and began to pace the floor. She should never have let him go — he was too young for this rough work. Sarah called from the dining room. 'There is a horse coming, Mama. I think it is Mr McKenzie — yes, and Friday.'

Lucy felt her pulse quicken. He had come back! She began to walk quickly to the front door. He had come back, and he would find Daniel as he had found Sarah, and — she halted, uncertain, remembering. She stood motionless behind the closed door, seeing again the cold blue stare. She lifted her hand from the doorknob and then stood listening to the horse canter past the homestead. She went back to the parlour to stand at the window again, and in the fading light she watched the Scot ride towards the barn. Then she saw Daniel, walking towards him leading the mare; he was home. She saw the tall figure lift the mare's offside foreleg and examine the hoof, then Daniel was leading the horse into the barn and McKenzie was back in the saddle, riding towards the hills.

'Come, Sarah, and set the table,' she said distractedly. The Scot was back. She did not ask herself why he was back, but she knew she did not want him here — did not want him here to undermine her determination to go home. Tensely she waited for Daniel to come in.

'Why has Mr McKenzie returned?' she asked sharply when he did.

'To help with the shearing, I expect.' Daniel raised his eyebrows at Sarah.

'We don't need him. There are more than enough people here.'

'Without me, Mama, there are only three. The mare has a stone-bruise and can't be ridden for a while. Last time, there were four to work the sheep.'

Lucy said no more, but prayed that Nobby Clark would bring the reply to her letter on his next trip, that there would be no delay.

The weather was holding and the shearing, according to Daniel who was never far away from the activities, was going well. The sheep in the yards and pens bleated and baaed incessantly, stretching Lucy's taut nerves to breaking point, and the dust and flies were an added trial. Deliberately, she kept distance between herself and the Scot, but at night, when the men were riding in on their way down to the hut, she sometimes heard the chestnut's distinctive ambling gait and her heart would beat faster. Angrily she promised herself that once they were safely home on English soil her obsession with McKenzie would become nothing but a nonsense and he a figure to be ridiculed. But this was a waiting time, an endless waiting time that had to be filled so that she was not tempted to find excuses that would cause her to cross his path. This was not easy to accomplish: in Lucy's mind everything she did in the homestead was temporary, and as a result her home-making activities were limited. With Sarah's help she bottled the peaches, the nectarines and the apples, and what was surplus to their requirements she enjoined Willie Good to take away to make his own pies and preserves. When the shelves in the lean-to were filled to capacity, that activity also ceased. Lucy was not of a mind to take up her embroidery or to reread the books in the small bookcase, and though on occasion she would sit at the piano to play simple airs from memory, the piano was so badly out of tune that the sound grated on her and that distraction also ended.

The shearing was finished and, as Ruby Gaunt had predicted, the wool clip was more than satisfactory. The flocks had moved up into the hills again, and Lucy now found the ensuing silence oppressive; her solitude under the brooding mountains was crushing her and she worked all the harder to fill the empty days. At night, overtired to the point where sleep eluded her, she would lie wide-eyed through the hours of darkness to fall asleep finally as dawn broke. She was in an emotional vortex with no way out, and as the days passed she became more brittle and more sharp-tongued.

'Why is Mr McKenzie still here?' she demanded of Willie

Good one day when he brought salmon from the river for their table. 'I'm not paying him to loll about in the hills, living off the fat of my land.'

Willie Good's round face sobered instantly. 'Eh, missus, nay, ye couldn't say farther from the truth. We've wild pig an' maraudin' dogs watchin' fer the chance ter worry yer sheep but McKenzie'll nay come down from them hills till 'e's shot every last one of 'em, be sure o' that.'

'I see. Then when he has done this, perhaps you would tell him to come and pick up his dues.'

''Tis never-endin', missus, there'll allus be summat ter prey on the flocks an' fifteen thousand acre is a biggish lump o' land fer three men ter watch over.' The cook had been concentrating on the brim of his hat, twirling it slowly in his plump fingers, but now he looked directly at Lucy. 'McKenzie an' 'is dog are the best ye'll ever find, missus — ye'd be wise ter keep 'im on, long as 'e'll stay — 'e'll save yer from big stock losses an' keep yer meat barrels full o' wild pig.' The blue eyes crinkled then. 'An' bein' a frugal kind o' feller, 'e don't eat much neither.'

Smiling a little in spite of herself, Lucy nodded. 'Very well, for the present we'll leave things as they are.' She thanked the cook for the salmon, then with a sigh returned to her butter-making. The day was very warm and, beat as she would, the butter would not turn. At last, losing patience, she scooped up the container and made her way wearily down to the river where she wedged it between rocks in the shade of the bank for the water to cool it.

On her way back to the homestead, she stopped to look

at her garden. Of the four rows of potatoes she and Daniel had planted, only one was left to dig and some of those must be saved for next year's planting if they had not left Chandler's Run by then. Ruby Gaunt had brought over a bag of kumara, the Maori sweet potato, to supplement their dwindling supply, but the family had considered them a poor substitute for the potato they had known all their lives. She would need to plant double the number of rows if they were not to run out again, she thought grimly, but God willing she might never need to grub in the dirt again.

The pumpkins and melons she saw were beginning to straggle among the rows of tomatoes, and as Lucy bent to pull them away she became aware of a horse approaching. She glanced up and her heart lurched as she saw James McKenzie riding towards her. Straightening up, she stood waiting until he reined his horse to a halt at the edge of the garden.

Lounging in his saddle he sat considering the vegetable patch, ignoring her, his demeanour clearly indicating that he had not paused to pass a friendly moment. The bitch Friday moved around her, sniffing at her boots, then losing interest began to wander among the pumpkins.

'Ge' oot!' the Scot said sharply and Lucy jumped. His pale eyes turned on her then, and covered her from head to foot with studied insolence.

Lucy felt her hackles rise. 'What is it Mr McKenzie, what do you want?'

'Nae wha' ye wad gie me,' he growled.

'I don't understand. What are you saying?'

'Aye, ye'll ken well enough nae doot.'

'I don't,' Lucy snapped, 'and I don't care for your attitude, sir. You'd best be about your business.'

With a humourless laugh, the Scot reined the chestnut about, whistled his dog and cantered off, leaving Lucy trembling and fighting angry tears. If he disliked her so much, she raged inwardly, why did he not spare both of them and move on?

Three days later he did.

Lucy had sent Sarah down to collect the eggs from the hen house and Daniel to fetch a leg of lamb from the meat barrel while she went off, bucket in hand, to dig some potatoes. That was where McKenzie found her. She did not hear his approach as she dug the potatoes under the hot sun and dropped them into her pail; was not aware of his presence until he spoke softly from behind her. 'Ah canna weel fix in ma mind which ye are, an' I fain wad ken — are ye a fuil or are ye a doxy?'

Lucy spun around, her cheeks scarlet. 'How do you dare to speak to me so!'

'Haud ya tongue.' The Scot towered over her. 'Did ye nae set yersel', brazen aye, tae owrhailet me, wi' ya twa een tellin' me o' tha pleasures ye wad gie tae me, an' ye'd nae own to the sin o' it, the puir mon doon there nae yet deid!' His hands were iron bands gripping Lucy's arms and she winced away from the fury in his eyes. Slowly, deliberately, he lowered his head and his mouth was crushing her own. She felt her anger drain away, felt her body melt against his, the longing in her banishing all resistance, until with brutal force he thrust her from him. 'Aye, 'tis a whore ye are, then,' he said in a low voice and Lucy's face blanched with shock.

She struggled then to free herself from his grip. 'Let go of me!'

'Nae, lass,' McKenzie drawled. 'Ye'll gang awa' wi me noo an' sure, ye body ah'll use as ye intended.'

Furiously Lucy began to fight, kicking, lashing out wildly with clenched fists while the Scot, holding her in a bruising embrace, laughed in her face. Then the toe of her New Zealand Company boot found its mark and, breathing an oath, McKenzie released her to clutch his shin. Lucy stepped back, her body rigid with outrage. 'I am no doxy, Mr McKenzie, but I admit to being a fool — and hear me now.' Her words fairly crackled. 'You will leave Chandler's Run and never, never return!'

In the pale eyes that were raised to hers there was anguish and no small measure of surprise, and Lucy glared back before turning on her heel to walk rapidly away, hating the tremor that had been in her voice, hating him and hating herself.

Chapter 11

ONLY A MONTH remained before the muster and Lucy knew she would have to do something about replacing James McKenzie with at least one extra musterer. She was reluctant to approach Ruby Gaunt for help, such was her shame and mortification over the Scot's behaviour, and she pondered the problem at length before she decided to take the initiative herself. Enlisting Jack Tanner as her guide and interpreter, she set off for the Ngai Tahu village to try again to persuade Ruben's former workers to return to Chandler's Run. Jack Tanner had difficulty hiding a grin as he assisted Lucy, in her long skirt, to mount the mare and try to ride decorously side-saddle on Ruben's heavy stock saddle. The mounting was a feat of comic ingenuity, but to remain sitting upright, one leg draped about the pommel, while the bombazine skirt billowed in the wind, causing the mare to baulk and shy, was in itself a remarkable achievement of balance. Tanner was obliged to cough a number of times to disguise his mirth.

The shepherd's Maori was only rudimentary. He spoke slowly and quietly to the snowy-headed chief and, pointing several times to Lucy, ended his request by smiling widely, spreading his hands and reassuring them: 'Everything ka pai now.' They waited while the chief sent someone to find the Maori Lucy sought, and when finally the men appeared they looked warily at the two Pakeha. When the chief had finished speaking to them, the men shook their heads with finality. The elderly Maori turned to Lucy and Tanner, and it was clear from his expression that they had failed. He spoke briefly to the shepherd; Tanner answered as briefly and the visit was over.

'What did the old man say, Mr Tanner, and what did you say in reply?' Lucy asked as they turned for home.

'Seems, missus, that those three lads were caught fair in the middle o' those raidin' devils an' carried along wi' 'em in the excitement until someone spotted 'em and tried to run 'em over t' edge o' the gorge.' The shepherd relapsed into silence.

'Did they tell you that Ruben Chandler was sent to his death that way?'

'Didn't say, missus, but they did say that they'd not work on yer run again 'til all the Rafferty brothers were dead.'

They rode on for a time until Lucy reined the gelding to a halt. 'There is another village not too far away, I believe. Do you know of it?'

'Nay, missus, an' effen I did, wouldn't make no nevermind — word'll 'ave travelled far an' wide by this time — like as not yer run is tapu now.'

'What does that mean — tapu?'

'Don't rightly know — means keep orf or summat.'

❧

After two near-incidents on the way home, Tanner delivered his mistress safely to her front steps where Ruby Gaunt, propped against the veranda post, her hat tipped over her eyes, awaited her.

'Been fraternizing with the help?' she asked, sitting up and pushing her hat to the back of her head.

Flushing, Lucy was obliged to explain.

'And are they comin' ter work fer yer?'

'It would seem not.' Lucy slipped awkwardly from the saddle and began to tie the reins to her stirrup.

"E'll roll on that, girl, an' split yer saddle tree, an' how in God's name yer didn't break yer neck ridin' like that I'll never know — 'ere, leave that ter me. Go an' put the kettle on.'

The kettle was simmering on the hob when Lucy entered the kitchen. As she set up the cups, she could hear Daniel and Sarah playing a game in the parlour that was causing some merriment. Listening to their laughter, she wondered how safe they really were; was it possible that the Rafferty brothers, or someone like them, could someday prey on them again?

The widow kicked her boots off in the kitchen doorway and dropped a roll of something on to the floor. 'Couple o' cowhides yer might like fer the parlour floor.' She plumped herself down at the long table. 'Now, gettin' back ter yer labour shortage; if yer can't get more workers, yer'll 'ave ter manage wi' your four fellas 'til I can spare some o' mine — take a bit longer is all.' She sipped at the hot tea and added, 'McKenzie an' 'is hound do the work of two anyhow.'

Into the silence that followed the widow's words Lucy

said quietly, 'McKenzie is no longer here.'

The widow raised her eyebrows. 'Yer tellin' me 'e's moved on right afore musterin'?'

'I had to put him off.' Lucy did not meet the older woman's eyes. 'I did not care for his manner.'

Ruby Gaunt digested this for a moment, then grunted and shook her head. ''E's somethin' of a rebel, an' antisocial ter the point o' rudeness, I grant yer, but 'tis a shame yer couldn't overlook 'is shortcomin's. 'E's a grand worker.'

'So people keep saying,' Lucy muttered.

'Well then, looks certain yer goin' ter need my boys, so they'll be across soon as they've finished my place. Put yer back some, 'avin' ter wait, but yer'd be late finishin' anyway wi' only three men.'

The widow finished her tea and, after unrolling the hides for Lucy to admire, she took her leave. A moist southerly wind blew in Lucy's face as she stood on her veranda and watched the cart trundle away down the track. Looking up to the mountains, she saw skiffs of early snow on the higher ground; winter was on its way and any day now Nobby Clark would be arriving. Lucy knew she was measuring her incarceration in the high country in months rather than years, and in doing so was setting herself up for intolerable disappointment should the decision from John Hamilton go against her expectations, but she would not contemplate a time when all hope was gone, when her destiny would be irrevocably sealed. She continued to count each day as one less to be spent in this place, and in this way she kept her spirits up.

~

The muster began on the first day of May and Ruby Gaunt's projected estimate promised to be correct. 'Yer've a decision ter make now, girl,' she rumbled. 'Either yer'll 'ave ter sell off some stock or risk over-grazin' yer land, which in time will reduce yer numbers anyway — or lease more land ter support yer increase.'

'I can make no decision at this time, as you very well know, Ruby.'

'Aye, an' if it's guts an' determination that'll set yer on yer way, yer'll be goin' home right enough.' The leathery countenance was sober. 'Well, yer'll not 'ave much longer ter wait.'

The two women were in the lean-to, and the widow was seated at the deal table watching Lucy make her butter. Then the older woman began to chuckle.

'They'll not believe yer when yer tell 'em at home that yer made yer own butter an' cheese an' had ter clay yer cookin' hearth yerself an' roast bloody lumps o' meat on that hearth ter feed yer empty bellies.'

'I think perhaps I'll tell them as little as possible about much of what we have to do here to survive. If I am to hold my head up in society again, I think I must learn to fib.'

At that moment Daniel burst through the doorway. 'Mama, Ruby's having her calf — can't you hear her bellowing — come and see!'

'Where is she?' Ruby Gaunt asked.

'In the barn. Sarah's there too.'

'Oh,' Lucy cried. 'Oh, she mustn't be! Wait, I have to change my shoes — oh, bring her away, Daniel!'

'Don't take on, girl. Will do the child no harm to see Ruby birth her calf — she's seen lambs come, hasn't she?'

'Of course not.'

'She has, Mama,' Daniel corrected, 'and she hasn't been worried.'

'*I* am worried,' Lucy snapped. 'It's unseemly for a young girl to be exposed to—'

'Don't be shuttin' the stable door after the horse has bolted, Lucy. Come, let's see what the girl is goin' ter deliver.'

Daniel and the widow left the lean-to. Lucy, pulling on her shoes, followed more slowly. On entering the barn she stood for a moment while her eyes adjusted to the gloom, and then Daniel called from somewhere to her left, 'Over here, Mama.' She moved towards the dim outline of the cow and of figures bending over something lying in the straw. 'You've a bonny heifer calf, Lucy,' Ruby Gaunt announced as Lucy went closer to her daughter and peered into the young face.

'Look at her long eyelashes, Mama,' Sarah whispered. Lucy relaxed: the birthing of Ruby's calf had harmed her not at all. The widow was right — and this was something else that would not be told to the folks at home.

'She is very pretty, dear.' Lucy smiled as she watched the little animal struggle to gain its feet on gangly legs that buckled fore and aft, until at last it stood uncertainly, measuring the distance between itself and Ruby's udder.

'This 'un'll not starve.' The widow chuckled. 'An' I'd best be on my way. I'll pick up the old cow next week some time — see me off, girl.'

Halfway to the homestead, Nobby Clark's team came into sight, the big animals pulling the heavy cart laboriously up the track.

'There yer are, then.' Ruby Gaunt's voice was low. 'You go on — I'll get me cart out of the way.'

Almost running, Lucy hurried towards the approaching wagon and prayed that it would be carrying the letter that would release them. Her heart was pounding as she forced herself to wait circumspectly before the homestead to greet the teamster and direct him around to the back door. The unloading began while Lucy made the tea and buttered thick slices of bread, spreading them liberally with raspberry jam. Her movements were jerky and distracted, impatience seething within her until Nobby Clark's bulk filled the doorway and he thrust a bundle of newspapers and letters at her.

'Come in, Mr Clark, come, sit here and have your tea.'

'All t'same ter you, missus, I'd as lief sup out ther'.'

'As you wish.' Lucy took the papers and letters from the giant, and picking up the mug of scalding tea she followed him outside. 'Sarah, bring the plate, please.'

Conversation was not necessary as Lucy waited to refill the mug; the big man was interested only in the food before him and getting his next delivery done before dark. Daniel came down from the barn to help with the last of the unloading and to water the horses, chatting guilelessly with the taciturn man, seemingly able to interpret the grunts and rumbles as they worked.

At last the team was again hitched to the wagon and the

teamster paid, and Lucy hurried inside. She riffled swiftly through the letters until that which she sought was in her hand. With trembling fingers, she broke the seal and quickly scanned the stilted wording. Daniel came through the kitchen doorway as several words leapt at her from the page: *Gone through probate . . . appeared to be of sound mind . . . see no reason to revoke it . . . wonderful opportunity for your son.* Words that sent Lucy's hopes crashing.

'Mama, you haven't given Mr Clark next year's order.'

'What?' Lucy looked blankly at her son.

'Next year's order, Mama. Mr Clark wants our order for next year.'

'Order?' Oh — dear God — we are not going home.' Lucy suppressed a senseless urge to laugh and forced herself to speak calmly, 'Yes, of course. Last year's list will suffice.'

'Are we not going to order things from Mr Clark's catalogues, Mama?' Sarah wanted to know. Lucy sat down slowly and faced her children. She felt suddenly tired, bloodless, and she wondered vaguely if she were about to faint. She heard herself murmur, 'Mr Clark might be prevailed upon to leave his catalogues with us a little longer.' And with an effort, Lucy pulled her wits together. 'Those letters on the mantel are to go with him, Daniel. Will you see to it, please?'

Lucy read John Hamilton's letter over and over again until every damning word was printed indelibly on her memory. Underlying those words was a hint of admonition, and, as the full implication of her helplessness began to register, Lucy felt actual hatred for Adam. In that feeling there was a total absence of guilt.

When the widow called to recover her cow one week later and learned that Lucy had failed, her words of comfort fell on barren ground. Lucy knew that Ruby Gaunt had hoped they would remain in the high country, and because of this her feeling of hatred only just fell short of Ruby also.

The muster was over and the sheep, having been examined for scab, had been dipped then returned to the hills. After the constant bleating and the activity surrounding her these past weeks, the solitude and the silence weighed on her as it had done after the shearing, only more so; and there were times when Lucy felt that the brooding mountains were crushing her. For her sanity's sake, she again filled the empty days cleaning, cooking, working in her garden, toiling until she was exhausted; making sure of the deep and dreamless sleep that was her only escape.

Long after Nobby Clark had delivered the letters and papers from home, they remained unread. To her they represented the cruellest of ironies, reminding her that the people and places within their pages were lost to her, perhaps forever. It was that thought that determined Lucy not to bow to one man's decision; she would write to the family lawyer in London. With hope reborn, she knew she was equal to whatever challenge the high country visited on her as long as her tenure here was of limited duration.

Having been refused once, Lucy wrote this letter with extra care. When she had finished it she then wrote to her father, begging him to support her. Only when this was done did she feel she could bear to read her letters and the newspapers from home; copies of the *Otago Witness* she put to one side.

~

'Hello, the house!' Ruby Gaunt scuffed her boots off at the kitchen door and, from the lean-to, Lucy bade her enter and went on beating. The widow stood in the doorway, contemplating the younger woman as she worked.

'You goin' ter order that churn?'

'I'm not ordering anything,' Lucy answered flatly. 'I am going home.'

'How can you if Adam's will is deemed to be in order?'

'I have written to our family lawyer at home. *He* will see the impossibility of the situation, I am certain, and will appeal on my behalf.'

'I wouldn't be too hopeful, Lucy. It's the same horse, only a different colour.'

'I have to try — if only for the children.'

'Hmm,' the widow murmured. 'Anyway, speaking of horses, come see what I have outside.'

Looking a question, Lucy followed Ruby Gaunt outside. A large bay mare stood dozing in the winter sunlight and cropping the grass near her was a black gelding.

'Mostly I ride the mare these days so this fellow is in need of exercise — I wouldn't part with him, mind, but you may borrow him if you wish. His name is Thomas.'

'Ah, you rode — I didn't think I had heard the cart arrive. I don't have riding clothes or a lady's saddle,' Lucy vacillated, remembering her painful experience on the mare's back. 'Thank you for your kind thought, though.'

'You have Ruben's saddle, and, for God's sake, ride astride — split an old skirt up the back.'

'Ride astride!' Lucy was indignant. 'I would never do that; it would be most unseemly.'

'And most sensible in this rough terrain. Side-saddle is for ladies in the park. Now, this chappie is experienced, sure-footed and a gentleman. He will look after you. Well, do you want him?'

'If I were prepared to do as you suggest, where would I ride?'

'Heavens, girl! Anywhere.' Ruby Gaunt thrust her arm out in a wide arc. 'Come with me on my calls to the villages, visit *me*, ride around your acres. This is the biggest park you could ever wish to ride in — to explore — to enjoy. What do you say?'

Lucy stroked the gelding's black neck, considering, then she turned to the widow. 'I'm not sure about the skirt, but yes, thank you, Ruby, I would like to ride him.'

'A wise decision. Ther's more to livin' than workin' from dawn 'til dark, day in an' day out — now, is that kettle on?'

When the children had come outside to admire the gelding and had taken him up to the barn, Lucy and the Widow Gaunt settled themselves at the kitchen table to drink their tea and talk over current happenings on both runs. During the course of the conversation, Ruby Gaunt said, 'What did yer make o' the story 'bout McKenzie?'

'What story?'

'In yer paper — yer got yer copies, didn't yer?'

'The *Otago Witness* — yes, but I haven't read them.'

'Then yer'll not know. McKenzie was arrested in March fer stealin' sheep — a thousand o' the buggers from the Levels Run — big place nor'west o' Timaru.'

'I see.' Lucy rose to her feet and went to the fire to replenish the teapot. 'Where is he now?' She spoke over her shoulder, her face averted.

'In gaol, sentenced to five years, last month. Sidebottom, the Levels' overseer, an' two Maori shepherds caught 'im with the sheep, but it seems 'e got away from them.'

'You said he was in gaol.'

'So I did, an' 'e is — the law caught up wi' 'im in someone's loft in Lyttelton.'

Lucy was silent for a time, then said, 'Poor Daniel.'

'Poor Daniel? Why?'

'Mr McKenzie was larger than life to Daniel, someone he admired tremendously.'

'Maybe he still can, girl. I don't see McKenzie as a sheep thief — not 'is way—'

'As he is in gaol, the law must have considered that it *was* his way,' Lucy stated bluntly. The widow, somewhat surprised, said no more.

When Ruby Gaunt had gone on her way, Lucy quickly looked out the Dunedin newspapers and flicked through their pages until she found the item about James McKenzie. There, in black and white, she read of his apprehension by the Levels' overseer, J.H.C. Sidebottom, and his two Maori shepherds, Taiko and Seventeen, caught red-handed driving one thousand of the Levels' sheep without authority. She went on to read of his escape from them and his arrest by Police Sergeant Edward Seagar when he was run to earth in a loft in Lyttelton. During his trial, the article stated, McKenzie had remained *mute of malice*, pleading neither guilty nor not guilty, but he had been convicted and sentenced to five years' imprisonment on existing evidence. Lucy's heart was thudding heavily in her chest as she finished reading. She was conscious of a momentary feeling of grief for the Scot as she thought of him languishing in a cell for five years, but the feeling was replaced by quick anger: five years in prison was no more than his due, presuming to take that which was not his to take. With burning cheeks, Lucy folded up the newspaper and placed it back on the table. As she turned away, she heard Daniel's excited call, 'Mama, come and see this.'

She walked through the dining room and into the hallway. Through the open doorway, she saw Tom Masters astride his horse with a wild pig slung across the animal's rump.

'It's a boar, isn't it, with tusks like that?'

'Aye, lad, 'tis a boar.' Masters raised his hat to Lucy as she stepped out on to the veranda.

'Look at the size of it.' Daniel addressed his mother. 'It's nothing like the pigs at home, is it?'

'No, it is not.'

Daniel turned back to the shepherd. 'Did you get him with a single shot?'

Masters grinned slightly and shook his head. 'Was my second shot that put 'im down.'

'Do you see wild pig often?' Daniel's hand rested on the bristly carcass.

'Flush 'em out o' the scrub from time ter time, aye.'

'Could we go up there and hunt for more?'

Masters looked at Lucy, who gently shook her head.

'Nay, lad, ye'd need ter learn ter shoot first an' ye'd need yer mama's agreement to that — 'tis a dangerous business is pig hunting, and I'd best get this one out o' the sun.'

The shepherd lifted his hat to Lucy again, smiled at Daniel, then turning his horse about he rode off towards the hut.

'Can I learn to shoot, Mama?' Daniel persisted. 'We should have a gun to protect ourselves with, and I would be careful not to put anyone in danger — you know I would.'

'Let me think about this, Daniel — it's not something I can make a decision on in a minute.'

Lucy rode most days and found that the exercise relaxed her and helped her to sleep. The gelding was everything that Ruby Gaunt had claimed, and Lucy adapted to riding astride very quickly, albeit her bellowing skirts were cumbersome and threatened her modesty. Daniel, riding the mare bareback, was sometimes her riding companion. On one occasion Lucy accompanied the widow to a Maori village two hours' ride away where she was attending to various ailing natives, but she was so sickened by the lancing of a putrescent carbuncle that she declined to go again. The letter to her family lawyer, however, was left with the village elders, who would see it safely on its way to the postmistress. It was on this occasion Lucy learned that her made-over skirts offered little protection against matagouri and speargrass.

'Cut down a pair of Adam's moleskin trousers, girl,' the widow had advised. 'They will serve yer better than those ridiculous skirts.' Lucy's reticence would not permit this radical act, however, until she again fell foul of a patch of matagouri and bush-lawyer, she and the gelding suffering badly as a result. She followed the widow's suggestion then, but for some time rode only where she was sure she would not be observed. Eventually she became bold enough to ride up into the hills with Daniel, and was encouraged to realize that the shepherds found nothing odd in her appearance.

Sarah rode the gelding twice with Daniel in attendance on the mare, but she was a timid rider and much preferred to remain on her own two feet and occupy herself with her self-appointed tasks in the homestead. Lucy, having little interest in keeping house now, gave the girl a free run, doing only what Sarah couldn't manage. When she wasn't riding, Lucy busied herself in her garden, and when Tom Masters arrived with bags of sheep manure and offered to dig it in for her she was happy to let him do so, and happier still to find him clearing the cold ground in preparation for spring planting, leaving her free to potter in her borders. Daniel's days were mostly occupied riding the lower hills and gullies tending the sheep, watching for cast animals and wild dogs, and ever-hopeful that Lucy would let him learn to shoot.

He came riding down to the barn on a day when the sky was the colour of pewter. As he rubbed the mare down, he remembered that Willie Good was in need of newspaper to light his fire, his wood being damp and difficult to start with flint and tinderbox. There was paper aplenty at the homestead, so when the mare was bedded down for the night he decided to run a bundle down to the hut before the snow began to fall.

'Don't take the papers from home, Daniel.'

'I've only the Dunedin papers here, Mama, these should be enough.'

And this was how Daniel learned of his hero's fall from grace.

'Why didn't you tell me, Mama?' he cried as he read the damning article.

'I could not see the need to upset you.'

'But you can't believe he would take somebody else's sheep — you don't think he is a thief — you can't!'

'I don't know what to believe, dear, and it doesn't really matter now; he has been found guilty and that's an end to it.'

'I hope he escapes again and comes back here. We'd help him, wouldn't we, Mama?'

Lucy did not reply and the boy, seeing her set face, rose from the table leaving his meal untouched, and went up to his room.

The following morning Ruby Gaunt paid a visit. There had been a snowfall during the night and the family had awoken to find a white mantle of silence cloaking their world, muting all sound, so until she shouted at the door nobody was aware of her presence.

'A body could perish out here!' she bellowed and Daniel, hurrying to let her in, said, 'We didn't hear the cart.'

'Came on' old Bess — took the liberty o' puttin' 'er in yer barn wi' a feed of oats.'

Lucy took the widow's ulster. 'We are about to eat. Sit down, Ruby, and join us.'

The raw-boned woman rubbed warmth into her hands before the fire then sat at the table, casting an appreciative eye over the food being served. 'My, yer can set a bonny meal now, girl; I mind the time when yer couldn't cook a gnat's ar— pardon me—' And the widow coughed into her hand, covering her grin.

Lucy, frowning slightly, replied, 'Courtesy of the *Soyer's* cook book and hints and advice from Mr Good, yes, I can now set a fair table.'

'Yer can indeed. Now, I believe, if memory serves me right, 'tis somebody's birthday.'

Lucy's brow puckered again, and then her face cleared. 'It's *my* birthday, the sixth of June. How would you have known that, Ruby?'

'Have to admit I didn't, girl. Sarah, last time yer were visitin', made mention o' forgotten birthdays. The date stuck in my head, an' from Daniel's long face here, I reckoned it weren't 'is birthday. Anyway,' here the widow rummaged in her pocket, 'ter celebrate birthdays past an' present, Cook has made yer some sweeties.' A brown paper bag was held aloft. 'A dish, missus, if yer please.'

Sarah's smile was broad as everyone began to eat, with the exception of Daniel, who continued to sit glumly silent.

Ruby Gaunt's gaze was on him as she forked food into her mouth, and eventually she said, 'The lad must be ailing if the sight of Cook's delectables can't raise even the hint of a smile. What's yer bother, boy?'

'Do you know about Mr McKenzie?'

'That 'e's in gaol, aye, I do.'

'Do you think he is a thief?'

'Daniel, hush now. Mrs Gaunt is not to be questioned.'

'Steamin' load of— No, lad. That man is a free spirit an' I don't believe 'e'd saddle 'imself wi' someone else's sheep or anythin' else as would hold 'im still.'

'You really *don't* believe he's guilty?'

'No, Daniel lad, I don't, but 'e's gone down for five years anyway.'

Ruby Gaunt chewed in silence for a moment, her eyes still on the boy, then turned to Lucy. 'The second reason fer my visit here today is that, weather allowing, I want to show you something tomorrow. Wrap up warm an' saddle up Thomas in the morning, early, ready to go on a longish ride.'

'No more Maori villages, visiting the sick?'

The widow grunted. 'Nothing ter do wi' Maori villages.'

The meal finished, the children left the room and Lucy rose to fill the teapot again. Ruby Gaunt's narrowed eyes were on the younger woman's face. 'You know it could be all of two years before word comes back from yer lawyer in England. Have yer thought about that an' what yer'll do in the meantime?'

'In the meantime?' Lucy sat down again and, refilling their teacups, passed one to the widow. 'In the meantime,

I suppose I will go on doing Adam's bidding, and in the event that our London lawyer is of the same opinion as John Hamilton, then I will simply have to carry on for Daniel's sake. But why do you ask?'

'Does Daniel know what is in his papa's will?'

'No, and I will only tell him if there is no reason not to.'

'Are you up to doing what Adam has asked of you?'

'I will have no choice but to abide by his wishes, but the thought of Sarah being forced to exist in this place with no prospects at all is breaking my heart. And Daniel — it is all very well his inheriting a large sheep station when he reaches his majority, but he also will be greatly disadvantaged for lack of a formal education.' Lucy stared at her hands clasped tightly before her on the table and said quietly, 'To answer your question: physically, yes, I am up to overseeing the run, but mentally and emotionally, I am not sure of my strengths.' She looked directly at the older woman. 'Today I have turned thirty-two years of age, but already my life is over; there is nothing left for me except to go through the motions of being alive until I am actually dead.'

Lucy's voice was so low that the widow strained to hear the last words. She leaned back in her chair, her hands spread on the table, and began to chuckle. Through her chuckles, the gravelly words emerged: 'Well, girl, when yer've dragged yerself out o' that morass o' self-pity an' martyrdom—'

Two bright spots of colour appeared in Lucy's cheeks.

'Aye, be angry, not defeated. An' when yer ready ter listen, I'll tell yer how ter live life as yer never could hope ter in the closed social structures of England and home.'

'I don't know what you have in mind,' Lucy replied stiffly, 'but nothing here will ever be able to replace those social structures or the dear ones I may never see again.'

'Nonsense. Has it never occurred to you, my dear, that your loved ones are as capable of visiting this country as you are of visiting home if you've a mind to?'

Lucy stared at her guest.

'I can see that it hasn't, and I would say to you now: there is no cloud on your horizon so hopelessly black that yer'll not find a chink of light somewheres. Keep that in mind.'

Ruby Gaunt pushed her chair back and stood up. The flint-grey eyes resting on Lucy were a little shinier than usual as she reached across the table to pat the clasped hands. 'I'll be on me way, lass, an' I'll be here early in the morning. Damn fine meal was that.'

Lucy walked the widow to the door, calling to Daniel to fetch the mare from the barn.

'Don't bother the lad,' the big woman growled. 'I'll see to it, 'tis cold out.'

Daniel came into the kitchen and took his jacket off the peg by the door.

'I've not been out today — I'll help you saddle up.'

~

The day was crisp and still, and pale sunlight touched the snow as the two women rode south. Lucy was quiet for the first few miles, brooding and distracted. Daniel was clearly piqued with her for not sharing Ruby Gaunt's faith in McKenzie's integrity, and Lucy's anger was rekindled as she relived the episode in her garden. Damn him, damn him, she thought savagely. Now he was coming between herself and her son — damn him to hell!

The widow's rough voice broke in on her bitter recollection. 'See that big outcrop up ahead — that's roughly in line with your southern boundary. Beyond that, between Chandler's Run an' Long Reach, ther's near enough to eighteen thousand acres o' prime sheep country.'

'And your reason for pointing this out?' Lucy's voice was flat.

'My reason, girl, is as I promised, to show you how to live your life to the full in this place — but only if you have the guts!'

They rode on in silence for another half-hour before Ruby Gaunt pointed again with a gloved finger. 'See them cabbage trees — they mark the best way down to where two rivers meet. Above the fork is a plateau ideally situated for a homestead!'

Lucy pulled the gelding to a halt and turned to face the widow. 'Why are you showing me this place and being so mysterious? Will you pay me the courtesy, please, of speaking in plain English?'

'As you wish.' Ruby Gaunt's face resembled a crumpled burlap bag more than ever, and her eyes disappeared among its folds. 'I'm showing you this desirable property in the hope that you will see the merit in purchasing it.'

'You must be mad!' Lucy's patience was at an end. 'I have no money to purchase anything, as you very well know, nor do I have the desire.'

'Bear with me. If my suggestion begins to make sense, there are ways an' means, girl. Yer've heard of a pastoral lease?'

'Yes.'

'An' grid-ironing?'

'Yes, but I'm not sure what it means.'

'Grid-ironing is the purchase of key areas of land that form a barrier to anyone who might try to lay claim to your leased land.' The Widow Gaunt peered into Lucy's face. 'You understanding me?'

'Yes.'

'Good. Now, if you want to become a run-owner in your own right—'

'Oh, Ruby, why would I?' Lucy laughed grimly. 'Am I not in enough of a sorry state without adding to my woes?'

'Pshaw, yer not thinking. Listen ter what I'm sayin' — the idea of bein' yer own man, as it were, an' draggin' up yer wiltin' self-esteem, bein' in charge o' yer own destiny — this *has* to appeal.'

'Of course it does, but I don't want to be tied here forever.'

'You don't have ter be. When yer ready to leave, whenever that is, sell it as a going concern — Sarah's legacy.'

'Oh, my goodness.'

'Now yer listenin'.' The big woman swung down off her mare and, brushing off the top of a large flat rock, she seated herself and indicated that Lucy should sit beside her. 'Now, I will tell you how we go about this. Firstly, as overseer, Chandler's Run must pay yer as it would pay a man in that role. Has Adam made provision for this in his will?'

'I don't know. I don't think he said so, and I haven't yet seen the will.'

'Well, you are entitled and yer salary would be in the vicinity of one hundred an' fifty pounds a year. Yer pastoral lease will cost five or so shillin's an acre annually an' it's essential that you purchase that spur down there. It's one o' the doors ter this property an', as I've said, the obvious place ter build yer homestead at a later date.'

'I can't grasp all this — you are going too fast.'

'Then let me explain it this way. First you tell the boy about his inheritance, then, instead of leasing more acres for Chandler's Run to accommodate this year's stock increase, you purchase six hundred ewes at thirty shillin's a head from Daniel, paying them off over time. I'll give yer three old rams in exchange fer two young 'uns when yer've got 'em, an' yer'll take a year's advance on yer salary ter secure that spur of land. With me so far?'

'Yes.'

'Good. Now, your boundary to the south abuts my property and your boundary to the north abuts Daniel's. They are secure, as is your western boundary, flanked by the mountains, but your eastern boundary is wide open in places so it is important, if you decide to do this and Daniel is in agreement with my suggestion, that we make application for your first thousand acres and grid-iron the eastern boundary as soon as possible. As your stock numbers grow and your wool clip grows with them, you will be able to pay Daniel back with interest and secure the remaining acres over a period of time. Have I painted a clearer picture for you now?'

'Yes. I understand now what you are saying, but, Ruby, if I feel I can do this there is still the question of workers. If Ruben's men won't come back and word has travelled far and wide, I am defeated before I start.'

'Not a bit of it, girl — this bonny piece of land is not Chandler's Run and we will call in on the Ngai Tahu lads on our way back from Dunedin town when you've made application for your grant.'

'We are to go all the way to Dunedin ourselves to do this?'

'Did you know that the Ngai Tahu tribes go all the way back to the Waitaki moa hunters? Of course we have to go to Dunedin, Lucy, how else can you make your application and have your grant and purchase registered? We will need to obtain a copy of Adam's will also.'

Lucy, more than a little overwhelmed by now, studied the craggy face for a long moment, then said quietly, 'I don't think I can do this. The very idea scares me to death.'

'You *can* do it, Lucy, of course you can. I did it when I was little older than yourself and determined to be my own person, and look where I am now; and you will have what I didn't have when I began — help! Go home and talk this over with that fine son of yours. Away with you now — just follow our tracks back and I'll see you in a day or so.'

∽

Lucy, Sarah and the Widow Gaunt left for Dunedin a week later. Daniel remained at home with assurances from the shepherds and Willie Good that he would be well looked after. The widow's cart was made comfortable for the journey with the tussock-filled mattresses that Lucy had made the year before, and these were covered with mackintoshes. A wooden box under the seat held a billy-can, an old teapot, four tin mugs and plates, and a bag of bannocks. Other bundles and boxes went unremarked next to the tailgate. Rewi accompanied them on horseback, taking the route to Dunedin that only the Maori knew. They slept in comparative comfort in native villages along the way, welcomed and fed by the friendly Maori, and in return Ruby Gaunt gave them unguents and potions for their ills, old clothes, worn tools and the odd blanket.

At the end of four days of difficult travel, most of the tracks being barely wide enough for the cart, they reached Dunedin. The rain had fallen incessantly overnight, and as the tired horses pulled the cart down the long main street, thick mud, almost to the axles in places, stretched ahead of them. In the fading light the few buildings they passed were nondescript and devoid of life. The stench from the mud was overpowering, and Lucy and Sarah were thankful when finally they pulled up before what appeared to be a small wooden rooming house or hotel, the dim light filtering through its windows their only welcome.

'Stay put,' Ruby Gaunt grunted. 'I'll carry yer.' She bent down and, pulling on high-sided boots, she stepped down into the noisome mud then turned to lift Sarah down and carry her across the intervening distance to deposit her on the wooden veranda. She returned for Lucy, cursing the mud that was sucking the boots from her feet. Having set Lucy down beside Sarah, she squelched back to the cart once more to retrieve her other boots and their clothes. While the widow changed her boots again, Rewi drove the cart away, leading his own mount.

'Hello, the house!' the widow bellowed, and pushed the low door open. The landlord came from behind his small desk and peered short-sightedly at the trio.

'Two single beds with a trundle, landlord, an' dinner if yer please.'

The landlord focused on the raw-boned woman. 'Certainly, sir, certainly — this way please.'

'We'll be needin' a hot tub too — quick as yer can,' the widow growled, hefting their bundles. She followed the man up the stairs, almost walking on his heels and grinning broadly.

The small room was clean but bitterly cold, and the water in the pitcher numbed their hands as they washed away the grime of travel.

'Ther'll be a fire in the parlour,' the widow rumbled. 'We'll get ourselves down ther' an' take a sup o' somethin' ter warm ourselves while our bath-water heats.'

The parlour was small, too, but a welcoming fire burned in the hearth and in a minute a young man entered to serve them. The widow ordered a small brandy for Lucy and herself and a mug of cocoa for Sarah. Curiously eyeing the big woman, the waiter served their drinks. He cast an appreciative glance at Lucy, then his eyes swung back to the widow, blatantly staring. Ruby Gaunt chuckled deep in her throat as she addressed her brandy.

Lucy and Sarah bathed in turn in a galvanized tin bath in a rough lean-to at the rear of the hotel. There was no way of barring the ill-fitting door, so each stood guard for the other. The water was uncomfortably hot for Sarah and barely tepid for Lucy, so cold were the draughts that came through the cracks in the walls, but both luxuriated in the cleansing water after four days on the road.

A small table had been placed near the fire for them when they returned to the parlour, and, while they waited for the widow to join them, two other people came into the room, both men. The curious waiter hovered about the doorway. When the widow reappeared, she was dressed in a clean woollen shirt, waistcoat and woollen serge trousers; she still wore her battered hat.

Once seated, she turned a cold sliver of eye on the loitering waiter, who quickly left.

'Where is Rewi?' Sarah asked.

'He stays at a Maori village near the beach. When do you suppose they are goin' ter feed us?' The Widow Gaunt stood up again and strode through the door. Almost immediately the waiter returned to serve their dinner of beef stew, dumplings and boiled onions. His hands fumbled the dishes and his eyes were cast down in a beet-red face. When he had left the room, Lucy murmured, 'What do you suppose was wrong with our waiter?'

The widow grinned an evil grin. 'Me reputation 'as gone afore me, I'm thinkin' — 'e'll not dilly dally again.'

Sarah was falling asleep as Lucy finished her treacle

pudding, so they went up to bed while Ruby Gaunt prowled off on a quest of her own. A small trundle bed had been placed beside Lucy's bed and, shivering in the cold room, they quickly undressed and burrowed under their quilts. Lucy did not hear the widow come to bed, but awoke in the pre-dawn to a symphony of stertorous snoring coming from the other bed.

~

In daylight the long main street of Dunedin was even less inviting than it had been the night before. They could see now the putrid mud, a brew of dirty snow, animal and vegetable remains, dead fish from the market along the street, and sewage which emitted evil bubbling gases; a source, the widow claimed, of typhoid and death.

The unhappy horses drew the cart through this porridge, snorting their disgust. There was a general store, and Lucy and Sarah stepped on to an unstable plank to enter this emporium in order to replenish their writing materials and search for something suitable for Daniel's birthday in September. They passed a small wooden kirk, two butchers, three bakers and several shops with large windows for the display of goods which Ruby Gaunt warned were priced twice as high as goods ordered from home. Lucy, however, stepped down to shop in one of these, buying for Daniel two blue shirts, priced at five shillings each, two pairs of moleskin trousers, sixteen shillings a pair, a pair of lace-up boots for each of them at two pounds a pair, and several yards of light calico at two shillings and sixpence a yard, to make curtains for the homestead's windows.

Nearer to the beach was the courthouse where the Land Office was to be found, and the gaol, surrounded by a high wooden fence. Lucy did not care to dwell on the possibility that McKenzie might be behind that fence, and hurried to follow Ruby Gaunt into the Land Office. Two gentlemen were in attendance, and Lucy saw a quick glance exchanged between them as the widow strode across the room to a wall where several maps were pinned. Selecting one of these, she withdrew the pins and, turning, placed the map on the counter before the older man. Without preamble, stabbing the map with a gloved finger, she stated, 'This here is Chandler's Run an' this here is Long Reach. Between the boundaries of them two runs is eighteen thousand acres of, I believe, unclaimed territory. Now this here,' and she pulled Lucy forward, 'is Adam Chandler's widow an' she's 'ere ter lodge a claim on them acres an' purchase the spur ther' to build a dwelling on at a later date.'

The older man bowed to Lucy then turned to confer with his companion. After a rather lengthy confab, he came back to Lucy. 'Am I to understand this is to be an extension of Chandler's Run?' He raised lofty eyebrows.

'It is not,' the widow's gravelly voice replied. 'This acreage is ter be registered under the title of — yer maiden name, girl?' she hissed in an aside.

'Camden,' Lucy whispered.

'Under the title o' Camden Station.'

'Well now,' the older man addressed Lucy, 'if you will kindly take a seat we'll see what we shall see.'

Lucy and Sarah sat on the straight-backed chairs while Ruby Gaunt stood impatiently beside them slapping a leather glove into the palm of her hand, her narrowed eyes fixed on the two men who were deliberating over several documents beyond her range of vision.

The older man, having come to a conclusion, muttered something to his colleague then addressed Lucy again. 'It appears that Chandler's Run was willed to your husband by his late uncle, Ruben Chandler, and that your husband has, in his turn, willed the property to your son. Would this be correct?'

'Yes.'

The man studied Lucy's face in silence, before continuing, 'And you have inherited no part, not even the homestead it would seem. So, madam, I need to ask you now, how can you suppose that you can extend this property under its present title, or the title it seems you have just invented, when you have no written authority to do so?' The man's eyes slid sideways to his companion in petty triumph.

Lucy stood up and approached the counter, her cheeks blooming; the widow, watching her closely, this time held her tongue.

'My husband has charged me with the responsibility of overseeing my son's estate. As he is yet a minor I am empowered to manage his affairs until he reaches his majority and in so doing use my own discretion.'

'Then you *are* purchasing and taking up leasehold of this tract of land in his name?'

'No, sir, I am not. Let me clarify again my intention.' Lucy's dark eyes glittered. 'In my own right, I intend to purchase key areas of this holding and over a period of time extend my leasehold to encompass the acres between the boundaries of Chandler's Run and Long Reach. I trust there will be no impediment to my doing this?'

'That will remain to be seen. You are aware, I suppose, that good merino stock is in short supply?'

'This will present no problem. Chandler's Run has had two good seasons and is now over-grazed. I intend to purchase my son's excess stock at the going rate — thirty shillings a head, I believe.' Lucy could not recall how she knew this, but the clerk nodded and Ruby Gaunt chuckled. An expression of reluctant admiration crept over the fellow's face and his younger assistant was smiling. By, this comely lass was nobody's fool.

'Hmmph.' The senior clerk cleared his throat and nodded grudgingly. 'Good, yes, good.' He drew a form towards him and laboriously outlined the land in question on a smaller map, which was then attached to the form. 'Unfortunately, the decision on these matters is not made in this office but will come from the Commissioner of Lands. However,' he went on, 'if you have the stock and the people to work the property . . . ?' He raised an eyebrow in query.

'She has,' the widow snapped.

'Then I can see little obstacle to your claim.' The hint of a smile was in the man's eyes as he placed pen and inkpot by Lucy's hand and turned the form around. 'Read this carefully before you sign it.'

The younger clerk leaned forward and murmured, 'You

might be better served if you do not prefix your signature with *Mrs* — if you see what I mean?' He started back when the widow snatched the document from under his nose with her gloved hand, perused it thoroughly then slapped it back on the counter. 'Looks in order, girl — go ahead.'

With a hand that shook slightly, Lucy signed the application form, then, looking squarely at the two men, she said quietly, 'In the event that my claim is approved, would you kindly advise my lawyer, Mr John Hamilton; the appropriate monies will be left with him. Thank you for your time.'

The widow nodded her approval as Lucy turned to the door, murmuring 'Come, Sarah', and swept from the small office. Ruby Gaunt chuckled deep in her throat as she followed. 'Yer did all right, girl — those gents were *both* ready ter lay their jackets over yer puddle. Now, shall we visit the postmistress an' see if she's anythin' fer us an' post yer letters?'

'Yes, and I shall ask her where Mr Hamilton has his office and also directions to Mrs Brand's address. I will take but a short visit with her, Ruby, if you agree.'

'As you wish, Lucy, but I shan't visit with you. The lady does not approve of me.'

The journey home was uneventful, but as they approached the high country slate-grey and white snow-cloud was gathering, darkening the hills, and a cold westerly blew in their faces. They stopped only briefly at the Ngai Tahu village while the widow spoke to an elder and Ruben's three shepherds. Her welcome into the village had been such that Lucy had no doubt that the natives held her in high regard. The meeting, though brief, ended with handshakes all round, and some of the women came forward to touch noses with the Widow Gaunt. Sarah was amused by the gestures but sobered quickly at Lucy's frown and Rewi's dark stare.

'You have yer workers,' Ruby Gaunt stated as they set off again, and for Lucy the reality of what she was about to do was beginning to set in. If her grant was approved, she would not only be overseer of Chandler's Run but be in charge of an additional eighteen thousand acres in her own right, and in charge of their respective animals and workers — she — Lucy Chandler, late of Tenbury, Worcestershire, England, and newly widowed wife of Adam Chandler. The situation was so absurd that she began to laugh.

'What's amusing yer, girl?'

'I feel at this moment that I am enacting a farcical comedy, a nonsense, and that none of the characters, including myself, are real.'

'It'll be real enough, missus, when you get yer grant. Now, 'ere's somethin' ter take yer mind off yerself. Got talkin' ter Hamilton's factotum whilst you were in the inner sanctum — unending source of information he was, an' I had ter wonder if the lawyer was aware that the fella was so free with 'is chitchat. Anyway, after 'e'd waded through all sorts o' stuff 'e moved on ter McKenzie: what we already knew 'bout 'is capture, 'is escape an' 'is capture again in Lyttelton. What did make me prick up me ears, though, was when 'e said that McKenzie, during the trial, claimed he had been hired by James Mossman to drive the sheep for the payment of twenty pounds and that, at 'is committal, twenty-one pounds an' eleven shillings were found on him.' Ruby Gaunt pushed her hat back off her brow and cast a sidelong glance at Lucy, who sat stony-faced on the high seat.

'An' did yer know that the word *mossman* is Gaelic fer cattle-thief?' The widow chuckled. 'An' McKenzie, the fellow says, got away once more an' hid his money somewhere in the bush before they caught 'im again. Canny Scot fer a fact, but a thief — it don't fit somehow, what say you, girl?'

'I have given the matter little thought either way, Ruby,' Lucy answered shortly, 'but if he is, then he has earned his sentence and I applaud the judge who handed it down.'

Nothing more was said on the subject as they bowed their heads before the biting wind and Ruby Gaunt gave her attention to getting them home before the snow came. Lucy turned her thoughts to Ruben's old housekeeper. Agatha Brand and her sister were forthright, God-fearing women who had left Lucy in no doubt that they did not approve of her association with the *black widow*, as they referred to her. 'She is no doubt everything she stands accused of, my dear,' Mrs Brand had stated bluntly, 'and I would be wary indeed of having dealings with her.'

Lucy rose to her friend's defence as best she could, but knew her words fell on deaf ears. The sisters also bluntly informed her that to purchase apparel of any kind in this country was to pay horrendous prices for the same items ordered from the old country and that furniture made here was sadly inferior. 'Be patient, my dear. The wait for your English goods will be well worthwhile, saving you money and frustration in the long run.' There was more advice in the same forceful manner, and Lucy, with the sisters little more than half an hour, was pleased to leave behind their strong opinions and the small, stuffy, over-furnished parlour that carried a hint of the meal from the night before.

She breathed deeply of the clean sharp air as they travelled ever higher, and was thankful that they need visit Dunedin only rarely.

It was four o'clock in the afternoon when the cart pulled up before the homestead. It was almost dark, and Lucy offered the widow and Rewi a bed for the night, fearing they might be caught in the pending storm. Over the last mile or so the wind had risen to near gale force.

'Nay, lass, we've a while afore that lot comes down.' The widow squinted up at the lowering clouds, then turned to Daniel as he emerged from the doorway. ''Ere, son, take hold o' these an' get yer sister indoors out o' the cold.' She passed parcels and bundles to the boy while Lucy clambered stiffly down from the cart, keeping hold of the letters from home and the long envelope she had brought from the lawyer's office. The Widow Gaunt helped Sarah alight and bustled her inside, then again took her place on the high seat and said, 'I'll not dally, 'tis goin' ter be a wild trip home an' I'll be seekin' me own bed early when we get there. You want me ter bring some shellac next time I'm over this way?'

'Shellac?'

'Varnish yer floors with it.'

'Is this what you have put on your floors?'

'Aye — yer'd be well-served ter cover yer white floorboards

afore they're past doin'. We're off — get in out o' the cold.'

Lucy hurried indoors as the cart went off down the track. She was cold to the bone, but a small glow dwelt within her as the homestead enveloped her in its clean newness, its warmth and the aroma of roasting pork. She did not envy the townspeople of Dunedin their stuffy, constantly closed-up rooms because of the proximity of those streets to the cottages.

'Did you get the land, Mama?'

'I have made application for it, Daniel, but we have to wait until the Land Office decides.'

'By, 'tis good ter see yer safe back home, missus.' Willie Good came into the hallway wiping his hands on his apron. 'A good trip, was it?'

'Rough, but uneventful for the most part — it's nice to be home.'

'Well now, yer dinner's on — the lad 'ere 'as lent a hand an' you can be sittin' down about six o' the clock. I'd best get down below an' see ter the lads' supper now; they'll be comin' in froze ter the marrer this night.'

A strong gust of wind hit the windows as Lucy and Sarah went upstairs to remove their capes and heavy outer skirts. Lucy looked through the glass to the early darkness beyond and was pleased that she had bought the calico for her curtains; she would begin stitching them tomorrow. From Mrs Brand too she had received a tiny plant of lily of the valley and the dried seeds of foxglove, sweet william and stock, to be planted when the weather turned warmer. She smiled to herself as she thought of the fine show they would make in her borders, and with surprise she found her thoughts turning to Nobby Clark's catalogues. Perhaps their sojourn in Dunedin had made her more appreciative of what she had here; perhaps, too, it was possible that because of it she might better be able to settle for the remainder of her time in the high country, be it two years, seven years or longer.

That night as Lucy lay in her bed, listening to the wind shrieking around the homestead, her thoughts turned briefly to James McKenzie. There was a deep emptiness within her as she acknowledged how unconditional the surrender of her heart would have been, and at what cost, when she found that not only was he a rebel but also a thief. She forced her thoughts away from him and drifted into sleep, trying to remember the contours of the land for which she had lodged a claim. Lucy awoke once in the early hours; the wind was gone, the night blanketed in silence, and before sleep reclaimed her she heard snow slide from the roof and dump on to the ground below. Dimly, she thought of the sheep out there in the freezing darkness, huddling together, weighed down by the snow on their backs and the new life in their bellies, and wondered how they survived year after year.

Chapter 12

DAY DAWNED COLD and grey. Lucy had slept late and arose to find the parlour and kitchen fires glowing brightly, but there was no sign of Daniel.

The snow was deep, piled high against the lean-to and all but burying the veranda steps, and she realized a little anxiously that her son had joined Masters, Tanner and Pitchin to rescue animals trapped in deep snow in the gullies and ravines. Dismissing her uneasiness, she set about making breakfast for Sarah. Later she would don her boots and make her way up to the barn with hot bannock cakes wrapped in a cloth; she suspected that Daniel would have left without breakfast.

When Sarah came downstairs and had eaten, Lucy set her about her morning tasks, then wrapped up the bannock cakes and left the homestead. Trudging through the deep snow was taxing, and from time to time she stopped to get her breath, scanning the white slopes for Daniel. A grey mist hung suspended below the ragged peaks hovering in the gorges and gullies, tendrils touching the black scrub-line with damp fingers. The jagged monoliths rose from its cold mantle, sombre and forbidding. The bleating of the sheep was muffled by the heavy snow-cover and Lucy experienced a sense of deafness, the thick silence pressing down on her as she struggled forward again.

The sheep did not move from her path when she reached the barn, and standing amongst them she again searched the hills. There was no movement of men or sheep. She lifted her gaze higher then and her breathing stilled. Just below the bush-line a lone horseman sat unmoving, facing her. He was mounted on a rangy chestnut and she could just discern a black-and-white collie at his side. Lucy strained her eyes against the whiteness of the snow, her pulse racing. How could this be? It could not: she was mistaken. But then the tall rider seemed to raise a hand in the familiar gesture of touching two fingers to the brim of his hat, before he turned his horse about and dissolved into the mist.

Lucy stood motionless, staring at the place where the Scot had disappeared, scanning the stunted trees and patches of mist. Her heartbeat thudding in her ears, she waited; waited for what? A further sighting? For him to ride down? She did not know. Her whole body was shaking. Clutching the warm bannocks to her breast, Lucy struggled into the barn and, pushing the big door shut behind her, she lowered herself unsteadily on to a wooden box. There she sat for an endless time until the barn door began slowly to open, and she stared at it transfixed, uneasy. Then she heard Tom Masters' voice and her son's in reply.

'Lay yer straw thick, lad, an' let's get 'em inside quick.'

'They'll be all right now, won't they?' Daniel was asking as he entered the barn leading the mare. 'Mama,' he said in surprise. 'Why are you sitting there? You must be freezing.'

'I have brought you some bannocks. They are still warm and there are enough for all of you.'

Tom Masters was pushing wide the big doors and urging the exhausted sheep into the barn.

'That's grand, Mama, but I need to bed the sheep down — some of them are in a bad way—'

'Yes, yes, I can see that they are.' Relief washed over her as she stood up. 'Let me help you, it will warm me to be doing something.'

She worked quickly, spreading the straw where Daniel indicated, and when Masters came into the barn half-carrying a beleaguered animal, she heard him mutter to Daniel, ''Tis no task fer a lady.'

'But a task befitting an overseer, you'll no doubt agree,' she said in reply. 'How many are you bringing in?'

'Fifty head, missus, an' ther'll be more if we can get 'em out in time.'

The thought had occurred to her that Masters and her son might have seen McKenzie; might even have spoken to him. She continued to lay the straw, waiting for something to be said, but, when after a time nothing was forthcoming, impatience overcame her.

'Who did I see riding in the hills west of here, quite high, near the scrub-line?'

Silence followed her question until Daniel turned and, looking at her a little oddly, replied, 'Mr Tanner and Pitchin are riding north of here, Mama. Is that who you saw?'

'No, Daniel, that is not who I saw.'

Both the boy and Masters shook their heads and concentrated again on the sheep. Lucy worked on for a while, then, brushing the straw from her skirts, she walked to the barn door and stood for a space, looking up to the hills. 'I'll expect you in for your dinner, Daniel,' she spoke over her shoulder, and began to thread her way through the sheep to make her way back to the homestead. Why had nobody else seen the Scot? She had to believe that Daniel would have told her had he seen him or talked to him. That he had escaped again was obvious, but where was he going and why was he here? A small thrill of something like fear ran through her and Lucy began to flounder faster through the drifts of snow, casting a wary eye towards the western hills as she went.

Shivering, she took her boots off at the kitchen door, struggling with the frozen laces, trying to hurry, but once inside the warm familiar kitchen her sense of proportion returned. Whatever the reason James McKenzie was here, she felt he had not come to harm her; frighten her, perhaps. But would he risk his freedom by coming too close? She thought not.

When Daniel came in for his dinner, he made no mention of his mother's odd question, his mind being occupied by the number of heavily pregnant ewes filling the barn and overflowing into the woolshed. 'I don't know how many more are buried up there, Mama, and we are going to lose some of the sheep we *have* brought down unless their condition begins to improve soon.'

Lucy looked at the worried young face across the table.

'Is there nothing we can do? What would Mrs Gaunt do if they were her sheep, do you think?'

Daniel shook his head. 'Mr Masters said we have to let nature take its course now — we've done all we can.'

'Then eat your dinner, dear — see what tomorrow brings.'

~

Twenty-five ewes had perished during the night and ten more had died by late morning; the first known losses the run had sustained. The unspoken word was that, had the Scot been with them, all the ewes would have been brought down to safety before the weather closed in.

The shepherds had been up and away by first light to search further afield while Daniel rode boundary, confining the mob to the lower pastures, and Willie Good left his kitchen to feed out. At noon the Widow Gaunt rode up to the homestead on her big red mare. Without preamble she kicked off her boots and ushered Lucy into the parlour out of earshot of Sarah, who was helping to prepare dinner.

'I've a word ter convey ter yer ears an' nobody else's,' she said cryptically, her shrewd eyes scanning Lucy's face. 'A visitor has come a-callin' ter Long Reach an' 'e's askin' yer permission ter call afore 'e moves on.'

'James McKenzie,' Lucy breathed.

'Aye. Yer did see 'im, then?'

'What does he want with me?' The tiny dart of fear had returned.

'Ter square summat away with yer, summat that's botherin'

'im a bushel.' The widow turned to the leather sofa and eased herself down on to it. 'Sit, girl,' she grunted, 'ther's a story ter tell afore yer give me yer answer.'

The widow was silent for a while, gathering her thoughts, then she began.

'Seems our Mr McKenzie is heir ter a goodly property in Scotland. Before 'e set sail out 'ere, 'e was courtin' a fair lassie with an eye ter gettin' wed. All in 'is world was rosy until 'is mama passed away. In no time at all, it seems that the fair lassie were payin' more attention ter the laird than ter 'imself, an' in less time than that, the laird an' the fair lassie were wed, leavin' our McKenzie bereft an' entirely out o' sorts.'

'Why are you telling *me* this?'

'I'm tellin' yer, child, because there was summat or nothin' atween yer — 'e's not sure — but either way 'e says 'e did you a disservice, misjudged you, and would put it right if yer'll allow 'im to.'

Lucy stared at the weathered face of her visitor and felt her own grow hot. 'Why would I be concerned with the opinion of a man who would steal another man's sheep?' she snapped. 'You may tell Mr McKenzie not to trouble himself.'

Ruby Gaunt stood up and, slowly pulling on her gloves, shot a keen glance at Lucy's flushed cheeks. 'Well, girl, it's plain ter see ther's more makin' yer smart than McKenzie's observations of yerself an' I'll not pry, but in fairness ter 'im I'll just add that he claims he had no inkling of mischief afoot when he was hired to drive those sheep. It wasn't 'til

335

Mossman — realizing that Sidebottom an' 'is fellas were on to 'im, said summat like "Stay put, yer didn't steal the sheep an' yer didn't know I had" — that the poor bugger knew 'e were in trouble.'

The Widow Gaunt's piercing eyes held Lucy's. 'Sidebottom, 'e says, admitted at the trial that they had followed two sets of prints — no point 'im sayin' that if it isn't true.'

Lucy stood up also and faced the widow. 'Are you saying that you believe him?'

'Aye. Must do, seein' I've put 'is bitch among my pack ter hide 'er 'til 'e comes back fer 'er.'

'Comes back — back from where?'

'From tracking down the only person who can clear 'is name: Mossman, or whatever that fella calls 'isself.'

Ruby Gaunt waited and watched as Lucy sat down again and stared at the logs burning in the grate, then said quietly, 'If you agree to see him, Lucy, he will come tonight — late when there is no chance that he will be seen.'

Lucy studied the widow's face for a moment, then returned her gaze to the fire. Her heart was pounding and her mouth was dry as she faced her dilemma — should she follow the longing in her heart, or use her head and steer clear of all involvement with the Scot? The emotions which she had tried to deny were at war with the memory of his rough words and rougher intention; she was afraid of him, afraid to trust him, and that was the truth. She looked up into the face of her friend, and slowly she shook her head. 'I fear it would be a mistake, Ruby,' she said in a low voice. 'Things are better left as they are.'

The widow leaned close then and placed a firm hand on Lucy's shoulder. Her face bore the expression that Lucy had seen when she had tended the distressed cow; so long ago, it seemed now.

'Be sure you're not doing something you'll regret, lass, in time to come. I've a feeling you might be — think on a bit.' And the big woman went quietly from the room, leaving Lucy to ponder her words.

The fire crackled in the silent room. Lucy, her eyes closed, sat with her hands clenched in her lap trying to bring the chaos within her to some kind of order. She made herself remember the Scot's obvious regard for Daniel, his patience and insight in bringing about Sarah's healing, his gentle attention to Adam's frailty when he had carried him up to the homestead, and his courage as he drove the marauders from Chandler's Run. In view of these things, could she fairly deny McKenzie his request? She could hear the rumble of Ruby Gaunt's voice in the kitchen. Reluctantly she rose to her feet and made her way there.

'Will you dine with us, Ruby?'

'Nay, I'll not take the time, but yer can see me to the door.' She patted Sarah's cheek. 'Goodbye, child, yer'e a good lass.' She strode to the door and as she straightened from tying her bootlaces she asked in a low voice, 'Well, girl, what answer am I to carry back with me?'

'You may tell Mr McKenzie I will see him. I owe him that at least.'

'Good, good. Then I'll be on me way.' The widow crammed the battered hat down firmly on to her head and, leaving the warmth of the kitchen, went out to her broad mare. Stepping up into the saddle she waved a hand at Lucy and rode out of sight around the lean-to.

∽

The day stretched out interminably as Lucy went about her daily tasks, her concentration such that time and again she would enter a room only to wonder why she had come there. There was a strange excitement in her, and at the same time a feeling of dread, which left her palms moist.

When Daniel came in for his dinner he said that more sheep had perished, and for fear of losing men and dogs in the treacherous conditions it had been decided that the animals in the intractable higher reaches would have to remain where they were; wethers for the most part, he thought, as ewes in lamb would not venture so high. They would not know the extent of their losses until after the snow thawed, Daniel added, and the muster the following April would confirm them.

'How did Long Reach fare, Mama? I saw Mrs Gaunt riding off.'

Lucy realized then that she had said nothing of their stock loss, nor had she thought to ask the widow about the situation at Long Reach.

'We did not speak of it, dear,' Lucy replied vaguely. Daniel stared at her in some surprise, then, frowning, turned his attention to his dinner. He ate without haste, in no hurry to join the men and the hapless sheep. In the past hours he had viewed more death than he could stomach. He loved the sheep, each and every one of them, as only a boy could. He did not think of the dead animals in terms of financial loss, but rather as woolly, trusting friends whose lives had been cut short by the onslaught of nature at its worst. Dinner over, he reluctantly donned his outerwear again and left the homestead.

After the dishes had been cleared away, Lucy set Sarah her lessons for the day, then, leaving her busy with her sums, she went into the parlour, needing to be alone to gather her composure and collect her thoughts. Soon she was to face the Scot and she felt very vulnerable. She sat for a space beside the fire, then, restlessly leaving her chair, began to pace the room, stopping to stare unseeingly through the window before pacing again as her agitation grew and, with it, renewed anger. What had possessed her to agree to see this man? What could ever come of it? He was an escaped prisoner, guilty or not, and she forgot her reasons for agreeing to the meeting; remembering only the slights, his brutal behaviour and his chilling dislike of her.

She ceased her pacing as she thought how ridiculous it was to upset herself so. She would see him as agreed, but for a few moments only. *She* would be in control, hear him out, then send him on his way. That would be the end of it.

~

The night was quiet and still. Sarah and Daniel had gone to their beds long since, and Lucy sat at the kitchen table stitching her curtains. A fine tremor in her fingers made her stitches erratic and her temper warm, as time and again she was obliged to unpick her work.

A little after midnight a light tap on the kitchen door stilled her hands, and for a long moment Lucy did not move. Slowly then she rose from her chair and went to open the door. She did not look at the Scot as he entered, but moved away to resume her seat at the table. 'You may stay for as long as it takes you to say what you wish to say,' she said coldly, 'then I must ask you to leave.'

The Scot closed the door softly and, removing his hat and boots, he stepped into the room to stand and regard her in silence. Still not looking at him, Lucy stabbed her needle in and out of the fabric and waited for him to speak. Save for the crackle of the fire and the ticking of the clock, which seemed inordinately loud, there was no other sound and the silence began to nibble at her nerves. At last she shot an angry glance at McKenzie, and the words she was about to snap died on her lips. His level gaze rested on her face, the pale eyes dark with pain, his mouth tense in his beardless face, and as their eyes met Lucy's anger cooled. He spoke then in a low voice, 'Ah mind the day ah first saw ye, strugglin' wi' ya washin'.' A faint smile touched his lips then was gone. 'The sight o' ye helplessness stirred me to ma soul. I was afeart o' the strength o' the feelin' inside o' me — aye, an' hatin' it, maun turn it to anger agen ye.' His eyes dropped to the hat in his hands. ''Tis me is the fuil, lass,' he said softly, 'turnin' ma back in the face o' ye need.'

Lucy felt her face flame and her heart pounded a hard, rapid beat beneath her bodice. Bewildered, she stood up quickly, pushed the big kettle into the flames and remained standing with her back to the Scot. Quietly he spoke again.

'Ye've been told tha tale o' she wi' tha spirit o' greed and duplicity — a bitter tale tha' drove me frae hearth an' hame. Ah looked at the fair face o' ye an' saw only tha face o' her an' ma need ta hurt ye — ta crush ye — was a sickness in me — aye. An' ah could nae stay awa' an' tha canker grew.'

Lucy was crying now, silent tears she could not hold back. McKenzie came to stand behind her and his hands were on her shoulders, turning her gently to press her face into the roughness of his coat until she grew quiet, and then he spoke against her hair. 'Ah didnae pay muckle heed ta the bairns' chatter — ma ears wa nae tuned ta ye innocence an' it wa' there fa tha listenin' — twa' me wa' the fuil.' He did not speak for a moment, then said in a low voice, 'Ca' ye forgive me lass? Ah'm nae expectin' ya ca' . . .'

Lucy leaned away and looked up into the strong face. 'I think perhaps I can — your own father — such betrayal.' Her eyes were soft in the lamplight. 'Yes, I can forgive you.'

'Och, lassie, ah'm a happy mon — ye'll nae regret it.'

'I wish Adam could have forgiven me,' Lucy murmured against McKenzie's chest. 'He sensed the change in me, I could not hide it, and it hurt him so — his eyes haunt me still.'

'Aye, but ye did nae wrong him wilfully an' ya love fa him didnae change.'

'No, but because I could not share with him what was happening — I did not understand it myself — he thought I was faithless — he died believing this.'

'Ma puir wee love. Weel, nae doot tha laddie kens different noo, sae leave it a' go.'

'I think I must.' After a moment, Lucy raised her head, and releasing herself from McKenzie's arms she asked softly, 'How is it that you are here?'

'Ah canna clear ma name frae behin' stone walls an' dinna be afeart ah'll pu' ye at risk wi' tha law; whe' ye've brewed a cup, ah'll gang awa' ta hunt oot tha fella tha' stole tha' sheep — 'aince ma name is cleared, och, then . . .' The Scot's blue eyes moved over Lucy's face, and the glint in them sent a frisson through her body and quick colour touched her cheeks. Desire rose in McKenzie; he struggled to subdue the urge to crush her in his arms, to possess her now while he could. Lucy sensed his passion as she set the cups on the long table, and she lowered her eyes in warm confusion, half-afraid, and McKenzie knew he must wait.

In the hush of the small hours, their secret moment was fleeting then gone, and McKenzie was at the kitchen door pulling on his boots. Lucy stood beside him, committing every part of him to memory; the rich glint of his hair in the lamplight, the long fingers tying his bootlaces, his hard, lean body and the brilliant blue of the eyes he raised to her as he straightened up. 'Ah fain wad stay, lassie,' he said softly, and Lucy waited for his arms to enfold her again — for him at last to claim her lips — but he simply placed his hands on her shoulders and pressed his mouth to her forehead in a long kiss, and then he was gone.

Lucy was too restless to seek her bed. The sense of anticlimax that came in the wake of the Scot's departure left her in turn empty, anxious, ecstatic and fearful, her mind darting from one obstacle to another that could come in the way of McKenzie returning to her. This won't do at all, she told herself as the bleak daylight filtered into the kitchen. She determined then to fill every waking hour, to keep herself busy until he came home, and, in so doing, to keep her spirits up and her fears at bay. There were many things needing her attention: the curtains to finish, the floors to varnish, her wardrobe of fine clothes, rarely worn, to be freshened ready to show off. At the thought, Lucy's cheeks grew warm as she reminded herself that she was still in mourning and would remain so for at least another year, but, she reflected, smiling a little, there were lace collars and discreet touches of ribbon and silk that could be added to relieve the deep black, the black of death. Lucy shivered as again she saw Adam's eyes, and quickly pushing the memory from her she bent to replenish the fire.

Breakfast was on the table and the bread-dough set on the hearth to rise when Daniel and Sarah came downstairs. The boy's face was drawn and pale, with shadows beneath his eyes, and Lucy remembered that today the pile of corpses behind the barn was to be burned. Watching Daniel toy with the food on his plate, she came to a conclusion. 'This morning, Daniel,' she said, 'I will require your help indoors. I am going to varnish the floors and with the three of us putting our energies together we will be finished with it the sooner.'

Daniel did not answer immediately, but then he looked directly at his mother and squaring his shoulders said firmly, 'I will be pleased to help you, Mama, but not today. I will not shirk my responsibility.'

'There will be time enough for such awful tasks, Daniel, when you are older — let grown men deal with it today.'

'I'm sorry, Mama, but I must do my part. If I allow you to baby me through the bad times I will lose my self-respect and the respect of those around me. Now — please, may I go?'

Surprised, Lucy faced the steady gaze of her son and saw the depth of his commitment, realizing in that instant that Daniel was fast approaching manhood, and she felt a tiny pang in her heart.

'You are right, of course,' she replied softly, and wondered as he left how she had not noticed his deepening voice or the down on his cheeks until this moment.

That evening there came a tap on the kitchen door and Lucy found Tom Masters on the doorstep. 'Nay, mistress, I'll not come in.' His eyes swept the kitchen. 'Master Daniel about?'

'He is in his room. Sarah, will you call him down?'

'Nay, nay, 'tis a word wi' ye I'm needin',' he said hastily, pulling his hat from his head. 'Yon lad worked along wi' us the day, never once turnin' aside, sickened though 'e were an' 'tis ower thought that 'e's now man enough ter handle a musket.' The hint of a grin played around the man's mouth. 'Wi' your permission, can ye think of owt best able ter take 'is mind from terday?'

Remembering the smudged, exhausted face of her son

and the stench of burned flesh and singed wool that he had carried into the kitchen earlier, Lucy hesitated only a moment. 'Sarah, fetch Daniel down, dear.' A soft smile answered the shepherd's question. 'Tell him that Mr Masters is here to see him.'

~

Within days of the burning, Daniel had little time to dwell on the loss of his sheep; riding boundary, learning to fire the heavy musket, and shellacking and waxing the homestead's floors, his days were filled. Some days earlier, Ruby Gaunt had sent a large bag of shellac, a container of methylated spirits and a big tin of beeswax across to Chandler's Run with clear instructions on how to apply them, and bit by bit the floors were taking on a soft golden shine. Sarah worked hard and happily, trying to ignore the fumes until on the third day Lucy sent her to sit for a time on the veranda. The girl's face was pale and her eyes were heavy, and when she began to shiver Lucy grew a little concerned. 'Do you feel unwell, dear?'

'My head aches, Mama, and it's very cold out here.'

It *was* cold but Sarah was warmly clad, and Lucy, reaching a hand to the soft cheek, found the skin hot and dry.

'Come, lie down for a while until you feel better. It is more than likely the fumes.'

Lucy tucked her up on the horsehair sofa before the parlour fire and left her to doze while she continued with her varnishing. It was some time later when she returned to the parlour and found the girl huddled in the blanket, shivering violently; her face was flushed and her eyes held the brightness of fever.

'May I go to bed, Mama? The sofa hurts me — it is too hard, and my head aches so.'

Seriously worried now, Lucy helped Sarah up to her bed. Returning downstairs she filled a basin with cold water, took up a soft cloth and hurried back to the bedside to bathe Sarah's forehead. The sick girl would take no tea that evening and spoke rarely, wanting only to sleep.

By morning, Lucy was becoming frightened. Sarah's fever was higher, and while she was bathing the burning face she discovered a swelling beneath Sarah's ear. At midday it had grown bigger and was quite inflamed. Lucy waited no longer. She ran to the higher pasture where Daniel rode around the perimeter of the flock. Panting, gripping her side, she sent him racing to the hills to bring down whoever was nearest, to go and fetch the Widow Gaunt.

'Make sure he remembers to tell her — about the fever — the swelling.'

Two and a half hours passed before the widow and Pitchin rode up the track, their lathered animals bearing testimony to the speed with which they had covered the miles between the two runs. It took only minutes for Ruby Gaunt to examine Sarah. By now the glands below her ear had become a painful knotted mass. The widow's seamed face was without expression as her fingers probed beneath the other ear and into the girl's armpits.

'Fetch me something to cover this pillow, girl,' she said then. 'Something you don't mind being stained.'

She turned to her bag as Lucy hurried to do her bidding. From it she extracted a small brown bottle and a piece of wadding, and when Lucy returned she placed the folded cloth under Sarah's head and proceeded to dab the liquid from the bottle on to the swelling beneath her ear.

'What is that? Do you know what is wrong with her?' Lucy whispered.

'Aye. Now, this is iodine and must be applied with persistence. If swelling occurs under her other ear as this one heals, treat that as diligently.' Ruby Gaunt straightened and passed the bottle to Lucy. 'I will leave this with you. The window there needs covering — it is too light in here and Sarah must sleep. You must also drink lots of water,' the widow addressed her young patient. 'Rest now. I will look in again in another day or so.'

Daniel waited for them in the kitchen. 'What is wrong with Sarah, Mama?' He turned to the widow. 'She is very sick, isn't she?'

'She is quite ill but not seriously so yet.' The big woman pulled out a chair and sat down at the table. 'Make me a cup of tea, girl, and I will explain.'

Lucy filled the teapot at the hearth before she also sat to the table, motioning Daniel to do the same. Their eyes were fixed on the Widow Gaunt, fearful of what she was about to tell them, and the widow without preamble began to speak. 'Sarah is suffering from a glandular disease; it is known as scrofula and I have treated native children for it on a number of occasions with some success.' She accepted the cup Lucy passed to her and continued.

347

'Caught early, there is no reason to expect other than a happy ending. However, left untreated or given insufficient treatment, the disease could move to the glands under the arms, resulting more often than not in death.'

'Dear God,' Lucy breathed. 'Where would she have caught such a disease?'

'We are not clear on this, Lucy. It can occur in poorly nourished children or following the measles. These two causes do not relate to Sarah.'

'Scrofula is a horrible word,' Daniel said.

'Aye. And tuberculosis of the lymph glands sounds just as unpleasant, which is what scrofula is.'

Lucy placed her cup carefully in its saucer and stared at the widow.

'Has she caught this from Adam?'

'No, my dear. She more than likely has become infected in one of the native villages where we passed the night or in Dunedin itself. This is a different form of the disease altogether.' Ruby Gaunt sipped her tea thoughtfully then glanced from Daniel to Lucy. 'This will be a tiring affair over the next few days, but I want you to apply the iodine every hour, day and night, until pus forms and the swelling breaks down. Daniel, will you help Mother? She cannot manage this on her own.' The gravelly voice was kindly and her face creased deeply as she looked at the boy.

'I will do anything, anything I can.'

Day followed night and night followed day, and between

them Lucy and Daniel shared the task of administering to Sarah. As the affected glands began to heal, new swellings appeared beneath the other ear, and Lucy, deeply afraid, doubled her efforts with the iodine.

During these worrying days, Willie Good added Lucy's tasks to his own; cooking the meals, baking the bread and making the butter. Tom Masters, along with his shepherding, applied himself to the woodpile and milking the cow. Pitchin and Tanner doubled the hours they rode boundary, and Ruby Gaunt faced the elements every second day on her big mare, covering the freezing miles to Chandler's Run. Every day Lucy prayed that James McKenzie would ride up the snow-covered track to take her again in his arms and soothe away her fears, but as each day passed her prayer remained unanswered.

Willie Good placed a steaming treacle pudding on the kitchen table the day that Sarah was well enough to come downstairs for dinner, and Lucy's heart swelled with gratitude towards these good people who had, in their quiet way, helped them through their trial. She felt a genuine warmth for each and every one of the shepherds, and had come to regard them not only as workers but as friends who cared. Each day one or other of them would come shyly to the homestead to enquire after Sarah. Ruby Gaunt had proved herself to be a pillar of strength with her comforting presence and her dedication to Sarah's recovery, which came swiftly once the swellings were gone.

Life resumed its usual pattern again; Daniel milking the cow and chopping the wood and working his stint with the sheep. He spent long hours in the saddle and absorbed every aspect of sheep management with avid interest. He was tall for his age, mature beyond his years, and carried himself in a manner that drew respect from the men. Lucy knew that Adam would have been proud of his son.

The stitching of the bedroom curtains was finished, and Lucy had spread them on the ground outside, anchored with stones, for the frost to bleach them. Later, when the calico had whitened, she would dye them a soft gold with onion skins before hanging them at the windows. The floors were stained throughout now, but much waxing was still required and could only be done in manageable portions lest the task became too taxing. Tom Masters, of his own volition, had come to turn over the heavy soil of the vegetable garden, reassuring Lucy in his quiet way that he regarded the time he spent doing this as recreation, 'an' 'twould need turnin' at least twice afore the spring planting.'

Almost a month had passed since James McKenzie's visit, and Lucy's tentative expectations were growing less as each day passed. Soon the thaw would be on them and the rivers dangerous to cross. Where would he be and at what risk when the melt-waters began their tumultuous descent from the frozen high ground? Firmly she pushed her anxiety away; he was a pathfinder and would overcome any obstacle to reach her if all was well. Then her thoughts would find another path to worry down. On nights when sleep evaded her, as it often did now, Lucy would sit long into the night penning letters home and writing long lists to send with them of the clothing and commodities they needed to make this remote place more like home. In the light of morning, she would look at her lists again and scratch out most of the items on them. Busy as she kept herself, Lucy found the days plodding by on leaden feet. Sometimes she rode the gelding, but never very far; always hoping that when she returned she would find the Scot awaiting her, and when he wasn't, her despondency deepened.

When the widow invited Lucy to visit for a few days, Lucy was more than ready to break the cycle of her anxieties. Putting Sarah up behind her, she set off on the gelding for Long Reach.

The air was keen as they followed the faint cart track, almost obliterated by the snow, but the gelding knew where he was going; with ears pricked forward, he headed for home. It was a pretty day, crisp snow sparkling, pristine; a tarn here, a stream there beginning to flow again as winter relinquished its hold. As they drew nearer to Long Reach, the black horse nickered and hastened his pace.

Ruby Gaunt stood on the veranda steps to greet them. 'Daniel's not come with yer, I see.'

'Daniel is taking his responsibilities very seriously. With lambing about to descend on us, wild horses could not drag him away.'

'An' that's how it should be. He's a good lad. When yer've freshened yerselves, come sit in the parlour — ther's a fire an' a cup o' tea waitin' ter warm yer.'

Parani came forward shyly as they entered the broad hall to take the flax kits from Lucy's hands, and she and Sarah followed her up the stairs to the room Lucy had occupied previously. Sarah was shown into the bedroom opposite, a room that would evoke no memories of her breakdown. A small chair had been placed before the window and beside it was a low table on which stood a slender vase of early daffodils and several books; a glowing fire warmed the room. There was an air of simple welcome about this room and Lucy was grateful for the widow's sensitivity.

When Lucy and Sarah joined their hostess in the parlour, Moana entered carrying a tea-tray. Placing it beside the big woman's chair she turned to Lucy and smilingly embraced her, then she faced Sarah and, taking the small hands in hers, she briefly touched her nose to the girl's before softly leaving the room. Again Lucy felt the warmth of caring people envelope her and she realized that, during these past weeks, the fear of isolation had almost been erased and she was now more at ease with the kinship they offered. These people of the high country were friends in a very different sense to those at home, even friends of very long standing. They were people of a different calibre entirely. Dealing with raw reality every day, they were hardy, loyal, generous and commonly bonded in the need to rely on each other for survival; and Lucy had received a hard lesson in reliance when Sarah was taken ill.

Smiling inwardly, Lucy recalled her first meeting with the Widow Gaunt. In all her life, she would never have considered friendship with the unprepossessing individual who had thrust herself into Lucy's naked presence that day almost two years before, yet here they were, sipping tea together, comfortable in a friendship that despite dubious beginnings had grown stronger with the passing of time. Each was privy to sensitive issues concerning the other, issues known only to themselves, and each woman instinctively knew that the other would honour the confidences she held.

Five enjoyable days were passed at Long Reach, riding, walking and spending comfortable hours before the parlour fire, conversing on many subjects. On their last day, Mrs Samuels invited the widow and her guests to her own house for afternoon tea.

After toiling uphill for ten minutes they arrived, not at the hut that Lucy had envisaged, but at a wattle and daub cottage. It was whitewashed with a tidy garden set before it, and, on entering through the low doorway, she was surprised again by the civilized appearance of this native home. The small room was furnished like any middle-class English parlour; lace curtains were at the windows, carpet on the floor and a tea-tray was set out on a low table. A silver-framed photo of a middle-aged white man stood on the mantle. Their hostess was completely at ease as she presided over the teacups whilst chatting in passable English. Lucy was intrigued by the Maori woman who, though not much older than herself, had wings of silver in her black hair. She was well versed in native legend and held them enthralled by the tales she told until, with regret, at the widow's signal they took their leave and set off back down the hill.

'The man in the photo, Edward Samuels, was my manager until three years ago — died of pneumonia. Aroha was much younger than he. He was a good man, came from good middle-class stock, and lost his first wife in childbirth on shipboard — married Aroha a year or so later.'

'Are there children?' Lucy asked.

'No, more's the pity. She must be lonely when she's not with us. She's not changed a thing in that cottage since 'er man died — did you see the boots on the hearth?'

The morning was fine with a nip in the air as Lucy and Sarah set off for home. There had been a frost, and ice diamonds glittered on bushes and tussock as they passed. The gelding was fresh and wanted to run but Lucy, mindful of Sarah's nervousness, kept him on a tight rein until they were on a level stretch of track where she lifted him into a rocking canter. She was eager now to be home. There had been several occasions at Long Reach when she thought she had glimpsed McKenzie in the distance, but always it had proved to be somebody else, so she prayed as they rode north that she would find him waiting for her at the homestead.

Tom Masters came from the garden to take the gelding. He smiled his quiet greeting as he helped Sarah down from the horse's back, then turned to steady Lucy as she dismounted.

'You've been working in the garden, Mr Masters?'

'Aye. One more turnin' an' we're about ready ter plant.'

'Would you not rather save your leisure time and spend some days in Dunedin or with friends?' Lucy asked.

'Nay, mistress. I'd not enjoy the smell o' that place an' my friends are here.' Colour dyed the man's throat and touched his weathered face as he took the gelding's reins from Lucy's hand.

'Please don't misunderstand me, Mr Masters. I do appreciate the help you are giving me,' Lucy said quickly, 'but you work all the time. Surely there must be times when you would like to be free to do the things you like doing?'

''Tis doin' summat I like, do ye see — an' — ' a faint grin twitched the shepherd's lips ' — vegetables don't bleat.' Gathering up the reins, he nodded briefly and led the gelding away. Sarah burst into laughter and Lucy shook her head as they went up the veranda steps. She was not going to argue further; if this quiet man was happy working in the garden in his own time, then she was content to let him. His proximity in this vast place was reassuring and company of a sort. He rarely conversed, even though there was much he could wish to talk about with this lovely woman if only his shyness did not keep his tongue tied in knots.

Embers glowed dully on the hearth as Lucy entered the kitchen but only cold ash was in the parlour grate; the homestead held a feeling of emptiness as she walked slowly to the window to search the hills. Only Daniel could she see, riding towards her, and he rode alone.

Chapter 13

IT WAS DANIEL'S fourteenth birthday. Lucy was putting the finishing touches to the dinner when Ruby Gaunt hailed her from the front path.

'Hello, the house! Come and take these — quickly, if you please!'

Sarah ran to open the door. The Widow Gaunt sat precariously in her saddle, a parcel clamped under her arm and a bag held aloft in the gloved hand. With her other hand she struggled to restrain the big mare which stamped, twitched and turned, half-bucking with ears laid back.

'Cook's made some sweetmeats for the lad's birthday,' the widow grunted. 'Get them inside afore I'm dumped an' the beast 'elps 'erself. Quite a sweet tooth has Bess!' Lucy approached the animal in quick, nervous darts, snatched the bag and parcel, and hastened up the veranda steps while the widow turned the recalcitrant mare towards the barn. 'Get along, yer old glutton — straw is good enough fer you.'

Lucy placed the parcel and the bag next to the gifts from Sarah and herself, to await Daniel's attention when he came in for his dinner. In pride of place on the kitchen table was a large apple pie — made from the previous year's preserved apples, Willie Good had stated when he'd delivered it to the kitchen door an hour earlier.

Setting the good china on the table, Lucy sang softly to herself and Sarah smiled as she listened. Mama seems happier today, she thought, which is as well, it being Daniel's birthday. Some days she sensed her mama's distraction and believed she understood why. She did not dwell on the why of it, however; her mind still tending to shy away from thoughts of her father. Better to centre her thoughts on Mama, ever busy making the homestead more like home. The portions of the floor that had been waxed were a rich gold, softly shining, and the curtains that they had stitched for the parlour and bedroom windows, Mama had dyed to a pale gold. The overall effect was one of sunshine and warmth, which gladdened Sarah's house-proud heart. It was a shame that they had used all the shellac, because the walls could be stained as well, but more could be coming she supposed, as would the new furniture if Mama ever got around to ordering it. It would truly be home then.

Sarah, almost twelve years of age, promised to be as lovely as her mother. Fair where Lucy was dark, her young figure had blossomed into early shapeliness, rapidly outgrowing the expertise of Lucy's needle on her existing garments. She crinkled her nose as she recalled the stench of Dunedin's long main street. Mama had said that, because it took so long for dresses to come from home, they might have to make another trip into the town next winter — the thought of which held no appeal for Sarah.

The kitchen door opened and Ruby Gaunt entered,

rubbing her hands together. 'By, 'tis a bonny day an' ther's twenty early lambs frolicking about on them bottom pastures.' She raised her head and sniffed. 'Summat smells good — the lad'll be down any minute, 'e says.'

'Go through to the parlour, Ruby,' Lucy smiled. 'Sarah will bring you a hot drink and I will join you directly.'

The widow cast an appreciative eye over the younger woman. Lucy wore her usual black, but had relieved it with a jade silk scarf draped about her shoulders. Her hair she wore in glossy coils on top of her head; her flawless skin glowed with health. She was a beauty, no doubt about it, and there was a subtle change in her, an inner something that had not been there before. Nodding sagely to herself, Ruby Gaunt stepped across the hall and into the parlour. McKenzie had said little to her about his visit to Chandler's Run and she could only guess at his reason for going there. Looking at Lucy now, as she followed Sarah into the room, she prayed that the Scot would be able to vindicate himself in the eyes of the law and that no more tragedy would be visited on her young friend. On her previous visits, the Widow Gaunt had exercised unusual tact, making no mention of McKenzie. In time, perhaps, Lucy would confide in her.

They chatted of mundane things beside the parlour fire, until they heard Daniel in the kitchen and there they joined him. He was smiling broadly as he held up a tooled leather belt that Jack Tanner had given him and a small wooden horse, carved in faithful detail from a block of pine, which young Pitchin had laboured over for weeks.

'And Mr Masters has given me the musket,' he said proudly.

'Ther's more ter come, young man,' the widow rumbled, indicating the parcels on the table. Daniel opened them quickly, his smile growing wider still as he unwrapped his mother's gift: two novels, Charles Dickens's *David Copperfield* and *Oliver Twist*, which Lucy had purchased from the general store while they were in Dunedin; a bright woollen scarf, knitted for him by Sarah; and a warm sheepskin jacket from Ruby Gaunt. 'Ther's a bag of sweetmeats an' all, from Cook,' she chuckled, pointing. 'Near cost me me life carryin' it acrost ter yer.' In comical detail she told him of Bess's addiction to sweet things and her antics on the ride over from Long Reach.

'As well, Daniel,' Lucy added when their laughter had ceased, 'Mr Good has baked you this apple pie.'

There was a small silence. Daniel's face sobered briefly and Lucy guessed that her son was remembering his last birthday, when McKenzie had been present. A tiny dart of hope went through her. Would he come today? Daniel was smiling again, hugging Sarah and his mother and placing a quick peck on the widow's seamed cheek.

'A chap couldn't have a better birthday — thank you, one and all — and Cook,' he laughed.

~

It was officially spring but still a little too cold to plant the vegetables or Lucy's borders. Tom Masters had suggested erecting a stout fence around the vegetable garden and the homestead to prevent the sheep from destroying the plants, and each day Lucy and Sarah went to gather small stones to make a pathway to the front gate and a path from the back door to the outhouse, thus enabling them to remain mud-free when it rained. Standing on the veranda admiring their efforts, Lucy visualized the flowers they would plant moving in a soft breeze, the colourful borders and the flowers growing in profusion below the veranda railing. Clematis and honeysuckle would climb the veranda posts busy with bees, and Lucy closed her eyes, envisaging the Scot on his chestnut horse ambling up the track, coming to make her life here complete.

But still he did not come and Lucy's spirits began to lag. Keeping busy by day she forced herself to be optimistic, but the nights betrayed her. Many times she lay warm and secure in his arms, delighting in his love, only to awaken to empty reality and hopeless tears. Listlessness was growing in her now, and Daniel, observing this, finally spoke. 'Mama, are you unwell?'

'No, dear.' Lucy saw the worry in her son's eyes and felt guilty. Closed away in her longing and anxiety, obsessively busy in the attempt to shut out her fears, Lucy realized she had unconsciously been shutting out her children. Daniel stood before her, taller and broader still, and she had not seen him growing. Had she also missed essential changes in Sarah? In that moment, she resolved that whatever the future held for her the children must not be neglected. Nor must their home; this very night they would sit down as a family and choose furniture and carpets from Nobby Clark's catalogues, and whatever else they required to complete their home.

That evening, as the list grew longer, Lucy found she was actually enjoying herself, and, when Sarah and Daniel had finally gone to bed, she sat quietly thinking, then on impulse added a butter churn and a saddle to the list and a note at the bottom of it to send for a piano tuner.

The following morning she intercepted Willie Good as he returned from his stint of riding boundary, to inform him that she would be sharing the cooking with him when lambing started in earnest; she would not neglect her workers either.

Willie was delighted with Lucy's decision and happily set about telling her what meals the men favoured. 'Mutton stew an' mashed potato, middle o' the day — I've a bag o' potatoes left — an' station brownie ter follow, made wi' flour, brown sugar, drippin' an' raisins. Pitchin or me will take it up to 'em, rather than have 'em comin' down one after t'other gettin' under ower feet.' He rubbed his hands together and continued. 'Supper will be beef-steak pie made wi' a good dripping pastry an' a plum-duff they can eat 'ot or cold — they'll come down fer their supper.'

'Should we roast some pork, Mr Good?'

'Nay, missus, the men'll prefer their stews an' their pies, as I've said.'

'Every day, the same food?' Lucy raised her eyebrows.

'Aye, every day the same.' The cook grinned. 'An' bread — heaps o' bread to sop up the gravy.'

When they had agreed on which meals each would cook,

Lucy returned to the homestead to sort out her cooking pots for the mutton stew and mashed potato.

'Tis as well ye'll be cookin' fer a small crew first-off — shearin', now, wi' all t'extra mouths ter feed — ye'd as like want ter pack it in quick,' Willie Good had asserted, but Lucy was experiencing an odd feeling of satisfaction, of being a part of the bigger picture for the first time since setting foot on Chandler's Run, and she looked forward to it. After dinner she sent Daniel off to instruct Masters to dispatch three five-year-old wethers to top up her meat barrels and to send the skins down to the homestead, please. She and Sarah, at the widow's urging, would be learning to tan them and make them into floor rugs, using tree bark in place of the mineral salts or tannic acid they did not have.

Sarah was excited at the prospect of helping her mother with the cooking, anticipating a certain amount of fancy fare to be added to the menu. Lucy brought her down to earth: 'Plain food, Sarah, and large quantities of it when the shearing begins in January, and lots of bread.'

'May I do the pudding, then?'

'Of course you may.'

'Perhaps I could make the plum-duff as well?'

'If Mr Good agrees, dear.' Lucy smiled. 'Now let us go and gather more stones for the paths — I would like them to be finished as quickly as we can manage now.'

Of late, Tom Masters had been bringing larger stones in his saddlebags to border the paths, and each time he came down from the hills at day's end Lucy looked forward to his brief visits as he set them in place. He was a quiet man, unassuming, as he went about his work around the homestead, and she was comfortable with his presence. For his part, Tom Masters was more than content just to be near the lovely widow, asking and expecting nothing more than to speak to her sometimes and be able to work in her garden. His devotion was humble and it was complete.

One evening when he was putting the finishing touches to the garden gate and Lucy was planting out her stock seed below the veranda rail, a lone rider came into sight around the corner of the track. He rode a rangy chestnut and Lucy's pulse leapt. Her feet carried her to the gate before she realized she was watching the approach of a stranger. Tom Masters, reading the naked disappointment on her face, knew then where his love's heart lay and he turned quickly away lest she see his own.

Lucy waited, hands clenched beneath her apron, for the rider to draw nearer.

'Is it Mrs Chandler you are, then?' he called. 'Jimmy O'Reilly, missus, come ter tune yer piano, so I have, at the biddin' o' the good Widow Gaunt.'

He drew his horse to a halt before the gate and removed his worn bowler. ''Tis hopin' ye've a place ter rest me head, I am, seein' it's late an'—' he reached into a copious saddle-bag '— 'tis yer letters an' a paper or two I've here as well.'

Struggling to regain her composure, Lucy thanked him and took the proffered bundle, then, without raising her eyes, she said, 'Would you see Mr O'Reilly settled, Mr Masters, please?' Turning to face the piano tuner she added, 'Come to the house in the morning. It is too late to start now.'

''Tis kind ye are an' all,' the man replied and, replacing his bowler hat, he turned his horse about and followed Tom Masters down to the hut.

'We can sing carols around the piano at Christmas, Mama,' Sarah said happily as she followed Lucy inside. 'It will be like it used to be at home.' Expectantly, she stood close to Lucy, waiting to see who the letters were from.

'Yes, pet, it will. Now — here are letters from Grandmama and Grandpapa. There is one from Auntie Charlotte, Uncle Christian and — I think these two are from Grandmama Chandler and, yes, Auntie Amelia. You may open Auntie Charlotte's letter, if you wish.' Lucy placed the letters and the papers on the kitchen table, keeping back a long envelope with the seal of the Land Office on it. Quickly she broke the seal and, withdrawing the contents, she read them twice before slowly seating herself at the table. Her claim had been granted; she had won. Elation began to spread through her and her elation carried her into her next expectation: James McKenzie would return to her. Together they would work these many acres, build their homestead — in time, when Daniel was older — and fill it with love and children. She smiled softly.

'Mama.' Sarah's voice broke into her daydream. 'Auntie Charlotte has had a baby. She was born in January and they've named her Anna Jane, for Grandmama Camden — isn't that wonderful?'

Lucy took the letter from Sarah's hand. 'Indeed it is!'

Lucy's younger sister had longed for a family, but, in spite of all care, had never carried to term. How the family at home would have celebrated the birth of this long-awaited child, who would now be eight or nine months old. A pang of homesickness smote Lucy as she visualized the love and devotion the family would be bestowing on this tiny new member, but it was quickly gone when she saw again in her mind's eye the way the Scot had looked at her and felt again his arms holding her. This was to be her life now, and her pulse quickened when she realized that it could be starting very soon. Lucy read her parents' letters, full of news from home and doting observations about the baby girl, then skimmed through the other letters, intending to read them in full later. When these letters had been written, her letters advising them of Adam's and Ruben's deaths had not yet arrived. She passed them to Sarah, and reaching for a copy of the *Otago Witness* she scanned the pages with a cursory glance.

Suddenly her body stiffened, her eyes riveted to the stark printed sentences on the page before her: James McKenzie had been recaptured and had begun to serve his long sentence. For a moment shock made the words meaningless, but, as their import began to register, Lucy's hopes crumbled to dust. The Scot would not be coming home; he had not cleared his name. What would five years behind stone walls do to him — would this further injustice embitter him again? Lucy longed to be with him, to comfort him, to share his pain.

Suddenly cold, she stood up and went to stand before the hearth. Sarah chatted on and Lucy answered, not attending to what was said or how she replied. She was in a dark and hopeless place that somehow seemed familiar — had she been here before? She knew that she had, but this time the darkness was deeper.

~

The empty days passed; each hour reluctant to move into the next, it seemed to Lucy. As busy as she kept herself in her waking hours, there were long periods where time was an aching vacuum that she had no power to fill. Her nights were sleepless or nightmare-filled and, even though she was an integral part of a working team, in her isolated state her loneliness was absolute. She was suspended once again, waiting for a future that might or might not eventuate, and her labours now seemed pointless.

In despair she began to ride again, going further and further from the homestead, heedless of the hours she was away, reluctant to return. Only Sarah was aware of her mother's long absences, but she said nothing. Many times the lessons Lucy set for her she had done before, and of this she also said nothing but used the time doing the tasks that were being neglected. It was Sarah now who made the stews and the station brownie and baked the bread.

In mid-October the thaw had begun and snow tussock, buried for months, appeared on the ridges again. Lucy set off early one morning, nodding to Willie Good as she rode past the hut.

'Watch 'ow yer go, missus,' he called, ''Twill be gettin' slushy up in them gullies.'

With a bellyful of spring grass, Thomas stepped out with a will and Lucy turned him, as she had several times earlier, on to the rugged hills of Camden Station. A warm north-westerly was at her back, and after a time, disregarding the cook's warning, she began to climb higher towards the scrub-line and the edge of the forest. She had been up there before on the sure-footed gelding, and the view was superb, but there were moments now when the snow underfoot was dangerously soft and the black horse plunged nervously until his hooves found solid ground. Lucy pushed him on, unheeding.

It took a long time to search out a path through the speargrass and bush-lawyer but eventually they reached the tree-line. Finding a vantage point where she could view the wide panorama spread out below her, Lucy dismounted, gave the gelding a rewarding pat and tied him to a tree. She found a niche in the rocks clear of snow, and settled herself to eat the food she had prepared that morning. Her hunger satisfied, Lucy leaned back against the rock face behind her and began to doze. She was warm in this sheltered place, and tired from lack of sleep and the long ride. As the noises of the bush and the peace enveloped her, she drifted into sleep.

She was chilled when she awoke; the sun was low. She had slept too long and the gelding was pawing the ground, nickering uneasily. The wind had risen and tugged at his mane and tail, and as Lucy left the shelter of the niche the strong north-wester buffeted her, making her stagger. She lifted her gaze to the skies, saw the grey banners of ragged cloud racing south, and quickly gathering up her saddlebag she untied the horse. 'We must go home, Thomas, and fast,' she muttered as she mounted. She swung the horse around to where they had come through the scrub earlier, but the wind, gusting fiercely now, laid the bush over, obscuring any sign of the passage the gelding had made.

Time and again, Lucy drove the animal into the thrashing bush, and time and again they had to retreat as impenetrable thickets of matagouri and bush-lawyer barred their way. It would soon be dusk and Lucy was growing afraid. Then she remembered McKenzie merging into the forest the day she had carried her bannocks up to the barn. He had not come down through the scrub but had surely found a safer path through the stunted pines. She turned the gelding back towards the trees. It was already dark beneath their swaying canopy, and the wind moaned and shrieked through the flailing branches. She leaned forward, stroking the animal's neck, and her palm came away sticky. Her legs beneath their covering of moleskin were stinging and felt sticky also, telling her she had not escaped the barbs and razors of the bush either. Swinging the horse into the wind, Lucy gave him his head. 'Take us home, Thomas, good boy, take us home!' she called over the wind.

Twigs and small branches flew in their faces as they moved forward. The gelding was edgy, swinging his head this way and that, stepping out erratically, stopping suddenly, snorting, then trotting on for a space only to hesitate again, nostrils flared, testing the wind.

The strength of the gale increased, and somewhere above a tree was uprooted and came down with a rending crash. The gelding leapt forward in fright and Lucy was almost unseated as he plunged through the darkness. There was no path, just stunted writhing trees coming at them from every direction, and she clung to the flying mane, branches whipping and tearing at her as the horse ran headlong. Then he came to a sudden sliding halt on the edge of a scree slope that fell away almost sheer below them. There was no forest or scrub here, just rock and snow and shale. Lucy could see no clear way ahead other than across the treacherous face, and in the growing gloom she could not see how far it extended.

Turning the horse obliquely into the wind Lucy urged him forward but he baulked, snorting and nickering in fear. Desperately she drove him with heels, hands and voice until he took a tentative step on to the unstable footing, and then another, until he was slipping and sliding on his haunches across the steep face, struggling to stay on his feet. With her heart thudding against her ribs she pushed him ever downwards, letting him choose his way; the path home was somewhere below them, and with God's help they would find it.

The wind was a screaming, tearing demon, tugging and battering horse and rider with stinging, continuous force, taking the breath from their lungs. When the gelding halted abruptly, trembling in every limb, Lucy peered ahead but could see nothing but the pale gleam of smooth snow. Why had he stopped? She shouted and struck the black horse with heels and fists; he would not budge. She screamed and hammered at him until at last he leapt forward, and suddenly they were floundering in soft, deep snow. The horse struggled violently to extricate himself, rearing back, plunging about until he found solid rock, but slick with ice his hooves could find no purchase and they were sliding out of control down the frozen face, then they were falling. With a whistle of sheer terror, the horse was gone from beneath her and Lucy was plunging downwards head-first. She felt her teeth jar through her lip as she hit something solid, then she knew no more.

～

Willie Good, breathing hard, hurried through the milling sheep. Tom Masters, hearing the cook's shout above the wind, turned his horse towards him and seeing the agitation on the cook's plump face called out, 'Summat amiss, Willie?'

'Aye, an' badly I fear.' The cook wiped a sleeve across his streaming face. 'She's not come back — the young missus. Rode out early this morn,' he panted. 'Should 'ave been back long afore this — 'twill be dark in an hour or so an' that lot'll be on us soon!' He waved an arm at the flying clouds above their heads.

Masters' face darkened. 'Which way did she go?'

'I'd not be knowin', but she'll 'ave left tracks, less'n ther wind's swept 'em away. Headed south is all I know.'

The shepherd moved swiftly. Putting heels to his horse, scattering sheep in every direction, he galloped off. 'Send Pitchin ter Long Reach — get help!' The urgent words came back on the wind.

Stopping briefly at the hut, Tom Masters gathered up bedroll, horse-blanket, flint and tinderbox, sugar, tea and pannikins. From the byre he snatched up clean straw, stuffed it into a gunnysack, and tying it behind his saddle he mounted again and rode on. The wind had scuffed the loose snow but he could see faint tracks left by the gelding and followed them on to the new run, losing them briefly among the tussock where Lucy had turned from the track, heading for higher ground.

The light was almost gone and the shepherd pushed his winded horse harder. The wind was obliterating the faint tracks even as he rode, and in the near-darkness he was forced to retrace his steps several times to pick the tracks up again. Then, as he approached the scrub-line, he lost the tracks altogether. Dismounting, he looped the horse's reins over a rock and went forward on foot, crouched low, straining his eyes to see any disturbance in the snow. Without success, he searched a hundred yards either side of the place where the tracks had ceased, then paced further afield trying to find a break in the dense scrub, but the wind beating and tearing at it obscured any path that might have been there.

Close to despair Tom Masters began to shout, but his voice was lost in the roar of the wind. He made himself stand still and think. The tracks he had followed were not fresh; in all probability they had been made before midday. If Lucy Chandler had found a way into the forest and had become lost, it was feasible that as the day wore on she would have turned her horse in the direction of home — if she had not become disorientated — hoping to find a place where she could pass through the scrub without injury to herself or her horse.

Masters returned to his mount, took up the reins and, still on foot, headed north, keeping to the scrub-line until rocky outcrops and gullies forced him to descend. Passing around them, in the rapidly falling darkness he stumbled knee-deep into soft snow time and again, snow that appeared firm. His concern for Lucy was growing. As he moved with care over the unfamiliar ground, he shouted until he was hoarse. There was little hope that she would hear him, but he kept shouting. The wind was changing, coming from the west, a cold blast howling down from the mountains. The shepherd mounted his horse and rode on slowly, knowing there was little chance of finding Lucy in the darkness — the area was too vast and too wild for one man to cover. A heavy lump of defeat sat in the pit of his stomach as he turned his mount downhill. To his left, faintly visible, was the edge of a stony moraine; to attempt to cross it would mean certain disaster. Following the dim outline until it ended in a deep gully, he then turned his horse west and began to climb again. Carried on the wind, he heard the distant sound of unstable snow crashing from the steep rock faces and the report of trees splitting asunder under the gale's onslaught. Then, over these noises, he heard the terrified scream of a horse and from somewhere above him dislodged stones and boulders were sliding and bouncing. Suddenly, Masters' horse squealed in protest, plunging away as rocks and shale pelted them. When they had subsided, the shepherd kicked his horse into motion.

Lightning stabbed the darkness as he urged his mount upwards. There had been only that single scream, and the savagery of the wind made it difficult to pinpoint its direction, but the fall of rock and snow had come from almost directly above him and that was where he would search. Masters was not a praying man, but he was praying now as the thunder rumbled and he pushed on higher and higher, dreading what he might find. He had never denied his feelings for Lucy Chandler and readily had accepted that she would never look on him as she did the Scot. He had believed he could be content while ever he was permitted to be close to her, in whatever capacity. Desperately, he kicked his heels into his labouring horse; if he found her dead now, he would have squandered any chance he might have had to win her, and bitter gall rose in his throat as he faced the stark possibility that this was likely.

With dramatic suddenness the wind ceased, and in the eerie stillness Masters heard the squealing cough of an animal in distress. It came from somewhere to his left. Dismounting, the shepherd crouched down, feeling about in the darkness for the source of the sound. If it proved to be Lucy's horse then she must be near. 'Lucy!' His voice was loud in the silence and his mount started away, dragging at the reins looped over his arm. 'Steady, lad, steady.'

Masters stood up, peering ahead. 'Lucy Chandler! Lucy, can yer hear me?' he called again, but only the sounds of the night came back to him.

The darkness was total and the cold bit his face and hands. He stepped forward slowly, aware that one wrongly placed foot could end it all, here and now. Depending on his horse's senses rather than his own, he climbed upwards until they were halted abruptly by an outcrop of rock. Masters moved along its face, touching its roughness, then without warning his hands were flailing at emptiness and he was falling forward, desperately clinging to the reins. The horse nickered in protest but stood firm while the shepherd regained his feet and moved carefully forward. The lightning flashed then, revealing a deep recess beneath the outcrop. The opening was blacker than the night as Masters entered and he rummaged in his saddlebags to find his flint and tinderbox, then grabbing a fistful of straw from the gunnysack he squatted down and struck the flint until he had a spark. With infinite care he blew the tiny ember until the straw caught alight. He peered beyond the small blaze into what appeared to be a deep cave. Rotting branches and dry tussock were banked against the rough walls, and the shepherd wasted no time gathering up armloads of these to feed his tiny fire. The feral smell of pig and wild dog was strong in his nostrils, and the horse stared warily about as Masters led him into the cave.

The lightning flashed and the thunder rolled as he took his bedroll from the pommel of his saddle and, kicking a space clear of rubble near the fire, he spread it out. Quickly he searched for a thick branch, and finding what he needed he thrust it into the flames until it became a fiery brand; then, leaving the shelter of the cave, he stumbled out into the cold darkness to begin his search. He found the gelding first. The horse lay still, cast; evidence of his struggles to rise lay in the broken rock and piled snow brought down by his flailing hooves. He rolled a white eye as Masters held his torch aloft but did not move. The shepherd stroked the matted neck. 'Rest, lad,' he muttered. 'I'll see to ye directly.' Then he raised the blazing torch high and again began to call. The silence was unnerving him. A dozen times he blundered towards Lucy's body lying in the snow only to find each time that it was exposed rock or a shadow cast by his torch. In the end he almost stood on her when he slipped on the slick surface of the moraine. She was frighteningly still and the coldness of death lay on her as Masters touched her cheek with a shaking hand. 'Eh, Lucy, girl — eh.' He rammed the end of his torch between the rocks and with infinite gentleness lifted her into his arms, holding her for a moment before beginning the slow descent to the shelter of the cave.

Lightning stabbed the darkness, aiding his erratic progress, and when at last he reached the over-hanging rock, he entered and laid the still form on his bedroll. In the light of the fire he could see the extent of her injuries; the lovely face was bloodied and bruised, and congealing blood filled her mouth. Tom Masters gathered her to him then and, cradling her in his arms, he wept. He did not hear the low moan of the returning wind or see the brilliant flash of the lightning. The thunder reverberated around the hills, crashing almost continuously overhead, but in his grief he was deaf to all of it. Time stood still while he knelt there holding her, then at last he pressed his lips to her cold forehead and laid her gently down.

Rising slowly to his feet, Masters went to his horse, removed the saddle and saddlebags, and lifting out the pannikins he walked to the cave entrance. There he scooped snow into them and turning to the fire he placed them near the edge to thaw. This done he returned to his horse, fed him a handful of straw and covered him with his blanket. The shepherd's movements were sluggish; he felt bone-weary as he did these simple tasks. He longed to lie down beside his beloved and do no more, but he knew he could not. The black horse was waiting for him, either to rescue him or put him out of his misery. But first there was something he would do.

Removing a pannikin from the embers he tugged his neckerchief from his neck and dipped it into the melted snow, then kneeling beside Lucy he washed the blood from her face and mouth. ''Tis an evil thing that has befallen ye, lass — that has taken ye from me.'

He lifted a bloodied hand and, tenderly, his rough fingers washed it clean. 'I would have cherished ye to me last breath — ye didn't know that, did ye?' He raised his eyes to the dear, dead face and, from beneath puffed lids, Lucy looked steadily back at him. His heart lurched into his throat. 'By, ye're alive,' he breathed. 'I thought never ter look into yer eyes again — by.'

Masters' haggard face expressed a gamut of emotions. He leaned closer as Lucy's swollen lips formed words he could not hear. 'What are ye tryin' ter say?'

'Horse — my horse?'

'Aye, lass, yer horse is out ther' an' I'll see ter 'im when I've tended ter ye.'

He picked up the pannikin and, taking it to the entrance

of the cave, he scrubbed it out with snow then packed it to the brim with fresh snow and pushed it into the glowing embers. Then, going back to Lucy, he lifted his saddle from the ground and placed it carefully under her head. As he straightened, he turned away, listening intently. Carried on the gusting wind he heard the shrill whistle of a horse in distress. Lucy heard it too and tried to rise. Masters pressed her back.

'Leave it ter me, lass, ther's nowt ye can do.'

He picked up his carbine, seized a blazing branch from the fire and strode away into the darkness. The wind gusted wildly beyond the cave opening and Lucy lay rigid, eyes closed, waiting, straining her ears. In a while she heard the crack of rifle shots. It seemed a long time before she heard the shepherd's voice nearby, beyond the fire, and she became aware that the wind had ceased. 'Come on, lad, there's nowt ter worry about — ye're safe in here, aye, an' warm — steady now — there.'

Lucy forced her eyes open as Masters came into the firelight leading the gelding. The horse was bloodied and very lame, snorting and nickering nervously as he was led into the cave, and Lucy began to cry, gasping sobs that hurt and tore at Masters' heart. He covered the black horse with the blanket he took from his own horse, then knelt again beside the weeping woman and placed a gentle hand on her shoulder.

'Ye thought I'd shot 'im, but 'twere wild dogs I shot that were about to sup on 'im. Aye, weep, lass, 'tis healin' ter weep—' The soothing words stopped in his throat as emotion overtook him, then after a space he muttered, 'Has been a hell of a do has this an' no mistake.' Rising stiffly to his feet, he set about making a brew of hot sweet tea and melting more snow for the horses.

A flash of lightning and a clap of thunder heralded the rain. Lucy had drifted into exhausted sleep after Masters had dribbled a little tea between her damaged lips. Now he attended to the horses' needs and built up the fire before lowering himself to the rough floor, there to prop himself against the cold stone and keep watch over the woman he had thought was lost to him. A dozen thoughts crowded into his mind while he feasted his eyes on the beloved face. By, he'd waste no more time; 'twas a miracle that she lived at all — he was as good as any man an' the Scot could take 'is chances — let the best man win — fair to say *he* was here an' the Scot was not. This was his time — he would woo this woman and he would treasure her to his last breath, aye. Help — immediate help was needed — had anyone seen his fire? He must not let it go out — poor bloody horse —

The gelding had sustained many injuries, among them a severely wrenched shoulder, but the shepherd had found no broken bones. He had applied liniment to the shoulder and covered the animal again; he could do no more until daylight came.

Lucy's injuries were more difficult to ascertain. She had barely moved since he had laid her in the cave, and he was reluctant to intrude on her modesty by searching her person for injury. If nobody came the next day, he would ride for the

Widow Gaunt — but how could he leave her? In a quandary, the shepherd closed his eyes.

The rain beyond the cave was torrential and, in spite of himself, Masters dozed fitfully, jerked awake at intervals by the roar of unstable snow and rock plunging down from rock faces and outcrops. He thanked God that he had found Lucy and the gelding when he had. There would have been little chance of finding either alive in these conditions, if indeed they could have been found at all.

A still, grey morning dawned and Masters stood at the cave entrance surveying the ravages wrought by the storm. Rushing torrents of water carrying dirty snow and debris from the hills above him posed a real danger to anyone trying to negotiate the rocky slopes, either going down or climbing up, until such time as the flow abated. He knew it would be folly to risk the journey to Long Reach alone; if he failed, Lucy might not be found. No. Urgent though the situation was, he'd best wait for conditions to improve. He turned back into the cave.

Lucy was awake. Supporting her, he held the pannikin to her swollen mouth and she tried to sip the cooling tea. In the daylight, Masters could see that her bottom lip was deeply lacerated, making drinking difficult and painful. 'Aye, 'twill hurt, lass, but ye need the sustenance — take yer time.'

When the light in the cave grew stronger, Masters was able to examine the gelding more closely. The shoulder was grossly swollen and his hooves were split and broken. Both of the animal's knees were bloody pulp, and his nose and chin were deeply grazed. The shepherd had been obliged to cut the wrecked saddle from the horse's back in order to roll him on to his feet, and he wondered if he should go and retrieve it. Remembering the tricky descent down to the cave, he decided against it. He applied more liniment to the animal's shoulder, then replaced his blanket. Picking up his hat, Masters went outside and packed clean snow into it. He had found a hollowed stone and this he filled with the snow, making a number of trips back and forth, then emptied hot water over the snow and stirred it about until the horses were able to drink.

Lucy lay watching him. The shepherd's rugged face was grey with fatigue as he plodded back and forth. She had never studied his face before but she did so now, and in it she recognized the heart of the man as he moved about, quietly attending to the needs of herself and the horses. But for him, she knew, she would not be alive now and neither would the black horse. Tears welled up and trickled from under her bruised eyelids. Masters was quickly beside her. 'Eh, lass, are ye hurtin'?'

Lucy moved her head fractionally towards him and forced words through her lips, 'So kind — thank you.'

'Nay, nay.' Masters gently touched her shoulder. 'Don't ye go upsettin' yerself - — rest — save yer strength.'

He watched her for a moment until she was calm, then urged her to sip more tea. When she had finished he got to his feet and walked wearily to the cave entrance, his mouth set in a grim line. Damn the Scot — damn him! he thought as he stared out at the desolate landscape. That sweet lass in ther' would be better served if the feller didn't come back with his wanderin' ways — damn him!

He stepped out on to the snow and walked a short distance from the cave, shielding his eyes against the glare as he looked for landmarks. A thin mist was rising from the valley floor, obscuring much that lay there. He could hear the deeper roar of a large body of water and wondered if it was the river that joined the fork below the plateau. If it was, then he knew where they were, but to be certain he would have to wait until the mist cleared.

His stomach rumbled with hunger. It had been many hours since he had eaten and the sweet tea gave only brief relief from the pangs. Why had he not thought to pack some bread in his saddlebags? Lucy would have benefited by having something more substantial to sustain her than tea. He turned back into the cave and found her again near to tears. 'What is it, lass?'

Closing her eyes she mumbled, 'Privy.'

'Privy?' Dark colour suffused Masters' face. 'Oh, aye—'

'I'm sorry,' Lucy whispered and silent tears fell.

The shepherd gathered his wits with an effort. 'Don't ye fret now — 'tis nothin' ter be bothered about — let me sort summat.' He stood for a space contemplating the fire at his feet, then picked up a dry branch and pushed its end into the flames. When it had caught alight he picked his way deeper into the rocky recess, holding the burning branch before him. The cave was much deeper than he had at first thought, ending in a jumble of rock and debris piled high against a low roof.

Masters wedged his branch into the rocks and set about

gathering flat-sided stones. These he placed one on top of the other to make a seat of sorts with a hole in the centre, careful to ensure that the small structure was stable. Working quickly he padded out the rough top with twists of dry grass then went back to Lucy. 'Can ye sit up a little? Aye, that's it.'

Lucy gasped with pain as Masters lifted her in his arms and carried her to the makeshift commode. 'Now, I'll not be looking at ye,' he said as he set her gently on to her feet, and divesting himself of his jacket he draped it about her, then turning away he said, 'When ye're ready I'll help ye ter sit.'

Lucy, barely able to stand, struggled with her clothing; sharp pain in her side made her gasp again and almost fall. She clung to Masters' shirt, half-laughing, half-crying, embarrassed and hurting, and the jacket fell to the floor.

''Tis all right.' With his face still averted Masters picked up the jacket and tied the arms firmly about Lucy's waist, and with commendable sensitivity on the shepherd's part the deed was done. Gently, he carried her back to the fire; she was shivering with cold and shock as he laid her down and Tom Masters began to worry anew. He would have to fetch the widow; he daren't wait any longer. Somewhere down there people would be looking for them now and somehow he must draw their attention. Hurrying to the rear of the cave again, he gathered up an armload of dry grass, and taking it outside he rubbed it in the snow then placed it on to the fire. It smoked as he had hoped it would but the smoke was pale and would not easily be seen. He went back inside the cave and squatted beside Lucy. 'Ye'll be alone fer a bit — need ter let the folks know where we are — I'll not be gone long.'

Taking up two long sticks he left her then, and prodding the soft snow beyond the cave he worked in a wide radius, looking for a safe descent. Rock and debris was still coming down but the torrent had eased a bit. He kept a wary eye on any movement above him as he worked his way to the edge of the treacherous slope, marking his path with the sticks for fear of losing his bearings.

He stopped abruptly. Over the noise of grinding stones and rushing water he had heard a shrill whistle. He watched the patchy mist that lay below him but could see nothing. Putting his fingers to his lips he whistled in reply. A whistle came back immediately, followed by a distant shout. Relief choked Masters' voice momentarily, but then he bellowed and bellowed again. By — help was coming!

Two voices were shouting now and he realized that they were not muffled by the mist but came clearly from the slopes north of his precarious position. As he picked his careful way towards the voices, two riders came into view over a low ridge and he recognized Daniel and Jack Tanner. He waved his arms and shouted a warning, pointing to the unstable scree above. Jack Tanner shouted something back and Masters watched as the riders dropped from sight.

For a long time there was no sign of them, then they appeared again, closer and on foot, leading their horses. The shepherd stood still on the edge of the moraine and awaited their approach. In spite of Masters' warning, Daniel pushed ahead. 'Mama — have you found Mama?'

The boy's eyes were dark hollows in his white face as he joined Masters.

'Aye, lad. She's up yonder 'neath that big outcrop — safe — but ye'll need ter ride fer the widder, Jack — the missus is hurt some.'

Tanner nodded and touched Daniel's arm. 'Go wi' Tom, lad, an' stay wi' yer mam.' Reading the anxiety in Masters' face he mounted quickly and turned his horse back the way they had come. 'The widder's south o' here — I'll fetch 'er up.'

Masters took the bay's reins from Daniel. 'Walk where I walk, slow an' careful an' ye'll come ter no harm.'

'Is Mama badly hurt?'

'Aye, she's in a lot o' pain — injuries yer can see an' some ye can't.'

'What happened?'

'Can't rightly say, lad. I'm guessin' she's come ter grief tryin' ter ride across this here scree slope in the dark. The geldin's right poorly an all.'

This was a long speech for Tom Masters and it indicated the measure of his anxiety.

Ruby Gaunt strode into the cave, took in the situation at a glance, and immediately took charge. 'Daniel, I'll need yer ter help me — you other gents, outside if you please.' She was still breathing hard from the long climb up to the cave as she knelt beside Lucy. 'Let's be seein' the damage, girl. Daniel, help me sit yer mama up — gently now — support her back.'

With deft fingers the widow searched out the painful areas and suppressed an oath when she saw the dark bruising on the pale skin.

'Ye've a couple o' cracked ribs an' a broken collar-bone so ye'll need ter be strapped up firm before we ride down to the cart — 'twill hurt some.'

When Lucy was trussed in broad strips of linen and dressed again, the widow turned to the black gelding. 'Yer poor old bugger,' she murmured, passing gently searching hands over his body and legs. 'Ye're in a right mess, but ye'll heal. Daniel, ther's a tin o' Stockholm tar in me bag ther' an' some rags — fetch 'em here.'

When she had applied the tar to each broken hoof and bound them firmly with coarse rags, she rose stiffly to her feet. 'Right, lad, we're ready. Bring the men in.'

Lucy was lifted on to Masters' horse with gentle hands, uttering no sound, holding her breath when her body protested. Masters supported her while Daniel led the animal. Jack Tanner went ahead leading the bay, keeping to the tracks they had made on the way up, and Ruby Gaunt brought up the rear with the gelding. The small cavalcade moved at a snail's pace, constantly alert for falling rock and snow slides, and the Widow Gaunt grunted her relief when finally they reached more stable ground and began the long descent to the track below where Rewi waited with the cart and Tanner's horse.

They were forced to stop frequently to rest both Lucy and the injured horse, and when at length they reached the track and the waiting Long Reach shepherds, Lucy was near collapse. Masters lifted her on to the bed in the cart himself, tucking the rugs around her with gentle hands, and the widow, seeing the expression on the man's weary face, read his heart. 'Aye,' she mused, 'though he be older and less dashing than the Scot, were it left to me, I know who I'd be choosin'.' She spoke quietly to her shepherds, then, taking up the reins of the big horses, the cavalcade moved off again. Daniel crouched beside his mother in the cart while Masters and Tanner nursed the black horse along behind it. Rewi, leading the bay, rode ahead, marking a smooth path home.

Chapter 14

LUCY KEPT TO HER BED for a week after her ordeal. Masters had carried her upstairs and laid her carefully down, standing for a moment, his gaze on her face, then gruffly he'd said, 'If yer need owt, send Daniel fer me — I'll not be far away.'

Sarah had cried out in dismay at the sight of her mother and had dissolved in great gulping sobs until the widow had turned a steely eye on her. 'Ye'll make no kind of a nurse wi' all that racket, girl — come now and help me ter get yer mama undressed.'

Willie Good had bustled back and forth between the hut and the homestead all week, making broths and custards and coddled eggs for the injured woman. He'd made the butter and baked the bread, as he had done when Sarah was ill, leaving the girl free to tend her mother. With the lambing well advanced and these tasks added to his other duties, he was on the run from before dawn until well after dark. Ruby Gaunt, coming into Lucy's bedroom at the end of the week, was chuckling as she approached the bed.

'I'll swear "Nanny" Good has shed a good ten pounds these past few days — 'ave yer seen 'im? His trews are like ter sail down 'is backside if 'e takes a good sneeze.'

'It's not fair to make fun of him, Ruby,' Lucy had smiled. 'The dear man is very caring and looks after us well.'

'Don't we all,' the widow had grunted, 'Let's have a look at ye. Aye, well, ye're all colours of the rainbow still.' She'd straightened and her face had creased into a grin. 'But ye've no need ter laze in that bed any longer — yer can get up tomorrow an' start pullin' yer weight again — a little at a time, mind.'

'Have you seen Thomas today?'

'Aye,' the widow had answered. 'He's mendin' well — lots of guts has that one, an' seein' as how you've near killed each other, I consider yer should stay together — he's yours.' She'd turned then and stalked from the room. 'Where's that girl — I need a mug o' tea.'

Five weeks had passed since the incident on Camden Station. Lucy had healed and, apart from scarred knees, so had the gelding. Tom Masters had brought the animal down to the homestead as soon as Lucy was on her feet again so that she could see for herself how he was faring. She had struggled with her guilt, knowing she had nearly brought about his death, and tears of contrition had welled in her eyes when she saw his healing body. Resting her head against the black neck and stroking the velvety muzzle her tears had come, and embarrassed by her weakness she'd turned away to walk quickly up the veranda steps. Thomas had nickered after her and Masters had said, "'E'd not say no ter a crust or two.'

'Wait, then,' Lucy had replied, not turning around, passing swiftly through the door while Masters grinned at the black horse.

～

She stood now at the end of the veranda looking at the rows of young vegetable plants. Masters had continued to tend the garden and had removed more rock and stones to make it larger, and every free moment would find him there or doing odd jobs about the homestead. Lucy had found no way to thank him for putting his life at risk to save her; the event was still too close, but when her emotions were less raw she knew she would. The words he had uttered in the cave when he'd thought she was dead were clear in her memory and they saddened her. Lucy's listlessness had left her during her convalescence; she had come to terms with her loneliness, accepting the long wait ahead before McKenzie was free, and had determined to keep the feeling between them alive by writing letters to him and visiting him if somehow she could make her way to Lyttelton.

In the meantime, she planned to return to the Ngai Tahu village and bring Ruben's boys back to Camden Station to begin work. There would be time to build their huts and cooking-shack before summer arrived, and time to burn off the rugged terrain to improve the forage before the first sheep were culled from Daniel's flock the following year. There would be time too for a barn to be erected if Daniel could spare Tom Masters or Jack Tanner for a while. She smiled to herself. She was already thinking like a run-holder.

Lucy also planned to visit Dunedin again when winter returned. She would see John Hamilton to tie up legal loose ends and do some shopping. She also intended to purchase a gig and a strong horse to pull it, and she would buy another saddle to replace the one she had lost. As well, she thought she might visit Mary Truscott in Port Chalmers if the journey was not too difficult. She felt she would like to renew their acquaintance and give that worthy lady her business, as she and Sarah were past due for new dresses. She wondered how the family had fared since leaving the *Rajah*, and if they were making a good living at their respective trades.

Lucy's optimism soared as she made her plans, all of which, in one way or another, involved James McKenzie. There was much to be done, and in no time at all he would be home again and then their life together could begin. She had outlined her plans to Ruby Gaunt on one of the older woman's visits, and the widow had promptly thrown cold water on several of them.

'A gig won't serve yer here, girl, as I've told yer before. A cart is what ye need, an' two strong horses. The wheels an' bits an' pieces of Ruben's cart are still up by the barn, all but buried in the tussock — order some timber an' have the lads repair it. An' while I remember, yer can have the geldin's saddle — 'tis old but serviceable. I'll not charge yer fer it.'

Ruby Gaunt sat herself down at the long table and reached for the teapot. 'This fresh made?'

'Yes. But, Ruby, I really would rather travel about in a gig. A cart isn't . . . it's not—'

'I'm assuming yer'd be wantin' me ter take yer to Dunedin?'

the widow cut in, raising a quizzical eyebrow.

'Would you be so kind?'

'In me *cart?*' the widow shot at her.

'Oh, Ruby, I didn't mean — I'd never for a moment . . . Oh damn!'

Ruby Gaunt, slapping a big hand down on to the table, shouted with glee. 'By, ye'd not make a diplomat, girl.' Wiping her eyes she picked up her cup. 'An' afore yer get ter plannin' a visit to this Truscott person, think on. If the wind's a mind ter be frivolous, yer could be hours gettin' ter Port Chalmers or be stuck out on the water fer the night comin' back — a most unpleasant experience, folk'll tell yer — eaten alive by sandflies in the daytime and frozen ter the bone after sundown.'

'Is there no road?'

'None that ye'd care ter travel.'

'I see.'

'The natives wi' their dugouts might be an option.' Ruby Gaunt's eyes disappeared into their pouches.

'I wouldn't consider it,' Lucy snapped, glaring at the widow; then she was laughing. 'What a dreadful tease you are, Ruby Gaunt. Anyway, although it would have been nice to see Mrs Truscott again, it was only a notion.'

'Aye. Now, me last bit of advice — do yer burnin' off *afore* yer build yer huts an' yer barn — wind changes, yer've lost the lot an' pit-sawn timber ain't cheap.'

Reluctantly, Lucy took the widow's advice. She would go to Dunedin in any event to order the timber for the barn and the cart and to see the lawyer. In the meantime she worked side by side with Tom Masters in the vegetable garden, enjoying his quiet companionship. Lucy had felt a certain reticence when she recalled the makeshift privy and her complete dependence on the shepherd, but before long, when neither by reference nor sign did he give any indication that he even remembered the event, she was again comfortable with him.

Masters had carried sack after sack of sheep droppings from the pastures to dig into the stony soil, and as a result the garden this year was thriving. He had spread the manure around the base of the fruit trees as well, and called Lucy to see the young fruit setting on the branches.

'Ye'll be busy wi' yer bottling, missus,' he said. 'Ther's many pounds of fruit on them branches.'

'I will need to find more bottles and jars,' Lucy replied. 'The berry fruits are flourishing too. Perhaps Mr Good has jars to spare.'

They walked down the rows of berry-canes and young vegetable plants, discussing the growing crops with satisfaction. Lucy's thoughts turned to McKenzie, and the future when *he* would be walking by her side, speaking of next year's planting as Masters was doing now. Warmth rose in her cheeks and the shepherd, glancing at her, saw the bloom that no healing scars could mar. He yearned for her but he gave no hint of the hunger within him, knowing he must win her with sensitivity, not haste. He'd give her the chance to know him, to learn to depend on him, and then perhaps he would dare to show her how he felt. Even then he might lose her if she could not see past the Scot, but that was a possibility he would not dwell on.

Lest she see his vulnerability, Masters turned aside to tie back a loose cane, his mind on McKenzie now. He'd always felt a certain respect for the man, but there were times when unworthy thoughts would not be denied, times when Tom Masters felt an active dislike for the Scot, and those were always followed by a sense of shame in the knowledge that there was no fair reason for it.

Lucy turned to Masters as he gained her side again, and smiled a whimsical smile. 'With peas and new potatoes for Christmas dinner, one could almost imagine oneself back home.'

'Aye, an' Willie will make 'is plum pudding as usual. We'll be wi'out the goose, though. Hogget an' fowl's as near as ye'll get, missus.'

'And we'll manage well enough with those.' Lucy walked a little way in silence, then said, 'What I do miss, living away up here, is the fish Cook would buy in the market. Steamed fish in parsley sauce — oh, yes!'

'Ye can be havin' yer fish, missus. Salmon's still spawnin'. Young Pitchin can go down to t' river when 'e's done 'is stint an' catch some fer yer supper.' He tipped his hat off his brow and pushed his fingers through his hair thoughtfully. 'Parsley now — ther's nowt o' that about as I'd be knowin' of.'

It was Christmas, and this Christmas of 1855 was of special significance to the eight people who sat around the long table in Lucy's kitchen. Not only was it a celebration of the birth of Christ, but it was also a celebration of Lucy's life spared.

She was deeply moved by the shepherds' quiet toasts given in her honour, and by Willie Good's extra culinary efforts to fill the Yuletide table with treats; his way of expressing his joy that the missus had not been taken from them.

Sarah had decorated the parlour mantelpiece with small branches of macrocarpa and rata flowers. It looked very festive, and after dinner everybody retired to the parlour to sing carols around the piano. Tom Masters' rich baritone surprised everybody, and when Lucy and Ruby Gaunt sang a duet the devotion on the shepherd's face was there for all to see.

On Christmas Eve, Lucy and the children had walked down to the hut with a bottle of whiskey, one of the six that Lucy had placed with the remaining brandy in the back of her kitchen cupboard. With the whiskey was a raspberry tart and a bowl of cream. Willie's plump face had lit up when he'd seen the whiskey. 'By, t' lads'll enjoy a nip o' this, missus — thank 'e, thank 'e.' Gazing at the bottle in his hand with reverence, he'd pulled the door wide. 'Will ye not step in an' take a sip o' cider — made from last year's windfalls.'

Sarah had not entered the hut since Adam had died, and the girl had held back, looking at her mother for reassurance.

'Come now, don't be shy,' the cook had urged, smiling broadly. 'Mother will let you taste Willie's cider, eh? Best in t' country.'

'Did ye know,' he'd chuckled as they'd moved into the kitchen, 'that ther whalers made *ther* whiskey out o' cabbage trees?'

'How would they do that?' Daniel had looked doubtful.

'Chopped out the young growth, they did, an' made it from that, an' the missionaries brewed ther beer from 'em.'

'Imagine that,' Lucy had murmured as she'd watched Sarah gaze around the room and visibly relax. This was the last ghost the child needed to lay to rest, and in Willie Good's jovial company it was happening. She'd been silent throughout the short visit. It was as they'd walked back up the track that she'd said; 'It's different, Mama.'

'What is different, dear?'

'Our old place — it feels happy, it *smells* happy!'

Lucy had looked down at her daughter's earnest face and her heart had swelled with pity: You poor child, you poor little soul — what I could have spared you had I the wit. But all she'd said was, 'I think it would have to be a brave smell indeed if it entered Mr Good's kitchen and it was *not* a happy one.'

Sarah had giggled and then replied, 'Could we take some flowers down to Papa for Christmas?' And Lucy had known then that her child was truly healed.

~

New Year's Eve saw the long front veranda of the homestead become the meeting place where everyone gathered to welcome the coming year. Moana, Rewi and Mrs Samuels came with Ruby Gaunt, Mrs Samuels seated sedately beside the widow dressed in her rusty black and holding a black parasol over her head. A hot zephyr blew from the north-west and heat radiated from the cart's timbers and the black leather seat, but if the Maori woman was uncomfortable in her widow's weeds, she gave no sign. As Lucy went to greet her, Mrs Samuels stepped down from the cart and stood for a time in the hot sun, politely admiring the flowers bordering the front path before mounting the steps, with unhurried dignity, to the veranda's shade. Lucy was somehow reminded of royalty.

Conversation turned to the inevitable subject of sheep and the shearing which was to commence on Long Reach within the next two days, and on Chandler's Run soon after. Lucy had already set up her pots and pans in readiness for the endless mutton stews, mashed potato and station brownie that she would be serving when the shearers arrived.

'We'll be lookin' fer more shearers next year, girl; higher stock numbers, the new run beginnin' ter operate — we'd best put the word about when we visit Dunedin town, an' ye'll be needin' more huts ter house 'em as well.'

'An' a couple more musterers, missus,' Tanner said, with feeling.

'Yes, indeed,' Lucy was quick to reply, whilst fearing that this would be no easier to accomplish than it had been before. The Rafferty brothers were still at large. 'As well, Mr Tanner, I will require you to accompany me to the Ngai Tahu village again when the shearing is finished, to bring back my workers. The burn-off on Camden Station will begin then and I'd like you to oversee it.' Grinning with surprise, the shepherd straightened from his customary slouch.

'Twill be me pleasure, missus.'

'You know how to back-burn, mister?' the widow growled.

'That I do,' Tanner replied quickly, 'an' when not ter burn an' all.'

'That would be when the wind is blowin' in *my* direction.'

∾

There were only pockets of snow on the mountains, and white cumulus cloud hovered motionless in a pale, misty sky. Heat shimmered above the hard, stony ground under the gelding's feet. This was the first time Lucy had ridden since her accident, and she was a little diffident as she rode along the track searching for the path down to the fork where the rivers came together. At supper the evening before she had told Daniel and Sarah of her intention to ride down to the plateau in order to decide on the site where a second homestead could be built.

'Won't you wait until I can go with you, Mama?'

Smiling gently at her son, Lucy had assured him that she would be careful.

'While the weather is so good it would be a pity not to take advantage of it. Besides,' she had added, 'when the shearing begins and the fruit is ready for bottling, there'll be no chance to go before the burning-off begins.'

'Then I will go with you — the sheep-washing can go on without me for a few hours.'

Lucy had remained thoughtful for a moment, her eyes on her son, then softly she had said, 'I understand your concern, dear, truly I do, but I'm recalling now your once saying to me: "If I am to be any kind of a run-holder, I can't allow you to coddle me."'

There had been a silence in the room while everyone remembered Lucy's terrible experience, then she had spoken again, 'You may be sure I will be cautious — very cautious indeed.'

Now she reined in the gelding and her eyes moved over the terrain above her. Was this where she had left the track on that fateful day? She could not be sure; the scorched purple hills looked very different. Turning away, she scanned the boulder-strewn slopes below the track. The glimpse of sparkling water seen earlier eluded her now, but she could plainly hear the river running in the hot, calm air.

Dismounting, she looked for a shady place to tether the gelding, then slowly she moved down the incline, watching where she placed her feet as she manoeuvred around flax bushes, tussock and rocks. She clambered down until she came to a small outcrop, and as she climbed up to its flat top, she heard Thomas neigh. The horse was out of her sight, but from this vantage point she could see the glint of fast-running water below. Her view was still restricted, however, and she could identify no landmarks.

Turning, she climbed down again then halted suddenly, listening. From somewhere above her came the sound of booted feet and dislodged rocks, and a small sense of disquiet sent her to stand below the outcrop. She remained still, silent, waiting to see who was approaching while the sun beat down on her, and her feelings were somewhere between relief and annoyance when Tom Masters came into sight. Stepping clear of the outcrop she said, 'Are you following me, Mr Masters?'

'Aye.'

'And why would you be doing this?'

'Young master's orders, missus.'

Lucy stared at the shepherd thoughtfully, then said, 'If I, as overseer, were to tell you to return to your work, what would you do?'

Masters, taking note of the flash in the dark eyes, scrubbed at his chin with an apologetic fist. 'I'd be in summat of a fix, missus.'

'Yes, I suppose you would be.' And she smiled. 'Well, as you are here, perhaps you could help me find the way down to the spur where the rivers join?'

'Ye've come too far south and missed t' best road down.' He held out a supporting hand and helped Lucy climb up to the track. Here, they mounted their horses and turned north.

'Best part o' two miles back ther's two cabbage trees — on t' edge of the track markin' the way.'

'Ah, yes — I recall.'

They rode in silence for a time, then Lucy asked, 'How do you know where the spur is, Mr Masters?'

'Ridden this way a time or two, missus — interested like.'

He lifted his horse into a canter and Lucy followed. In a while he raised his arm and pointed. 'Do yer see ther'?'

Lucy, following the line of his pointing finger, saw the tall cabbage trees, and soon they were riding down the relatively easy slope that the Widow Gaunt had shown her earlier. The rougher aspect of the higher ground gave way to rolling hills and gentle valleys where tussock spread a tawny carpet before them, and flax and cabbage trees rattled in the soft breeze as they passed.

The horses could smell the water long before their riders saw it, and stepped out eagerly. At the head of a wide valley, Masters drew rein and pointed. 'Over ther', missus, is yer spur.'

'Let us go and look at it.'

Impatient to reach the water, the horses needed no urging to canter down the gentle slope and across the river gravel until they were hock-deep in the cool water. They drank their fill while Lucy and Masters sat in their saddles, enjoying the peace of this tranquil place; then they moved on, riding in the shallows until the water grew deeper as the two rivers merged, running swift and milky-green over its stony bed. Turning north-west, they rode along the spur and up on to the plateau. Robins and fantails darted through the low scrub, and somewhere high above a lark sang its euphoric song.

'This *would* be most suitable for a homestead,' Lucy spoke dreamily. 'Should it face north, Mr Masters, or should it face east?'

Tom Masters felt the tranquillity of the day slip from him. He turned searching eyes on the beloved face before him and saw in his mind's eye what she was seeing: the homestead set in this idyllic place and the *Scot* sharing it with her — this woman who meant more to him than life. He turned his gaze from her, and for a long moment he stared at the tumbling waters beyond the spur before at the last he muttered, 'Compromise, missus, face it nor'east.' He pulled his horse's head around. 'Best be headin' home — ye'd not be wantin' ter worry folk.'

About to speak, Lucy saw the man's closed face and followed him in silence as he pushed ahead of her up the hill.

Chapter 15

THEY CAME DOWN from the hills, their stealthy progress marked only by the flickering lightning. The night was hot and black, and distant thunder masked any sound they made as they began to circle the mob. On the far side of the pasture the two shepherds drew their mounts to a halt, unaware. 'Wa kapu ti?' 'Ae, kia takitaro taua ka haere.' Yes, it would be time for their tea-break soon. They sat easily in their saddles, talking and laughing for a space, then gave each other a friendly punch and parted company, riding in opposite directions around the flock. The lightning flared, throwing the purple mountains and sun-dried hills into stark relief, and the sheep began to mill about uneasily.

The thunder rumbled, coming closer, and the shepherds, watching the approaching storm and fascinated by the brilliant display in the night sky, knew there would be no tea until the storm had passed; the flighty merinos would require all the shepherds' efforts to keep them contained.

Forked lightning stabbed the hills and sheep broke from the restive mob. One of the shepherds whistled sharply to set his dogs to retrieve them. He did not see the crouching man, did not see the hurled rock that crushed his skull or hear his dogs' frenzied barking as he fell to the sun-baked ground.

His companion wheeled his horse about, then, to listen intently. Whistling his own dogs, he dug his heels into his horse's belly and galloped towards the sound, circling the flock as swiftly as the darkness would allow. Somewhere near the homestead a shot rang out, but he raced on; there was trouble here that would not wait.

Lightning bleached the scene ahead of him and he saw his hoa, his friend, lying in a dark pool on the ground; the dogs barking and whining, backing away from the still form; the grey mare, spooked, ready for flight. In the instant before the light faded he saw all this, and a horseman, rifle levelled, riding straight at him. The bullet hurled him from his saddle and his horse bolted into the night. A terrified header-dog leapt at the oncoming rider, teeth bared, and was shot dead in mid-air. Thunder tumbled and rolled, then all was quiet.

Darkness laid its blanket over the carnage and the cringing dogs, and covered the nine riders as they rounded up the flock and turned it towards the western hills. Soon the rain would come and it would wash away their tracks. Fortune was on their side — this would be a good night's work.

Ruby Gaunt came out of a deep sleep, not knowing what had woken her. Summer lightning played on the hills beyond her window and thunder rumbled distantly. For a space she lay still, gathering her wits, listening to the silence. Was it the thunder that had woken her? Then she heard the sheep bleating and dogs in full voice. Nearer, the dogs penned for the night were suddenly barking furiously in reply.

The widow was quickly out of bed, dragging on her trousers and boots, cramming her hat on to her head. She snatched up her gun and a handful of bullets as she left her bedroom, and was loading the gun as she thundered down the stairs and out on to the wide veranda. The night was black and she could see nothing, but the commotion seemed to be coming from the southern pastures. Wild dog or pig gettin' at me sheep, was her thought as she leapt down from the veranda and hurried through the garden gate. Once clear of the homestead, she fired her carbine into the air to hasten the predators on their way and hurried on down the hill, the lightning illuminating her way. As she went she wondered where her shepherds were and why they weren't discharging their own guns.

She heard a shot then, followed quickly by another, and in a minute or two she heard a horse coming towards her, running fast. As the sky lit up she saw that the animal was riderless. Ruby Gaunt was running then, hampered by the nightshirt she still wore, shouting, 'Who's out ther'? Where the hell are me shepherds?'

Lightning crackled across the sky and the widow saw the riders, a number of them circling her shorn flock, sending them scurrying in terrified bunches first this way and then that. Thunder almost overhead crashed deafeningly, pounding through her chest, shaking the ground, and she ran faster. 'Yer thievin' mongrels!' she screamed. 'Get yer scurvy backsides off my land!' She stopped to reload, fumbling in the darkness, then lightning blazed across the sky. A massive fist punched into her shoulder and the Widow Gaunt was flat on her back.

She lay stunned for an instant, then realized she'd been shot and fury galvanized her. 'By God, ye'll not,' she muttered. Scrambling to her feet she loaded her carbine and stood waiting for the next flash of lightning, her rifle at the ready, and when it came her finger squeezed the trigger and she smiled grimly when she heard a man scream.

Moving quickly to a different vantage point, she reloaded and again waited for the lightning. Her hand was slippery on the rifle barrel but she felt no pain. The sky lit up and she pulled the trigger. In the blinding flash she saw two things: her man go down and a horse bearing down on her from her left. There was no time to reload. Turning to face her attacker, the widow clutched her rifle by its barrel and as the man fired at point-blank range she was leaping at him and heard the satisfying sound of crunching bone as the butt of her weapon crashed into his face. Ruby Gaunt sank to the ground then. All at once there was no sound, no feeling; she was numb and immeasurably tired. By — the bastard 'as done fer me, was her last vague thought.

The Widow Gaunt lay in her bed. Slowly she opened her eyes to see the shadowy form of Aroha Samuels moving quietly about the room. The heavy curtains were closed and she wondered what time of day it was. 'I'm all right, then?' she growled. 'Thought I'd set off on the pearly mile.' Gingerly she touched the padding on her shoulder. 'Is the bullet out?'

'Yes. Moana has learned well.' The housekeeper came to stand beside the bed, hands folded, her expression firm. 'Rest. You must keep in your bed — much blood was lost.'

'Pshaw! We're shearin'. I've no time ter be layin' about.' Ruby Gaunt made to rise, then was still as a thought occurred to her. With searching fingers she felt her face, her chest, her stomach, then she glared up at her housekeeper. 'Yer not tellin' me somethin', are yer? That second bullet — where did it get me?'

'Not worry, my dear. You must not—'

'Where?' the widow thundered.

'Ah.' Aroha Samuels regarded the widow, then slowly stepped away from the bed. In a moment she returned and with reverence she laid the remains of Ruby Gaunt's battered hat on the counterpane; it had been shot in half.

'Me hat — me bloody hat!' the widow howled. 'I'll see them buggers in hell fer this!'

'Already you have done this,' the housekeeper stated. 'Your gun spoke, as did Kahu's and some others. The Rafferty brothers are no more and three of their kind also are no more.'

'You sayin' — all three o' them mongrels? How d'yer know it's them?'

'The boss shearer, Mr Turnbull — he know how they look.'

'An' three others, you say? Should 'ave stayed awake ter see that!'

The Widow Gaunt lay quietly, digesting this welcome piece of news. Lucy Chandler must be informed. In a moment she turned to the housekeeper.

'Did any of 'em get away?'

'Two — three perhaps — up into the hills.' Mrs Samuels waved an arm to the west, then fastened stern eyes on the woman in the bed. 'Rest now. Please.'

'Headin' fer the pass,' the widow murmured, then on a thought: 'Our lads — I saw a riderless horse — are our boys all right?'

Aroha Samuels dropped her gaze. 'Curly Rewiti. He lies on the marae.'

'Ah.' There was a silence then the widow spoke softly, 'Poor lad — I'll need ter go down.'

'But rest now,' the housekeeper insisted. 'There is time for that.'

'Anybody else? You'd best tell me; I'll not rest 'til I know.'

'Ae, other boy with the sheep, he shot in his arm, and a shearer — half his ear gone.'

To forestall any further questions, Aroha Samuels turned on her heel then and left the room.

Hurriedly, Lucy packed a flax kit with the items she would need during her stay at Long Reach. Rewi had ridden across early that morning to tell what had happened and clearly he expected her to return with him.

'Yes, Rewi, I will come but there are things I must see to first. Go now and I will follow tomorrow.'

Concerned for her friend, worried for Sarah being left

alone at the homestead, and uneasy about the ride across Camden Station alone, Lucy was finding it difficult to concentrate on the instructions she must leave for Daniel and Sarah; things to be done in her absence that could not wait.

Rewi had left nothing to her imagination in describing the events of the night before, the killing of one shepherd and the wounding of the widow and two others, and he told of digging graves for the six marauders so they could be buried before the heat of the day, and how the Long Reach shepherds and the shearers had descended on the thieves in an avenging hoard when they'd found the Widow Gaunt and her attacker lying side by side on the scorched grass. 'Him dead, she not.' And he'd added proudly, 'Boss lady not be killed easy, eh?'

Lucy felt some apprehension when she learned that three of the Rafferty brothers' men were still on the loose, and as she finished her preparations she wondered if she should take Daniel's musket as well. Smiling grimly to herself she decided against the idea. She'd never been acquainted with guns, so she was reasonably sure that anybody approaching her in a threatening manner would be perfectly safe even though *she* held a musket.

'I want you to stay here to see to things, Sarah. Our own shearing will be starting soon, so we must not fall behind. Do you think you can manage on your own for these few days?'

Sarah, never keen to venture out on horseback, assured her mother that she would manage very well and Daniel would be there to help if need be. Tom Masters, learning that Lucy was about to make the long trek to Long Reach alone, was quickly on the doorstep. 'Ye'd never be wise ter ride out ther' on yer own, missus. Ther likely ter still be in t' vicinity, them three that got away.'

'I have to go in any event, Mr Masters, if only to satisfy myself that Mrs Gaunt is mending.'

'Then ye'll not mind if I ride along wi' ye ter see yer safely ther' an' home again?'

'You cannot be spared, Mr Masters, you are needed here at this time.'

Lucy read the anxiety in the man's eyes and a sense of disquiet caused her to compromise. 'I shall have Pitchin accompany me, then — will that do?'

'Pitchin's but a lad an''e'd be no match fer them ruffians — best that I go.'

The words were said with finality. Lucy studied the shepherd's open face in silence. 'Very well,' she said at length. Then softly, 'Thank you.'

To avoid the heat they set off early the following morning and passed the journey mostly in easy silence. With the shepherd riding alongside her, she was not fearful but enjoyed the exhilaration of the early-morning exercise, and their horses, being fresh, covered the miles in little more than an hour.

Aroha Samuels waited on the veranda to greet Lucy, and when Tom Masters had helped her to dismount and led the gelding away they went directly to the parlour where the widow sat propped up in her chair, a wide bandage supporting her arm. Lucy could see at a glance that her mood was difficult, and the first words the invalid uttered confirmed this. 'I was ter be at the lad's tangi termorrer, but me bloody shoulder's infected — hurts like hell!' The lower lip jutted. 'An' I'll not make an ass o' meself expirin' away in the heat down ther' — so here I sit — no use ter man or beast.'

'Come now, Ruby, be thankful that it's not *your* funeral; that you *are* able to sit there,' Lucy soothed. 'We might have lost you, too.'

'Aye, an' I'm delighted 'tis *not* me goin' inter the ground — course I am.' She scowled at Lucy. 'Not used ter bein' the fella in the bed — goes against the grain.'

'Is your wound beginning to improve?'

'I'd doubt it. Moana's killin' me — keeps pourin' iodine over the damned thing — sendin' me through the bloody roof. I keep tellin''er — beggin''er — "use titoki berry lotion", but she must needs use both.'

'Oh dear,' Lucy sympathized, 'can I do anything for you?'

'Aye. Yer can attend the tangi in my place,' the widow growled. 'Rewi, Moana, Aroha and some of the boys will be goin' — yer could do that fer me.'

Lucy, remembering Ruben's funeral — the heat, the flies and the smell — was dismayed by the very idea. 'Oh, Ruby, I couldn't. Please don't ask that of me.'

'If yer plan ter live yer life up here an' employ native workers, 'tis a duty and a protocol that'll be demanded of yer sooner or later,' the Widow Gaunt snapped.

'Perhaps, but I can't think that this is *my* duty. The young man was not employed by me.'

'Quite so. He was employed by me an' *I* can't be there. Now, I have a white face an' *you* have a white face, an' out o' respect one of 'em should be down at that tangi.' The steely eyes glittered. 'An' ther's Alf Turnbull's statement ter be sent off ter the police via the villages — that's ter be taken ter the rangatira down ther' an' all.'

Lucy greeted the unrelenting words with silence, every fibre of her being in revolt. I can't do this, she stormed inwardly. It should not be expected of me. Then she remembered the ancient tohunga who had presided over Ruben's funeral and the Maori boys who had buried him, and she knew that she must. 'You are right. Of course I will go, and Mr Masters will go with me.'

Lucy knew she would remember forever the funeral of Curly Rewiti: the keening of the women that made the hair rise on her nape, the dignity of the elders who solemnly made them welcome, and the plank table loaded with food, its centrepiece a whole roast boar. Children languidly waved bundles of flax over the table to keep the fat blowflies away, and long stems of toi toi were passed gently over the bier that stood on the far side of the meeting house. Lucy and Tom Masters stood at a respectful distance while the boy's whanau sat close around him, touching him, talking to him. Lucy felt her eyes fill and tears roll down her cheeks. There was nothing to fear here, nothing to revolt her, just the universal grief of a loved one lost, and she was not ashamed to weep.

~

Lucy remained at Long Reach for four days, an exercise in patience. The house-bound widow was querulous and picky on the one hand, and grumpily apologetic on the other. It was a credit to Lucy's ingenuity that she could divert the woman's frustration away from the shearing for even short periods of time; playing the piano and singing to her, reading to her, pitting her brains against the widow's over the chessboard, and making elaborate floral arrangements from the flowers in Ruby Gaunt's garden.

Satisfied at last that the wound was clean and healing well, Lucy and Tom Masters set out for home. They rode in silence for a time, until Lucy asked, 'Do you think those men will trouble us again, Mr Masters?'

'I were thinkin' summat along the same lines, missus,' the shepherd replied, 'but I'm surmisin' that wi' these days gone by an' no sign of 'em that ther long gone an' as well as that, wi' ther leaders put down, they'd need ter be daft ter show therselves 'ereabouts again.'

'I'm relieved to hear you say so, and perhaps, when word gets out what took place here, we can hope to be spared from this sort of trouble in the future.' Lucy was silent for a moment, then added sadly, 'But at what a terrible cost — that poor young man.'

'Aye, but best not dwell on t' bad of it. Think on — yer can employ yer Ngai Tahu lads on yer *two* runs now, as many of 'em as will work. Ther's good ter dwell on an' all.'

Lucy nodded, and glancing at the shepherd she smiled to herself. This quiet man, she thought, was in danger of becoming quite voluble, and what a comfort he was, bless him. Her thoughts turned back to the widow, and Lucy shivered as she realized how different the outcome might have been if the second bullet aimed at her had found its mark. Life without the Widow Gaunt was not to be contemplated, and Lucy freely admitted that the ugly, volatile woman had won her deepest respect and a large, warm space in her heart. Never demonstrative, Ruby Gaunt had surprised Lucy as she was taking her leave by placing her good arm about her and hugging her. There had been no parting thanks, just a wide stretching of the deep wrinkles about the mouth and a light in the steely eyes.

The miles passed under the horses' feet, and by mid-morning the heat was dancing ahead of them in shimmering waves. There was no breath of wind to give relief, and the horses' chests and necks were flecked with foam even though they'd travelled at no faster gait than a trot. When they reached the sentinel cabbage trees, Masters pulled his mount to a halt. Lucy's tender English skin was beet-red beneath the brim of her hat and tendrils of hair dripped sweat. The shepherd had no desire to go near the spur again, but, realizing that he had little choice, he made the decision to ride down, water the horses and themselves, and rest in the shade of the scrub for a time; he'd be a fool to put the missus in the way of heat stroke.

The day *was* exceptionally hot, and in truth they should

have set out much earlier. Had Lucy been so inclined they would have done this, but she had dawdled, so here they were. He turned his horse off the track. 'Ye're needin' a drink an' so are t'horses,' the shepherd said over his shoulder, 'an' we'll rest fer a spell.'

'Indeed, yes,' Lucy murmured, turning the gelding to follow him down the hill. When they reached the river, Masters allowed the horses to drink briefly, then led them away from the water and up to the shade where he tethered them.

'When they're cooled down some they can drink ther fill, then we'll get back on t'track an' head fer home,' he said as he came back. He drank from his cupped hands, then, dipping his neckerchief into the shallows, he washed the dust from his face before moving back to the shade. Lucy longed to take off her boots and cool her burning feet, but decorum dictated that she move out of sight of the shepherd before rolling up her trouser legs. She looked about for a suitable place to wade and set off for what appeared to be a tiny inlet.

''Ere now, missus,' Tom Masters called as she crunched across the pebbles. 'Don't ye be goin' too far — 'tis not a river ter be trifled wi'.'

'I wish to bathe my feet,' Lucy called back, 'and I need privacy to do this.'

'Aye, so ye do, an' I'll not be lookin' if ye'll come back an' do it 'ere.'

Lucy scrunched back across the pebbles again and watched Masters stretch out in the shade with his hat over his eyes before she removed her boots and rolled up the legs of her trousers. The water was so cold that her feet and legs ached, and she gasped as she splashed her face and her throat. Refreshed then, and her thirst quenched, she pulled on her boots and joined the shepherd.

'It is so hot today,' she remarked, 'even the birds are still. We should have set out for home much earlier, I think.'

'Aye,' came the dry reply.

~

The sun was high when they rode up to the homestead. It blazed down from a brazen sky, scorching everything beneath it, and the sheep panted under the weight of their heavy fleece.

'Shearin' won't be comin' too quick fer them poor woollies,' Tom Masters observed, and then pointed a finger to where Sarah worked along the rows of berry canes, unaware of her mother's arrival.

'Oh, poor child — look at the colour of her face. Sarah!' Lucy called. 'Come indoors, dear, it's much too hot to be picking now.'

The girl raised her head and, giving her mother a tight smile, she picked up her pail and walked towards them. 'It *is* too hot, Mama, but the birds are eating the berries faster than I can pick them.'

Lucy dismounted and, passing her reins to the shepherd, went to take the pail from Sarah's hand. 'You are burned to a crisp, child — if need be the birds can have them; you will ruin your skin. In future we will pick only in the cool of the morning, and when the shearing starts we will pick in the evening.' Tom Masters kept his face straight as he led the gelding away.

Willie Good had delivered his surplus bottles and jars up to the homestead during Lucy's absence, and Sarah had commenced the bottling on her own. Proudly she showed her mother the preserves already on the shelves in the lean-to. As well, the weekly supply of bread had been baked and the butter made, and a stew bubbled on the hob. Everything in the homestead was orderly and Lucy felt blessed as she kissed her daughter's tired young face.

'Tomorrow morning, immediately after breakfast, dear, we will pick until it grows too hot to stay outdoors and we will bottle as we go, so that the fruit does not spoil. Do you agree?'

'Yes, Mama. I am so glad you are home.'

Lucy slept fitfully that night, her mind busy planning the work ahead of her. Daniel had told her at dinner that the shearing would commence in four days' time, and she lay in her bed mentally lining up all the cooking pots and utensils she would need to cater to the shearers. Her thoughts passed from this to how best to utilize the jars and bottles in the lean-to. Even allowing for the extra ones and Willie Good using a good quantity of fruit for his own preserves, there would still be waste; one could only eat so much fruit and the men could not be tempted, clearly showing a preference for puddings and plum duff, albeit with fruit in them, to finish their meals. Lucy could not recall seeing fruit trees at Long Reach. Perhaps Cook would be pleased to have any surplus fruit sent across. This is ridiculous, she fretted as she tossed and turned. *I can think about all this tomorrow. I must go to sleep.*

But sleep still eluded her and, as day was breaking, Lucy left her bed and dressing quickly tiptoed downstairs. She built up the kitchen fire and placed the kettle on the hob, then, cutting herself a slab of bread, she went into the lean-to to collect the pails. Chewing on the bread she set off for the garden.

It was barely light enough to distinguish the colour of the berries but the air was already warm, presaging another hot day. She worked steadily for half an hour then realized that she was no longer alone. Tom Masters was approaching the garden fence carrying a wooden box.

'Good morning, Mr Masters,' Lucy called. 'What have you there?'

'Windfalls, missus, an' ther's more'n these 'ere. Happen I could empty t' box an' bring in another load.'

'This is kind of you. Could you perhaps empty it on to the table in the lean-to?' Lucy smiled.

'Aye, an' I'll do a stint o' berry-pickin' an' all if ye'd like.'

'Oh, indeed yes, if you can spare the time.'

''Tis an hour ter breakfast. Yer can pick a heap o' berries in an hour — 'twill gi' ye more time fer yer bottling.'

'Sarah will be pleased. She had far too much sun yesterday.'

'A good girl is that, missus,' the shepherd remarked as he went off to empty his box.

~

With the arrival of the shearers, Chandler's Run was working at top speed, and Lucy and Sarah toiled from dawn until well after dark. While Willie Good baked his pies and made his plum duff, they baked endless loaves of bread, cooked endless pots of mutton stew and mashed potato, and pan upon pan of station brownie. Along with these activities the fruit still had to be picked, cleaned and bottled, and the butter had to be made, a task which became more trying as the days grew hotter and the cream refused to turn. At the end of each day, hampered by the heat, the dust, the flies and the eternal wind, they would go to their beds exhausted but with a sense of adversity conquered.

Into this mêlée of bleating sheep, barking dogs and sweating men rode the Widow Gaunt. Shouting encouragement to this one, quipping mildly with that one, she circled the mob watching procedures for a time, then turned her mare back to the homestead where she dismounted and strode to the open kitchen doorway. 'Hello, the house,' she called as she stepped inside. Sarah, face flushed, was tipping fresh-baked loaves on to the long table and Lucy was mashing a huge pot of boiled potatoes with a wooden pestle.

'By,' the widow chortled, 'when I first clapped me eyes on you, girl, I'd not 'ave given tuppence for yer chances of surviving the rigours o' this place, but dam'me, look at yer — up ter yer elbows, slavin' away an' lovin' it, both o' ye.'

'Not the butter-making, though.' Sarah pulled a face. 'The cream simply won't turn today.'

'Then give it ter me lass — let me wash me 'ands first.

You ordered that churn, missus?' Ruby Gaunt shouted from outside the kitchen doorway.

'Yes, among a number of other things,' Lucy replied as the widow entered the kitchen again, removing a different but equally battered hat from her head.

'Yer plannin' on stayin', dare I hope?'

Lucy avoided the sharp eyes. 'It is possible,' she murmured.

Nodding sagely, the big woman took the bowl of cream from Sarah's hands and marched off down to the river. Lucy stood in the doorway to watch her go, marvelling at the widow's resilience, the tireless energy of the woman, the dry humour and her strength. These qualities were all still there in spite of her being shot less than two weeks ago. This was a woman to be reckoned with; what a pity it was that her papa could never know the fine person she had become. For a moment Lucy thought of her own father. Would he be proud of her and the children, struggling every day for subsistence in this wild, cruel place? She knew that he would, and she wished that her family in England would leave their safe haven to come and see their endeavours: her sister Amelia and her husband, Hubert; dear Charlotte with her baby girl and her husband Charles; Christian, the brother she adored, his wife Felicity and their children; and, above all, her beloved Mama and Papa. How she longed to see all of them, even if, as Ruby Gaunt had suggested, it was only to visit. She smiled ruefully. If all these dear people were to visit, where in God's name would she put them all?

Lucy turned back into the kitchen as she saw Pitchin

striding down to the homestead to take the midday meal up to the men.

'Are we ready?' She went to the hearth to lift down the heavy pot of stew.

'Yes, Mama, but we'll have to make up more baking powder if I'm to bake soda scones for tea and I can't find the *Soyer's* book.'

'Don't worry about the book, dear, just mix together four ounces of tartaric acid, six ounces of carbonate of soda, two ounces of sugar — finely ground, mind — and an ounce of salt. Can you remember all that?'

'Yes, I think so. All we'll need then is the buttermilk, if there is any.'

'And there is,' the Widow Gaunt said as she came into the kitchen and placed the bowl on the table. 'I'll expect a nice cup o' tea when I've patted up yer butter an' all.' She raised her head and sniffed. 'Summat smells good — puddin', is it, or cake?'

'Station brownie,' Sarah replied, pointing.

The widow moved closer to look. 'Allus a bit dubious o' station brownie,' she muttered. 'Can't never tell if it's a raisin in yer mouth or a fly 'til it's too late.'

'Yer've never got flies in that ther' puddin', Miss Sarah — 'ave yer?' Young Pitchin stood in the doorway, grinning.

Daniel sat in his saddle and turned the mare to face the way they had come. The bay was lathered with sweat and her sides heaved as he slowly dismounted and stood gazing down over the hills, the patches of scrub, the rolling grassland turned brown, and the glint of water far below.

It was hot, very hot. He could see the heat radiating off the scree slope to his left; and the gentians, ranunculi and other vegetation were wilting under the onslaught of the continuing dry spell. The wethers that he had rounded up to drive down to the holding pens made no effort to scatter but stood calmly, watching the dog slowly circle them. Daniel pulled his drink bottle from his saddlebag and sipped the tepid water, then poured a little into his hat and let the mare drink. Above him the sky was a misty blue and white cumulus clouds hung motionless, looking like lumps of kapok. He drank again, wetting his cracked lips, then dampening his neckerchief he wiped the sweat and dust from his face.

Looking down, he could not see the homestead but he could see the woolshed, the holding pens and a corner of the barn, and Pitchin riding the circuit; at least he supposed it was Pitchin he was seeing through the shimmering heat haze. He turned around to the bay. 'Come on, girl, let's get on down, must be close to dinner time.' About to mount, he was stilled by the sharp crack of a rifle shot. It echoed about the hills, that single shot, and it seemed to have come from the tree-line above him. The sheep stirred, and quickly, in a low voice, Daniel commanded the dog to 'hold'. Thoughts of the three raiders still at large made him draw the mare behind the shelter of a low outcrop of rock. Here he crouched for a while, waiting for further shots to follow. When none came, he slowly stood and peered up towards the tree-line but he could see nothing. He shifted his gaze to the rider below.

The boy's face was raised to him; obviously he had heard the shot for he was gesticulating with a widely sweeping arm to Daniel's right. Again he searched the tree-line but whatever the boy was seeing, Daniel could not, and he could not fathom his signal.

Carefully he pulled himself a little higher up the rocky outcrop, the better to see, but the stone was too hot to touch and he quickly stepped down again, brushing the brittle lichen from his palms. Uncertainly, Daniel stood there feeling the sun peel the skin from his sunburned face. What could he do if it *was* the Rafferty brothers' rabble coming to drive off the sheep? He glanced again at the small figure below him, still now but still watching, and he came to a decision. Reaching for the musket tied to the back of his saddle, he set about loading it, trying to ignore the tremor in his fingers, then he stood waiting for whatever was about to happen.

On the hot still air he heard metal strike stone and he knew the riders were coming, slowly, furtively, down the hill towards him. Were they approaching from the near side of the gully or from the scrub behind him? He could not tell. He pulled the mare in closer to the outcrop and laid his musket across its top, not feeling the hot rock scorching the skin on his knuckles as he lined up his sights with the leeward side of the patch of scrub.

The riders were so close now he could hear the creak of leather and Daniel gritted his teeth, his finger ready on the trigger. Then from somewhere below him he heard a faint but shrill whistle, and chancing a quick glance downwards he saw Pitchin again waving his arms, this time with seeming urgency. In the distance he looked like a tiny human windmill, and Daniel recognized the gesturing as a warning. Fearfully, he swung back to keep his eyes on the patch of scrub and suddenly he was aware of the silence.

Nothing moved; the riders were still. What were they doing? Daniel's legs began to tremble. For an endless time he stood there, his musket levelled, the tension in him mounting until he could stand the silence no longer. 'I know you're there!' he shouted, his voice an octave higher than normal. 'Come on — show yourselves!'

And Jack Tanner, carefully emerging from the patch of scrub, looked down the barrel of Daniel's musket. ''Ere, now,' he called, 'Don't shoot the man wi' the bacon!' He sheathed his gun as he rode forward and Daniel, lowering his own, saw the boar slung across the rump of Tanner's horse.

'I heard the shot,' Daniel said apologetically, 'and when I saw Pitchin waving his arms about down there, I thought he was warning me of trouble.'

'An' I thought 'e were warnin' *me*,' Jack Tanner chuckled. 'No 'arm done this time, but yer can't be too careful an' that's a fact,' he said with feeling.

He studied the boy's face then and asked quietly, 'Effen I *'ad* been them fellas, 'an I expect yer thought I were, what would yer 'ave done effen all three of 'em 'ad jumped yer at the same time?'

Daniel grimaced. 'I'd have tried to shoot one of them at least and that would have been that, I suppose.'

'Aye, an' I'd as like 'ave done ther same. Let's get this tusker an' yer sheep down — feels like dinner time ter me.'

A soft breeze touched their faces as they rode down to the lower pastures, rattling the flax bushes and the cabbage trees and gently lifting the horses' manes. They were grateful for the slight relief it gave, it being the first breeze they had felt in days.

Their gratitude, however, was soon to turn to frustration. By late afternoon, the breeze had become a stifling blast from the north-west, buffeting man and beast alike, choking them and blinding them as the dust rose in swirling clouds from the parched ground. Dark clouds were gathering around the mountain peaks, and shearers and shepherds watched uneasily as flying banners broke free to obscure the sun.

'We're in fer a dousin'.' Alf Turnbull squinted up at the racing cloud. 'Best get as many woollies under cover as we're able — I ain't shearin' wet wool!'

There was a scurry of activity as sheep were driven into the barn and the woolshed, a bleating, stamping mob, crushed together in the heat. They bleated incessantly throughout the night until the wind dropped at four o'clock in the morning and the rain descended in a warm, solid sheet, drowning their noise.

It rained for two days and the shearers sweated and swore, trying to work in the confined space. When the rain stopped, they cursed again as the sandflies found the softer flesh under their clothing. To ease the shearers' torment, Lucy sent her supply of ngaio juice up to the woolshed with Daniel with instructions to apply it to their skin to prevent them being bitten. When none was left, she went herself to make bitter smoke to kill the insects by burning wet leaves and twigs from the kawakawa tree. Ruby Gaunt had supplied both remedies from her immense fount of knowledge.

With the return of the sun, Chandler's Run went back to normal. Willie Good came trundling up to the homestead with a haunch of pork in a bag of muslin, carried high on his shoulder. ''Tis pickled pork, missus,' he said, lowering the haunch on to the kitchen table. 'Soon as ther beast were skint, thought I'd best pickle it fer yer, what wi' ther weather breakin' an' all.'

'As well you did, Mr Good, thank you. I've never pickled pork; I don't know how to.'

''Twill more'n likely be in yer recipe books. Yer just rub layers o' salt an' saltpetre onter ther meat soon as yer pig is cold — ain't hard ter do.'

'We have saltpetre here, Mr Good. It was in Uncle Ruben's order of dry goods when we first arrived. We didn't know what it was for but thought it wise not to throw it away. It's been in my cupboard all this time.'

'Then ther very next porker we shoot, missus, I'll show yer how it's done.' He turned to leave, then turned back again. ''Ere, while I think on it, ther's a barrel down yonder, had ale in it. 'Tis a good size fer a water butt. Made o' oak it is, an' has a spigot an' all. One o' the lads could put it where 'twill catch t' runoff from yer lean-to-roof — save a trip or two down to t' river.'

'What a wonderful idea, Mr Good. Indeed, that would be such a help. Thank you again.'

'Well, missus, yer' welcome. I can't readily use two less'n I'm ter go outside fer the water. Ower barrel is set up ter feed t' water through t' porch wall. Ye've not noticed it when yer were down?'

'No. No, I didn't.'

'Anyroad, if yer've a length o' pipe mayhap yers could be fetched through t' lean-to wall as well.'

'I haven't any pipe, Mr Good, but it will be on my shopping list when next we visit Dunedin.'

It seemed to Lucy, as the shearing continued, that the days were unending; there was so much to do. She felt overwhelmed as her energy dwindled in the heat. They were still picking and bottling fruit; there were peas to be picked and dried, onions to string and hang in the lean-to, and potatoes to dig and bag up. Latterly, Ruby Gaunt had ridden across, bringing with her mineral salts to show Lucy how to tan her sheepskins. These must be done before the skins spoiled — one more task to add to Lucy's already heavy load.

'Yer need ter get someone in ter help yer, girl,' the widow had growled. 'Some young lass from the village down ther' would be happy ter work fer yer.'

'There is nowhere for her to sleep here,' Lucy answered tiredly, 'and it's too far to come each day.'

'When yer shearin's done get the lads ter build 'er a room — on to yer lean-to or somesuch. Yer killin' yerself an' young Sarah wi' the work ye're tryin' ter get through each day. I'm a deal stronger than you are, Lucy, an' *I'd* not tackle it.'

'I try to spare Sarah, Ruby, truly I do, but whilst ever I

am working she must needs do the same and I fear the tasks are never-ending.'

'An' have become more'n a challenge — I can see ye're at the end o' yer tethers, the pair o' ye. So now, shall I go down ter the Ngai Tahu village an' sort yer out a likely young woman? She can sleep in the kitchen as Moana did down below until a room can be built fer her.'

Lucy looked doubtful as she considered the older woman's suggestion, then said, 'I think I am better to continue as I am for the time being, Ruby, rather than take on the added task of training some native girl, especially if she has no English.'

'Aye, I can see ther sense in what yer' sayin', lass, but I'd urge yer ter get a girl inter harness afore the muster else yer'll be in much the same fix as yer are now.'

'I shall, Ruby, I shall, and I would be grateful if you would choose her for me.'

So Lucy and Sarah continued to carry the heavy workload and, to spare her child, Lucy worked harder than ever. Overtired many nights, she found sleep would not come, and the nights when it did come she had nightmares; nightmares so intensely real that they remained with her throughout the next day and still troubled her when she could finally go to her bed. Adam and Ruben played a dominant role in her dreams, and she would awaken sobbing with terror, the accusing dead eyes and the stench of carrion so real that she would flee her bed and spend the remainder of the night in the kitchen, trying not to see the shadows that moved in the flickering candlelight.

During these days, Tom Masters was a pillar of strength.

He watched Lucy's growing exhaustion with concern, and at the end of his stint each day he came unfailingly to relieve Lucy and Sarah of as many tasks as he could. He even took on the job of butter-making, a chore that taxed Lucy severely in the January heat. His presence about the homestead was constant so that the other shepherds and shearers began mildly to tease him, and even Daniel was beginning to wonder. Lucy, however, was oblivious to her growing dependence on the shepherd as she pushed her tired body and mind to deal with the demands of each day. At the end of one particularly trying day, when the hot wind had buffeted the workers relentlessly and blown grit and choking dust into every crack and cranny of the homestead, settling on food and flesh alike, Lucy crawled into her bed, fatigued to the point of tears.

Again she lay sleepless, her tired body hot and aching, unable to find comfort however much she tossed and turned. Eventually, accepting that she wouldn't sleep, she allowed her restless thoughts to focus on the Scot, conjuring up his face, his voice, the way he rode his horse, his touch. She longed for his touch with a longing that was a physical, unbearable pain, and her throat ached with the need to cry. Deliberately, she made herself think of the future, comforting herself with the vision of Camden Station and its development under McKenzie's guiding hand. Daniel would be nineteen when the Scot was released from prison, and by the time the new run was operating and its homestead built, the boy would be well able to manage alone. Later, he would find a wife and have a family of his own.

But what of Sarah? What did the future hold for Sarah? Would she ever have the chance to find a suitable husband or would she be forced to remain a spinster for lack of suitable choices? The child's sweet face came before her mind's eye, and again Lucy's throat ached. In any event, she consoled herself, Sarah would have her legacy; as Adam had willed Chandler's Run to Daniel, so, on her death, would Sarah inherit Camden Station. Still thinking of the child, Lucy drifted into sleep.

In the small hours she emerged slowly out of a heavy slumber to hear the sound of a lone horse passing the homestead. Sleepily, she wondered who would be riding out at such an hour. Then suddenly she was wide awake, listening intently, straining to hear the distinctive ambling gait of an animal heading towards the hills. In an instant Lucy was out of bed, running to the window, pushing it wide. The sound was gone and she could see nothing. Except for a handful of stars the night was pitch-dark. For a time Lucy stood at her window, straining to hear over the pounding of her heart, staring out into the velvety darkness, but only the usual night sounds came to her. Eventually she turned away from the window and returned slowly to her bed. Her disappointment was keen as she lay there, realizing that, of course, she had been dreaming. McKenzie had been uppermost in her mind before she had fallen sleep, so of course he would be the product of her dreams, but the ambling horse had sounded so real.

Chapter 16

Lucy, rising later than usual, felt jaded and irritable. She was very tired and it was going to be another very hot day. She performed her toilet in a perfunctory manner, brushing her hair less than the usual one hundred strokes before twisting the dark tresses into an impatient knot on the nape of her neck.

'Mama — Mama, can you come down!'

Daniel was calling from the foot of the stairs, but when Lucy went to the landing he was gone. She could hear his voice in the kitchen joined by Sarah's quick laughter, and when she entered the room Willie Good stepped forward, smiling broadly. 'Eh, missus, 'tis good news I bring ye this morn. Ower lad's back — McKenzie, that is — rode in late the night.'

Lucy gripped the back of a chair and stared at the cook as elation swept through her. She had not been dreaming!

'How—'

'Aye, well — pardoned, 'e were, missus, by Governor Brown 'isself on the eleventh day o' this month. Can yer believe it?' The plump cook rubbed his hands together and chuckled. "E's all but dodged the shearin', but by gum 'e'll be 'ere fer t' muster — beggin' yer pardon, missus—' A cloud passed over the ruddy face. 'Effen, that is, yer can see yer way ter put 'im on t' pay-roll again.'

'We'll have him work for us again, Mama, won't we?'

Lucy shifted her gaze to her son. A tiny voice inside her whispered, 'Oh Daniel, if only you knew . . .' Her pulse was dancing a jig throughout her body.

'Yes, of course,' she murmured. 'Where is Mr McKenzie now?'

'Up in t' hills bringin' down t' last o' the wethers. Took some tucker wi' 'im. Said 'e'd stay put 'til yer sent fer 'im — by.'

Lucy's thoughts were shambolic. Why had McKenzie not come to her directly? Today was the twenty-fourth day of January. If he was released on the eleventh, where had he been for these thirteen days past? Why had he not come to her this morning? Had he begun to doubt her constancy, or was he simply being discreet? She became aware that the three people in the room were waiting for her to do something. With an effort Lucy gathered her scattered thoughts.

'Yes, very well. Daniel, when Mr McKenzie is sighted, will you have somebody fetch him down?' Lucy turned to the cook. 'Thank you, Mr Good. Now, I must get on.' And she quickly left the kitchen and hurried through the dining room and across to the parlour to stand at the back window. She searched the scorched hills for the rangy chestnut and its tall rider, but there were no riders to be seen. Quelling her impatience, Lucy returned to the kitchen to eat the breakfast Sarah had prepared. Later she would go back upstairs and take more pains with her toilet in readiness for her visit with McKenzie. Her heart beat faster at the thought.

Half-listening to Sarah's chatter, Lucy performed the morning's tasks automatically; the excitement of McKenzie's nearness was making her dizzy. Daniel came in for his dinner and she turned quickly, expectantly, but did not speak. She waited while he talked about a problem with the wool-press, and waited again while he explained that he would take the food up to the men today because Pitchin was still up in the hills, and waited yet again until he assured her that he would hurry back and not keep their own dinner waiting. Lucy was bursting with frustration when he added happily, 'Oh, we found Mr McKenzie, Mama. He's bringing a mob down from the eastern hills. They're heavy with wool and very thirsty, so he said he would take his time and might be a little late.'

Lucy nodded, pushing the damp hair away from her forehead as she served slices of lamb and gravy and mashed potato into two large pots in readiness for Daniel to carry them up to the barn.

When their own dinner had been eaten, and the dishes washed and put away, Lucy retired to her bedroom where she removed every stitch of clothing and washed herself from top to toe with a cake of her dwindling supply of lavender soap. Dressed in a fresh gown, her hair coiled in a shining mass on top of her head, she went downstairs to wait. She would not watch for the Scot's approach, but made herself sit at the kitchen table and set Sarah's lessons for the next day.

Every fibre of her being was alive and tuned to McKenzie's coming. She imagined how he would look, how it would feel to be in his arms again, and a frisson passed through her, leaving her weak. She pushed Sarah's lessons aside, her concentration gone, and then he was there, standing in the open doorway, the slow grin on his face at odds with the expression in his eyes. 'Nae doot ye'll be needin' a guid musterer, lassie,' he drawled softly and stepped into the room. Lucy was lifted from her feet and held close while his lips touched her hair and caressed her throat, then, slowly, he set her back on her feet and filled his eyes with her glowing beauty.

'Where is the wee girl?' he asked hoarsely.

'In her bedroom — oh, James—' she could say no more as McKenzie's fingers traced her face and she read the urgent desire in his gaze. Then his mouth was claiming hers, gently at first, then demanding, in a long kiss that left them both shaken. 'Ye'll not be lookin' after havin' a long courtship, lassie, will ye?' he murmured into her hair. 'Because ye'll nae be gettin' it.'

Lucy laughed softly. 'Were it possible, I would marry you tomorrow. It has been so long — oh, how I have missed you.'

'Hello, the house!' The widow's rough voice caused them to draw quickly apart, and as she entered the kitchen her sharp eyes were on Lucy's heightened colour. 'Got yer musterer back, then,' she rumbled. 'Yer goin' ter keep 'im?'

'Yes — I am.' Lucy could not look at the Scot as she replied.

'Good. Well, young man,' Ruby Gaunt's quizzical gaze rested on McKenzie briefly, 'ye'd best get about yer business less'n she changes 'er mind.'

McKenzie grinned at Lucy, pushed his hat back on to his red hair and, touching two fingers to its brim, he strode from the room.

The widow pulled out a chair and sat herself down at the table. 'Silly bugger,' she grunted. 'Woulda been 'ere sooner but 'e'd stashed 'is savin's in a patch o' bush way off the beaten track, not knowin' the place were tapu ter the local Maori. They wouldn't let 'im go an' dig 'em up — took 'im a while to out-fox 'em.'

Lucy frowned, puzzled. 'I don't understand — how did he come to be pardoned? Was more evidence . . . ?'

'Not as such — no — but it seems our lad 'as escaped more times than we know about an' 'e was becoming an expensive fella ter keep behind bars. Henry Tancred, his gaoler, when 'e forwarded McKenzie's petition for clemency, urged the Governor ter grant 'im a free pardon owin' ter the fact that ther' were some discrepancies in the evidence.' The widow touched the teapot and raised an eyebrow. Lucy took the pot to the hearth to freshen it.

'So his good name has been restored then?'

'Aye, James Fitzgerald, the superintendent of Canterbury, said 'e were inclined ter believe McKenzie's claim that 'e'd been hired an' agreed with the gaoler — so our lad got 'is pardon. How's that tea, girl?'

'An amazing tale,' Lucy murmured, pouring the tea. 'How do you know all this?'

'McKenzie came ter Long Reach first ter get cleaned up an' fetch 'is dog. I got the story then.' There was a short silence, then the widow asked, 'Yer glad 'e's back?'

'Yes.' Lucy looked directly into the keen eyes then.

~

Bringing a bunch of stragglers down to the lower pastures, Masters recognized the Scot as he was leaving the homestead, and the shepherd's mouth set in a grim line. He reined his horse in and sat watching the tall figure ride down to the hut while his mind grappled with the implications of McKenzie's early return. Having camped out overnight he knew nothing of what had transpired in his absence; he assumed that the Scot had escaped again and was taking refuge on Chandler's Run, and cursed under his breath.

Whistling sharply to his dogs, he pressed his heels into his horse's sides, and as he continued on down the hill he saw Ruby Gaunt's big bay dozing in the sun at the homestead's back door. In that instant he knew that what he had just seen did not bode well for Lucy or anyone else, and the sooner the law caught up with the Scot again the better it would be for all concerned. He wondered what part the Widow Gaunt played in the man's presence.

He marvelled at the gall of the Scot, showing himself so brazenly, and wondered how he could bring himself to involve Lucy in his lawlessness if his feelings for her were genuine. Masters cursed again, knowing that because *he* cared he was bound to silence. In helpless anger he followed the slow-moving mob down to the lower pastures, and when the dogs had driven them into the holding pens, he rode on down to the hut. There were questions to be answered.

$\sim$

The shearing was nearing its end and only a few animals were left to be shorn when Lucy carried McKenzie off to ride with her over the lower acres of Camden Station.

The Ngai Tahu shepherds would be arriving any day now to begin the burn-off, and Lucy wished the Scot to see it before its acres were blackened by fire. She wished also to have him to herself at last; there had been no further opportunity for them to be alone together. Even in this remote place, proprieties had to be observed, and Lucy would obey them until a decent interval had passed; then it could be known that she and James McKenzie were courting. The Scot appeared to agree, but in fact there were more urgent requirements on his mind.

They set off early in the day, carrying food and water for themselves, and Tanner, coming from the woolshed, watched them leave with jealous eyes. ''Ere,' he grumbled, 'why's she takin' 'im over ther'? I'm ter be overseer — she said so — not 'im.'

Masters, standing beside the big door, turned back inside, making no comment but guarding his own eyes as he went about his work with a heavy heart.

McKenzie and Lucy rode at a leisurely pace over the lower hills of the run, stopping at intervals to rest the horses. At these times they caressed only briefly, knowing that their hunger for each other was a fuse that once lit would not easily be extinguished.

At midday they returned to the track, riding north again. Lucy pointed out the sentinel cabbage trees. 'Down there where the rivers join is a spur of land and above this is a plateau where I can visualize our homestead standing.'

'Then ye'll maun gang awa' doon wi' me an' take a wee look — ah mind ye'll be getting' hungry.'

They passed between the cabbage trees and Lucy led the way until they reached the gently rolling hills. The rivers were quieter that day, even where they merged, and the bird and insect chorus was all about them.

When the horses had been watered, they found a shady place to spread McKenzie's plaid, and Lucy, setting out the food, realized that she was hungry indeed. She smiled softly as her gaze rested on this man who was soon to become her husband, and watched with pleasure his deft hands slice the lamb with economy of movement and place it neatly on the thickly buttered bread. Within her, as she watched, were feelings she had never experienced with Adam. She was half-afraid of them, yet gloried in the living excitement that coursed through her. He was so close that if she wished she could stroke the thick auburn hair, touch the brown arms and cover the firm mouth with her own. McKenzie, raising his head, saw the ripe beauty of her set against the shade of the trees and, carefully putting the food aside, he took her in his arms. He kissed her eyes, her throat and her hungry mouth, filling his senses with the essence of her, and Lucy, tasting his passion, threw caution to the wind and propriety after it; the fuse was lit and in this place where she planned to build their home, they abandoned themselves in primal, instinctive need. In the urgency of their lovemaking nothing existed beyond their fever, and, when at last they lay spent in each other's arms, Lucy knew that something deep within her had changed for all time.

~

The wind blew from the south-east and the hills of Camden Station sweltered already in the mid-morning sun as Tanner and the three Maori boys torched the tinder-dry tussock and pockets of scrub. Three days before, when the wind had been blowing gently from the west, they had back-burned the scrub-line starting at Long Reach's boundary, and the Widow Gaunt had ridden across to keep an eye on proceedings.

'Yer doin' good, Jack,' she'd rumbled, 'but ye're keepin' in mind that ye'll need ter back-burn my entire boundary afore the wind changes? A nor'wester could wipe me out.'

'Aye, missus, aye. Leave it ter me,' Tanner had scowled as he'd worked on, the widow at his heels.

'An' effen yer section yer territory inter strips in yer mind's eye, an' burn each alternate one, keepin' the wind behind yer, ye'll not get yerself inter trouble 'cause yer back-burnin' as yer go — see what I'm sayin'?'

'Aye,' the shepherd had growled. 'As I said, leave it ter me.' By, ye'd think she were t' flamin' overseer, he'd grumbled to himself and, calling to the three Maori boys, he'd pointedly headed north.

For a week they worked in the middle section of the big

holding and the wind held, veering only slightly. McKenzie rode across when it began to blow again from the west, and ordered the shepherd to go back to torching the scrub-line while the westerly continued. Again Tanner took exception, and when the Scot had ridden off he resumed working the middle section as though nothing had been said. The Maori boys looked at each other uneasily then went back to work.

With the shearing season over, life on Chandler's Run resumed its normal rhythm. Seventy thousand pounds of wool had been clipped, and the bales were stacked high on the platform in the woolshed awaiting the arrival of the big wool-wagons. Lucy, with Sarah, sorted through their clothes and made a list of new ones to be purchased when next they made the journey to Dunedin. Lucy had expected that McKenzie would accompany them, and when he had appeared reluctant to do so, choosing to remain behind to build the extra room for Lucy's native girl, she had been disappointed. Apart from that, for Lucy the days were magic; every mundane task was lightened by thoughts of the Scot, and everywhere she went there was the chance she would see him. Though they exercised admirable discretion during daylight hours, there were nights when McKenzie came to her bed, leaving only as dawn's grey mantle was lifting.

Masters saw the Scot return silently to the hut on two occasions, and, with a sick heart, he removed his swag to one of the empty shearers' huts, wondering as he did so why he didn't just shake the dust of Chandler's Run from his feet and search for work elsewhere. McKenzie's early return had removed all hope of being able to woo Lucy, and to remain here was only to turn the knife in the wound, but somehow he couldn't bring himself to go. He still worked in Lucy's garden, but less often, choosing to remain in the hills for days on end. Nobody teased him now; his morose countenance was an effective deterrent.

The blistering heat seared his eyes and was heavy in his lungs as Masters, slumped in his saddle, rode slowly around the flock. Momentarily he dozed, then became aware of a faint stirring in the hot February air. He drew his mount to a halt and looked out across the hills to the blue mountains, seeing puffs of white cloud lifting from behind them. The faint smell of smoke from the burn-off had been in his nostrils for days, but it was now gone and he knew that the wind had changed and was no longer coming from the south.

For a further hour he circled the mob, and during that time the zephyr became a steady wind blowing from the north-west. Miles away to the south, white smoke rose up into the blue sky and, as he watched, the smoke began to roll towards Long Reach's boundary.

'Twill be hell down ther' burnin'-off in this heat, he thought. "'E'll not be so keen ter oversee a burn-off in t' future, I'm thinkin',' Masters said to his horse's ears and grinned. He pressed his heels to the gelding's sides and continued on his leisurely vigil. Some while later he drew the animal to a halt again and surveyed the billowing smoke. 'By, ther lad's coverin' some ground terday,' he said aloud again. 'Ther widow'll not be best pleased breathin' that lot.' His gaze dropped to the rolling hills below him, and through the shimmering heat haze he saw a rider pushing his horse hard, coming up the hill towards him. Masters frowned. 'Who'd run an animal like that in this heat? Damned fool is like ter kill 'im!'

As the rider drew nearer, Masters recognized young Pitchin. 'Slow down, lad,' he bellowed. 'Ye'll break yer bloody neck!'

Masters urged his own horse forward as the boy slowed his labouring mount to a walk, and when the shepherd reached him he growled, 'What der yer think yer playin' at, drivin' t' poor beast so hard?'

''Tis Mr Willie — Jack's on t' wrong side o' t' burn-off, an' Mr Willie sent me up ter fetch yer.' The boy wiped an arm across his streaming face.

'Couple o' t' Maori boys have rode in — in a right state they were. We're guessin' Jack's caught up somewheres wi' t' other Maori fella an' t' fire's spreadin' quick!'

Masters stared beyond Pitchin at the growing area of smoke, then turned to the boy. 'Where's the Scot?'

'Can't rightly say, Tom, 'e were west o' 'ere yesterdy.'

'Aye, well, stay wi' ther flock, lad. I'll get down yonder an' see what's ter be done.'

When Masters reached the hut, Willie Good had his own horse saddled ready to join the search for Tanner. Lucy and Daniel and the two Maori shepherds were with him, Daniel having brought the news to his mother when he had come in for his dinner. 'Ye'd best stay here, Willie,' Masters said. 'Ther's nowt ter be gained wi' all o' us goin' — t' Maori lads'll come back wi' me.'

Willie Good nodded. 'Aye, well, take me mare then —
she's fresh.'

'Shouldn't I come too?' Daniel asked quickly.

'Nay, lad, ther's nowt ye can do. Stay put.'

Tom Masters changed horses and, nodding briefly to Lucy,
he set off at a canter towards Camden Station, the Maori
shepherds riding close beside him.

The edge of the fire was little more than half an hour's
ride from the Chandler's Run boundary, and one of the
Maoris pointed up the hill to a scrub-filled gully. Driven by
the wind, the fire was racing through the stunted trees and
bush, devouring the tall, tinder-dry tussock that bordered it.
The red of the fire could be plainly seen creeping down the
hill towards the track where they had halted their horses.

'Boss man up there. Rangi up there.' The Maori pointed
again.

'In t' gully? Above t' gully?'

'Roto.'

'Inside?'

'Ae.'

Staring up at the fire, Masters thought quickly. On the
northern side of the gully the fire burned more slowly. From
where they stood the distance was more than likely to be
deceptive, but he thought he could see a rocky outcrop that
might form a natural fire-break, enabling them to gain access
to the lower end of the gully. This would probably be the only
area that was not ablaze, where they might find Tanner and
the boy, Rangi. Pressing his heels to his horse's belly, Masters
swung back along the track for a hundred yards then put the

animal to the hill. It was a steep, rugged climb, and the mare tackled it valiantly, the Maori shepherds riding close behind, their wary gaze fixed on the fire eating its way through the tussock towards them. As they drew nearer to the inferno, the heat increased incredibly and the horse behind Masters reared and tried to bolt, nearly unseating its rider. The boy fought to control it, but it reared again and again, whistling in fear, and Masters, shaking his head, waved the Maori boy away and pointed down to the track. 'Taringa!' he shouted to the boy to wait, then pushed on up the hill turning obliquely north, his intention being to reach the outcrop of rock before the fire cut him and the remaining shepherd off.

The outcrop, when they reached it, loomed much larger than Masters had estimated, and as they rode beneath it they breathed the cooler air into their lungs in great gulps.

'By, if Jack's in t' middle o' that lot, lad, I'd not much care fer 'is chances!' he shouted. Waving an arm he shouted again, 'Boss man, Rangi — kia whea?'

The Maori stared at the blazing scrub uncertainly and shook his head, pointing vaguely.

'Aye. Looks a bit different now, eh?' Masters muttered. 'Effen I'd a better grasp o' yer language, I'd know better what we're about an' all.' He scrubbed a hand over his face. ''Tis bloody daft, is this.' He turned to the Maori boy then and shouted, 'Nohanga!' The roar of the fire was deafening as he turned Willie's mare towards the gully and urged her forward with little hope of finding Tanner.

The outcrop proved to be a shelf of rock which ran across the face of the hill, ending in a series of broken steps that took Masters down to the eastern side of the gully. Here it had subsided to form a massive slide of rock and shale; the fire had not yet reached here. He drove the frightened mare to the very edge and shouted. Then he listened. Again he shouted, and again he listened but nothing came back to him but the explosion of burning trees and the roar of the fire. He had begun to rein the mare away when a movement caught his eye and, turning back, he peered more closely through the smoke to the rocks and debris below. Just visible against a fall of boulders was Tanner's horse. The animal whistled at that moment and Willie's mare answered.

Tom Masters searched for a way down, frantic now as the fire came ever closer fanned by the high wind. Tanner was down there and he had to reach him before the fire did. But there was no safe way down that Masters could see, so he gritted his teeth and sent the mare plunging down the treacherous slope. Somehow she stayed on her feet, and when they reached the bottom at last she nickered in protest. Through the smoke Masters could see the gelding, but of Tanner, the Maori boy and the Maori boy's horse, there was no sign. He could also see the great red maw of the approaching fire and, as he pushed the mare forward, the smoke and the heat searing his lungs, he wondered why Tanner's animal had not fled. The horse neighed as they drew closer and began to paw the ground and swing about, and then Masters saw the reason. Tanner was slumped almost to the ground, his arm through his stirrup leather, and he appeared to be unconscious. Masters shouted and urged the mare forward. The fire was overhead now, leaping from treetop to treetop, and both animals were frantic. Somehow the shepherd freed Tanner's arm and heaved him up into his saddle, winding his reins about his wrists and thrusting his feet into the stirrups while he fought to hold the frenzied horses, a feat he would never have accomplished if terror had not been driving him. There was a loud report overhead as he leapt into his own saddle and burning branches crashed down on them. The horses bolted and Masters made no attempt to stop them, knowing it would be futile, but he prayed, at every jolting step, that Tanner would not be dislodged from his saddle.

The shepherd had no clear recollection of coming up out of the gully, but when the horses at last reached the top and stood blown and trembling, their heads drooping, Tanner was still in his saddle, barely conscious, his hair and clothing singed, and Masters noted dully that his own shirt was almost burned from his body. When he saw them on the edge of the gully, the Maori shepherd left the shelter of the outcrop and made his way silently down the hill. As he reached Masters there was a question in his eyes.

'Rangi, kea whea?'

Masters shook his head as Tanner, rising up in his saddle, began to cough and retch. With the return of his senses he turned smoke-reddened, streaming eyes to Masters and croaked, 'By, Tom — thought I were a goner—' He could say no more as a paroxysm of coughing took his breath.

In the heat, Tom Masters was shivering and the Maori shepherd rode forward to look at the seared flesh on his arms, neck and shoulders.

Quickly, he unwound the reins from Tanner's wrists and pointed down in the direction of the track. 'Heke! Go down!' he shouted and flicking the reins of both animals over their heads, he gathered them up in a fist and, turning his own horse down the hill, dragged the beleaguered mare and gelding behind him to the safety of the track below.

For Masters, the ride back to Chandler's Run was blurred by pain. Mercifully the sun had gone in, but the hot wind brushing his burns was an agony. They did not immediately go up to the hut, but turned aside from the track and stopped in the shallows of the river at the bottom of the gorge. Here the two Maori boys helped Masters to dismount and carefully lowered him into the cool water to lie among the spawning salmon. There they left him while they filled their hats with water and emptied them slowly over the horses' scorched hides. Jack Tanner had minor burns only and, sitting on the rocks beside Masters, his face grim, he now had time to reflect on why this terrible thing had happened. From time to time he shook his head; the Maori shepherds did not look at him.

It was late afternoon when the wind dropped and the rain came. Masters was helped on to his horse and the small cavalcade rode slowly home. It rained steadily all night, and by morning the fire on Camden Station, except for smouldering pockets here and there, had been extinguished.

That same afternoon, Rangi, singed and smoke-grimed, rode his pony up the track to the hut; it was an amazing tale he had to tell. In the midst of the heat and the noise, as he and Tanner were fleeing for their lives, he had smelt rather than seen the water. He had shouted to the boss man to come back, not to run further, but the man had not heeded him. Rangi had turned aside and, quickly searching, had found the tarn. He and his pony had taken refuge under the overhang of rock behind a curtain of clear spring water. Here he had remained through the long night as the flames raged overhead and all around them, dousing himself and his horse with water when the rocks grew uncomfortably hot. It was afternoon before he felt it would be safe to leave. Then he'd led his pony slowly out.

Tom Masters suffered his burns with stoicism, able only to lie on his stomach, as far from the kitchen fire as possible, but when the blisters burst and the raw flesh became edged with yellow he developed a fever. McKenzie rode for the widow. She came within hours, examined the burns and immediately applied warmed elderberry leaves dipped in oil to the affected areas, an extremely painful exercise. When that was done, she gently applied soft cloth bandages. From her saddlebags she then took two small sacks, and ordered Willie Good to scatter the chloride of lime from one on the dirt floor and burn the sulphur in the other twice daily to disinfect the area where Masters lay.

'I can do nowt about the scarrin', lad,' she muttered. 'Ther'll be some, I've no doubt, but I'll not let ye die o' blood poisonin'. Rest up an' drink plenty o' water ter flush yerself out.'

She stepped out into the kitchen then and turned to Willie Good. 'Where'll I find Tanner?' she grated.

"E'll be in fer 'is dinner—'

The door opened as the cook was speaking and Jack Tanner walked in.

'Outside, mister,' she growled, 'I've summat ter say ter ye.'

With the flat of her hand against his chest, the Widow Gaunt walked the shepherd backwards through the doorway. In the porch she turned on him.

'Yer great oaf,' she roared, 'ye've not got the brains of a louse! I were back-burnin' whilst you were still in petticoats, but yer wouldn't be told, would yer, yer fat-headed know-it-all!' Ruby Gaunt's angry face was three inches from Tanner's nose. 'Yer put the lives of my people at risk, the lives of my animals at risk, an' years o' bloody hard work at risk — an' not satisfied wi' all that, yer left the lad Rangi ter fry. Were it up ter me I'd not put yer in charge o' emptyin' the privies!'

Jack Tanner wilted visibly under the widow's attack, and at the end of it he mumbled a humble 'Sorry.'

'Sorry, is it?' she snapped. 'Ye'd be a good man, Tanner, were ye ter use yer ears instead o' yer pride!'

With that, the Widow Gaunt turned back into the kitchen and said, almost amiably, 'I'll be back day after termorrer ter see to the lad — don't remove them bandages!'

～

In an attempt to take his mind off his pain, Lucy made time each day to walk down to the hut to read to Masters. He was grateful, but Thackeray and Brontë did not hold his attention; Lucy could just as readily have been reading

Urdu. It was not the words but the sound of her voice that calmed his pain, and after a week, when with care he was able to sit up, he enjoyed the added pleasure of watching her face.

Ruby Gaunt rode across from Long Reach every second day to dress the shepherd's burns. Lucy, when she first saw them uncovered, was aghast at the severity of them.

'Had it not been fer the Ngai Tahu lads soakin' 'im in the river 'e'd 'ave been much worse off — burns go on burnin' an' it were nearly an hour as it was afore they could get 'im ter the water.'

'I am so sorry.' Tears were gathering in Lucy's eyes as she looked at Masters, and his colour deepened.

''Ere now, missus,' he murmured. ''Twere not o' yer makin' an 'tis healin'.'

The burns were healing well after a week or so of the Widow Gaunt's ministrations, but this time, as Lucy helped to dress them, the smell suddenly made her feel queasy. She thought little of it until two days later, when, sipping her morning cup of tea, the flavour did not please her and again she felt a little unwell. Seated at the long table she became very still and slowly began to reckon the days since her last menses. When she found that six weeks had passed, she felt her skin prickle with apprehension. For a time she sat there casting about in her mind for reassurance, forcing herself to be calm as she told herself there was nothing to worry about; she was a little late as sometimes happened, and this was the reason for her feeling slightly unwell.

Banishing her fears, Lucy went about her daily tasks with

a light heart. She took more care of her appearance than usual, using lime juice and glycerine on her hair to give it a deep gloss, and dusting a little rose leaf powder on her face. She still wore black but took care now to relieve it with a bit of colour or a piece of jewellery, and she basked in the glow of McKenzie's eyes when he looked at her. Could life ever have been this wonderful before? she wondered as she began to plan a celebration for Sarah's birthday. On the twentieth day of March her little girl would be twelve years old and was fast becoming a young woman. She had Adam's fair colouring and Lucy's beauty, and looking at her daughter Lucy thought: It will be a lucky man indeed who wins her heart, then frowned as she wondered how her child was to meet this lucky young man.

As the hot days of February gave way to the balmy days of late March, Lucy had to finally accept that she was indeed pregnant. There was an urgency in her now to share her news with McKenzie and arrange an early wedding — time was passing. But then, with a jolt, she recalled Adam's words. 'Should you remarry and there is other issue, had I willed the run to you, Daniel could lose his heritage.'

This was the sense of his words and suddenly Lucy was uneasy; she needed to talk to John Hamilton. Safe in the cocoon of McKenzie's love, concerns involving the possibility of an extended family had been far from her mind, but now, forced to face the unknown intricacies of the legal world, Lucy feared there could be decisions ahead of her that she would shrink from making. The law took little account of women's rights, she knew, and she also knew that when she married McKenzie, Camden Station would, by right of law, belong to her husband. Daniel was still a minor and there *was* other issue; would her son's legacy be safe? And what of Sarah's legacy? Camden Station was to be *her* inheritance. In the event that Sarah did not wed, would she then have nothing?

Lucy worried at her problems as a dog worries at his bone. She knew she should be telling the Scot about her condition and was troubled that she was reluctant to do so. With the misery of morning sickness on her and the fragile emotions that sometimes accompany early pregnancy, her problems loomed large; the time *was* passing and for decency's sake she must soon be wed, but this she could not do until she had talked to John Hamilton, and she could not do this until the glacier-fed rivers that they must cross on their way to Dunedin had reduced in volume. This would not happen until well into April; the muster was in April — she would have to be here for the muster. Dear God! Her head was bursting! Then one morning she awoke clear-headed and clear-eyed. How stupid I am, she thought. Why can we not, in time, extend our holding? What lies beyond the northern boundary of Chandler's Run? In all probability they would find more prime sheep country, and Lucy smiled softly as she lay in her bed. This child too would have his legacy and she rested a warm hand on her stomach. Today she would tell James that she was with child.

But when the chance came that night to do so, a small insistent voice inside her head urged her to wait until she had seen John Hamilton.

Sarah's birthday was a lively affair. The Widow Gaunt rode across from Long Reach for the occasion, bringing with her a bag of sweetmeats from Cook; struggling most of the way to contain the bay mare's sweet tooth. She also brought a small greenstone pendant strung on finely plaited flax, a gift from Aroha Samuels, and a book of fairy tales written by the brothers Grimm, from the widow's own library.

Willie Good baked his famous apple pie, placing it with a flourish on the kitchen table while wishing Sarah 'Happy birthday.' He turned to hug her, but hesitated as he took in the sight of her in her blue gown. 'By,' he murmured. This was never the gangly child he knew, but a gracious young woman who thanked him politely with a soft smile. 'By,' he repeated.

Lucy had spent many nights, after the homestead had settled to sleep, making over one of her newer gowns. With its simple lines, made from a soft blue fabric and with a touch of lace at the throat, it transformed Sarah's indeterminate shape into one of tall elegance.

Young Pitchin, when he called, became tongue-tied when he saw Sarah and wordlessly thrust his gift into her hand, a sheepdog carved out of pine that closely resembled the bitch Friday. He stood awkwardly then, clutching the mug of cider that Lucy had placed in his hands, his eyes never leaving Sarah for a moment while everybody admired his handiwork. Lucy, becoming aware of the enraptured young face, sighed softly and looked away.

'Clever is this,' Willie Good was saying. 'Ye could make a name fer yerself wi' carvin's the like o' this an' Master Daniel's horse last yer — aye, yer could.'

The boy, blushing furiously, moved to stand behind Masters, who had just arrived bearing a sheepskin rug. 'Ter keep yer toes warm when yer step out o' bed on a cold morn,' the shepherd smiled. Daniel's present to his sister was a charcoal drawing on a piece of smooth boxwood. It depicted mountains, cabbage trees and streams, and was framed with pressed mountain daisies glued around its edge with a thick paste made by boiling flour and water together. A string was attached to the back so that it could be hung on the wall.

Jack Tanner, still dubious of his reception, did not join the people in the kitchen, and James McKenzie also was absent, watching over the sheep in the western hills. The seven people in the room toasted Sarah's birthday with Willie Good's apple cider and set about demolishing the large apple pie. Stories and amusing anecdotes were passed around the table, and Lucy, who had been feeling slightly unwell, began to feel better. The Widow Gaunt and Willie Good danced an impromptu jig around the room while everybody sang the lively air and clapped their hands in time, and, amid the laughter that followed, the cook scooped up Sarah and whirled her around the kitchen in a giddy waltz.

Later, when everybody had left and dusk was falling, the Scot arrived at the kitchen door. 'Ye'd nae be imaginin' ah'd forget ye, lassie,' he laughed and pressed a golden sovereign into Sarah's palm. 'Wud ye ha' kept a wee bitty piece o' Willie's pie fer me an' puir Jack up yonder?' he wheedled in a high voice and Sarah giggled. McKenzie's blue gaze passed over her fair head to rest on Lucy's face and there was a message in them that could not be misread.

That night as Lucy lay in his arms she heard his soft whisper against her hair, 'Let us be wed, lassie, ah canna bear ta wait longer.' And before sleep claimed her she wondered how Adam's family and her own would receive the news that she had married again less than twenty-four months after Adam's death and, furthermore, how they would deal with the knowledge that she had already been pregnant when she did. Thinking of Sarah and Daniel, then, she bit her lip in the darkness and quickly pushed these thoughts away.

Chapter 17

THE GREAT DRAYS rumbled past the homestead on their way to the woolshed, their iron-shod wheels passing over the stony ground causing the wooden floors to tremble briefly.

Sarah ran from the parlour out to the veranda, calling excitedly to her mother as she went, 'Come and see, Mama, it's the wool-wagons!'

Lucy, who was with Willie Good in the kitchen discussing the meals to be provided during the muster, quickly joined the girl. They stepped from the veranda to watch as the drays made their ponderous way up the hill.

'I counted sixteen bullocks pulling the first dray, Mr Good,' Sarah said, 'and eighteen bullocks pulling the second and the third one. But why are their tails tied together?' she asked with a laugh.

'So's they can't turn in t' yoke,' Willie Good replied. 'D'ye see — them as has ther tails tied is all shorthorn bullocks. The leadin' dray ther' is bein' pulled along be longhorns, an' I'll wager ther tails aren't tied, bein' as 'ow ther better mannered an' not fidgety like them shorthorns.'

The cumbersome wagons were manoeuvred into position

to load the bales as they watched. 'Next year Camden Station will be producing, too.' Lucy's voice was light as she anticipated the happy, busy years ahead. Jack Tanner and Daniel were helping to unhitch the teams so they could be led to the lower river to drink, and one of the teamsters pointed to the smaller wagon. Daniel moved towards it to climb up and reach beneath the high seat.

'They must have brought our letters, Mama, look.'

'Yes, I think they have, dear.' Lucy thought of the unfinished letters upstairs in her bedroom, difficult letters advising the family of her approaching wedding; equally difficult was the task of telling her children. Adam had been dead for eighteen months. At home, her coming marriage would be considered to be precipitate, scandalous in fact, and she feared that Daniel and Sarah would share their view.

Absently, as she stood there, Lucy saw McKenzie lead his chestnut gelding from the barn. Mounting, he headed for the western hills without looking back, his black-and-white bitch at his heels.

'I'll get away down, missus,' the cook spoke from behind her. 'If ther's owt yer needin', send young Pitchin down ter the hut wi' a note.'

Lucy nodded, watching McKenzie's diminishing figure. Above him, the intense blue of the summer sky had faded and snow covered the jagged peaks that thrust up through the hovering cloud. There was a nip in the air and it would soon be time to think of journeying to Dunedin. When the muster was over at the end of May they would go.

Sarah had gone indoors and, turning to go in also, Lucy

looked across to the vegetable garden: it had an unkempt appearance. There were potatoes still to be dug and pumpkins to be lifted. Masters had not worked in the garden since he'd been burned and she missed his quiet company. The tendons in his right arm had been damaged and though he could still do his work as a shepherd, heavy digging and lifting presented a problem. Before the muster began she would have Daniel and Pitchin attend to the garden, and perhaps in time Tom Masters would be able to continue with the work he had enjoyed doing in the past.

When Daniel came in for his tea he brought the mail and a bundle of newspapers with him. Sifting quickly through the letters, Lucy came upon a letter from the family lawyer. Quickly she broke the seal and read the single page that the envelope contained. Almost word for word, the lawyer reiterated John Hamilton's advice; the stilted wording held an underlying kindness but left the reader in no doubt that she must obey her husband's dying wishes. Folding the letter carefully, Lucy pushed it into the pocket of her skirt and reached for a letter from her mother. It did not matter; her life and her children's lives would be lived here with the man she loved, and the family lawyer's letter served only to reinforce John Hamilton's edict that Adam's bequest to his son could not be nullified.

By mid-afternoon the following day, ninety-five bales of wool had been loaded and the wool-wagons were ready to leave. With the wool receipt in her hand, Lucy wondered why it was Tom Masters who stood at her side as the heavily loaded drays pulled away and not James McKenzie.

The Scot had not returned the night before, and Willie Good had been a little surprised to find the drover's swag still in the hut.

"Appen 'e were a ways off be nightfall,' he commented to Masters, 'an' 'twere not cold the night. Anyroad, 'e can look arter 'isself.'

Tom Masters did not voice his own thoughts but went about his work. In the early afternoon McKenzie rode in. He gave no explanation for his absence and nobody asked for one. Lucy knew nothing of the incident. In the wake of the burn-off, the Ngai Tahu shepherds had returned to Camden Station to erect temporary living quarters. These were raupo whares, primitive huts — without floors, doors, windows or chimneys; draughty and damp, the rain soon finding its way through the thin thatch of the roof and turning the floor beneath into a quagmire. They would serve only until such time as more substantial materials could be brought from Dunedin to build permanent huts, and this would need to be done as soon as possible. To discourage the building of raupo huts, the Governor had imposed on run-holders an annual tax of twenty pounds while ever the huts remained in use.

Lucy and McKenzie had ridden across to see where the Maori boys were building their huts, and to inspect also the blackened hills and gullies and the scrub-line up to the forest. It was a depressing sight; twisted trees and scrub stood stark and limbless, with here and there the carcasses of the hapless animals and birds which had been caught in the fire.

The Scot had seemed preoccupied as they'd moved over the ravaged landscape, and Lucy, feeling more unwell than usual, was pleased to be able to ride in silence.

McKenzie reined his horse to a halt below the gully where Masters had been burned, and quietly surveyed the area for a moment before turning the gelding back the way they had come. 'We'll nae be findin' the twa lads beyond this,' he said. 'Their hoose'll be doon frae here, near tha river.'

When they came to the sentinel cabbage trees, the Scot turned down the path. The trees were scorched and would probably survive but the tussock grass was gone, leaving only ash where it had grown, and, as they rode down the hill, the horses' hooves raised it in grey clouds that dried their mouths and left a bitter taste on their tongues. As they came down from the path on to rolling pasture they found where the fire had burned itself out, and the horses, snorting the acrid dust from their nostrils, moved eagerly forward over the short tussock towards the sound of the river below.

When they reached the river, Lucy and McKenzie washed the grime from their faces while their horses drank, then found a place to sit and rest for a while and watch the river's milky green flow moving south-east, slower now as the tarns above were beginning to freeze.

'We must decide soon where the barn and the woolshed are to be built.' Lucy broke the silence.

'Ah've nae gi'en muckle thought tae it but ye'd nae be wantin' ta pu' ye hame doon-wind o' ye pens.'

The Scot's reply was distracted, and Lucy, turning to look

at him, saw that his attention was focused on something across the river, his expression sober. Silently she followed his gaze but could see nothing that was untoward.

'I only mention this, James,' Lucy continued, 'because in the spring, when the grass here begins to grow and there is enough fodder to feed them, we will be cutting out six hundred of Daniel's ewes and bringing them to Camden Station. There will be need of a barn then to shelter the new lambs.'

'Aye.' He turned then to look at her, a long, probing look that searched deep. 'Ah wou' ken tha' strength o' ye love,' he murmured, 'aye, lass, I wou'.'

Lucy stared at McKenzie uncertainly. 'What are you saying? I don't understand.'

Gently, he took her face between his two hands and his blue gaze held hers. Slowly he bent his head and softly kissed her mouth. He released her, then and said quietly, 'Aye, an ah'd nae be lookin' ta test it, were God on ma side.' He stood up and, taking her hands in his own, he pulled Lucy to her feet. 'We'll gang awa' hame noo.' He was smiling his sweet smile and Lucy relaxed. 'Tha's rain hangin' aboot abeen them peaks an' ah'm nae lookin' ta ge' a wettin'.'

In the end it was the Widow Gaunt who advised Lucy where the barn, woolshed and holding pens should be erected and the best site to build the shepherds' and shearers' huts.

As good as her word, the widow had ridden with Lucy down to the Ngai Tahu village to select a suitable young woman to be trained to work in the homestead on Chandler's Run. The room that McKenzie and young Pitchin had been working on was almost completed, and, with the muster soon to begin, Ruby Gaunt wanted to see the native girl settled in as quickly as possible. Lucy had been looking decidedly peaky these past few weeks, and the widow had been keeping a surreptitious eye on her young friend whilst exercising admirable reticence in holding her tongue. There was no doubt in her mind that between Lucy and the Scot there was an affiliation of some kind, but because of its discreet, one could almost say furtive, nature, the widow could not assess the seriousness of it.

In the meantime, the Widow Gaunt had chosen a strong, young Maori woman — who was known by the name Hapara, which in English meant 'dawn' — to come and work for Lucy.

'She'll not need a bed, girl; like Moana she'll not use it. Just a warm, dry room an' she'll surround herself wi' her own things. Maybe some o' yours as well effen she's not honest.' On the way back from the Maori village they turned aside on to Camden Station. The widow sat her horse and squinted up to the plateau where the homestead would be built, and pointed to a low rise about a quarter of a mile south of the plateau and elevated by about the same distance. 'Up ther' is where I'd build me woolshed an' holdin' pens an' yer shearers' huts — the wind can blow from any quarter an' ye'll rarely have the stink o' sheep up yer nose. Yer barn, fer convenience sake,' she rumbled on, 'yer could build a bit closer along wi' yer shepherds' huts.' Raising a gloved hand to shield her eyes from the sun she added, 'Seems somebody else shares me opinion — see the wisp o' smoke — ther's where yer shepherds 'ave set up ther huts.'

So the decision had been made, along with a rough estimate of the materials to be ordered when they made the journey to Dunedin. Lucy was grateful, for it enabled her to visualize her holding with more realism. They discussed several issues before they parted on the track above, then went their separate ways. Lucy feeling happier in herself; Ruby Gaunt vaguely bothered as she urged Bess homewards.

The muster began in the first week of April, earlier that year since they had a full complement of workers without having to call on the widow's shepherds for help. With the three Ngai Tahu shepherds and four of Hapara's brothers who were eager to work, and counting Daniel, there were twelve people to muster and examine the sheep for scab. Lucy's morning-sickness had almost left her until the smell of the sheep dip — a mixture of salt water, sulphur, saltpetre and tobacco — wafted down to the homestead when the dipping commenced. Then she felt queasy for a while, but at length the nausea passed.

Hapara proved to be a quick learner and a willing worker. The mutton stews, the pots of mashed potato and the station brownie that Pitchin took to the workers came from Lucy's hearth in short order, allowing Lucy precious moments when she could stand at the parlour window and watch her love at work. She was impatient for the muster to be finished, for then she would be free to go to Dunedin. Once there, she would enquire after a travelling missionary in the hope that one could be found who would agree to come to Chandler's Run to perform the marriage ceremony. McKenzie had again shown a marked reluctance to journey to Dunedin. 'Abeen is God's kirk, lassie.' He had swept an arm up to the mountains. 'An' here ah wou' ha' him sanctify our joinin', do ye ken?' Lucy, remembering the words in Ruben's letter and Adam's strange searching and preoccupation with the mountains, nodded thoughtfully and agreed, and as she did so she saw John Hamilton's office in her mind's eye and the man himself sitting behind his desk, and the sun seemed to dim a little.

Sarah was excited at the prospect of visiting Dunedin again in spite of her memories of its noisome streets. She would have new dresses and new shoes. Her own shoes pinched her toes and blistered her heels now, and Mama had said that she would try to make contact with that Mrs Truscott from the ship in order to have her sew their dresses from the material Mama would order from home. Sarah chattered to anybody who would listen, including Hapara, who understood not a word, about the colours and textures of the gowns she would like, and the scented soaps and the ribbons she needed to buy — oh, and a present for Mama whose birthday it would be on the sixth day of June.

Lucy smiled at this lovely daughter of hers and wondered again how and when she would tell her of the wedding soon to take place and of the tiny life that was growing within her.

～

Sitting at the dining table eating her evening meal, Ruby Gaunt became aware of movement outside in the hall. In a moment there was a light tap on the door and Aroha Samuels entered. 'Can you come, please? Three policemen are at our door.'

'Take them into the parlour, Aroha. I will come directly.' The widow frowned and resumed her meal. She knew why the constabulary were here; they'd come to take up her time asking fool questions. They'd better not be expecting her to dig up the dead marauders. She clicked her tongue impatiently — she'd not do it.

Her meal finished, she left the dining room and strode down the hall to the parlour where the constables stood awkwardly about the hearth awaiting her.

'Good evening, gentlemen,' the widow grated, ''ave yer come ter arrest me for the murder o' six good men?'

'Nay, we've not,' the older of the three replied soberly. 'We've Mr Alfred Turnbull's statement as ter wot took place 'ere an' I'd 'ave ter say yer've done the country a service.'

'Kind o' yer ter say so, an' 'avin' established that, what brings yer all ther way up 'ere wastin' me time in ther midst o' musterin'?'

By, she's an ugly old crone, the man was thinking. An' she's got a tongue on 'er an' all. 'We'll be takin' no more o' yer time than can be 'elped,' he replied tersely, 'but we've statements ter take an' the scene o' the attack ter examine—'

'An' do ye want ter examine me bullet wound while yer'

464

about it? Good God, man, ther'll be nowt left o' anything after all this time an' the sheep all over it.' She scowled at the constable for a moment, then shook her head.

'Well, get on wi' it then, so's we can get about our work the sooner.' She began to turn to the door and the senior constable cleared his throat. 'We're here on another matter as well, madam,' he said doggedly.

'Is that so — what other matter would that be, then?'

'We've been led ter believe that one James McKenzie is in 'idin' 'ereabouts.'

'What are yer sayin', man? McKenzie's no fugitive, 'e were pardoned — by ther Governor 'isself, no less.'

'Aye, so 'e were — a provisional pardon, madam — providin' 'e left ower fair shores on t' first ship available. Three month on 'e's still in t' country, 'idin' 'isself up 'ere in t' high country an' we've reason ter believe 'e's got 'imself a cosy billet across t' way.'

Ruby Gaunt's eyes were slivers of steel. 'An' this information 'as come from where?'

'One of them drivers on t' wool-wagons — 'e'd no reason ter mislead us as we knows of — got a look at McKenzie 'eadin' fer ther hills. You seen 'im, missus?'

The Widow Gaunt thought quickly and adopted a more moderate tone. 'Aye, I've seen 'im. Came ter pick up 'is bitch as I were lookin' after, 'an 'e'd been pardoned then. 'E worked 'ere, yer know, afore 'is arrest, an' across ther way as well.'

'Were you not aware o' the conditions o' 'is pardon?'

'I was not,' the widow replied bluntly, 'and neither were others 'ereabouts. What 'appens to 'im *if* yer catch 'im?'

'We'll catch 'im, an' 'e'll be put on t' first ship that's 'eadin' back ter the auld country. Will yer answer me this now: is ower man still likely ter be on yer neighbour's run?'

The Widow Gaunt shook her head. 'Far as I know 'e's long gone — stayed around long enough ter earn 'is passage 'ome then skedaddled.'

Silence fell over the room as three pairs of interrogating eyes were turned on the widow and the three policemen digested this last statement. Ruby Gaunt's brain was running along a fast track, searching for pitfalls that could be in wait for the uninformed on Chandler's Run.

'To ower certain knowledge 'e were in possession o' twenty-one pound an' some shillin's,' a younger constable spoke into the silence.

'Were 'e now?' the widow replied sardonically. 'I saw none of it fer me trouble. That bitch o' his ate like a starvin' wolf.' She dismissed the man with a glance, turning to the senior policeman. 'Now — we've all 'ad a wearyin' day an' ther's more o' the same ter be dealt with termorrer. Yer welcome ter stay 'ere the night an' rest up. I'll 'ave a word wi' Cook ter set up a meal fer yer, then I'm off ter me bed — 'tis an early start fer me.'

'That's obligin' o' ye, mistress.' The senior constable unbent a little. 'We'd not want ter put ye out, but a hot meal an' a warm bed we'd be grateful for.'

'Then I'll say goodnight, gentlemen. The girl will show yer where ye're sleeping when yer've eaten.'

Ruby Gaunt stepped out into the hall and saw Aroha Samuels hovering near the dining room door. The widow strode down to her and, taking the housekeeper's arm, she urged her into the dining room, shutting the door behind them.

'Listen ter me carefully, Aroha,' she said in a low voice. 'I've ter ride across ter Chandler's Run an' those gentlemen in the parlour are ter think I'm abed. Tell Cook ter make 'em a meal, summat hot an' quick, an serve it in 'ere. Then I want yer ter help Moana make up beds for 'em, on t' south side so's they'll not see me goin' or comin' back. When you fetch Moana, 'ave Rewi saddle up Bess an' lead 'er down the hill a bit — an' not a sound. I'll see 'im ther' soon as I've changed me clothes. 'Ave yer got all that now?'

'Ae. You be careful.'

'I will, lass, I will. Don't ye worry, an' I'll see yer in the morning.'

The Widow Gaunt opened the door then, and, walking towards the stairs, said in a voice that would be heard in the parlour, 'Get ter yer beds as soon as ye can — we've a big day ahead o' us termorrer. Goodnight now.' And she walked purposefully up the stairs.

The first few miles were covered at a steady canter with the moon to light their way. Ruby Gaunt murmured to herself from time to time as she rode and shook her head. 'By, ther's summat brewin' 'ere that I don't even want to think about, Bess,' she muttered, pressing her heels harder into the mare's sides. 'Get a move on, can't yer — we've not got all night.'

Half an hour later the bay was beginning to labour and the widow was obliged to slow her to a walk. 'Yer too soft an' too fat, an' likely gettin' too old fer this kind o' caper.' And the mare grunted in protest when after a few minutes she was lifted again into a canter.

It was little short of ten o'clock when Ruby Gaunt tapped softly on the door of the hut. Tom Masters opened it.

'Where's the Scot?' she muttered. 'Where's McKenzie?'

'In 'is bunk, asleep,' Masters replied, peering beyond her to the blown mare at the entrance to the porch. 'What's amiss?'

'Well you may ask — the law is at my place an' in a while they'll be over 'ere ter take 'im inter custody.'

"E were pardoned, weren't 'e?'

'Conditional on his leavin' the country, it seems.' The Widow Gaunt hitched her trousers and growled. 'Fetch 'im out an' tell 'im ter get 'imself up ter the barn.' She lowered her voice. 'An' not a word, Tom. When the buggers get 'ere — warn everybody — yer don't know where 'e is, an' be hazy about when 'e left. The missus, like yerselves, knew nowt o' this an' is not ter be put on t' wrong side o' the law cause she's taken 'im on. Are ye takin' me meanin'?'

'Aye.'

'Good man. Now, will ye tend ter Bess as well while I go up to the homestead? Poor old girl's past 'er best an' she's yet ter get me home.'

Tom Masters stood still for a space after the widow had left, the bay's reins in his hand, and thought over what she had said. Then, shaking his head, he led the animal into the porch and threw a rug over her steaming hide. He turned then to see the Scot standing in the kitchen doorway.

Ruby Gaunt strode up the track to the homestead and saw with relief the light shining through the kitchen window. With every step she had tried to plan what she would say to her young friend, but now, standing at the garden gate, she had still found no easy way to deliver her news. Through the window she could see Lucy sitting at the long table, darning socks. Her hair was loose about her shoulders and the lamp cast a soft glow across her face. The Widow Gaunt watched her with pity, knowing that in a few moments the serene picture would be destroyed completely by the words she must utter. Wearily, she walked around to the kitchen door and called softly, 'Hello, the house.'

With the light behind Lucy, the widow could not see her face, but she heard the thread of anxiety in her voice as she invited the older woman to enter. 'You are a late caller, Ruby. I hope nothing is amiss.'

'I fear there is, my dear, I fear there is.' Ruby Gaunt pulled a chair out from the table. 'Sit down, girl, and I'll tell you what I must.'

She seated herself, facing Lucy. 'The police are at Long Reach in connection with the raid on us, but in a day or so they will be coming here to take James McKenzie into custody.'

Lucy stared at the craggy face. 'I don't understand. Why? He was—'

'Pardoned. Yes, he was — but only on the understanding that he leave the country and never return. Unfortunately, one of the wool-wagon drivers recognized McKenzie and has informed the law that he is still here.'

Lucy's colour fled. Suddenly faint, she bowed her head and closed her eyes. The widow waited until she raised her head, then said quietly, 'If the police find him here, they will take him back to gaol until there is a ship to take him back to Scotland.'

There was a look in Lucy's eyes that made the older woman uneasy. 'Aye, I've guessed there was summat atween yer — an' I were right, eh?'

Lucy was staring at the fire and slowly she nodded. 'We have become close, yes,' she murmured.

The widow studied the lovely face and the lines in her own deepened. 'I'm sorry, lass — so very sorry.' She placed a gentle hand on the younger woman's arm. 'Go now, child — he's waiting for you in the barn. I'd best get back afore I'm missed. An' remember: whatever happens you can depend on my help.'

Disbelieving and dazed, Lucy watched her friend as she stood up and walked to the door. 'It is a mistake, Ruby — there has been a mistake.'

'No, girl, ther's no mistake. God knows I wish ther' were.'

Lucy turned her gaze back to the fire and listened to the widow's boots clump around the side of the homestead. In a while she too stood up and left the kitchen, closing the door quietly behind her.

～

Friday's eyes glowed in the lamplight as she entered the barn and McKenzie came out of the shadows towards her. 'Ma wee love.' He opened his arms, but Lucy stepped back, tense and alarmingly pale.

'Mother of God, James, what have you done?'

'Aye, an' ah've scarce slept these months gone, fearin' this vera thing.'

'Why did you not tell me the truth? Why? You let me trust you, you have let me love you — completely. You are my life — do you know what you have done?'

Lucy's eyes were dark pools of pain as she stared at him, her fists clenched against her stomach. 'You knew there was never a chance for us — No!' as McKenzie stepped forward again.

'I don't know how I can ever—' She began to gulp air in great, dry sobs, moving backwards away from him, her eyes huge. Friday thrust a cold nose into her palm, but she did not feel it.

In helpless pity, McKenzie stood motionless, choking on his own pain, unable to ease hers, but when her tears came he moved to her and taking hold of her wrists he drew her gently to him. Tenderly he held her, stroking her hair. 'Ye ah tha reason my heart beats, lassie,' he murmured, 'I cou' nae turn frae ye then an' a canna turn frae ye noo; tellin' ye tha truth wou' ha been ta lose ye.'

For a long time they stood together, close, silent, needing the comfort of their closeness to face their fears. At length Lucy whispered, 'How could you think that you'd not be found out? Sooner or later this had to happen.'

McKenzie shook his head. 'Were it no' fa tha' wagon-driver an' his gob, ah'd a had tame ta wed ye an' whisk ye an' tha bairns awa' ta Sco'land.'

'I cannot leave this place. It is Daniel's legacy.' Lucy raised tormented eyes. 'You know I can't — not for years.'

'Aye, ya can. One da' ah'll be laird an ye'll forfeit nothin' when ye gang awa' frae here — awa' ta Dunraeth, my hame in tha Highlands. Daniel wi' ha' his legacy, ye ken, an' tha's ma promise tae ye.'

Lucy thought of the child in her womb, and heard again Adam's words. Desperately she shut them out.

'Bide wi' me, ma love, an' a grand Highland weddin' we'll be havin' noo.' McKenzie spoke against her hair and Lucy winced; in the time it would take to reach Scotland, she would be very pregnant indeed. Another disturbing thought came to her. 'What of "she with the spirit of duplicity"?' she asked. 'Would she live with us also?'

McKenzie laughed grimly. 'Tha place is sae vast ye'd walk fae a week an' ne're cross heer path — leave a' this, Lucy, an' gang awa' wi' me.'

Thoughts, emotions and anxieties clogged Lucy's brain, and on a half-sob she said, 'I can't think — I need time — there are too many considerations.'

'There's nae tame, lassie, twa days is a' ah'd dare.' The Scot's eyes pleaded. 'Take wa ye canna do wi'out, nae mair, an' we'll gang awa' in tha morn.'

They stood locked in each other's arms, his eyes holding hers in the lamplight, and he seemed to search into her very heart for the reassurance he craved. 'Ma bonnie love, be nae afeart, ah'd dei afore ah'd harm ye or tha bairns.' His lips touched her forehead. 'Gang awa' noo an' in tha' morn tell me wha' ah maun wud hear.'

With the taste of his kiss on her lips, Lucy walked down to the homestead. She was bemused by what had happened; in less than an hour her life had been turned upside-down. Dear God, how could she make a decision of such impossible magnitude; one that could adversely affect Daniel's future. If the child she carried was male, Daniel, at best, could only ever be a stepson to James, and this surely would be the measure of his prospects. Sarah would have the chance to marry well, and Lucy would see her beloved family again, but what of Chandler's Run and Camden Station? What of the people here who trusted her? What of Ruby Gaunt — dear, ugly Ruby, loyal friend?

Desperately, Lucy paced the kitchen floor. James. She could not contemplate life without him, but she saw them all as fugitives running from the law. She saw herself, too, in her mother's arms, all of her loved ones safe together on English soil, and she saw Daniel asking her in years to come why his inheritance had been made forfeit. There could be no decision.

Exhausted and deeply distressed, Lucy at last went up to bed. She lay in the dark for a long time, wishing that, this night of all nights, McKenzie would come to hold her in his arms and talk away her fears; would soothe her with his love. Finally, with the tears of despair on her cheeks, she fell asleep. She sensed his presence in the room and her pulse quickened. 'Oh, my love,' she whispered. 'I thought you were not coming.'

She lay in the darkness, waiting for his touch, her eyes

heavy with sleep, and then she smelt it, the sweet, putrescent stench of decaying flesh, and her eyes widened in shock as Adam leaned over her, the rotting flesh of his face dribbling down on to her own. Deep in the black sockets of his eyes a malevolent light gleamed. 'Yes, Lucy, I have come,' he hissed. He leaned nearer as though he would touch her and Lucy recoiled, tried to scream, but her throat had closed. Frantically she tried to claw herself away from him, but all power of movement had left her limbs. 'You cannot escape me, Lucy,' Adam Chandler whispered. 'You are as helpless now as I was when you betrayed me.'

The terrifying face loomed closer and the putrid smell filled her nostrils. His whisper was hoarse with disgust, 'You lie with him while you still wear my ring, and will you now betray our children — lose Daniel's inheritance to the bastard in your belly? No, Lucy,' the whisper grew louder. 'You are the guardian of my trust and you will honour it or there will be a reckoning!'

Fleshless fingers lingered below Lucy's heart where the tiny life lay. So cold were they that they burned her flesh and she screamed out in terror, a long, soundless scream. Then she was tearing herself free of the tangled bedding, throwing herself from the bed to cower shivering, sobbing, staring into the darkness, and suddenly she was running; fleeing on leaden limbs from the horror behind her, through the door, half-falling down the stairs, blundering across the hall, across the dining room, to shut herself in the kitchen. With shaking hands, she lit every lamp and candle she could find, and then she sat, huddled in a chair, throughout the long hours until daylight came, her eyes fixed on the dining-room door.

~

Pale light was filtering through the window when Lucy rose stiffly from her chair. She snuffed the guttering candles and extinguished the lamps, then slowly opened the door into the dining room and listened: there was no sound.

The fire had burned down, but despite that the kitchen was hot and the smoke from the candles caught at her throat. Wearily Lucy walked to the kitchen door and opened it wide, and, standing in the open doorway, she raised her eyes to the mountains. The sun just touched their uppermost peaks, turning them into spires of rose and palest gold. These were the spires of 'God's kirk' where she was to have been wed, and the enormity of her loss hit her with a force that made her stagger.

'James. Oh, James,' she whispered, and stumbled outside on to the cold stones of the path. In her bare feet she walked back and forth, back and forth over the frosty ground, not feeling the cold or the sharpness of the stones, and her hands cradled the soft mound of her stomach. 'Perhaps I would have left all this, James, and gone with you,' she sobbed softly, 'but now — you see — I can't.' She turned then and went back into the kitchen. Automatically, she built up the fire and placed the kettle on the hob, then she stood in the dining-room doorway and again she listened.

She could hear Daniel and Sarah moving about upstairs; everything seemed so normal in the light of day. She could hear the sheep bleating in the lower pastures, the dogs barking and a shepherd whistling. Had the night's horror been a dream? Shuddering, Lucy savoured the everyday sounds, the doorknob in her hand. *Had* it been a nightmare — a particularly vivid nightmare, but a nightmare nonetheless? This morning, as the sun cast its early rays across the upper hills, she could almost believe that it had been. Had this not happened before?

Slowly she walked across the dining room, across the hall to the bottom of the stairs, and one step at a time she made her way up to the landing. Her bedroom door was shut. She gripped the doorknob and, turning it, she pushed the door wide and stared into the room. There was no stench of decay; the room was as it had been the night before when she had readied herself for bed. The room was as it had been, except that the covers had been dragged on to the floor. Lucy shivered suddenly, her fingers shrinking from the cold doorknob: she could not recall shutting the bedroom door as she had fled.

She made herself enter the room, and hurriedly she dressed, finishing her toilet with hands that shook. In vain she tried to shut her mind to the obscenity of the night. It *was* a dream, she had to believe it had been a dream or she would not be able to commit her life and those of her children irrevocably to James McKenzie. She moaned aloud as she envisaged the empty years without him, never to feel his arms about her or his questing mouth on her own as he claimed her. How could she survive such desolation?

∾

Daniel had left for the upper pastures shortly after breakfast and had taken his dinner with him. Lucy performed her usual tasks numbly, vaguely aware of time passing, relentlessly passing, carrying her to the moment when she must say the words that would end their hopes and their dreams, or the words that would allow them to live.

Her heart throbbed slowly and heavily as she worked at her bread-making, shaping the dough into loaves and placing them in the camp-oven on the hearth. She bent to scoop hot embers on to its lid, a familiar task in her familiar kitchen, yet today the action carried a sense of the unreal. Sarah was beating cream in the lean-to to make into butter, another ordinary task, but there was a different quality to the sound, a somehow disquieting sound.

Lucy wiped the flour from her hands and slowly lowered herself on to a chair to sit staring into the fire.

Disjointed thoughts passed through her mind. Did James suffer from seasickness? The captain of the ship would marry them. What would become of Friday? She pressed her fingers to her temples and closed her eyes, and the measured beating continued. In a while it became interspersed with the counterpoint of a horse's ambling hooves, and Lucy rose to her feet and turned to the window. The Scot was riding towards the homestead, Friday loping along beside him. Drawing a deep breath, Lucy went slowly to meet him. She waited on the veranda steps watching him approach, and she sensed the tension in him. Now that the moment was here, she felt strangely calm; she had made her decision.

From somewhere there came a faint shout and McKenzie

turned in his saddle. Lucy looked beyond him and saw the three constables coming fast up the track. They were still some distance away, but their intention was plain; the widow's warning had been in vain. There was another shout and McKenzie kicked his gelding into a canter, and Lucy was running. He was only yards from her when a shot rang out, and hauling the gelding back on its haunches he called a warning, 'Ge' awa' back, Lucy, come nae closer.' Slowly he raised his arms and slowly his blue gaze moved over her face. 'Ah'll pu' ye a' risk nae further.'

The constables were riding past the hut and had slowed to a trot now. McKenzie sat erect in his saddle, his arms still raised, his gaze fixed on Lucy's face. 'Ye are ma heart's life, lassie, an' ah'll love ye tae ma deith.' There was a yearning in his voice that went beyond grief.

Lucy could not speak. Adam's spectre was at her shoulder. Hungrily, she filled her eyes with James, his tall frame, the richness of his hair in the sunlight, the clear blue of his eyes, the way he sat his horse. These images she would keep in her memory forever. He lowered his arms then, and for the space of a heartbeat his sweet smile was on his lips, then, touching two fingers to the brim of his hat in the gesture she knew so well, he swung the chestnut about and rode to meet his captors.

Dry-eyed, Lucy watched him go; saw him hold out his wrists for the manacles then move off down the hill with the constables, one each side of him and one leading the way. The bitch Friday trotted at the gelding's heels. Lucy saw Willie Good intercept them to tie a sack on to McKenzie's pommel. She saw Tom Masters step forward and shake the Scot's hand, and she saw the Widow Gaunt moving slowly up the track towards them, saw her stop briefly to speak and grip the Scot's arm, then pull the bay mare aside as the cavalcade moved on.

They reached the bend in the track and went from her sight. McKenzie had not looked back.

All this Lucy saw in sharp relief before she turned to walk carefully into the homestead.

POSTSCRIPT

George Rhodes, manager of the Levels Run,
took possession of Friday as James McKenzie
was being deported.